DO NOT REMOVE
CARDS FROM POCKET

BORDER CROSSINGS

BORDER
CROSSINGS

DAVID L. FLEMING

Texas Christian University Press
Fort Worth

Copyright © 1993 by David Fleming

Library of Congress Cataloging-in-Publication Data

Fleming, David L., 1951–
   Border crossings : a novel / David L. Fleming.
      p.   cm.
   ISBN 0-87565-116-X.—ISBN 0-87565-117-8 (pbk.)
   1. Mexico—History—Revolution, 1910–1920—Fiction.   I. Title.
PS3556.L437B65   1993
813'.54—dc20   92-43653
                              CIP

10   9   8   7   6   5   4   3   2

Design and illustrations by Barbara Whitehead

for Gail

PART I

TRAILS
COME
TOGETHER

ONE

THE two riders for the Palomas Land and Cattle Company sat their horses on a low rise and watched the bunch of cattle move slowly across the flat below. Tiny Stott, a big man with black hair, wrote down the number in a record book the size of his palm, and the other man, Clay Smith, took off his hat and wiped his forehead.

"I'm goin' to bring me some cattle to my weddin' church," Clay Smith sang unevenly to a tune he made up with the words.

"You got to make up a song for ever'thing?" Tiny shook his head. "I swear. This is the last time I ride with you."

"You don't like songs?" Clay asked, fitting his hat back on his head with two seesaw pulls.

"I like songs I heard of."

Tiny closed the record book and slipped it and the pencil into his coat pocket.

"That's the last bunch," he said. "Time to ride for the house."

"I'm a-ridin' to the house," Clay sang.

"Oh, cut it out, Clay. I swear."

Tiny unwound the reins from the pommel of his saddle and turned his horse toward the New Mexico border, sixteen miles away. Before Clay followed, he looked once more at the cattle, then back to the southeast, the way they had ridden that morning. A haze of dust caught his eye.

"Hey," he said.

Tiny turned in his saddle. "What now?"

"Look at that." Clay pointed.

Tiny rode back to Clay. They sat their horses watching the dust, waiting to see what was causing it.

"Comin' this way," Tiny said, squinting. "Whatever it is."

"Might be a wagonload of girls," Clay said.

Tiny felt uneasy. "Don't count on it."

Abruptly, half a mile away, riders broke the top of a hill. Their dark coats and wide, black sombreros left little doubt as to what they were.

"Damn!" Tiny hissed. "Them's bandits. Let's get the hell out of here."

They spun their horses together and spurred to the north. Behind them, the bandits kept coming, faster now that they had seen the two riders.

"Split up!" Tiny yelled over his shoulder.

Clay veered to the right as they hit level ground, and they were a hundred yards apart, then two hundred, then three hundred. Clay turned his horse north again. A mile farther he hit a rocky hill. "I'm just a lonesome cowboy," he sang as he topped the rise with a feeling of challenge and adventure.

He jerked back on the reins. Tiny was still in the flat, pulling away. Clay looked back. All of the bandits were on his trail, and they were gaining. Something in his chest tightened, and the exhilaration he felt climbing the hill turned to one of desperation.

"Come on," Clay urged his horse, and they plunged off the hill. It was still a long way to the border, and Clay prayed his horse was equal to the race.

He stayed ahead of the bandits for the next four miles, but then felt the horse weakening, resisting the urging, and slowing down. They hit another rise, and the horse stumbled in the loose rock, recovered, and went on.

Clay had lost his hat. His long brown hair blew back from his forehead as he leaned into the wind.

Behind him, fifty Mexican bandits broke the rim of the hill in quick pursuit. The front line was ten across, and the leaders were backed closely by the others. Their sombreros had slipped to their backs, held by rough lengths of string. The bandoleers that crossed their chests were full.

Clay Smith spurred his horse, blood already streaming back from its flanks, and took a quick look over his shoulder. The bandits were less than a hundred yards behind him. Panic and disbelief alternated in his mind. Before he covered another mile, the bandits would be abreast of him. There was no place to hide. He had six rounds in his pistol, but the rest of his bullets were in a pouch at the bottom of a tied saddlebag. He was caught.

Abruptly, Clay Smith pulled back on the reins and slowed his horse. Before he stopped, he began to smell the desert dust that swirled around him on the breeze. He turned his horse and faced the bandits, the reins loose on the pommel and his hands in the air. He picked out the face of one man in the leading line and kept his eyes on the man's face, ignoring the rest. He could feel the sides of his horse quiver against his knees.

The bandits rode forward, saying nothing, their faces grim, but neither angry nor triumphant. They brought their own dust on the easterly breeze, and, like the dust, they surrounded Clay Smith and his nervous, blown horse. Somewhere to the north, Tiny Stott kept riding, too intent on the land ahead of him to ever look back. "I give up, boys. You got better horses than I do," Clay Smith said in Spanish. The man he had been watching had moved behind him. Clay Smith noticed several women in the band, their eyes as blank and waiting as the eyes of the men. A horse brushed his leg, and his pistol was jerked from his hip.

"Get down!"

Clay Smith turned to face a man who seemed to be the leader. He was fitting his sombrero back on his head, throwing his features in shadow.

"Get down," the man said again.

Clay swung down and stood beside his horse. He could feel his legs shaking, and his mouth was dry. He looked up at the men in front of him, their forms silhouetted against the bright March sky.

"I got nothin' against you fellas," Clay said in a casual way.

"Tie him," the leader said.

The bandits began to dismount. Clay crossed his wrists behind his back and waited, hoping to show he was willing to do whatever they said, that he was not their enemy.

Rope cut the skin. Clay tossed his head to shake back the strands of loose hair that tickled his forehead and stung his eyes. The horses began to move to the east, led by their riders. Clay was pushed after them by a man whose face he never saw.

They walked off the hill into a draw where catclaw and prickly pear had choked out an ironwood tree. The horses were led a little way off and held, but the majority of the band circled around Clay. The leader sat down on a protruding rock, and Clay was pushed to his knees in front of him.

"You talk Mexican?" the leader said in Spanish. From his coat pocket, he pulled forth a small bundle of sticks the size of kitchen matches tied together with a piece of hemp thread.

"Yes," Clay said in Spanish. "Yes, sir."

"What are you doing in Mexico?"

"I was herding cows."

"Your cows?"

"I work for the Palomas Land and Cattle Company."

"I don't think you do anymore," the man said.

As Clay watched, the man formed a cross with two sticks and put the others back in his pocket. From the ground beside him, the man pulled blades of dried bunch grass and wrapped them around the cross until he had made a skirt of them.

Clay Smith swallowed. "You can have my horse and saddle," he said. "I give them to you. I don't have anything else. Just let me go."

The man held up what he had been making. Clay saw that it was a small figure with a kind of skirt, a female doll.

"Do you know what this is?" the man asked.

"No," Clay said. He tried to swallow again.

"*La muñeca*," the man said. "The doll. It is the doll of the Virgin Mary. You work for her now."

The man jerked his head, and Clay was pulled to his feet. A looped rope was put over his head and pulled tight around his throat. When the rough braids scratched over his face, he went wild. He broke away from the two men holding him, but only fell sideways on the rocks. He was picked up again and dragged into the finger shadows of the ironwood. The end of the rope was thrown over one of the stouter limbs and was caught by four men.

4

"I didn't do nothin' to you," Clay cried, his voice high and tight.

The leader looked back at him as if he were only looking into the desert distance.

"I'll see you again, Mister," Clay said.

"I believe not," the leader said and jerked his head.

The men on the other end of the rope backed with it. Clay was lifted off his feet. He tried to stiffen the muscles of his neck, but his fear and the weight of his own body overcame his strength of will, and he began to strangle. The figures in front of him blurred, but he continued to stare at the leader. His ears rang with the force of a train whistle. Something rose inside of him like a silver bubble released under water, and when it hit the surface, Clay Smith was dead.

After the ropes were removed, the leader of the bandits stood over the dead man for a moment, no expression on his face, and nothing in his eyes. Then he dropped the crude doll on Clay Smith's chest and turned away.

"We are close to the border, then," one of his men said.

"Yes. We meet Villa tomorrow. We will cross soon."

Both men faced north, where, miles away, Tiny Stott pulled his horse to a stop. He looked around, but saw neither dust nor movement.

"Him and his damned made-up songs," Tiny said aloud. "I ought to just leave him." He shook his head. The border and safety was less than ten miles away. Tiny swore and turned his horse back to the southeast, moving at a lope, his rifle across the saddle in front of him, but he had no idea how many Villistas had come to be in that part of the desert.

Like his partner, he would never reach the border.

TWO

JAMES Hampton rode up to the barn just as the sun went behind the foothills of the Tres Hermanas Mountains on the western lip of the Mimbres Valley in southern New Mexico. The strong northwest wind caught at his collar and was cold against his thighs where the denim of his trousers was stretched tight. He lowered his chin into the wind and pulled his mare, Lady, to a stop at the barn door where Billy Dunbar was coiling a length of rope.

"Evenin', Mr. Hampton," Billy said. He threw his left arm out until he had the right length, then brought the coil back into his right fist.

"That my rope?"

"No, sir. This is Mr. Frank's rope. Want me to put away your rig?"

"I wouldn't be sorry to let you, Billy," Hampton said.

"Where did you go?" Billy asked, whipping the last three or four feet into his right fist and tying the loose end around the coil to hold it.

"Around the Sisters, almost to the back line," Hampton said, swinging down out of the saddle. When his boots were on the ground, he stood holding the reins against the saddlehorn until he straightened his back.

"See any Villistas?"

"What's that?"

"See any Villistas?"

"I wasn't looking for Villistas."

6

"Rueben says there's plenty of them around waiting for a chance to strike."

"Is that so," Hampton said, but he was not asking a question. He was tired and stiff, and he did not want to hear anything about Rueben Satterwhite whom he thought of as perpetually full of talk and empty of do.

Billy went into the tack room and came back without the rope. He was a likable boy of sixteen, big for his age, the son of one of the farmers who worked for Frank MacPherson, the owner of the ranch. Hampton passed Billy the reins and patted the mare's neck as he stepped back to the saddlebags where, among other things, he had enough crackers and jerky left to make a good enough supper. He slipped the knot on the leather thong that held the bags to the cantle and pulled them off.

"Want your rifle, Mr. Hampton?"

"Yeah. I might have to shoot me some Villistas on the way to the house."

Billy slid the Winchester out of the saddle scabbard and looked at it for a minute in the cold twilight that was quickly turning to dark.

"I'm going to get me one of these some day," he said.

"Uh-huh, but that one's mine."

"Satterwhite says I can ride shotgun with him when I get my own rifle."

"He does, does he?"

"That's what he says."

Hampton took his rifle in his free hand. "You need any help with the mare?"

"No sir. I'm already halfway through."

"Don't put my saddle on the ground."

"No, sir."

Billy was leading the mare into the barn when he stopped. "By the way, Mr. Hampton, you got company waitin' at your place."

"Who?"

"The preacher and some other fella."

"No Villistas?"

"No, sir."

Hampton nodded at the boy's back. "Appreciate it," he said.

Billy tossed his head in acknowledgment and took the mare through the high, wide door of the barn. Hampton turned toward his house, which was beyond the windmill and in line with the big house. He had already seen the preacher's buggy tied to the end rail of the porch. It was a familiar sight.

There was a hail from the big house, and Mr. Frank stepped out on his porch pulling the wings of his vest together against the chill.

"Hamp!"

"Yes, sir," Hampton said. He walked over to the porch and stood under the bare limbs of the big cottonwood. Mr. Frank put a hand up on one of the cedar posts supporting the porch roof. He was a tall man of seventy-two, with receding gray hair and a stoop and a rolling walk from breaking mustangs when he was younger.

"Are you just gettin' in?" he asked, standing in the lee of the wind at the edge of the porch.

"Yes, sir."

"What does it look like?"

"I've seen worse this time of year."

"Stock?"

"There's enough to go after."

"More than Rueben said?"

"We must have seen two different places. The place I saw had thirty or forty calves."

"Look all right?"

"Plenty good. Even rangin' around those hills. There's some green showing on the slopes."

"They must have been in a draw when Rueben was back there." Hampton looked away, hawked, and spit. Satterwhite was Mr. Frank's nephew, and that made a difference to him that it did not make to Hampton. He doubted that Satterwhite had even followed the trail around the last of the Tres Hermanas when he had left the ranch to do so.

"It is my opinion," Hampton said, "that there is enough young stock to make goin' after them worthwhile."

"Make a camp at the well?"

"Could."

"How long?"

"A couple of days."

"Mr. John Adams rode over here this afternoon. He seems to think we might have Villista trouble in the area."

"What does the army say?"

Mr. Frank laughed. "Most of them are over at Fort Bliss playing polo."

"We missed all that action," Hampton said. He turned and looked through the last haze of evening toward the south. The valley slid down between the foothills all the way to Mexico, and Hampton could just see the darker outlines of the water tower and two-story depot of the El Paso & Southwestern Railroad in Columbus.

"Long way to ride just to shoot things up," he said. "Don't sound like the army is too worried about it. Mr. Adams got some special information?"

"There's been talk in Palomas, across the border, along with the usual gunfire."

"Uh-huh," Hampton said.

"It may not be a good idea to get too far from the house. Two men from the Johnson ranch been missing since day before yesterday."

Hampton shook the saddlebags against his leg and raised the barrel of the Winchester up and down.

"You're the boss," he said. "I'm just the foreman. All I do is advise. That's the easy part. You have to do the decidin'."

Mr. Frank nodded. "Well," he said. "They need to be brought in. I'm not sayin' they don't. Guess I'm just a little nervous. Got a telegram from San Antonio today. Mary is on her way home."

Hampton looked up. "That right? What's the occasion?"

"She didn't say, but she's travelin' alone."

"Little Mary," Hampton said thoughtfully.

"I figured you'd be glad to know," Mr. Frank said. "You two used to get along so well."

Hampton looked down, remembering Mr. Frank's daughter, her gray eyes and her way of following him around, always talking. Even as a child, she had had a way of bridging the thirty-two year difference in their ages.

"Yeah," he said slowly. "She broke my heart when she married that man from Tennessee."

"Yours and mine both," Mr. Frank said with a laugh.

Hampton was beginning to smell supper mixed in with the smell of wood smoke from the big house. He wondered briefly what the preacher was up to and who the other man with him might be.

The door opened behind Mr. Frank, and a woman's figure was silhouetted in the light of the room beyond. When she closed the door, the twilight took her. It was Billy's mother, Betty. She wore a light jacket over her dress and a brown scarf was tied over her red hair.

"Goin' to the house, Betty?" Mr. Frank said, removing his hand from the post and turning around.

"Time to," Betty said. "Hello, Hamp."

"Evenin'. May I escort you as far as the corral?"

"Oh go on," Betty smiled.

"All right, Hamp," Mr. Frank said. "I just thought I'd check with you, see that you got back in one piece."

"Such a piece as it is," Hampton said, looking at Betty as she stepped close to him. The wind was catching the ears of her scarf and he could see a lock of her red hair blowing across her forehead.

As they walked away, Mr. Frank went back inside, and Betty said, "You were late getting back."

"Things slow down in those hills. I got slowed down and didn't ever pick up again."

"What's it like up there?"

Hampton looked sideways at her as they walked along. "Ride up there with me sometime, and I'll show it to you."

"Would you?"

"I said I would."

They walked slowly in the windy twilight like the old friends they were. Betty's step was light, and Hampton could smell her: the scent of woodsmoke and food, and the other sweet scent that was hers naturally.

"It would be better than you going off up there by yourself," Betty said, half teasing.

"Uh-huh," Hampton said. "I'll ask Tom about it sometime."

10

Hampton looked at the ground as he walked. They veered to the left toward the corral. The Dunbar cabin was a hundred yards beyond it, surrounded by a bare sand yard with one mesquite tree at the back corner.

"No you won't," Betty said.

"Probably not. Here's the corral. Think you can make it the rest of the way?"

Betty stopped and looked at the horses in the corral. The wind was blowing harder here, and it was cold. She looked at Hampton and smiled again.

"I thought you might be late. I built a good fire in your stove so you can cook some supper if you want."

"Why don't you come cook it for me?"

"Go on. I left you some bread, too."

"Betty," Hampton said, swinging the saddlebags away and half bowing, "you are a treasure. Thank you. I mean that."

Betty looked away, then looked back at him. "I guess I had better get home. Tom and Billy will be looking for me, I reckon."

"Yes, they will. They better," Hampton said, serious for a moment. He looked at her intently, watching the lock of hair catch the wind.

"Well," she said, like a schoolgirl.

"Thank you, Betty."

"You just keep coming back to this old ranch, James Hampton. A lot of wind can blow and animals live and die and crops make, but you just be sure you keep coming back, because otherwise none of the rest of it will make any sense."

"Why wouldn't I?"

"Oh, I don't know. I get the feeling sometimes when you go off somewhere that you'd just as soon keep going."

Hampton looked down, then raised his head and looked around. He was a big man with a habit of wearing suspenders with his belt and tucking his work gloves under the left strap while he cut himself a chew of tobacco or rolled himself a cigarette. He was nearsighted and wore goldrimmed glasses that caught the sunlight beneath the brim of his worn campaign hat.

"Well, good night," Betty said.

She hesitated the beat of an eyelid, then moved off in the darkness, stepping neither quickly nor slowly toward the light of her cabin.

He watched her for a moment, then turned and walked across the open space between the barn and the big house. Orion began to appear in the western sky, his belt stars first, then the point of his sword. The twilight had completely faded by the time Hampton passed the windmill. The fan had been turned off, but the strain of the wind against the blades made the metal creak and whine. Somewhere out beyond the big house, some cows bawled; all of the other usual sounds were taken away by the wind like the puffs of sand under Hampton's boots.

Hampton could feel the chill of the night press against his face, but he did not think about it. As he walked, he looked at the rocky ground in front of his boots.

It had been Satterwhite's job to check those pastures and draws where the Tres Hermanas leveled down onto the floor of the desert. He had been gone half a day and gotten back before noon, claiming to have seen only a handful of calves and two dozen head of four- and five-year-old stock.

Hampton had been going over seed orders with Tom Dunbar when he had heard him come in. He had gone out for Satterwhite's account, trying to watch the younger man's eyes, but he found that impossible since Satterwhite never turned his head to look at him.

"That's all you saw, fella?" Hampton asked him.

"What do you want to know for?" Satterwhite returned, licking at the ghost of a mustache he thought he had growing on his upper lip.

"Well, for one thing, it's my job to know. And for another thing, calves need to be branded and cut so as to avoid confusion later on. You understand that, do you?"

"You can go take a look yourself if you don't believe me."

"I may just do that," Hampton said.

Satterwhite had walked away then toward the big house with Hampton staring after him. The younger man had been in New Mexico only two years, and he still had the Oklahoma City walk he had the winter day that Hampton rode into Columbus to meet his train. From behind, Hampton thought Satterwhite looked like a man trying to walk across a set of box springs.

When Hampton was close to his house, he looked up from the ground and saw a light shining weakly out of the northeast window from the room where the wood heater was. The preacher would be in there with whomever he had brought with him from town. The preacher knew where everything was, and Hampton was glad the house would be warm when he got there. He hoped the preacher had taken the liberty of making some coffee.

At the low steps, he kicked at the sand on his boots and stepped up. The preacher's bay looked at him. For a moment he had the impression that he was about to enter another man's house. He could tell he was tired.

"By God," he said, stepping inside, "somebody better have some coffee on the stove."

Hampton was about to say something else when he saw the other man rise from the oak captain's chair pulled up to the wood heater in the front room. He knew that profile and the small, stocky frame, although it had been a long time since he had seen either one. It was Bud Tyler.

"Now look at that," Hampton said, dropping the saddlebags and standing the Winchester in the corner by the door.

"Hello, Hamp," Bud Tyler said, taking a step forward. He ducked his head slightly as if he were shy. "I hope you don't mind the preacher showin' me on up here."

"Bud Tyler," Hampton said. His eyes were bright in the warm room, watering from the wind. He sniffed.

"Yeah, it's me. Wish it was somebody else sometimes, but it's just me."

Hampton looked past Tyler's shoulder and saw the preacher standing with his back to the wood heater wearing his black wool coat. He was a young man for a preacher, tall and serious with blue eyes that could nail a sinner to the wall with sadness. Hampton was not a formally religious man, but he and the preacher had been friends since the preacher had come to live in Columbus five years before.

"Hello, Preacher," Hampton said.

He looked back at Tyler. He noticed the grayness of his hair and mustache and the salt-and-pepper gray of his whiskers. He looked like an old Confederate general retired from active service.

"You may not believe this, Preacher," Hampton said, "but me and this old man was born the same day of May in 1860."

"You could be twins," the preacher said.

"Cut from the same rock, maybe," Tyler said. "Hamp's mama wouldn't take kindly to adoptin' me."

"She's past decidin' that now," Hampton said.

Tyler abruptly extended his hand, and Hampton took it in a strong grip, a grip greater than one given in greeting, more expressive of how he felt about seeing his friend again.

"What is it?" Hampton asked.

Tyler ducked his head again. "I've got a proposition for you. I've made up my mind about somethin', and I want to include you in on it."

The two men stood looking at each other a minute more. In their eyes was an exchange of history that began in the south-central woodlands of Tennessee and had moved westward with parents into Texas through hard, dreary Reconstruction years, drought, outlawry, deaths in the family, eventual separation from family, across Texas into New Mexico, up to Colorado for Tyler who drifted with prospectors, staying just busy enough to pretend he was working, and just broke enough to keep at it, taking odd jobs in towns during the winters and following the sunset in the springs. Hampton had settled into ranching and had known it in the days of the open range and the big roundups, and now, in the infancy of automobiles and telephones and aeroplanes.

"I didn't know it till just now, but I been half a man since I saw you last," Hampton said.

Tyler dropped his hand and nodded. "I know what you mean," he said.

THREE

HAMPTON decided against the jerky and crackers in his saddlebags, and instead fried some slices of cured ham, opened a can of peaches, and melted two pounds of longhorn cheese in a pan with half a cup of milk and some pepper. He sliced the loaf of bread that Betty had left him and ate the end piece as he stood in front of the stove. A pot of coffee finished the table. The preacher had added wood to the fire Betty made, and it did not take Hampton long to fix the meal. Tyler and the preacher sat at the table talking quietly to each other or to Hampton while he cooked. In those moments when Hampton turned for a fork or for a cup towel to wipe his hands, he glanced toward his two friends, and, once, a restlessness he did not understand made a knot in his stomach. He thought it was impatience to be done with the cooking, but he knew it ran deeper than that, and it was something he had felt before.

At the table, the men ate solemnly and heartily, but without talking. Hampton had never been one to talk while a meal was before him, a practice begun by his father who had been a Methodist preacher and who had demanded silence at the table.

Afterwards, Hampton carried the kerosene lamp to the front room and the wood heater and the chairs there. It was a narrow room, fifteen by twelve, with a spare bunk against the far wall where Hampton sometimes slept on the coldest nights. On the floor by the bunk, there was a large duffel bag and a saddle tied up in a feed sack.

Hampton set the lamp on a small table and added wood to the fire. He cut himself a chew of tobacco before sliding the cuspidor along the floor with his boot to a place between his chair and Tyler's.

When he sat down, he felt the stiffness in his back and shoulders from the long ride, and he was tired.

There is a different kind of ease between men who are busy and men who are resting, and for several minutes there was an uneasy silence as the men got used to each other.

"You want a chew, Preacher?" Hampton asked, looking across at him.

The preacher smiled. "I think not. Another cup of coffee sounds better to me."

The room was silent again except for the chipping and cracking of the burning wood behind the iron door, and the occasional creak of the rafters as the cool air above strained to meet the warm air in the room. The preacher got up and went for the coffee.

"It ain't the church that keeps him from chewin'," Hampton said. "He doesn't have the stomach for it."

"You ever chew pipe tobacco?" Tyler asked, and spit. His graying hair was peaked on top from the pressure of his hat which now lay upside down on the bunk.

Hampton laughed shortly. "No, thank you."

"I did last winter. Makes for a knotty spit."

The preacher came back with a cup and sat down again. Hampton looked at him, and their eyes met across the wood heater. Hampton's eyes held a question, but the preacher's declined to answer. Tyler spit, then wiped his bottom lip with the full length of his index finger.

"You ever hunt bear, Mr. Leggitt?" Tyler asked the preacher.

"No, sir. I've seen them from a distance, but never hunted them."

"I'm talkin' about grizzly bears, killer bears, up in Colorado on one of them high meadows."

"Never been there," Hampton said. He had settled his chew in against his jaw and held it there without chewing. His hands were folded loosely in his lap.

"You would like it, Hamp," Tyler turned toward him.

"Been to Pueblo, though. I rode up there with Mr. Frank a few years ago. Didn't care for it. Hot. Looks like Columbus, only bigger."

16

"Columbus wasn't hot when I came through it. I thought I would blow away to Mexico before I got to Powers' drugstore."

"That's where I found him," the preacher said.

"I was havin' a sody," Tyler explained.

"He was taking hats down off the wall and trying them on."

"Nothin' wrong with that," Hampton said.

"The women's hats too," the preacher added.

"Some of them hats is real pretty," Tyler said.

Hampton snorted, then he said, "You hangin' out in drugstores these days, Preacher?"

"It was more in the order of business," the preacher said.

"Uh-huh," Hampton said. "I wonder whose."

Tyler spit. "I think y'all turned off on a side trail somewhere."

"Never mind," Hampton said, one corner of his mouth turned down in a kind of frown-smile. "You were talkin' about bears."

"I was talkin' about bears, but it was somethin' else I was thinkin' about. I was goin' to say that there is somethin' about huntin' an old grizzly bear up in one of them meadows that's a whole lot like goin' to war."

"When have you ever been in a war?" Hampton looked at him.

"Me and you both, down on the Rio Grande."

"I ain't sure that was a war," Hampton shook his head. His fingers clasped together, then relaxed again. "That was more in the nature of an extended saloon fight."

"I remember a lot more canebrakes than saloons," Tyler said.

The two older men chewed silently for a few minutes while the wood in the heater popped softly and the wind left the blades of the windmill, shook the bare limbs of the cottonwoods around the ranch headquarters, and creaked along the north wall of Hampton's little house.

"What is this about war and canebrakes?" the preacher asked, both hands around the cup of coffee.

"You mean Hamp never told you we used to be Texas Rangers down on the Rio Grande with the Captain himself?"

"No," the preacher said, looking at the two men for a sign of a shared joke. Tyler had the glimmer of a smile on his lips, but

Hampton's jaws, prickled with short gray whiskers, were set, locked in thought, or memory.

"Which captain do you mean?"

"Captain McNelly," Hampton said with force and reverence.

"The Captain himself," Tyler added.

"Should I know that name?" the preacher asked apologetically.

"You should," Tyler said, "but few remember."

"Texas Rangers," the preacher said.

"It seemed like a good idea," Hampton said. "We didn't have any money in those days anyway, so we thought we'd run with some other boys in the same shape."

Tyler nodded, then spit. "We was all preachers' kids."

A gust of wind howled around the corners of the house and swept across the foothills below the ranch toward Mexico.

"March winds," Hampton said.

"Sounds like riders sometimes," the preacher said.

Hampton and Tyler exchanged glances. Hampton moved his tobacco again, working it now, tasting the bitter, slightly smoky flavor of the heart of his chew.

"Maybe it's Pancho Villa," Tyler said.

The preacher looked up, caught Tyler's expression, then returned his stare to the wood heater.

"There would be more than just howlin' if it was that son of a bitch," Hampton said.

Tyler said, "That's what I was gettin' at about huntin' bears."

The preacher laughed shortly at Tyler's patient tenacity in making a point. Hampton followed suit.

"Listen," Tyler said. "Stalkin' one of them grizzlies up there in the mountains is a lot like a war. You get up there and go to lookin' for that bear, and you can't help thinkin' all the time that he knows more about where you are than you know about him. Holdin' that gun don't make you anywhere near the hunter he is. You get the feelin' you ain't huntin' at all, but just tryin' to stay alive. That bear could be waitin' not twenty steps from you.

"This Pancho Villa is the same way. When I came down here, I had a prickly feelin' I was walkin' into that bear's territory, and he knew more about it than I did."

"He probably fixed you that sody at Powers'," Hampton said.

"Miss Clark did that," the preacher said. "I believe that's what led to the hats."

"Did you say Miss?"

"She ain't Miss for an old bear hunter like you," Hampton said.

"Well, anyway, I got the feelin' I was walkin' into the territory of somethin' that knows more about me than I know about him," Tyler spit.

"I have heard more and more anxiety myself," the preacher said. "Problems with the Mexicans seem to be a matter of patriotism around here, for both sides. Been going on a long time, from what I gather. But lately it has been different. I don't know for certain what it is."

"There's been a bunch of talk around Columbus about a border war ever since the revolution started," Hampton said. "Anybody that's got time to listen can get his ears flushed with war talk."

"It doesn't seem to be just talk," the preacher said. "It's a feeling."

"See there," Tyler said.

"I go into town," the preacher continued, "and it seems like there isn't a wagon tied where there usually is one, or the barracks seem quieter, or there are four men standing by the depot instead of one or two. There's been a lot of strange Mexicans around too."

"You a sign reader, Preacher?" Hampton asked.

The preacher looked across the wood heater into the serious blue eyes of Hampton. "My father showed me a little about it when he was horse doctor for the army."

"I am," Tyler said. "And I read the sign of a loco grizzly."

Hampton and the preacher held their stare a second longer, then Hampton spit and the preacher dropped his eyes back to the firelight that leaked out through cracks around the iron door of the wood heater.

"Well that's good to know," Hampton said then. "Long as I hang around you, I won't have to worry about no grizzly Mexican bear sneakin' up on me."

"That's what it feels like to me," Tyler said.

The sound of the wind deepened around the house and early

night slipped into late night. There would be frost higher up where moisture was allowed to cling long enough to freeze, perhaps in the Florida Mountains to the east. The ground at the ranch would be hard and dry and cold in the morning.

"I could make some more coffee," Hampton offered. "Wouldn't take but about three hours."

"What are you waitin' for then," Tyler said.

"Not for me," the preacher said and shifted in his chair so that he was leaning forward with his elbows on his knees. His black wool coat bunched at the shoulders and fell open at his waist. "I need to be getting back. I've already stayed too long."

"It sounds like a cold night," Tyler said, listening to the wind.

"Book, chapter, and verse," Hampton said. Then he said, "I'd be glad to put you up."

"I know. I think I had better go on back. Rosie and Marcos will be looking for me."

"That's his mother and father," Hampton said with a short laugh.

"They came with the congregation," the preacher explained. "Rosie looks after the house. Marcos helps me with the church."

The preacher dropped his eyes to the fire, and although Hampton waited, the preacher continued to stare at the wood heater as if he wanted to memorize its warmth to recall it on the ride home. Hampton knew something was on the preacher's mind. The younger man was full of restlessness and yearning, but he seldom let anyone else see it, and the bond between the preacher and Hampton had sprung from shared secrets.

"Let me get my coat on, and I'll see you get on your way without being carried off by a grizzly bear," Hampton said. "Bud, that coffee's in the galley if you want it."

"I'll think on it a while."

Hampton sat forward, put his hands on the arms of the chair, then got to his feet slowly with a catch in his breath as he straightened his back. "I never know how tall I am until I have to stand all the way up."

The preacher got to his feet as well. "No need to bother, Hamp."

20

"No bother. Let me get my coat."

Hampton left the room, and the preacher backed up to the wood heater. He felt the heat rise along his back. In a moment, his legs began to cook. He put his empty cup on the seat of his chair.

"I appreciate you seein' me out here," Tyler said, looking up at the younger man.

"There isn't much I wouldn't do for Hamp," the preacher said. "I think a lot of him."

"So do I," Tyler said. "Me and him been down some pretty hard trails and rode some rough rivers. Used to be, we didn't even have to speak to one another, just look and go on. He can read signals better than any man I ever knew."

Hampton came back into the room. He shrugged on his worn, brown coat and shook his head.

"It's a two-blanket night for sure," he said. "Makes a man wish he'd patched up his quilts long before now. I'll be right back, Bud."

"Pleasure meeting you, Mr. Tyler," the preacher said.

"Same here," Tyler returned. He stood up and extended his hand to the preacher. A smile lit up his brown eyes and deepened the wrinkles around them.

Hampton and the preacher stepped out on the porch, and Hampton pulled the door closed behind him. He felt the cold immediately on his cheeks and on his hands, but it was not a bitter cold. In the winter that was already passing, he had felt much worse. They stood together in the shadow of the porch roof and looked at the night.

"Plenty of stars to see by," Hampton said.

"It'll be a short ride."

"Yeah," Hampton said.

"Mr. Tyler seems to be a good man."

Hampton glanced at the preacher's horse and buggy. "It's peculiar, him showin' up like this, but he's one man I always knew I'd see again, even if it wasn't in this life. Me and him been around a long time."

"Mr. Satterwhite said you were riding the hills."

"He ain't no mister."

The preacher laughed, knowing how little Hampton cared for

Satterwhite. His values were different, and Hampton was the kind of man who placed a heavy importance on values. It was another thing that brought Hampton and the young preacher together. Their values were the same.

Hampton stepped forward, raising his head to the wind as if checking it for scents. The stars were bright overhead, but hazy near the horizon.

"You got somethin' on your mind, Preacher?"

The preacher looked at the dark ground in front of the house, then up, past the pens and sheds and small collection of adobe farm houses that made up the ranch headquarters.

"I don't know, Hamp," he said, his voice low and hoarse from a sort of perpetual hayfever that gave the fervent parts of his sermons an affecting, husky earnestness.

"Uh-huh," Hampton said. "Been that way once or twice myself."

"I've been here five years," the preacher said. "I have a small but loyal congregation."

"Too close to the border for a big Protestant congregation," Hampton interrupted.

The preacher nodded in the darkness. "It isn't the size of the church, or even the church, or maybe it is the church, but lately I've been less and less satisfied with things here. I go through the motions, but sometimes I feel like I'm outside of myself watching myself. Or I feel split. Part of me just isn't in it."

"You losin' faith?"

The preacher took a step forward. "No," he said, looking at the night. "It isn't that. I believe in the sanctity of what I'm doing, I just don't get the same thing from doing it that I used to when I first left the seminary."

"It was new then, maybe."

The preacher looked down in the darkness. Something banged softly from the direction of the barn.

"It's still a challenge," the preacher said, then he shrugged. "I don't know what I'm trying to say. Maybe I'm just lonely. A preacher is supposed to have all the answers. People are quick to come to me when they are in need of something, but they never think that I might need something too. That sounds selfish, doesn't it?"

The preacher was quiet. The wind blew his words away. Hampton spit and moved the chew around in his cheek.

"Understandable," he said.

"I've been thinking about my father lately, the life we had after my mother died. I always think about him in the spring. I'm not sure why."

"You could have been a fair horse doctor yourself," Hampton said. "What made you turn to preachin' in the first place?"

"My mother. She was religious, an insistent kind of religious, but loving and warm on the human level, too."

"Best kind of religious. Looks good on a woman. You were pretty young when she died though, weren't you?"

"Twelve," the preacher said. "But her influence didn't stop with her death. I remember once when the weather was cold and wet, and my father had to leave the house for the afternoon and part of the night. It couldn't have been but a couple of years after she had died. It got dark, and the fire began to go out. The woodbox was empty, so I had to go into the storm for wood. I didn't want to, but it was a nasty night, and I knew my father would be put out if he came back and there was no fire.

"The woodshed was at an angle to the house, and I ran through the rain toward it. It was dark as death when I got there. A screech owl flew out at me screeching like the devil himself. It scared me so bad — you can imagine — I just froze. I couldn't move to leave the shed, nor could I remain in that terrible darkness."

Hampton was silent, his eyes going to each building or pen in sight, checking, noticing.

"I stood there in the dark, shivering, unable to move for several minutes, when suddenly a gust of wind roared across the clearing and blew open the front door of the house. It swung back with a bang that nearly made me jump out of my shoes. I saw the light from inside shining like a path, and I ran for it. After I was inside, I noticed my mother's picture had fallen from the wall."

Hampton spit and wiped his mouth on the sleeve of his coat. He pushed his hands down in his coat pockets.

"Is that a ghost story, Preacher?"

"I felt I owed her something, Hamp. My father and I had a good life. When he died, I felt I owed her memory something."

"There's a lot worse reasons for goin' into preachin'."

"I'm just not sure anymore that it's a good enough reason to stay."

"That's something I can't help you with," Hampton said.

"I just wish I didn't feel like such a traitor for it. Haven't you ever had the feeling it was time to move on to something else?"

Hampton was quiet a while, then he spit. "There was a man a few miles west of here. He's gone on now. Land developer in Deming has all his land. He used to plant about a hundred acres of the best damn corn you ever tasted. Every March, about this time, he'd go to work and plant corn, and everybody in Columbus would watch him. Hell, the mule deer up in the Floridas would watch him. And every June, there was all this beautiful corn. It was a sight to see, Preacher.

"He planted it between the house and the road, and anybody goin' down that way had to stop and admire it. Some of the boys used to go down there the first part of June and steal ears for supper. Mabry was his name, and he finally had to build a deer fence around the corn, but the boys would take a pair of fence pliers in their boot and ride down there about the time the chickens behind Mabry's house were wakin' up. They figured any man who had set out to guard that corn at night would be sleepiest at that hour.

"Other times, some of us would ride down there and offer to buy some of that corn. He had a tight little old adobe house with one of the best sittin' porches I have ever seen. Mabry would come out from somewhere and say, 'What happened to all of that you stold the other night?'

"He had him a young wife, and she was a picture, too. Lived a hard, lonely life down there, but she was a picture. To tell you the truth, I'd go down there just to see her walk by, as much as for that corn. Had hair the color of last year's penny."

Hampton spit again. The preacher was standing beside him,

24

listening to the sound of Hampton's voice as much as to his words. Hampton had a deep, certain way of speaking that made people give him close attention.

"Yes, sir," Hampton said. "That was good corn."

"What about it?"

"In July the stalks would be dry and yeller and crackle like river water in the wind. Dust devils would get in that patch and lift leaves and shucks two or three hundred yards up into the sky and carry them clear to Deming, if the wind was right. Sometimes I'd find those leaves way up on the slopes of the Sisters."

"What happened?"

Hampton spit. "This is between you and me, Preacher."

"It always is."

"Today, when I was up in the hills, I was ridin' along like nothin', then something catches my eye. I think it's a bird at first, but when I look again, it's one of those corn leaves driftin' down."

The preacher shook his head. "Hamp."

"You think I'm kiddin' don't you?"

"Aren't you?"

"No, sir. Now I'm not sayin' that was one of Mabry's. It could have been a leaf of cane, but I don't think so. It looked like corn to me."

"Say that it was," the preacher said, trying to follow where Hampton's story was taking him.

Hampton shook his head. "I don't know, but somethin' got to gnawin' on my insides after that. I felt I was guilty of great wrong-doing, yet nothin' other than the usual would come to mind."

"I think you've lost me," the preacher said.

"I've always wanted to raise corn like Mabry's," Hampton said. "This is a good life here at the ranch, but sometimes I wish I had a place of my own, a place with trees."

"I like the part about the trees."

"A man forgets about trees in this country. But sometimes, when the moon is too bright to find shade from, I think about it, and I think about a lady livin' out those days with me. She would be young and fair. On an evenin' in early June, she'd take a basket made of oak splints, like the one my mama used to have, and go into the corn field to pull a dozen ears for supper."

The preacher shifted and moved to the first step, but Hampton did not seem to notice. He was a thousand miles away.

"She'd come back to the house and I'd say, 'What have you got there, darlin'?' But you know something, Preacher?" Hampton asked, his voice changing. "She doesn't answer, because she ain't there. Not for an old man like me. I will be fifty-six years old in two more months, and I'm not what I used to be. No, sir. I figure whatever chance I had at that pipe dream is gone now."

The preacher could think of nothing to say. He stood beside Hampton and looked out in the night. A coyote cried, and the bay twitched its ears.

"Anyway," Hampton shrugged, "it makes me restless and short-tempered for a while to think about it, but I always get over it. Maybe you will too."

"Maybe you're right. It seems worse at times than at others."

They were quiet for a while, and Hampton knew something had been settled, at least for the moment. "You can stay, if you want," he said.

"No, Hamp. I need to get back. The ride will do me good."

"Did Bud get all his stuff inside?"

"He said once or twice it wasn't much for a man who had lived as long as he had. I think he was embarrassed about it."

"He's up to somethin'," Hampton said.

"Well, goodnight, Hamp," the preacher said, and stepped off the porch. Hampton moved to the post where the horse was tied and slipped the knot on the long leather reins. He threw them to the preacher and watched him climb in the buggy and turn it toward Columbus. Hampton no longer had the feeling something had been settled. He spit and went back inside the house.

Tyler was still in his chair by the wood heater, but he was holding a cup of coffee. He turned his dark brown eyes on Hampton as Hampton backed up to the wood heater.

"I feel a little in the way," Tyler said, crossing his legs and resting the cup on his thigh.

"Nope."

"I don't mean to be."

"You're not. The preacher is a little shy about some things. He's feelin' some doubts about his calling."

"I wonder if our fathers ever felt that way?" Tyler said.

"If they did, they never said it out loud. That's the difference between them and young fellas like the preacher. Folks nowadays talk more about what's on their minds."

"I reckon so. Pa never said nothin' but do or be damned."

Hampton felt the heat go into his muscles, and he yawned. He unbuttoned his coat and draped it over the back of the preacher's chair. The preacher's empty cup was still on the seat.

"What do you think of the place?" Hampton asked.

"It's real nice. Feels like a home."

"Yeah. I didn't want the bunkhouse. Like to sit by myself without somebody askin' me what's on my mind. Gettin' cranky in my old age, I guess."

"It's real nice, Hamp," Tyler said again.

"Thank you."

Hampton turned to the wood heater and held his palms down to it. His knuckles were lined and brown and scarred. "How you been, Bud?" he asked quietly.

"Well, I been in the hospital since last Christmas, Hamp. Horse rolled over on me and put a rib through my lung. Liked to come out my back into the dirt. Doctors worked on me and kept me alive, but I went through one kind of sickness after another before it was over."

"Pneumonia?" Hampton asked, looking at his friend.

"That liked to got me."

"I always figured that's how it would be," Hampton said. "You'd be off somewhere, and there would be an accident. Or I would be, and the other would never know about it."

"Yeah," Tyler said, "I know. I had plenty of time to think about it, lyin' up there in Denver in a room facin' west, wonderin' which sunset would be my last."

"You could have sent word."

"A man never thinks like that when he's laid up. But I did think about what I'd do if I ever got out of that hospital."

Hampton reached down and lifted the lid on the wood heater with the handle he kept there. He spit his chew into the coals, hawked, and spit again.

"Any more of that coffee, Bud?"

"Sure. Let me get you a cup."

Tyler put his own cup on the floor by his chair, then got up and went into the kitchen. While he was gone, Hampton sat down heavily. A lot of people had come in and out of his life through the years — men, women, girls, boys — and each had left a mark on him, good or bad, but Tyler had been the constant. As he sat down, the thought of almost losing Tyler brought back other faces to him. One was that of his little brother Homer, and one was Mr. Frank's gray-eyed daughter, Mary.

When Tyler came back, Hampton was sitting in his chair staring at the wood heater.

"Thank you, Bud. Smells just right."

Tyler sat down, and true night settled into the room. Hampton was getting sleepy.

"I could sleep in this chair tonight and never think twice about it," Hampton said.

Tyler sipped his coffee. "I mean."

"How is it now?"

"I get a little sore at night, otherwise okay. Doc said I'd probably have bouts with pneumonia the rest of my life, but I guess every man's got to have somethin' chasin' him."

Hampton smiled. "I reckon," he said, then, "You goin' to stay a few days?"

"I ain't in no big hurry."

"Got to bring some stock in. Like to help?"

"I done worse. You'll have to get me a horse. I sold the one that laid me up."

They drank their coffee and looked at the wood heater.

"Hamp," Tyler said after a pause, "I'm ready to go back to Texas."

"Texas?"

"Yeah, and I want you to come with me."

Hampton held his cup close to his face for the heat of the steam.

"I been roamin' around a long time," Tyler went on, "but I haven't felt good about myself since we left Texas. I figured maybe we could get us a place on the Brazos or the Navasota River and settle down like gentlemen farmers."

"I don't know, Bud. After Homer died, I swore I'd never go back to East Texas."

"I thought maybe all this time would have taken care of that."

"There's some things that time don't help."

Tyler was silent, then he said, "Think about it, Hamp. I don't want to take you away from a good thing here. I just want you to think about it."

Hampton finished his coffee and lowered the cup, letting it dangle from two fingers beside his leg. He remembered a sunny clearing in the pines of East Texas that he had walked into one day while hunting, and the way the sunlight and the wind had played upon the winter rye.

"I'll think about it," he said.

FOUR

T H E town of Columbus, New Mexico, lay three miles from the
Mexican border in open country of brush and cactus and mesquite. The dusty, dirt roads of the small town tilted to the south
visibly, as if the Florida and Tres Hermanas ranges to the north were
the heels of giant palms pouring the desert into Mexico. Established
fourteen years earlier in 1902 as a rail watering stop, the town had
grown slowly, basing its economy first on ranching and farming,
which was good if the fields were irrigated, then on the army, which,
as the revolution in Mexico heated up, created a ranging military
outpost there known as Camp Furlong.

Five miles to the northwest, in a straight line with the nearest
peak of the Tres Hermanas and the water tower at the depot in town,
was the MacPherson Ranch. Barely noticeable except for the cottonwoods around the low buildings, the ranch had been James Hampton's home for the past eleven years while he was foreman there.
Although he had been born and raised in river bottoms under the
shade of evergreens and oaks, something about the desert appealed to
him, suited him. He had watched Columbus grow, and, while he
never had much hope for the town, he enjoyed the rhythms of its
people and the solid, though bleak, aspect of its buildings and streets.

Now, in the bright March morning, Hampton and Tyler
walked past the windmill and crossed the open yard to the big house.
The sun had already warmed the desert, and only a few thin feathers
of high cirrus lingered toward the south. Both of the men were
wearing their coats, already unbuttoned.

"Looks like a nice layout," Tyler said, matching Hampton's determined step.

"Is. Been here a long time. Mr. Frank's father had to cut some deals with the Apaches and Spanish both when he settled here. There's good water under this whole valley."

When Hampton and Tyler got to the big house, they stepped up on the porch, and Hampton knocked. Then, he turned and looked across the yard and out through the front gate. He never liked knocking on doors and waiting, and his natural pride would not let him stand staring at the door until it was opened. Only a slight easterly breeze was blowing, and there was no movement at all in the desert, neither bird nor animal nor windblown dust.

"We'll be shuckin' these coats by dinnertime," Hampton said.

"Not like the mountains," Tyler nodded. "Gets cold up there, it stays cold."

The door opened, and both men turned to face Rueben Satterwhite, Mr. Frank's nephew, who stood with his hand on the knob as if he meant to shut the door again. Satterwhite was six feet tall, but thin, without much shoulder. At twenty-one, his sandy hair made him seem still a boy in appearance, and the sparse mustache did not make the difference Satterwhite hoped it would.

"Mornin'," Hampton said, speaking first. He looked Satterwhite up and down as if he had never seen him before. "Mr. Frank up and around?"

"Come on in."

"Don't mind if we do."

Hampton and Tyler passed through the doorway, and Satterwhite closed the door. The front room was Mrs. MacPherson's parlor and reflected her disinclination to decorate in the Mexican-western style that was so popular in Silver City. It was filled with an overabundance of stuffed furniture, a cut-down upright piano their daughter Mary used to play hymns on, and pictures suspended from nails in the plaster walls. A large rug covered most of the concrete floor in the middle of the room.

"He's in the kitchen," Satterwhite said, looking curiously at Tyler.

Hampton did not bother with introductions but nodded, crossed the room, and went through the arched doorway of the dining room. The kitchen door was always open except when company was seated at table, and Hampton was met by the smell of woodsmoke, fried bacon, and the coffee with chicory that Mr. Frank preferred. In another moment, they were in the kitchen.

"Mornin', Hamp. How about some coffee?" Mr. Frank asked. "Who's that you got with you?"

"Name's Bud Tyler," Tyler said. "Mr. Leggitt, the preacher, brought me over from town last night."

Mr. Frank shook his hand. "Frank MacPherson," he said. "You ain't a preacher yourself, are you?"

Tyler ducked his head and glanced sideways at Hampton who had leaned back against the counter where the tin sink was. "No, sir. I'm more of the sinner persuasion."

"Bud's here visitin', but I volunteered him to help bring stock out of the hills," Hampton said.

Mrs. MacPherson walked into the kitchen then with Betty Dunbar. Each carried a plucked chicken that Billy had probably cleaned for them, and their attitude was brisk from being in the cold air.

Hampton and Tyler removed their hats and said good morning to the women. Tyler looked at Hampton again and moved closer to him. Hampton noticed the movement and found it hard to believe that after all these years, Tyler was still as shy as he had been when their families were neighbors in Longview, Texas, and the two of them had served as ushers at Mr. Hampton's Methodist church. Tyler had blushed and hidden his face each time he had to escort a woman down the church aisle.

"Good morning, Hamp," Mrs. MacPherson said in her busy way. Betty looked at him and smiled as she went to the sink.

"This is Bud Tyler, a friend of mine."

Mrs. MacPherson nodded at him. "Frank, did you offer these gentlemen some coffee, or were you waiting for us to get back?"

"Gentlemen?" Hampton laughed.

"I'll get the gentlemen some," Betty said.

"Hamp knows where the cups are," Mr. Frank said, pausing in

32

the sharpening of his sheath knife on the whetstone that was permanently attached to the worktable before him.

"Rueben, do you want another cup?" Betty asked, and the men turned to the doorway of the dining room where Satterwhite still stood, his hands in his pockets and his tongue licking at his upper lip.

"No, ma'am," he said.

"I didn't know it was Sunday," Hampton said to Mrs. MacPherson, indicating the chickens as he took the hot cup from Betty.

"We may as well eat them as the coyotes," Mrs. MacPherson said, laying the chickens out on a cutting board for Betty, then wiping her hands on a cup towel.

"Yes, ma'am," Hampton said.

"So you're a friend of Hamp's," Betty said to Tyler, handing him a cup of the bitter coffee.

Tyler took the cup and nodded his head.

"Oh, he don't speak, Betty. We've tried to teach him how, but it never took."

Betty smiled at Tyler which caused him to duck his head a little lower. In the warm air of the kitchen, his cheeks were flushed, and his eyes were bright.

"You think there's enough calves to bother bringing the whole bunch down?" Mr. Frank said, picking up the cup towel his wife laid down and wiping the blade of his knife with it.

"There were yesterday," Hampton said, glancing at Satterwhite.

"Rueben was saying this morning that some of those you saw might have drifted up there from the Lightning Tree Range."

Hampton and Tyler both looked at Satterwhite, who pulled his hands out of his pockets and crossed his arms. Hampton noticed that he was wearing the striped pants and heavy cotton shirt he was so fond of.

"That so?"

"I didn't see that many head up in the hills," Satterwhite said. "If you saw so many, maybe they got out through a break in the fence."

"You see any breaks in the fence?" Hampton asked.

"If there are," Mrs. MacPherson said, "a certain red bull is sure to have an explanation."

"I saw that red bull myself just two days ago," Mr. Frank said.

"I didn't look for breaks," Satterwhite said.

Hampton started to say something, then bit it off and sipped his coffee instead. Satterwhite put his hands back in his pockets and looked at the floor.

"What is your plan, Hamp?" Mr. Frank asked, sliding his knife into the sheath that hung from his belt.

"I think it's time to bring them down, put them close to the house so we can cut and brand them."

"How many men you think you'll need?" Mr. Frank looked sideways at his wife, then meaningfully at Hampton. Hampton understood.

"Tyler here is about as good a brush popper as I've ever seen, if you'll put a horse under him. I'll go myself. How about one other?"

Mr. Frank picked up his own coffee cup and drank from it. Hampton did not particularly like the taste of coffee with chicory in it, but he had drunk it that way more times than not.

"You planning to stay overnight?"

"Maybe two," Hampton said. "Can't get much done when you're trying to beat darkness off the hill."

Mr. Frank nodded. Hampton knew he was going over men's names in his mind, some of whom worked for him more or less regularly but lived in town. Ordinarily Hampton would not have gone himself, but he wanted to be there to prove Satterwhite wrong.

"That's fine," Mr. Frank said finally. "Get together what you need. Betty will help you as usual. You can take Rueben with you."

Satterwhite uncrossed his arms and started to speak.

"Yes, sir," Hampton said, with a slight smile. "I'll be glad to."

"Guess what?" Mrs. MacPherson said then. "Mary's on her way home."

Hampton looked up and lowered his coffee cup. "That's what Frank said. Did she say when to look for her?"

"Depends on the trains, I 'magine," Mr. Frank said.

"What's the occasion?"

"She didn't say, but she's traveling alone."

"Little Mary," Hampton said, mostly to himself, as if he were trying out an old memory.

"I thought you would be glad to know," Mrs. MacPherson said, turning away toward the sink. "You two used to get along so well."

Hampton remembered the times he had watched Mary moving around the kitchen helping Betty or just getting in the way. She had a knack of knowing when he looked at her and would turn, anticipating him, her eyebrows raised in question over her gray eyes.

"It will be lovely to have her home again, don't you think?" Mrs. MacPherson asked.

"Yes, ma'am," Hampton said. "Yes, it will."

Hampton sipped his coffee and looked sideways at Tyler.

Before two o'clock, Hampton led the packhorse up to the big house, where Betty was collecting the groceries. Hampton had his own trail kit of coffee pot and frying pan and the Dutch oven for boiling water and doing dishes, but he often let Betty pack the ones Mr. Frank kept in the big house. Since Betty also packed the food, she knew better which utensils the men would need and which ones would be unnecessary. This time she had put in coffee, canned bacon, eggs packed in cardboard, canned fruit, crackers, bread wrapped in wax paper, a fruit cake, jerky, condensed milk, sugar, and six rings of deer and pork sausage.

Hampton stood in the kitchen as Betty went through the list of things, each put away in appropriate cotton sacks tied at the neck. Hampton had already tied the sack containing his own necessaries — paper, matches, chewing tobacco, face towels, ammunition, a change of clothes — to the packsaddle.

"Betty, that's enough stuff to feed Camp Furlong for a week," Hampton said.

"There's potatoes, too, in this bundle, or that one. That one. So you can fry potatoes or make a stew with the sausage, however you want it."

"You know, Betty, you could just come with us if you had a mind to."

"I'm sure Tom would approve of that."

"We could forget to tell him."

"I could just see me riding up into the hills with you. Wouldn't that be a story for my grandchildren?"

"It might be," Hampton said. "What's in this sack — airtights?"

"I put all the cans together. Is it too heavy?"

"I'll let Satterwhite carry it."

"Where is your friend?"

"Mr. Frank was helpin' him pick out a horse, the last time I looked."

Betty tied the last sack with a slip knot at the neck as she always did. The activity and the room suited her. She was a busy, hardy woman with a keen instinct where others were concerned but a stubborn lack of insight about her own affairs. Hampton had immediately liked her when they were introduced eleven years before, and, although he felt that he had aged, he did not think she had. Her high cheekbones and red hair would probably keep her looking young all of her life.

"Tom will be havin' his hands full pretty soon with the planting," Hampton said, thinking. "Billy's old enough to help out."

"Billy doesn't have the knack of it, seems to me," Betty said. She pushed the sack along the counter toward the others.

Hampton looked out the kitchen window to the small smokehouse, flanked by stacks of wood. It was a bright day, and the absence of green made the shadows appear darker.

"He'll learn it," he said.

Betty went to the sink and pumped a bucket of water for some other chore she had on her mental list. Hampton glanced sideways at her back and noticed the way her dress grew tight across her thin, strong shoulders. He returned his glance to the smokehouse, ignoring the sacks. Betty dried her hands on her apron and looked at him.

"You seem a little preoccupied today, Hamp. Is something on your mind?"

"I was just thinkin'," Hampton said, looking at the floor of the kitchen and noticing a stray bit of thread along the crack where the wall met the floor. He paused.

"Yes?" Betty moved against the counter and stopped, one hand palm down on the clean surface, the other at her side.

"I was wonderin' how you manage so well — your place and Constance's."

Betty smiled. "I have a job to do. So do you. We both manage."

"You work in another woman's kitchen."

Betty looked at Hampton's profile, her green eyes catching the light from the window in the slightly smoky room. "And you work another man's ranch."

"Yes, ma'am, I do."

"That's our job in this world."

Hampton turned to the sacks, but he didn't touch them. "Wonder how it got to be that way, Betty?"

"Hamp," Betty said.

Hampton shook his head. "Oh, it ain't nothin'. Bud showin' up all the sudden got me to thinkin' about things, I guess."

Betty smiled. "What sort of things?"

Hampton shook his head. The expression on his face was hidden in profile by his winter beard and mustache.

"Bud left home back in Texas when I did. Me and him been down some rough trails together."

"I feel like he's going to take you away from us," she said.

Hampton turned to the sacks and gathered the necks of them in his wide, brown hands while Betty stood at the counter watching him. When he had them like he wanted them, he lifted them from the table and looked at her.

"Thank you, Betty, as usual."

Betty smiled and joined her hands in front of her.

"Hamp," she started, "we let it get this way. No one did it to us. We chose it."

She stopped, and Hampton watched her eyes. After a minute, he nodded and said, "Would you mind gettin' the door for me?"

Bud Tyler and Rueben Satterwhite were waiting at the barn when Hampton walked up, leading the packhorse. They were standing apart, Tyler checking the rigging on his horse while Satterwhite kicked at the hay and dust spread like a delta in front of the barn doors.

"Ready?" Tyler asked.

"Yeah. Hold the reins for me, will you?"

Tyler took the reins of the packhorse. Both horses raised their heads to each other, seeing what the one had that the other did not. Hampton walked past Tyler and cut Satterwhite a look through his glasses.

"Good day to go ridin', don't you think?" he asked.

Satterwhite gave him a half-hurt, half-defiant look, but Hampton brushed on by.

"Billy! Where the devil is that boy? Asleep?"

"Here, Mr. Hampton," Billy said, stepping down out of the separate tack room.

"Didn't mean to wake you up, Billy, but we got to go. We'll be lucky to find firewood before dark as it is."

"Lady's all ready to go. I wish I was going with y'all."

"You help your father, son, and your mother when she needs it. That's how a man starts out. He can't be no help to himself until he's been a help to others. Book, chapter, and verse."

"Yes, sir."

Hampton caught the reins for the mare and moved along beside her to the stirrups. He put one boot in and swung himself up. Billy was watching him from beneath the brim of a ragged felt hat his father had worn out years before.

"What is it?" Hampton asked.

"I wish I was going with you," Billy said again.

"Well, I'll tell you a secret, Billy. There's one person goin' along whose place I wish you could take. You mind to your business and keep the barn doors shut until you see our dust."

"Yes, sir," Billy said, but this time with more conviction in his wavering adolescent voice.

Hampton rode through the middle of the high barn, feeling the coolness of the shade. When he got to the doors, Satterwhite mounted. Tyler was already on the gelding Mr. Frank had loaned him and was holding the reins of the packhorse in his left hand. He looked cheerful and almost eager in the bright sunlight.

38

"Goddammit, Bud, it's good to see your face."

"Same here," Tyler smiled.

"Let's go, Satterwhite," Hampton said. "But try not to sing no songs of joy on the way up."

They rode out of the yard with Hampton in the lead, then Tyler, then Satterwhite, and from the barn Billy watched them go: Hampton, his shoulders erect and slightly rocking to the rhythm of the mare's gait, Tyler, compact and gray, and lastly Rueben Satterwhite, with his striped pants and white shirt, scowling and sulking behind.

For Hampton, who had ridden the same trail around the big fenced pasture and up into the hills just the day before, the ride was uninteresting in itself, but Tyler was curious about the operation and asked questions. Both men ignored Satterwhite. He rode watching their backs and wished he were some other place. Still young enough to resent Hampton's apparent indifference to his welfare, he did not enjoy the feeling that he was in the presence of someone who would probably not help him if he got into trouble. At one point on a slope that led around the nearest of the Tres Hermanas peaks, they stopped and got off their horses. Hampton was leading the packhorse and tied both it and the mare to a stunted mesquite. They were at the edge of a rocky trail wide enough to be almost level.

"Got to stretch my legs out," he said.

"Me too," Tyler smiled.

They walked to the edge of the trail and looked back toward the ranch which lay four miles away to the south. The afternoon was warm, but Hampton felt a cool breeze under his hatband when he shifted his hat. He unbuttoned his right breast pocket and took out his tobacco.

"Want a chew, Bud?"

"Thank you."

Satterwhite moved up beside them, but about five feet away. He was looking down the slope the way they had come.

"How about you, Satterwhite? You want a chew?"

"I can't stand that stuff," Satterwhite said with disgust.

"Oh yeah," Hampton said. "You like smokin' better, don't you?"

For answer, Satterwhite pulled his pouch of cigarette tobacco out of his pocket and shook it in the air in front of him like it was a sack of bells.

"Uh-huh," Hampton said. "I see that. Heap plenty medicine you got there."

"We're headin' north here, ain't we?" Tyler asked.

"Yes, sir," Hampton answered. "Got to. Mr. Frank's boundary goes on along until the morning shadow of the last Sister."

"There's another trail goes west," Satterwhite said. "It's a lot easier."

"That the trail you took the other day?" Hampton looked at him and raised his eyebrows.

"It's easier."

"Uh-huh," Hampton said and spit. "Well, sometimes easier ain't better."

"Ranch looks a long way off," Tyler said. "That Columbus?"

Far enough away that height and depth were lost, the dark cluster of color that was Columbus spread out like a patch of burnt ground on the floor of the valley.

"That's it," Hampton said. "Down there. That's Mexico."

The men turned to look, Hampton and Tyler spitting, while Satterwhite put his rolled and pinched cigarette in his mouth. The sky near the horizon was hazy and white, giving the mountains in Mexico a light, transparent blue color. To the southwest, a cloud of dust hung in the air just at the point where the rim of the next hill cut off their view of the desert. Hampton squinted at the cloud, trying to justify it in his mind. He could think of no good reason for it, traced the land back to the El Paso & Southwestern Railroad tracks, saw nothing, then looked at the dust again.

"Something stirrin' up dust down there," he said.

Tyler nodded.

"Where?" Satterwhite asked.

Hampton pointed.

Satterwhite looked at the two men. "Think they might be Villistas?"

"Could be the army wearin' out horses," Hampton said.

Tyler looked back toward the ranch and spit. He wiped his lip with his index finger. "It's settlin', whatever caused it. At least from what we can see. The dust is movin' away from us."

"What if it is Villistas?" Satterwhite asked.

"What if it is?" Hampton echoed.

"Then we got no business chasin' cows up here. We need to be back at the ranch with the others."

"Uh-huh," Hampton said. "Let me worry about that. If I see any Villistas, I'll just tell them to skeedaddle, we got work to do."

Hampton started to say something else, when Tyler elbowed his arm and said beneath his breath, "Rider sittin' his horse up the trail, Hamp."

Hampton turned and looked at Tyler, then looked past him. A man had appeared on the down slope ahead of them and was sitting calmly astride his horse watching them. When he saw Hampton, then Tyler and Satterwhite looking at him, he gently spurred the horse, twitched the reins, and started up the slope toward them.

"Friend of yours?" Tyler asked, then spit. He glanced at the saddle scabbard on Lady.

"Who is it?" Satterwhite asked, nervousness telling in his voice.

"Shut up, Satterwhite," Hampton said. Then he said, "I know him. His name's Casoose. He lives in Palomas but works over here whenever he can find it."

They waited as the man rode up the trail toward them slowly, working his horse easily around rocks and cactus, riding smoothly and erect as if he were a part of the horse rather than a rider. Satterwhite stepped over to his saddle and opened a saddlebag. The rider rode to within ten feet of them and stopped. The horses and the men looked at one another.

"*Buenas días*, Casoose," Hampton said, speaking first, then spitting. He stepped a little forward. Tyler glanced at Satterwhite with his instinct for placing everyone and saw that Satterwhite had his hand on something inside the saddlebag. Tyler stepped over to him and stared him in the eye until he brought his hand out empty.

"*Buenas días*, Diego," the man said. "*Cómo está?*"

"Old," Hampton said. "Same as you, Casoose."

Casoose laughed, and Hampton spit, looking all the while at the horse Casoose rode, at its face and chest and flanks.

"Maybe not too old," Casoose said, still speaking Spanish. He laughed again, a hoarse, cigarette laugh, then moved his hat back on his head. "Going on a trip, *Diego?*"

"No, sir. Workin'. Time to bring the calves down and check on them."

"These helping you?" Casoose asked, tilting his head up at Tyler and Satterwhite.

Hampton nodded and spit.

"How is Mr. Frank's nephew?"

"The ass of a horse," Hampton said in Spanish. "But who can choose his relatives?"

"That's true," Casoose said, still speaking Spanish. "How long you men going to be in these cold hills?"

"Day or two," Hampton said.

"*Bueno.*"

"Want to ride with us? Dollar a day and found."

Casoose laughed. "I can't."

"What's got you so busy?"

Casoose shrugged. His horse shifted.

"See any calves back of the Hermanas?" Hampton asked.

Casoose looked over his shoulder, back the way he had come. "Some," he said.

"Where?"

Casoose shrugged again and looked back at Hampton. "How long did you say you were going to be chasing the calves, *Diego?*"

"Couple of days."

"*Bueno.*"

"Why?"

Casoose shifted in the saddle and glanced toward the south. His horse took a step back. Casoose looked at Hampton. "Maybe I'll come up and join you," he said.

"Uh-huh," Hampton said. "You do that."

"Well, *adiós,*" Casoose said. He eased his horse past Hampton on the trail and rode by Tyler and Satterwhite without looking at them. Hampton watched him for a minute, then spit.

"What did he say?" Satterwhite asked.

"He said two-legged jackasses were the worst kind."

Tyler moved up beside Hampton and watched the Mexican ride along the trail back toward Columbus. "Junior here was goin' for his piece," he said.

Hampton cut Satterwhite a look.

"Well, how was I to know he was friendly?"

"Because I didn't tell you he wasn't. You got that? When you ride with me, you wait for my word."

"What was he doing up here?" Satterwhite said after a hurt pause.

"He didn't say, and I didn't ask him."

"Why not?"

"A man's business is his own, that's why. Saddle up and quit askin' so many damned questions."

Satterwhite turned away mumbling. Beside Hampton, Tyler spit. "He have any reason for bein' up here?" Tyler asked quietly.

Hampton squinted at Casoose's retreating figure, glanced toward the south, then said, "No."

FIVE

EIGHTY miles to the east, Mary Alison MacPherson opened the door of a taxi parked at the curb in front of the Rio Grande Hotel in El Paso, pinched her skirt above the knee with her right hand, and got out, pulling her single valise along with her. She shut the door behind her and walked up the steps and through the archway of the hotel.

Everyone in the lobby looked at her. Besides her beauty, there was about her an air of energy and intelligence that drew people's attention to her the way it is drawn to staring eyes in a crowd. Some turned away again immediately, but others continued to watch in interest, wondering perhaps what her voice would sound like when she spoke, or whom she might be meeting.

If Mary was aware of the looks she got, she did not in any way acknowledge them. Her gray eyes were on the young man behind the desk when she entered the lobby, and she kept them there as she crossed the room.

She was in her early twenties, with long dark hair only partly hidden by her hat, but she moved with the assurance of someone much older. There was a confidence in her attitude which was still, in 1916, something of a novelty. Young women were expected to walk with less haste and directness, like someone in the aisle of a church. No one watching her guessed at how much of an act her attitude was.

"I telegraphed from San Antonio about a room," Mary said when she reached the desk. "My name is Mary Wells," she added, giving her married name.

The clerk smiled broadly, pretending to be more important than he was. "We have your room, Mrs. Wells," he said, turning to the pigeonholes above the long writing table behind the counter and snatching out a key.

Mary raised her right hand and pulled a long, amber-tipped hatpin from her hat. She took off her hat, holding it by the brim the way a man would, and slid the hatpin back through the blue satin.

"It is a pleasure to. . . ."

"Thank you," she interrupted him, taking the key.

A man in a dark wool suit was standing at the counter watching her. When she picked up the key, he said, "Excuse me. May I be of service to you?"

Mary looked at him directly and saw the pass for what it was. "What kind of service did you have in mind?"

His eyes were no match for hers, and he looked to the side. "Why, no service in particular," he said. "I just thought as you were traveling alone, you might. . . ."

Mary looked around the lobby, still holding her hat by the brim, then she looked back at the man. She was tired and had no patience for him. "Are you from around here?" she asked.

"I'm from St. Louis. My name is. . . ."

"Well, I was born and raised in this country," Mary cut him off again, "and I don't honestly believe anybody from St. Louis can be of any service to me."

Mary picked up her valise and crossed the lobby to the stairs, leaving the gentleman from St. Louis with a red face and nothing to say. The clerk snickered, then picked up a pen and put it down again.

Her room was on the second floor, facing west, and once inside, she dropped her valise on the bed, her hat and key on the bureau. She walked to the window and parted the linen curtains. The sun was going down. It threw a blue haze over the rocky slopes of the Franklin Mountains to the north and highlighted the contours of her face in soft, golden tones.

She let her eyes linger over the rooftops to the west, thinking about the ranch at Columbus, her life there, and the homecoming she could expect. She felt a longing for the bare, abrupt walls of the house and barns, the rugged lift of the Tres Hermanas, but her homesickness was mitigated by the circumstances of her return. She was divorcing her husband after five years of marriage in a time when divorce implied infidelity or physical cruelty, and her only reason was that she was not happy.

In many ways, Leonard Wells had been an important man in Murfreesboro, but he had not been the man she had fallen in love with six years before when they had met in Las Cruces at the Christmas party given by the matrons of the city.

She dropped her hand from the curtains and turned back into the room. Leonard was still knowledgeable and important, a branch manager of the shipping company he worked for, a man others looked to for decisions. But at home, without the routine and impersonality that made him so effective in his career, Leonard became passive and helpless. Mary found herself scolding him and making domestic decisions she felt were his to make.

She sat down on the edge of the hotel bed and put her hands on her knees, physically aware of the dark weight of her emotions. She felt bad and wrong and did not like the feelings, but she had been lonely among the things he owned.

It impressed her now as being a long time ago, when, in reality, only a month had gone by. She had not ever been the kind who made friends easily, and, without them, she could not stay in Tennessee. She could not make the passage from wife to independent woman. She had, as would be said of a man, no prospects, no talents, no bright, shining gifts, just two trunks of clothes that she liked, some silver dinnerware, a few books, some jewelry.

When the soft glow of the setting sun faded from the walls of her room, Mary washed her face and hands and went down to the dining room. An older couple and two soldiers were waiting for tables. Mary hesitated, then moved up behind them. In a moment a young woman with a small boy appeared behind Mary. The boy brushed Mary's leg by accident, and Mary turned and smiled down at him without really looking at him. The couple and the soldiers were seated almost immediately.

When the headwaiter returned, he nodded at Mary and asked, "How many?"

"One, for dinner," Mary said.

The headwaiter nodded again, then looked past Mary.

"How many?"

"Just the two of us," the woman said nervously. "Will it be long?"

"Twenty minutes?"

"Oh, that's too long," the woman said.

Mary glanced at the woman's face, then looked down at the boy's. He smiled at her, then looked around the room. A waiter came up to them.

"I have a table," the headwaiter said.

Mary turned back to the woman. "Will you join me?" she asked. "I never liked eating alone. I would enjoy the company."

"Thank you," the woman said. "I'm kind of in a hurry, you see, but Joey was hungry, so I thought. . . ." She tried to smile but only looked worried.

"Join me," Mary said.

Mary introduced herself at the table. The woman's name was Alma. She and her son Joey were leaving that night for Las Cruces. Joey was a good boy, the woman explained, a good traveler, too, and a big help to his mother. They were both dressed in gray winter wools that appeared several seasons old. The boy was about six with black hair and small hands that were busy pulling the linen napkin through the ring.

"Are you going to California?" the woman asked Mary suddenly with a deference that confused her.

"No. My parents live in Columbus. I'm going home tomorrow."

"You must be glad."

"I am. It's been a long time."

"I don't know about my parents," the woman said, sipping her water, then putting the glass carefully back on the table. "They was in Mexico last I heard, but that was a long time ago too. Joey ain't never seen them, but maybe he will someday if things work out in Las Cruces."

"I hope they do," Mary said. Something, a tone in the woman's voice, perhaps, reminded her of Tennessee in such a way that she saw clearly in her mind the sandy drive up to the front door of her house there and heard the sound of the wind from the west in the trees of the yard. There were no people in her image — it was an image of landscape only, a memory of a place that had accepted her apart from the humans who inhabited that place.

While they ate their dinner of steak and potatoes and green beans grown in fields of silt and sand along the river, the boy told a story about a man with two cats who had ridden on the streetcar with them the day before. The orange cat got away, and Joey chased it under the seats trying to catch it. His mother cautioned him to eat, they had to hurry, and each time someone came in the dining room, she looked up with a nervousness that was difficult for Mary to ignore. The woman barely touched her own plate.

At the door of the dining room, Mary told them goodbye.

"Thank you so much for sharing your table," the woman said, then abruptly she touched Mary's arm. "I'm glad you're going home," she said. "You seem like a nice person."

Mary looked down at Joey. "Take care of your mother," she said.

"I can jump four feet," the boy said.

Mary watched them cross the lobby to the front desk. To one side, three men were sitting in blue velvet wingback chairs. Through their cigar smoke, Mary recognized one of them as the gentleman from St. Louis. The boy stood beside the front desk with his mother who was talking hurriedly with the desk clerk. Mary glanced at them and started for the stairs.

"Alma!" a man's voice ripped across the room.

Mary, startled, broke her stride and turned toward the door where a thin man with dark eyebrows stood, his eyes angry and his lips twisted in a snarl of rage.

The woman at the desk turned around so quickly the buttons of her jacket scraped against the wood. Her eyes widened, and, without looking away from the man, she bent and put her hands on the little boy's shoulders.

"Run, Joey," she hissed and pushed him away.

The boy faltered a few steps, then not quite ran toward Mary.

"Here," she said quietly, and Joey went to her. She felt his shoulders against her thighs. Across the room, the three men paused

48

in their smoking and looked from the woman to the man who had called her name.

The woman turned to the clerk, both of her hands palm down on the counter top. "Call the police," she pleaded. "Call the police."

The man hurried across the lobby toward her. He caught her arms above the elbows and turned her around roughly. His clothes and haircut matched his emotion. They were careless, angry, and rough.

"Where do you think you're goin'?" he asked, shaking her.

"Please," the woman cried, tears in her voice, her hair loosened beside her temples with the violent shaking.

"I told you what I'd do if I caught you runnin' away again, didn't I?"

"I was going to come back. I just needed. . . ."

Mary put her hands down on the boy's shoulders. She felt him trembling under her touch, or perhaps it was her own hands that trembled. The desk clerk had stepped away from the counter and was watching almost guiltily, as if he might be somehow to blame for helping the woman. The three men had stood, their cigars poised somewhere between their belts and their chests.

"See here," the gentleman from St. Louis said, raising his voice.

"Shut up," the man growled. "This ain't none of your business."

The woman twisted free and tried to push by the man, but he caught her and threw her firmly back into the counter. The register fell to the floor. The woman gasped in pain.

Mary turned the boy's face into her skirt and said, "Leave her alone." Her voice was even and tight.

"Go to hell," the man said.

Alma raised her hands suddenly and scratched the man's face. He hit at her, but she ducked and began trying to punch him out of her way. He took a step back, then hit her with his fist. She fell against the counter again, and the man jabbed his left hand into his coat pocket. Mary saw the razor in her mind before the man had cleared it from the pocket.

"Stop it!" Mary screamed, looking quickly from them to the

desk clerk then to the three men, all of whom stood motionless in horror and surprise.

The woman twisted back and forth, trying to get away, but the man rushed her up against the counter, bending her backward over it with his right arm across her chest.

Mary pushed the boy behind her toward a row of chairs and ran to the man. She grabbed his left arm, but he wrenched it free and clubbed her away with his forearm. The blow caught Mary in the face, and she fell. No one made a move to help her.

The man flicked the razor open and raised it above his head. Before Mary closed her eyes, she was aware of several people moving up behind her from the dining room. There were shouts, then a scream, more shouts and cursing. Someone pulled Mary to her feet. She pushed through to the boy, caught his shoulders, and hid his face in her skirt while she watched.

The three men were still standing across the lobby, their cigars held low now. The two soldiers from the dining room were wrestling with the man on the floor. The woman was slumped sideways against the base of the counter, blood on the wool of her jacket.

"Oh, God," Mary sighed. She was hot and trembling and breathless.

One of the men had captured the arm with the razor and the other was repeatedly hitting the man in the face. His curses were mumbled and choked off. Finally he lay still, and the razor was snatched from his bloody hand.

"Call the police!" one of the soldiers shouted, breathing hard.

This time, the clerk stepped over to the wall where the telephone hung, picked up the earpiece and turned the crank. Mary sat down in the chair behind her and pulled the sniffling boy against her. She was aware that he was saying something, perhaps a name, but she didn't answer. The soldier rolled the man over on his stomach. He was conscious, but his fight was gone. There were murmurs of shock and horror behind her as people from the dining room crowded in the doorway.

The other soldier turned to the woman and, putting the razor on the floor, eased her position so that he could look at her. The woman's head tilted back, and Mary knew that she was dead. Mary held the boy against her and slowly stood up. With an effort no one noticed, she walked the boy into the dining room to wait.

The police had been at the hotel half an hour before one of them approached Mary. She was sitting in a corner of the empty dining room beside the boy. She had drawn two chairs together and was sitting close to the boy, her right arm around his narrow shoulders, her hand curving and resting on the pocket of his jacket. The boy's head was against her side, his black hair flattened against her blouse. Without thinking about it, Mary was softly humming one of her favorite hymns.

The policeman in charge walked up to them. He was a short man with dark stubble on his chin, and he had been on duty since noon.

"Is this the kid?" the policeman asked.

"Change your tone," Mary said evenly, softly, looking up at the man.

"Is it or isn't it?"

"Yes."

"Let me have him. Come with me, kid."

"His name is Joey."

"Oh yeah? You his grandma?"

Mary stood in one quick motion and slapped the policeman on his left cheek. It so surprised the man that he stepped back and glanced around as if further attack awaited him.

"Goddam," he said.

"I will not be talked to in this way," Mary said, her voice now shaky with emotion. "You'll either treat me and this child with respect, or you'll go get someone who can."

"Now wait just a damned minute," the policeman said.

"I will not wait. I do not care to wait. This child needs to know that there are adults in this world who behave like adults."

The policeman looked at Mary and shook his head, his cheek still stinging. Her face was angry and set, a dark blush on her cheek where the man had hit her, and the policeman knew she was right.

"Take it easy, now, ma'am. I don't mean to be rough with you or the boy, but I'm a policeman, not a preacher. I seen a lot of this kind of stuff."

Mary looked at him evenly, her breath coming fast.

"Can I take the boy now?" he squinted at her.

"Where are you taking him?"

"To the station," the policeman said, deliberately keeping his patience. "At least to begin with. Then we'll have to find out if he has any relatives. You don't know the boy's family by any chance, do you?"

"No."

"We'll do what's best for him, ma'am."

Mary dropped her eyes and took a deep breath. The boy was looking solemnly at her, waiting for her to decide what would happen to him.

"His name is Joey," she said.

"Yes, ma'am. Come along, Joey," the policeman said.

The boy looked at the policeman, then looked at Mary. His face was mostly empty, but tinged with fear.

Mary knelt beside him and looked in his eyes. "It will be all right, Joey. This man will take care of you."

"Have I done something wrong?" he asked. It was the first time he had spoken since it happened, and it made her lips quiver to hear his voice.

"No. This man. . . ."

"Albert."

"Albert is going to look after you for a while. He will make sure that you are all right. Go with him now."

Mary stood and reached for the boy's small hand.

"That's a good boy," the policeman said, taking the hand from Mary. "We'll go for a ride now. You'll see."

Mary stood trembling, watching them. The policeman looked up at her. The look on her face dissolved any remnants of his anger.

"He'll be fine, ma'am," he said. When Mary's expression did not change, he added, "I'm sorry I was rough."

Mary looked at him and nodded. "I'm sorry too."

"There'll be some detectives around tomorrow to get a statement from you. It's a formality since we have the . . ." he paused, "man in custody."

"I have an early train to catch."

"We'll try to be here early then. Goodnight, miss."

Mary watched the little boy's head as they left the dining room. The faint smell of cigar smoke drifted past, and she felt sick to her stomach. She hurried unnoticed to her room.

That night she held herself tightly in, shutting out images of the woman's death with a strength she did not know she had. Leonard was too far away both physically and emotionally to help her. Columbus was only eighty miles to the west, but she felt cut off from there, too. If her father walked into her room at that moment, she was sure his inarticulateness would be of no help to her, and her mother, in her busy way, would only be confused by her feelings.

Then she remembered Hampton. He was a brusque, lonely man who had always been understanding in the talks they shared. Something about him was different from anyone she had ever known. He had once killed a rattlesnake that had cornered her in the barn. When the snake was dead, and Hampton had thrown it out past the corral fence, he had not asked her if she were all right. She remembered that specifically because it had seemed to her that they had been talking the whole time, that even though she had not cried out in the first place, he had heard her.

Perhaps Hamp could be of some comfort to her, but even there, she was not sure she could approach him as a grown woman as easily as she had approached him as a child.

Perhaps, after all, she really was wrong in leaving Tennessee. Perhaps she should go back, live the life that she had thought she wanted. But she couldn't. No one spoke her language there. No one understood her when she was quiet.

Outside her window, El Paso slipped into the patterns of the western night. Sleep, when it did come to her, was one unrestful nightmare after another.

SIX

HAMPTON, Tyler, and Satterwhite reached the northwest corner of Mr. Frank's land as the sun was dipping low above the desert, and Hampton decided to spend the night there, working back out of the hills toward the first fenced pasture. They made camp in a low spot out of the wind. On the level ground above them was a windmill that pumped water into a concrete tank. The sand around it was well churned with cattle tracks.

Satterwhite staked out the horses while Hampton and Tyler unloaded the packs and spread out the utensils, bedrolls, and food. It took them until sundown to secure everything in its place and get supper going, Satterwhite reluctantly dragging broken limbs into the camp for the fire.

"What the hell is that stuff?" Hampton said. "The smoke smells like somebody pissed in the fire."

"It's just wood," Satterwhite returned, with an edge on his voice.

Hampton looked at him. Tyler spit and glanced sideways at Satterwhite with a squint.

"No, it ain't," Hampton said. "There's a dead mesquite under the windmill. Get some of that."

Tyler picked up a short branch as big around as a pencil and turned it in his hands, cutting grooves in the soft wood with his thumbnails as if they were miniature lathes. He was content to leave Satterwhite to Hampton, letting the younger man fend for himself if he could.

Satterwhite turned away abruptly and went to his saddle where it lay on the ground on last year's grass. He jerked at one thing and another until he came up with his wool coat. He pulled it on as if he were mad at it, his wrists flying out of the cuffs almost to his elbow before he shook the sleeves down again. Still facing the other way, he snatched out his tobacco pouch and began building a cigarette in the failing light.

"Coat doesn't seem too bad an idea," Tyler said. "I got to where I feel the chill a lot more than I used to."

"How much ridin' you done since that horse fell on you?"

"Not much, and most of that has been on trains."

"How do you feel now?"

"I'm all right, Hamp. Hell," Tyler said.

"Just makin' sure. I ain't used to babysittin' old men."

"I don't aim to give you no practice, neither," Tyler said and spit.

The first thing that went on the coals was the coffeepot, and after they ate and piled the dishes to be washed, the coffeepot was still blackening near the edge of the replenished fire. From somewhere above the camp a coyote howled briefly twice, then was silent for the rest of the night which spread above them clear and cold and full of stars. The moon set early.

Hampton and Tyler pulled their saddles and bedrolls closer to the fire while Satterwhite grumbled and clanged over the dishes.

"Good thing those ain't china," Tyler said.

"Satterwhite, you got to bang those things around like you was some Fourth of July band gone loco?" Hampton threw out, looking up from his bedroll.

"I didn't come along to wash dishes," Satterwhite said.

"Youngest man always does the dishes and gets the firewood, Satterwhite," Hampton said. "It's the rules of the trail."

"Says who?"

"Says me, for one," Hampton said.

Satterwhite banged and splashed and slung the wet rag from one dish to the other. The sleeves of his coat were wet, as were the thighs and knees of his trousers.

"Now I seen misery," Tyler laughed.

They kicked protruding rocks out from under their bedrolls

with their boots and placed their saddles at the head. Hampton put his rifle and personal bag close by to the left. Both he and Tyler poured fresh coffee in their metal cups, stepped back, and sat down on their bedrolls. Hampton's glasses reflected the orange light of the fire.

When Satterwhite finished with the dishes, he pulled his bedroll closer too and was angry at having the two older men watch him.

"What?" he said finally, after a long silence.

"Nothin'," Hampton shrugged.

"I thought maybe you didn't like the way I put my bed down," Satterwhite said with an edge on his voice.

"Oh no," Hampton said after a minute of staring. "It's fine. But if it was me, I'd be a little uncomfortable sleepin' in all that spilled dishwater."

"Goddammit," Satterwhite said. He jerked his bedroll away from the damp ground.

Tyler shook his head and laughed softly. When Satterwhite had smoothed out his blankets in a new place, he sat down on them, partly turned away from Hampton and Tyler, and proceeded to roll a cigarette. He slipped a paper out of the sheaf, opened the pouch with his teeth and right hand, and tapped the rough cut tobacco out on the paper. He closed the pouch the same way he opened it and set it on the blanket beside him while he rolled the cigarette. As he licked the edge of the paper, he noticed the other two men staring at him.

"You act like you've never seen anything before," Satterwhite said angrily.

"I've seen stuff before," Hampton said.

"I saw a man in Pagosa Springs, said he had the mummy of Geronimo in a box on the back of his wagon," Tyler said.

"What was he doing with Geronimo's mother?" Satterwhite asked, slipping the end of the cigarette in his mouth and reaching forward for a stick to light it with.

"A mummy is a corpse, Satterwhite," Hampton said.

Satterwhite lit his cigarette and puffed it. He threw the stick back on the fire. "Oh, yeah," he said.

"This fella would let you have a look at that mummy for twenty-five cents," Tyler said.

56

"Did you look?" Satterwhite asked, smoking. Hampton sipped his coffee and looked at the fire.

"Yeah," Tyler said. "I gave him twenty-five cents, and he let me climb in the back of his wagon."

"What did the mummy look like?"

"It looked like a man's bones wrapped up in dirty rags."

"Was it Geronimo?"

"I never saw Geronimo before."

"Maybe it was," Satterwhite said.

"A couple of days later, an old Indian fighter paid to see that mummy. He stayed in the wagon so long, the man had to go in there and get him out. The Indian fighter had unwrapped the bones, and they turned out to be part dog, part horse, and part cow, along with a human skull. I got my twenty-five cents back. So did a lot of other folks."

"I wonder what really happened to Geronimo," Satterwhite said.

"He died," Hampton said. "Seven years ago."

The fire crackled and smoked as if the wood had too much sand in it, and sparks rose six feet in the air. For a while none of them said anything, and the cold night began to slip under their collarless shirts.

"Better turn in," Hampton said, emptying his cup and hanging it upside down on the horn of his saddle. "We have a lot of ridin' to do tomorrow."

"You seem pretty sure," Satterwhite said, throwing his cigarette in the fire.

"I make a habit out of it," Hampton said.

Satterwhite pulled off his boots and emptied his pockets into them. He took his coat off and rolled in the blankets. He was asleep before he could think of anything to say to Hampton.

Sometime in the night Hampton woke suddenly, his eyes wide open and his senses alert. His shoulders were cold and stiff, and his head hurt. Smoke from the dying fire wavered in his direction before floating away, and he choked a little on it when he came awake. The night was deep and still and cold. He reached for his glasses that were propped carefully on the shank of one of his boots.

He had been dreaming, and at first, he thought he still was. In the dream, Tyler had been talking to him about buying five mules from a young girl who lived alone in a mud house on the banks of a river. Tyler was pointing to the mules when one by one they began to drop dead. The young girl came out of the house and asked him what had happened to the mules. Hampton looked around, but Tyler was gone. When he looked back at the girl, he noticed that her arms were tied behind her back, and a trail of blood was crawling away from her bottom lip like a red worm.

It had either been that last image or the frightening incongruity of the girl's arms being tied that had waked Hampton, but it was the blood on the girl's lip he remembered first. He shuddered, trying to remember the girl's identity. She was not anybody he knew now, but she seemed so familiar, he felt sure he had known her at one time, perhaps a long time ago. He could not remember her features, just the way she made him feel.

He rolled over, his glasses on now, and looked through the gloom at Tyler's bedroll. He saw the outline of Tyler's shoulders, but his head was hidden beneath the rim of his blanket. Satterwhite was sleeping soundly on his back with his coat over his face like a dead man. The smoke wavered like a ghost over the camp. Hampton shuddered again, fully awake, with a bad feeling in his chest and along his spine. He sat up and threw his blankets back. The top one was damp with condensation.

Hampton pulled on his boots and stood up, glancing at the two sleeping men again. The depression where they slept was full of shadows, any one of them big enough to hide several men or a large animal. He reached down for his rifle but could not convince himself that something was wrong enough to justify waking Tyler and Satterwhite.

The horses were staked nearby, one idly nipping at dead grass, while the other three stood perfectly still except for the occasional twitch of an ear. Like most men used to being around animals, Hampton knew he could trust the horses to sense things he could not sense. But now their apparent lack of concern or anxiety puzzled Hampton, who trusted his own instincts too.

Quietly, choosing his steps with care, looking at the ground first, then looking up to step, then looking down again, then up and stepping, Hampton walked away from the smoke of the fire. The browsing horse, Lady, looked over at him with curiosity, then looked at the other horses. Hampton moved past them and away from the windmill. Out of the range of his vision, where the shadows were deepest, Hampton thought he heard something, a bird perhaps, one of those that flit about at night with their night whistles. He turned his eyes in that direction, searching the shadows for movement, for some reason for the feeling he had. At the first stunted mesquite bush, he stopped and looked around. There was no movement at all.

Hampton stepped around the mesquite, his eyes going quickly from the ground to any area around him that might hide a danger. He was old enough and experienced enough in the outdoors not to be skittish, but something had him skittish now, and he was determined to find out what it was.

He remembered another walk like this on a summer night along the Nueces River in Texas, when a wounded horse thief and murderer had gotten away in the brush. There had been a full moon that night, which made the search both better and worse. The man was armed with a .45 revolver he had stolen from a gun shop in Uvalde. Hampton had been one of five trackers, including Tyler.

At first they thought they knew where he was and had surrounded the mesquite thicket, but when they rushed it, they found nothing. Any bush or tree or depression in the ground could have been a death trap for one of them. They had spread out then, whispering their plan, and moving slowly and soundlessly along the banks of the Nueces, dry at that point, the moon descending.

Hampton remembered the eerie shapes of prickly pear cactus and the dense shadows under and in huisache and mesquite trees. Then, the hair on his neck rising, he had turned to the right where a mesquite tree with a base split into six ascending trunks sheltered a dark shadow in its center. He had crouched low, trying to get a fix on the shape, trying to discern features or arms, a man's back, when there were several shots down river and a shout that the man had been killed. Hampton stood slowly, walked to a clearing, then, for no good reason, went back to the place where he had crouched. The shadow was gone, the tree perfectly transparent in the moonlight.

But there was no moon now, just stars spinning thickly around the haze of the Milky Way. Occasionally a falling star pointed down to the horizon. Hampton stepped his way far enough from camp to lose sight of the coals of the fire and of the ghost-like smoke. As he walked, he seemed drawn forward, as if being led to a certain specific destination by an obvious and determined trail, yet there was no sign of any trail where he stepped.

Hampton felt a chill on his back and neck and shivered. He could feel the cold now, and he stopped. He looked to his right, letting the muzzle of the rifle swing up and down in his hand. Almost at the instant of turning, he heard what sounded like a spoken word, and there was a blur of movement in his peripheral vision to the left. He chilled, then spun to the left, both hands on the rifle now, his finger against the trigger and his eyes wide open to get the most of the weak light. Something, not larger than a man, perhaps smaller, was running in a swift lope toward a sandy, brush-covered hill.

Hampton squinted, trying to see it more clearly . . . an antelope perhaps, a deer, a coyote, a . . . what? He brought the rifle up, but whatever it was had disappeared without a sound into the shadows.

Hampton shivered again, aware suddenly of his isolation, of the fact that he was alone in a dark place with no one to watch his backside. He waited a moment longer, then turned back toward camp. He no longer felt nervous and uneasy, but the cold had found its way into his clothes. He walked quickly back the way he had come.

Tyler rolled over and sat up as Hampton approached. "What is it, Hamp?" he asked quietly.

"Don't know." He looked over at the horses and leaned his rifle against his saddle. He coughed in the smoke and threw some wood on the fire.

Tyler watched him, with eyes red and watering from the smoke. He switched his stare to the fire as flames caught at the tiny branches on the sticks of wood. Satterwhite was still asleep.

"Did you see somethin'?" Tyler asked.

Hampton had not looked at the fire since it caught up, but was standing with his back to it looking out into the dark. Smoke and sparks silhouetted his heavy frame.

"Don't know, Bud. Horses weren't skittish, but I was. I walked out yonder a ways, then thought I saw somethin' runnin' away. Damndest thing, though. It had me goosebumps all over."

"Maybe it was a ghost," Tyler said, seriously.

"Could have been," Hampton said. "Can't say. The horses didn't smell it up or sense it. How come me to wake up and go out there to it?"

"Maybe you was the one it was after."

"Where is it now? I don't feel it now."

"It's gone, I guess," Tyler said, pulling the blankets up around his shoulders.

"Uh-huh," Hampton said. "Did you call me or say something while I was out there?"

"Nope. Was that ghost talkin' to you?"

"I don't know," Hampton said. "Thought I heard a voice. Sounded like singing."

"Singing?"

Hampton looked out into the night and did not say anything. He rubbed his hands together behind his back.

"I don't know," he said. Then he said, "I wish the Oklahoma Kid would wake up. I didn't pack any smokin' tobacco, and I sure could use a smoke."

SEVEN

WHEN it was almost time to leave the hotel for her train, the desk clerk gave Mary a message saying that the detective had been detained, would she please not leave until he had talked to her, a talk now might prevent a court appearance at a later date. Since she had left her room, and the lobby made her shudder, she again found herself sitting in the dining room. Sunlight flashed through the tall windows in the south wall.

She was tired and felt sick. She could not keep away the images from the night before, and they rushed through her mind with cruel clarity. If she had been more confident in the course she had chosen, or if she had not felt so alone, the emotional impact might not have been as great. But as she sat there, she saw again the woman's face and the three men with cigars who had stood watching the whole incident without even so much as knocking the ash off their smokes. She felt sick.

When the police detective walked up to her table, she was trembling with weariness and emotion. The detective looked at her profile, moved until he could see her face, then hesitated.

"Mrs. Mary Wells?" he asked. "I'm sorry to have to do this, but we would like your account of what happened last night. We have several men who are willing to testify as to what happened, but we like to talk to all the witnesses if we can. You understand, it's something we have to do."

"Where is the boy?" Mary asked with difficulty.

"He's with relatives in town, I believe. May I sit down?"

Mary nodded without looking at him. She had never liked loose ends. She liked things to be taken care of. Otherwise she would have already left El Paso and been on her way home.

"What will happen to him?"

"I don't really know, Mrs. Wells. Did you know the woman?"

"Those men did nothing to stop it," she said.

"What men?"

"There were some men in the lobby. They didn't do anything."

"Sometimes shock makes folks. . . ."

"They didn't do anything."

"How do you mean that?"

"They didn't do anything."

"Now, Mrs. Wells," the detective said in a different voice, a voice that was at once friendly and authoritative.

Mary looked at him. His eyes were blue in a heavy western face. His lips were pressed together in seriousness and concern.

"They could have helped her," she said softly, realizing how lost she was. "She was alone, and no one helped her. I don't understand that," Mary said. Tears filled her eyes and ran quickly down her cheeks. "I don't know. . . ." She shook her head and tried again. "I don't know . . . I don't understand that."

Drawn by her face, the detective leaned forward and patted her shoulder briefly as if calling her attention to something. "If I had been here," he said, "I would have done something, Mrs. Wells."

Mary looked at him. "But shouldn't everyone?"

The detective sat back and shook his head. "Some can and some can't. Like playing the piano or drawing a picture. Some men just got no knack for it. Does it bother you so much?"

"Yes. I wasn't raised that way."

The detective looked at the painting of a locomotive on the opposite wall of the dining room. He had always liked the painting. "Are you from around here, Mrs. Wells?" he asked.

"I grew up on a ranch outside of Columbus."

The detective nodded. "Did you know the woman and the boy?"

"No. I shared my table with them last night. She seemed in a hurry. She said they were going to Las Cruces."

"Had you ever seen the man before?"

"No."

The detective looked at her. "Henry, at the desk, said you tried to stop him. Henry said the man knocked you down."

Mary dropped her eyes.

"You're lucky he didn't kill you too." When Mary did not say anything, he added, "Your husband in Columbus?"

"No."

The detective looked at her hands in her lap. She covered her left hand with her right hand.

"Anything else you can tell me?"

Mary shook her head.

"All right," the detective said. "Sorry to keep you, Mrs. Wells." He stood up and looked down at her. Her eyes were on her hands. "By the way, one of my men said to offer his apologies to you. You met him last night. He said he was a little rough and was sorry for it."

Mary nodded. She felt empty and numb. On his way out, the detective paused at the door of the dining room and looked around at the feminine shoulders and straight back. Sunlight reached across the floor toward her. In the lobby the desk clerk was pointing to the floor and telling the story of the murder to two younger men.

"Mrs. Wells?"

Mary raised her eyes to a point across the dining room at the sound of the man's voice, but did not at first realize he was talking to her.

"Mrs. Wells?"

"Yes?"

"Could I get you something, send for something?"

Mary looked at the man's face. He could easily have been a friend of her father's. He had the same rough, gentlemanly cut, the same apologetic tenderness. His eyes were concerned, and his appeal was the first emotional anchor she had had since she left Tennessee.

"I don't know your name," she said with a weak smile.

"Walker, ma'am, and I'm awfully sorry you had to be a part of this. Lots of these fellas been driftin' through here ever since the Indian danger ended. They come with the railroad and the land speculators, fringing around hoping to make it big. Then they realize they're as lowdown here as they were someplace else, and next thing you know they're killin' one another.

"The woman last night may have seemed to a casual stranger like yourself to have been respectable, but she had been supportin' her commonlaw husband by, well . . . she wasn't what she may have seemed to you. I don't know if that makes a difference, but. . . ."

The man stopped abruptly. Mary's eyes were watching his in a direct way that made him feel there was something else he was supposed to say or do. Her eyes seemed filled with patient expectation. When he stopped, however, she blinked quickly several times and dropped her eyes.

"Look," Walker said. "I only thought, as you were alone, that I could help you somehow."

"Thank you, Mr. Walker. I just want to see a schedule of train departures, and I will be on the first train to Columbus."

"That may not be until tonight," Walker said. "The El Paso and Southwestern runs a late westbound. They call it the 'Drunkard's Special.' Mostly soldiers and drummers ride at that hour."

Mary closed her eyes but did not say anything.

"At any rate, I will speak to the desk about a place for you to rest until you are ready to leave."

Mary sat immobile with her eyes still closed. The sunlight reaching across the floor threw a golden glow upward over her face, and the man saw again how beautiful she was, but, at the same time, how complicated and sad, as the modern women tended to be.

"I appreciate your help, Mrs. Wells. I hope the rest of your trip is better. I'll speak to the desk, now." He turned to leave, a sensation of guilt and regret puzzling him.

"Mr. Walker?" Mary rose and extended her hand to him. He took it and felt a strong western grip in her long fingers. "Thank you for your thoughtfulness. I believe that if you had been here, you would have done something, and that poor woman would still be alive."

Walker nodded, then looked into her eyes. He thought of the way shadows of clouds moved along the slopes of the Franklin Mountains to the north. He let go of her hand.

"Fellows nowadays don't think the way we used to, Mrs. Wells. The new style is to go about your own business and look the other way. But there's a few good men left. That seems to matter to you, so I want you to remember it."

"Thank you."

Mary watched his back as he walked away. She dropped one hand to the table beside her to steady herself. In a minute he returned with the desk clerk whom Mary could not bring herself to look at.

"Henry says there's a room where you can be alone if you wish," Walker spoke slowly. "He says he'll look after your things until it's time to go to the station."

"Thank you, Mr. Walker."

"Yes, ma'am," he said. Then, turning to the clerk, he added in a stern voice, almost as if he were angry, "You see to it, by God."

Alone in the narrow room, Mary took off her hat and lay slowly down on the bed, letting the heels of her shoes hang over the edge. Then she became like a photograph. The light in the room changed as the day turned to afternoon and evening, but the sad, dry-eyed expression on Mary's face never wavered. She was less than a hundred miles from home but had never felt farther.

When the light had begun to dim, Mary rose and returned once more to the dining room where she pretended to eat a tasteless meal. The memory of the night before came back to her, and she thought of the little boy who in twenty-four hours had become a virtual orphan. She wished she were an orphan. She so little wanted to go home that the idea of no home at all appealed to her. All the things and places and people she knew now were strangers to her. She could never belong to them again.

Shortly before ten she left the hotel and was driven to the train station in a hotel taxi. The desert air was chill, the sky hazy and distant. At the station she purchased her ticket and watched through a window as her trunks were ferried aboard. Then she herself boarded, along with several troopers, drummers, and an older man who hummed songs for a while, or the same song over and over, until he finally went to sleep.

It was hard to resist the sleepy motion of the train, and soon Mary was asleep as well, her arms folded tightly across her breast, hugging herself. The moon set across the desert, and the train rolled heavily on through the darkness.

At Columbus, the movement of men in the aisle woke her, and she clutched her valise and stood up. The thing that impressed her most as she stepped off the train was the darkness of the town under the March night. For a moment, she hesitated, simply looking at the undistinguished skyline. Then her eyes drifted to the northwest and the dark bulk of the Tres Hermanas.

"Need some help, ma'am?"

She turned and found a trooper standing beside her. He struck a match with his thumbnail and put it to a bent briar pipe he held in his teeth. Mary could see his young bearded face, then the match went out. The aroma of the tobacco swirled around them both for a moment.

"Need some help?" the trooper repeated, stepping with her out of the way of the others leaving the train, mostly soldiers. The drummers looked once at Columbus and decided to go farther west. "Name's John Lucas. I'm stationed here."

"No, thank you," Mary nodded. "My parents live here. I'm no stranger to Columbus."

"Do I know them?" Lucas asked.

"Perhaps. My father is Frank MacPherson. He has a ranch at the base of the Hermanas."

"Sure," Lucas said. "You going out there tonight?"

Now that Mary was in Columbus, she was anxious to be home, but, late as it was, she knew it would be difficult to find someone who would take her.

"No. I believe it would be better just to spend the night here and go out to the ranch tomorrow."

"Goodnight to you, then," Lucas tipped his campaign hat. "Maybe I'll see you around town."

"Thank you," Mary said as the trooper turned away.

The night was clear and cold, and the unpaved street ahead of her was dark and empty. The sound of the locomotive echoed through the town as she walked toward the hotel.

At the front door of the hotel, Mary paused and looked up and down the sleeping street. It was fitting that her arrival was so unheralded, that no one was there to meet her, and it added to her feeling of being disconnected. "I'm no stranger to Columbus," she had told the trooper, but she said it as a ghost might say it: *I'm no stranger, but I don't belong here, either.*

She could smell the sweet perfume of the desert. A dog barked in an alley two streets over. She pushed open the door and went inside.

EIGHT

J U S T before daybreak, over coffee, Hampton lined out what the
   work would be. The morning air was chilled, but there had been
no frost. It would be a clear day without wind.

"Most of the cattle will be feedin' together, but spread out,
especially on the hillsides. It'll be easy to spot them. The hard part
will be workin' through the flats and draws where the brush is
thickest. If we keep movin' whatever we find toward the southeast,
we'll hit the fence at the property line, and it'll be no problem pushin'
them toward the house from there."

"That won't take long," Satterwhite said, red-eyed and sullen.
Although he slept all night without stirring, he felt exhausted.

"Take longer than you think, young fella. You didn't see all the
stock I saw."

"You're still saying I didn't look for them."

"That's right," Hampton said.

"How come so many are back up here, when MacPherson has
good pasture closer to the house?" Tyler asked.

"He turns them out in winter to take advantage of available
forage. Our rainy season starts early in the desert, then stops, then
picks up again midsummer."

"Seems like a way to lose a lot of head."

"He knows what he's doing," Satterwhite said.

"I'm sure he does," Tyler said, looking at him.

"That ain't the question, Satterwhite, goddammit."

"Sounded like it to me."

"How would you like to catch on fire?" Hampton asked, sipping his coffee.

Satterwhite stood up and poured the rest of his coffee on the ground. He dropped the cup on his bedroll and walked away toward the horses. Hampton watched him.

"That's his answer to everything. He just walks away."

Tyler glanced at Hampton and worked his lips over his teeth, tasting his coffee. "You two are somethin' to watch in action," he said. "Reminds me a little bit of the way you and. . . ." Tyler paused, then he said, "Reminds me a little of you and Homer."

Hampton sipped his coffee and looked over the rim of the cup at the fire, remembering his younger brother.

"He's got the makin's, but he ain't no Homer," Hampton said.

Hampton and Tyler both knew that when cattle spend most of their time in the hills, foraging for food in competition with deer, living like them, fending off the same predators, drinking at the same water holes, they become as wild and difficult to herd as deer. But Satterwhite had scarcely any idea of the difficulty that lay ahead of them.

By noon they had worked out about sixty head with at least twenty good-looking calves among the cows. Hampton had warmed to the work which had been second nature to him for so many years, but Satterwhite managed his flank only by cursing and stumbling and running headlong into brush, once falling from his horse, which seemed in no particular hurry to be recaught for more of the same work. Satterwhite would have been afoot the rest of the day if Tyler had not ridden his horse down.

About the time Mary was talking to the detective in El Paso, they stopped for lunch. Hampton dismounted next to Tyler and laughed shortly like he had been told a joke that was not very funny.

"Should one of us ride with them, or are you goin' to let them get away?" Tyler asked, pointing a handful of reins at the backs of the cattle as they slipped away through the brush, some of them bawling, others leaving a rich wet trail behind them.

"That's the wrong way to think about it, Bud. They're cows. They ain't gettin' away."

"Don't seem like cows," Tyler said, swinging down from his horse. "Seem more like jackrabbits."

"That reminds me of a story I heard about an easterner roundin' up jackrabbits thinkin' they were lambs."

"I feel like I've had his job."

Satterwhite came loping up then and got off beside them. "Damn," he said. "Mr. Frank ought to just let the mountain lions eat these stubborn bastards and be done with it."

"You tell him," Hampton said.

Satterwhite cut him a dark look and tied his horse to the nearest bush. Hampton pulled his saddlebags from behind his saddle and carried them over to a level patch of ground under a scrappy mesquite tree.

"Time to eat," he said.

The other two joined him. In the sun it was hot now, and each of them showed sweat, but even the smallest web of shade was cool. Hampton pulled the jerky and crackers out of his saddlebags. With his pocket knife he sliced the jerky onto the top of his saddlebags. They ate in silence for a while.

"Wish we had an onion," Tyler said.

"Be good," Hampton nodded. "Water would be good too."

Both of them looked at Satterwhite who stopped in mid-chew and shook his head.

"Youngest man gets the water," Hampton said.

"Water sure would make the difference," Tyler said.

Satterwhite stood up grumbling and went back to his horse for a canteen.

"Be easier just to shoot him," Tyler said.

"May have to."

It was late in the day when they had flushed the hills back of the Tres Hermanas peaks and had close to two hundred head of cattle moving across some low, dry hills. That morning they had packed everything and left the packhorse tied where Satterwhite could go back for it while Hampton and Tyler pushed the cattle out of the hills. But it was late now, and they knew they would spend another night before making it back to the ranch house.

Hampton rode up and fell in beside Tyler in the dust of the cattle.

"Going to have to make another camp, Bud. There's a flat up ahead with some grass, but no water. We can bed them down there if they'll let us and make a camp."

"Sounds good to me. I'm about ready to feel ground beneath my boots."

"Satterwhite will be along with the packhorse in a little while if he don't get lost."

"Go ahead and set up camp when he gets back," Tyler said. "I'll bunch these ladies and gentlemen and try to calm them down."

"It'll be dark soon."

"I'll come in by the light of the fire."

Hampton nodded and swung to the left to flank the herd while Tyler spurred forward to keep them moving. They were tired and ready to stop but still skittish enough to keep both men alert. It would take only one determined heifer turning back for the hills to start the whole bunch running, but they moved well and were soon on an open flat.

At sundown, Satterwhite appeared on the trail behind them and came on slowly until he saw Hampton wave and point to the place they would make camp. It would be well after dark before they ate, this time a cold supper since it was a dry camp, but they had plenty of water for coffee.

The moon was low on the horizon before Tyler rode up to the fire. He was tired and moving slowly as he stepped down from his horse. He stood beside it a minute, then loosened the cinch and tied the reins to a low bush.

"Satterwhite, you got some oats for this old boy? He's earned them today."

"They're in the. . . ."

"Get them," Hampton said.

"I'm getting pretty tired of waiting on. . . ."

"Get them," Hampton said again.

Satterwhite snorted and stood up.

"And don't make a lot of noise about it unless you want them cows headin' back up in the hills."

Tyler walked over to the fire. "I don't ever want no cows I got to ride after," he said.

"How you feelin'?"

"Beat into little pieces."

"Here's your cup."

"Thanks. I've spit so much I have dust for blood."

"Tomorrow is bath day," Hampton said. "Goin' to feel good. My head itches."

Tyler sat down cross-legged, then felt his back catch and leaned back to straighten it. "Goddammit," he said. "Trains is a lot easier on the back."

"You ready to eat?"

"In a minute. Let me sit a while."

"Not too hungry myself," Hampton said. "Betty always packs more than we need."

"Was she the redhead?"

"Yeah," Hampton said.

"Fine lookin' woman."

"Yeah."

"Had a real sweet face."

"Yep."

"She's married," Satterwhite said, walking up to the fire.

Tyler looked up.

"Listen," Hampton said, "give me some of them makin's. I've been needin' a smoke ever since last night."

"I thought you only liked to chew," Satterwhite said. He bent over his bedroll and his hat fell off.

"Satterwhite, you got to be a horse's ass ever' time you open your mouth?" Hampton asked. "Pass over those makin's."

Tyler looked at him. Hampton's face was blank in the light of the fire. The reflection on his glasses hid his eyes.

"Here," Satterwhite said, "help yourself."

"Thanks."

Hampton rolled two cigarettes of the coarse, dry tobacco. He sat down on his bedroll and did it carefully and slowly. Tyler began to remember Hampton's ability to seem entirely alone, no matter how many people were around. Hampton put both cigarettes on his blanket, then tossed the pouch back to Satterwhite.

"Got some more matches around here somewhere," Satterwhite said, looking. His attitude seemed to change after being asked a favor.

"Don't need 'em," Hampton said. "I'll use the fire."

The men lapsed into silence. They could hear the cows from time to time, but none of them wanted to think about the cattle. The wood on the fire crackled and burned, and the smell of the desert cooling was mixed in with the smell of woodsmoke and coffee.

Tyler yawned and straightened his back again. "I think I could go to sleep right now and eat in the mornin'."

Hampton stared at the fire, but he did not seem to see it. He might have been a statue or a picture of a man painted on his bedroll. The firelight flickered on his face and across his shirt, but he remained immobile.

"Not me," Satterwhite said. "I'm hungry. Runnin' them cows did me in."

Tyler looked at him, moving only his eyes across the fire.

"I never knew a cow could move that fast. One of them turned up the side of a hill in that loose rock, and I swear I was lyin' down on my horse's back. It was one foot up and two feet back."

"I saw you," Tyler said. "You was flappin' in the saddle like a loose sheet."

"I should have just shot the son of a bitch," Satterwhite said, getting carried away.

"Yeah," Hampton said. "Good way to build a herd."

"I wouldn't have really done it."

"Then don't say you would have."

They were quiet for a few minutes, Satterwhite nursing his new wound.

"A man shouldn't say things he don't mean," Tyler said softly. "Makes him seem insincere."

"I'll remember that," Satterwhite said with an edge on his voice.

Hampton sighed and picked up one of his cigarettes. He got to his feet and carried a small limb to the fire, let it catch, lit his cigarette with it, then dropped the stick on the fire. Tyler watched him. When the cigarette was burning evenly, Hampton stood by the fire, feeling its warmth. He took a deep pull on the cigarette and blew smoke out. It mingled with the smoke from the fire and wafted away into the night.

"I don't believe in ghosts," Hampton said.

"That's bad luck," Satterwhite said, rolling a smoke for himself.

"Something's brewin'," Hampton said, ignoring Satterwhite, "but it ain't ghosts, and it ain't weather."

"It's that old bear," Tyler said.

"There aren't any bears left in these hills," Satterwhite said.

"One might be passin' through," Tyler said.

Hampton looked down at his friend. Their eyes met. "I don't like the way it feels," he said.

"I know."

Hampton shrugged and smoked. He took the cigarette out of his mouth and looked at its length. "I'm goin' to put Satterwhite in the saddle for the first watch. I'll relieve him after midnight."

"Good," Tyler said. "I'll pick you up before daybreak."

"You got somethin' to say about the first watch?" Hampton asked Satterwhite.

"Would it matter?"

"Nope. Keep 'em still out there. And listen, you see anything you don't like, you slip back here real easy just as fast as you can."

"See anything like what?"

"You'll know it when you see it," Hampton said and threw his first cigarette in the fire. "Let's eat."

Hampton awoke when he felt sand blowing down his neck. He shook his head and threw back the blankets. He was instantly cold and could see that the fire had burned down. The moon was gone, and Orion was on the horizon, so he knew it was after midnight. He pulled on his boots and glasses and stood up. Tyler was rolled in his blankets with his head down low against his saddle out of the chill wind.

"I hope that damned Satterwhite didn't fall off his horse out there," Hampton said under his breath as he pulled on his coat. He looked through the darkness and located the cattle, but he could not see Satterwhite.

Buttoning his coat, he walked away from the dead fire toward his horse that was still saddled and staked about fifty feet away. Hampton tightened the cinch, slipped off the rope, and stepped up in the saddle.

"Time to get some exercise," he whispered and nudged her gently forward.

He rode around the other two horses and started across the flat toward the cattle. The stars were so bright overhead that they were almost confusing in their density. As he rode, he felt the chill deepen, then lessen to a bearable degree, and the stiff muscles began to stretch. He slowed the mare and walked the edge of the cattle. They were lying down, mostly, but a few were pacing aimlessly around the others.

Hampton rode three-quarters of a circle before he found Satterwhite sitting his horse in a shallow draw and smoking a cigarette. He turned down in the draw and stopped beside him.

"Well at least you had sense enough to get out of sight to smoke," Hampton said.

"I'm about to freeze to death," Satterwhite said.

"Go on back, then. Put some more wood on the fire, but not a lot. My stake rope is lyin' on the ground. Use it, but don't unsaddle. Try not to wake Bud."

Satterwhite finished his cigarette and mashed it out against his boot. Hampton pulled back on the reins to turn Lady away.

"Wait a minute," Satterwhite said, picking up his own reins.

"What."

"I guess I was wrong about these cows."

"You were."

Satterwhite looked left through the darkness, then looked back at Hampton, whose glasses reflected the stars. Satterwhite was glad he could not see his eyes.

"I been thinkin', ridin' around out here. I don't feel bad about not counting the cows. I didn't care much about them. I still think they're too much trouble. But I do feel bad about thinkin' I could slip somethin' past you."

"Uh-huh," Hampton said.

"I don't plan to do it again," Satterwhite said.

Hampton looked around, then back at the dim reins trailing out of his left hand. "Go on back," he said.

Satterwhite nodded and rode by him. Hampton backed the mare and sat in his saddle watching his dark form crest the draw and disappear. He shook his head and said to no one, perhaps to Lady, "He still ain't no Homer."

NINE

AS the sun went down on Hampton and Tyler and Satterwhite, a chill, easterly wind began to blow through the virtually empty streets of Columbus. The faint light of kerosene lamps burned in the windows of the Commercial Hotel and in the train depot where the stationmaster sat smoking next to the wood heater and reading a copy of the *Deming Graphic*. Faint lights also showed in the houses near the center of town, and farther out their glow tinted windows where farmers and businessmen rested.

In the preacher's house, three lamps burned — one in the kitchen, where Rosie was washing dishes from the evening meal, and two in the parlor, which was really only a front bedroom that the preacher received guests in and held a Bible study class in on Wednesday evenings. There was a wood heater in that room, not unlike the one in Hampton's house, but bigger and newer with two hot plates on top and curving ornamental legs holding it off the wooden floor. The heater was flanked by two stuffed wing-back chairs on one side and a horsehair settee on the other. Opposite the heater was the oak table where the members of the Bible study class sat. It was a warm room, with a rug on the floor and religious pictures on the walls.

It was just past seven o'clock, and the preacher was leading the discussion of miracles recounted in the Acts of the Apostles. They were beginning chapter twenty, examining the miracles of Paul, having already discussed the strength of his faith as he struck Elymas with blindness, healed a cripple at Lystra, cast out the spirit of divination from a girl, and performed various other miracles at Ephesus during his third missionary journey.

The Bible study class consisted on this evening of Carter Addison and his wife, Jessie Lee, Aunt Phoebe and her sister, Mrs. Strickland, and a young schoolteacher from Santa Fe who had moved to Columbus to help his cousin in the freighting business when he was not teaching school. Each had their King James version of the Bible open on the table in front of them.

The preacher sat at the head of the table, away from the heater, where he could see the room and through the doorway into the kitchen. His elbows were propped on the table, his arms crossed just under his book, and he leaned forward, ready to continue.

"I saw a picture in *Liberty* of the very dress I would like to wear on Easter," Jessie Lee said abruptly.

The preacher looked up and smiled slightly. Jessie Lee was eleven years younger than her husband and had a penchant for fashion as practiced in the East.

Aunt Phoebe and Mrs. Strickland looked at her with interest, but Addison said, "Now what does that have to do with miracles?"

"Well," Jessie Lee said with a pout, "it would be a miracle if I got the dress. Ladies in the big cities are so lucky. They can find in an afternoon anything they want. We have to wait so long when we order from the store, don't you think?"

"Yes, I do," Mrs. Strickland said. She was a thin woman who wore a narrow-brimmed black hat. "I ordered a coat and bag from Mr. Harlan, and it took well over a month to get it."

Aunt Phoebe looked on with interest. The schoolteacher licked his lips and folded his arms to match the preacher, a patient but confused look on his face.

"This isn't the time to talk about your dress," Addison said, picking up his Bible and laying it down again.

Jessie Lee smiled coquettishly at the preacher. "But I'm talking about the dress I'm going to wear to church."

"No one said you were getting the dress," Addison looked at her.

Jessie Lee frowned at her husband, then smiled at the preacher again. "I guess I'm just being vain when I talk about it," she said. "Do you think I'm being vain, Mr. Leggitt?"

"Human, perhaps," the preacher said and looked down at the page. He focused on the chapter number.

"I just don't think it's too much to ask to have a new dress for Easter," Jessie Lee said. She pulled her Bible closer to her, then pushed it away again.

"I have mine," Aunt Phoebe said. "It's the same one I've worn for ten years."

"You're sweet," Jessie Lee said, looking across the table at her.

"We were moving on to chapter twenty," the preacher said without looking up, his impatience showing only in an added degree of hoarseness in his voice.

They all looked at their Bibles, all but the schoolteacher skimming the verses quickly, trying to remember what the miracle was. Jessie Lee giggled when she read the verse that described Eutychus going to sleep during Paul's preaching and falling out of a third-story window.

"In this chapter," the preacher said, "Paul brings a young man back to life who had fallen from a window."

"That's silly," Jessie Lee said.

The schoolteacher looked at her, as did the other two women. The preacher did not look up.

"It's a good thing people don't sit in windows during my sermons," he said.

"Your sermons aren't boring," the schoolteacher said quickly.

"Not in the least," Mrs. Strickland added.

"Thank you." The preacher looked up and smiled.

"I don't believe this was a true miracle," Addison said, squinting at the page in his Bible. "I mean, it seems to me that this man, whatever his name is, might have just been unconscious and not dead at all."

"I still think it's silly," Jessie Lee said.

"I suppose that is possible," the preacher said, looking at Addison, "but all we have to go on are the words in the text. It says he was brought to Paul dead."

"But he could have just seemed to be dead. Maybe he had the breath knocked out of him. I've seen that happen before."

Aunt Phoebe looked across the table at Addison. "Are you questioning the holy word of God?" she asked.

"Not at all," Addison said. "I was merely pointing out what may have really happened."

"The point may be that Paul had the faith to know what was right or what was real, when the others didn't. If you interpret the text in such a way as to believe the man was only unconscious, Paul still had the ability to see the truth. If Eutychus was really dead, the Lord worked through Paul and gave him life again. As, indeed, the Lord has promised to do with each of us."

"Amen," Mrs. Strickland said.

"I think it's one of the more silly passages in the Bible," Jessie Lee said and closed her book, signaling all at the table that she had had enough for one night.

One by one, the others closed their Bibles and looked at the preacher. He smiled patiently, not feeling the smile beyond his lips, and led them in a prayer.

The preacher said goodnight to each of them at the door. "I hope you get your dress, Jessie Lee," he said as he opened the door for her.

She smiled, but Addison said, "Don't encourage her, Mr. Leggitt."

Mrs. Strickland and Aunt Phoebe followed them out, but the schoolteacher hung back. The preacher closed the door. Rosie came into the room, gathered cups and saucers from the table, and carried them back into the kitchen.

The schoolteacher shrugged on his coat and put his hands deep in the pockets. "Do you believe in these miracles, Mr. Leggitt?" he asked.

The preacher put his hands in his pants pockets. "If I believe in any of the Bible, I have to believe in all of it," he said.

"I don't doubt that," the schoolteacher said. "I was just asking. You see, I believe in them."

"That's good," the preacher said. He liked the schoolteacher, but he had the feeling, each time the man spoke, that he already knew what he was going to say. It was sometimes a struggle not to go ahead and say the words for him and save them both a lot of time.

"I have a reason to believe in them."

"You do?"

"Yes. I saw a miracle one time," the schoolteacher said, looking at the floor.

"Oh?"

"Yes. I used to live in Santa Fe. I was in love — courting a girl there. One day she was struck by lightning. I was with her. We were walking, and I had gone ahead. A thunderstorm came up from the desert suddenly. I heard the noise, then looked back, and she was on the ground. I ran up to her, and she was dead. Her eyes were still open, but she wasn't breathing."

The preacher took a deep breath and looked toward the kitchen.

"I was really scared, so I prayed. I prayed that she would come back to me. It began to rain, and the wind blew from first one direction, then the other. I opened my eyes, and saw her blink. The rain was hitting her face, and she blinked. She was all right, Mr. Leggitt."

"That was indeed a miracle."

"Yes," the schoolteacher said. He took his hands out of his coat pockets and put them back in again.

"Did you marry the girl?" the preacher asked after a pause.

"No. No, I didn't. She married someone else."

"I'm sorry," the preacher said.

The schoolteacher shrugged and looked up at the preacher, then looked down again.

"It doesn't matter," he said. "I just wanted to tell you that what you do means a great deal to me. I don't want you to let Jessie Lee make you think none of us really cares about these meetings. I look forward to them."

"Thank you," the preacher said. "Jessie Lee has a good heart. I try to remember that when she tries my patience."

"Of course," the schoolteacher said. "Well, I better be going. I just wanted you to know that I think you are a great preacher."

"Thank you again," the preacher said, and shook the school-teacher's hand. "God bless you."

"Goodnight, Mr. Leggitt."

"Goodnight."

When the door was closed, the preacher looked across the room for a minute, then walked into the kitchen. Rosie was finishing the dishes. The preacher leaned against the counter and watched her.

"You did a great job, Rosie," he said after a while.

"I think it is you who do the great job by not slapping Mrs. Addison each time she opens her mouth."

The preacher smiled. "Think it would do any good?"

"It would do me very much good," Rosie said. She carried the dishpan to the side door, opened it with one hand while she held the pan against her apron with the other, and threw the water out into the night. She closed the door again and looked at the preacher.

"You are too sad, I think," she said.

The preacher smiled slowly but did not look up. "Each time it seems to get harder, Rosie," he said.

Her dark eyes watched his face for a minute, then she wiped off the cabinet and left the dishcloth hanging on the side of the pan. She untied the apron and hung it on a nail by the door.

"Marcos better have a hot fire when I get home," she said.

"Let me walk you."

"There is no need for that."

"I want to."

The wind was steady and cold when they left the preacher's house and walked up the dirt street toward Rosie's house.

"Mr. John before you also did not have an easy time with his preaching," Rosie said as they walked. "He used to drink."

"I'm not quite ready for that," the preacher said. "I don't know what it is, Rosie. Spring is coming. Perhaps I'm just restless because of that. I need to mix some of my father's 'spring tonic' he used to call it."

"That sounds like drinking to me."

"But as I remember it, it wasn't something a man would want on a regular basis."

Rosie laughed, and they reached her house in the dark. "You can come in and get warm, if you want to, Mr. Leggitt."

"No thank you. Goodnight, Rosie. I'll see you in the morning. Tell Marcos we may go to Deming in the afternoon."

"He'll like that. Goodnight."

Rosie went in, and the preacher turned back down the street, his hands in his pockets. He felt as lonely as he was alone. The town was dark and still, and he could smell woodsmoke in the cold air. There was an emptiness in him like a hunger. He tried to push it aside, but couldn't.

After the preacher was back in his house, Rosie's last words echoed ironically in his head. He sat up late, reading until the sound of the midnight train broke his concentration. He fed wood into the heater and walked around the room several times, then finally went to bed.

Sometime later, when darkness was deep about the house, he got up and put on the same clothes he had taken off only a few hours before. He had no idea what time it was. The room was cold, but dawn was still hours away. He went out of the room in the dark to the kitchen where he lit the kerosene lamp. He pulled open the firebox on his wood stove. He kept old newspapers on a bottom shelf of his cabinet for starting fires. He stuffed several sheets in the stove on the cold ashes, put kindling on top of them, and lit the paper with a match he kept in a Sir Walter Raleigh tobacco tin on the shelf above the stove.

He stepped back while he waited, shivering, and rubbed his hand across his face. It was not the first time his restlessness had brought him out of sleep to question his life. If he prayed, he said the same words over and over again. They carried little meaning. He asked for strength but felt weak while he did so. He asked for an answer but posed new questions in his mind. He thought of his mother who had died when he was twelve, and her caring attention, then lost her image to that of his father, the army veterinarian, taking him hunting or into the field on one of his doctoring trips.

The paper caught the kindling and drew air in through the damper with a small roar. The preacher rubbed his hand over his face again and yawned. He bent and opened the door of the firebox and fed it some larger chunks of ironwood. When he closed the door, the roar continued, and the stove and flue began to tick with heat.

The preacher filled his coffeepot with water and added coffee. He put it on the stove. The smell of coffee cooking was always better than the taste of it. He sat down at the small table and waited.

There were too many things to think about. He was thirty years old and had been a preacher for nine years, had never known any other trade except for the times he had ridden with his father to help with surgery or birthing. For the majority of his life, he had been separated from the society of females. The early death of his mother, the absence of girl cousins, the scarcity of girls his age in schools, and finally the aloofness of his calling had prevented him from long or close association with the opposite sex.

He was alone, and he was not happy. He knew what his problem was. Why did he have to feel so guilty about it? Why couldn't he put on a different set of clothes and be someone else for a while?

Jessie Lee's facetious giggle echoed in his brain, along with the schoolteacher's appreciation. It was a difficult balance.

He slammed his palm down on the tabletop, then stood and turned away from the sound in the quiet house. He went to the window above the sink. Faintly there, he could see his reflection in the glass. A few bright stars were visible in the shadow of his image. His eyes were sad, deep-set, shadowed.

"What do you think I should do?" he asked.

His reflection waited for an answer. A sound like thunder reached his ears. It grew in intensity, and he leaned forward. About the time he saw the first man on horseback, there was a flash from a rifle. The windowpane burst inward on him in a shower of broken glass.

Part II

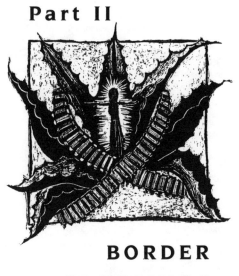

BORDER
CROSSINGS

TEN

JUST after midnight, Julio Salazar crossed through the cut boundary wires west of Palomas. He was one of nearly a thousand revolutionaries loyal to Pancho Villa who were making the crossing, but he did not see himself as one of many. After the decimation of his *Dorados* at Celaya less than a year before, Villa had come to rely on bandit chiefs in the northern desert of Chihuahua for added support to his dwindling personal army, and one of them was Julio Salazar. His band numbered close to fifty, including some women, wives or girlfriends, who travelled with the men, taking care of them and fighting when necessary.

Salazar was forty years old and had a wife named Carmen, but no children. He had been born the son of peasants. His father worked for an American mining company in Chihuahua, where Salazar eventually joined him. When the revolution began, he saw an opportunity to take the things he had never had from the people he felt had always withheld them.

His success as a leader derived from his harshness and his daring in battle, as well as from a mystical, almost religious quality. Although sensitive to irony, he was a man with virtually no sense of humor or compassion. But he was not a fanatic. He did not believe in any cause except his own, whatever it happened to be at the moment. In battle, he was immediately resourceful, seldom having to think as he fought, and his careless bravery earned him the respect of his men.

His mystical quality stemmed from something that happened when he was twenty years old. A meteorite fell with a crackling explosion on Christmas Eve, 1896, and dug a pit the size of a room in the desert floor fifty yards from his front door. Salazar had been the first and only one to explore the pit, where he found a dark chunk of rock buried in the sand. When he showed it around the village, he was told that anything that fell from the sky belonged to the church, so Salazar left his home and travelled to the church in Juarez to give the stone to the priests there.

This, in itself, raised him in the estimation of the other peasants in the mining community, but there was another thing. After he returned from Juarez, he compulsively began to make dolls from sticks and grass, mud, or bits of cloth. They were female figures, and the story spread that they were images of the Virgin Mary and that he had been blessed in some singular way. He became known as *El Hacedor de Muñecas*, The Dollmaker.

Once across the border, the raiders halted while the leaders moved forward under the windy night sky to work through their plan one last time. Spies had identified the homes of the army officers, and one group of raiders was to find these and surround them, while another attacked the barracks at Camp Furlong, south of the railroad tracks. Afterward, they would raid, sack, and burn the town.

Salazar listened to the plan, but made a new one in his mind. He would wait until the soldiers were engaged, then ride directly into the town. The prospect of looting American stores filled him with anticipation and excitement. He returned to his band. Carmen spurred up beside him. She wore two bandoleers and carried a rifle, a Mauser.

"I will hold the horses," she said.

"No. We will ride the horses," Salazar said. "Antonio!"

A man appeared, his face black in the shade of his sombrero, the same face Clay Smith had stared into as the bandits bore down on him.

"You ride with me. We will go behind the others to the road, but we will not cross it. We will follow the road into the town. Do you understand?"

"Yes, *jefe*."

"Tell the others. It is time."

Salazar trotted forward, and his band followed after him. All across the desert were men on horseback or afoot, moving north under the cold sky.

Mary had taken a room overlooking the street on the second floor of the Commercial Hotel. She was in the habit of sleeping with a window open, and when the eastbound train was half a mile from the depot, the sound of it through her window woke her. The chill of the night air was in the room, but the covers on her bed were heavy and warm and pressed around her. She lay on her side facing the window. Her loose, dark hair flowed down diagonally across her cheek, along the curve of her jaw, and disappeared under the quilts at her throat.

The train was slowing down but would not stop. Under the chuff of the locomotive, Mary heard another sound. Men were shouting briefly, and horses were in the street. Mary listened for a moment, on the edge between going back to sleep and getting up. Then, curious, she got up and went to her window.

Across the way, in front of the Lemmon & Romney grocery store, there were men and horses showing darkly against the sand of the street. Mary felt a cold spot grow in her stomach. As she continued to watch, she saw that there were more men than horses, and that those on foot were bringing supplies out of the store and tying sacks onto the horses. Other men came up the street on foot. They were carrying rifles and wearing the wide black sombreros common to Mexican bandits.

Mary stepped away from the window. The sound of the eastbound filled the room for a moment. She was sure she heard rifle shots but did not yet understand what was happening. She thought she had seen a robbery taking place, but her common sense told her it was more than a robbery.

The store was being looted by Mexican bandits. The town was full of them.

Shivering now, Mary opened the wardrobe and began to dress in the same wool skirt and cotton blouse she had worn the day before. All of her other belongings were in her trunks at the depot. She dressed quickly in the dark, her valise open on the bed ready to take whatever she threw in it. She gathered her hair at the back of her head, twisted it into a bun and put two long pins in it to hold it.

The train was on its way out of town, and the sound of rifle fire was unmistakable. Mary pulled on her coat and went to the window. There was more movement in the street now. Men on foot and horseback were sweeping by. Some opened fire, shooting into dark windows, and the desert-loud shots were followed by screams of *"Mata a los gringos!"*

"Oh, sweet Lord," Mary said under her breath. For a moment, the memory of El Paso filled her mind. She shuddered.

Mary turned to the bed, closed the snaps on her valise, grabbed it up, and ran out into the hall.

A door downstairs was broken inward with a crack of splintering wood and broken glass. Rifle shots followed, and heavy, quick steps drummed on the wooden stairs. Mary hesitated in the dark. She knew without thinking that the rooms would be searched. She turned toward the end of the hall and ran swiftly to the fire escape door. It was locked. To her left was the bathroom. She opened the paneled door and ducked inside. As the heavy bootsteps reached the top of the stairs, she slipped between a linen hutch and the corner, leaving her valise against the wall.

Confusion broke out. Mary heard excited Mexican voices ordering occupants out of the rooms. Doors were kicked in. Women screamed. Men asked questions in angry, startled voices and were either ordered outside by the bandits or shot where they stood. Two bullets splintered the paneled door of Mary's hiding place. She put her knuckles in her mouth to stifle a scream and huddled lower against the wall.

Mary felt her eyelids press against her eyes as she squeezed them shut. Where were the soldiers? Surely they would come soon and put a stop to this. Or were they all dead? Mary remembered the young lieutenant who had spoken to her when she got off the train. Where was he?

Footsteps came down the hall toward Mary. The splintered door was kicked open. Mary closed her eyes. A rifle went off in the doorway, the flash like that of a camera in the dark room, and the bullet rang on the iron bathtub and ricocheted into the plaster wall. Mary pressed her knuckles against her teeth, but in the darkness, the man did not see her.

"Burn it!" someone shouted in Spanish.

With the bathroom door open, the noise in the hall was terrific. Men were running, shooting, and breaking things. Light showed, firelight. The heavy boots went back down the stairs, but the gunfire never slowed. It was all around Mary, both inside the hotel and outside. In rhythm to the explosions, Mary heard the muffled chants, "*Mata a los gringos!*" and "*Viva Villa!*"

At the moment the window shattered inward, the preacher felt a numbing blow in his right arm just below the shoulder. He spun to the left, instinctively shielding his injured arm. There were more shots from outside, and he heard bullets hitting the stove and the table and the far wall of the kitchen. He ducked under the window, saw a splintered hole erupt in the wall near him, and crawled to the cabinet where the lamp burned. He reached up and pulled it to the floor and blew it out. Forcing himself to ignore the bullets, he crawled across the floor and threw his back against the wall on the other side of the stove.

Outside, the sounds of the horsemen lessened, and the gunshots went by him like the sound of thunder in a passing storm. His arm was beginning to burn now, and he put his hand to it, feeling the extent of damage and fighting back the shock of being hit by a bullet. His apprenticeship with his father had taught him what to look for. The muscle had been cut, but the bullet had missed the humerus. It would be a painful, but not a serious wound.

He turned his face toward the window in the dark room. Night air rushed in through the broken glass. He did not wonder what was happening. He knew the town was being attacked, as illogical as it seemed. He got to his feet and went to the chest of drawers in his bedroom. Pulling a red bandana from the top drawer, he held it in his teeth while he took off his jacket. He put the bandana around his arm, and, still using his teeth, tied a firm knot in it. The cut was burning fiercely, but there was nothing to be done about it now, not with the town under siege.

The preacher pulled his jacket back on. In the wardrobe was his Winchester Model '92. He took it out and emptied a new box of .38-.40 shells in his coat pocket.

Gunfire was all over town. The bandits whose job it was to

isolate the officers had been successful, but those sent to attack the barracks confused the long adobe stable with the living quarters of the troopers, pouring round after round into the stalls, killing horses and mules. Lieutenant John Lucas ran from his small house barefooted, carrying his .45. He had one of the keys to the munitions shed in his pocket. If he could get there, he could put the Benét Mercié machine guns into operation. As he raced across the cold ground, he was sure he was the only officer in the fight, and it was his intention to make it a good one.

The preacher hesitated in the shadow of his front steps for a moment, trying to get a fix on the movement. He began to load his rifle. Taking the cartridges out of his pocket one at a time, he slid thirteen into the magazine, breaking his thumbnail on the spring cover. He cocked the lever and put one more round in the magazine.

Most of the shooting was in the main street up from the depot and in the vicinity of Camp Furlong, but there was scattered shooting everywhere. The preacher couldn't tell how large the force in the town was, but it had to be several hundred. A sudden orange glow outlined the rooftops toward the center of town.

My God, the preacher thought, *they are burning the town.*

A lone rider approached, dodging in and out of buildings, shooting into houses and howling. The preacher stepped further back in the shadow and raised the Winchester to his shoulder. The movement pulled at the cut on his arm, but he set his teeth and ignored it. The rider veered off toward town. The preacher lowered his rifle, but the rider appeared suddenly again around the corner of a building not fifty feet away in the gloom. The preacher raised his rifle and fired the moment the sights landed on the chest of the rider. The Mexican spun around, still holding the reins, and fell sideways off the horse.

The preacher ran toward him, ejecting the spent shell. The adrenalin was flowing now, and he felt nothing but cold determination and anger. The Mexican was not dead and had not released the reins, but he could not move his arms. The preacher had cut his spine.

There was shooting to the north of where the preacher stood, and he thought of Rosie and Marcos. The preacher whipped the reins from the man's hand. He grabbed the saddlehorn and swung up on the horse, the pain in his shoulder completely forgotten now. As he turned the horse up the street, he heard the furious sound of the Benét Mercié machine guns that Lucas had successfully brought into the battle. The sound encouraged him, and, holding the rifle in his right hand and the reins in his left, he urged the bandit's horse toward the north end of town.

Six miles away, Tyler rode up to Hampton around the cattle which had begun to stir and stand and browse warily on the new grass.

"Get enough rest?" Hampton asked.

"I didn't come out here to rest," Tyler answered quietly. "I might have known you'd put me to work."

Hampton looked away and worked his shoulders under the chill weight of his coat. There was not any part of him that was warm, but seeing Tyler beside him made a difference in the night.

"Did you bring your tobacco?" Hampton asked. "I chewed mine all up."

Tyler pulled his plug out of his coat pocket and reached it to Hampton.

"Looks like I'm gettin' in the habit of borryin' tobacco off other men."

"Did you notice Satterwhite perk up when you asked him for a smoke?"

"Hate to be in his debt, but I needed that smoke." Hampton cut a piece off the plug of tobacco and passed it back to Tyler who took it and did the same.

"You think anymore about my proposition?" Tyler asked.

"Yes, sir, I have."

"Well, you have a good thing here. Don't let me pull you away from it if you ain't ready to leave."

Hampton looked down, feeling the slight burn of the tobacco in his cheek. He had been thinking most of the night, remembering his life in Texas, the good and the bad of it. He looked up, facing east, and started to answer. On the horizon, the orange glow of fire in

Columbus caught his eye. He stared for a minute, making sure, but the tight feeling in his chest had already convinced him. He pulled the reins up in his hand and pointed.

"What?" Tyler said, turning to look.

"It's your goddamned bear."

Tyler saw the uneven wavering glow and gathered his own reins tighter. "Lead the way," he said. "I'll back you up, just like the old days."

Hampton jerked the reins on Lady and turned back to the camp at a full run. The nervous cattle jumped away, scattering again. When Hampton and Tyler got to the camp, they dismounted before their horses had stopped. The familiar energy of battle was in their blood.

"Get up, Satterwhite," Hampton barked, going to the packhorse and untying the sack with his gunbelt and rifle ammunition in it.

"What? I just got warm. I'm not going. . . ."

"Get up, goddammit. Columbus is on fire. Get your gun and all your bullets."

"Villistas?" Satterwhite asked, kicking out of his bedroll. He stood up and squinted to the east. The orange glow was growing.

"Hurry up, Satterwhite," Hampton barked, tying on his gunbelt and carrying the sack with ammuniton over to Lady. He tied it on behind his saddle, but didn't check his rifle. He knew it was full. He untied the packhorse and let it go.

Satterwhite pulled on his boots. "What about the cows?"

"Forget 'em. You ready, Bud?"

"Yeah."

"Let's ride."

"Wait for me," Satterwhite said, but they didn't.

When smoke began to fill the hall, Mary heard steps on the stairs again. She was trapped and helpless, and she knew she was going to die. She heard voices calling out in English, the crying of women, and hurried steps back down the stairs. The gunfire was so continuous, she couldn't believe the voices she had heard had been American. The smoke was choking her. She had to get out of the hotel.

She reached for her useless valise and stood up. Her legs were shaky, and she leaned against the splintered jamb of the bathroom door to get her balance. She coughed and pushed down the hall. Two of the rooms were burning. The dark form of a man lay in the doorway of one of them; clothes and broken furniture were scattered everywhere.

Mary stumbled toward the head of the stairs, tears running down her cheeks. She could see flames at the bottom of the stairs, but went on. The heat and smoke were about to overcome her. She raised her left arm against her face and jumped down the last steps. It was almost impossible to breathe now. She crossed the short hall and fell out the back door of the hotel.

For several minutes, all she could do was cough and try to breathe in the cold, night air. Her eyes were streaming tears so that she could see nothing but blurs of shapes. The sounds of the battle were louder. She heard the rattle of a machine gun, shouts and screams of men and horses, and the steady, unbroken return of rifle fire.

Getting to her feet, she ran forward to the wall of a dark house. The roar of the wind fueling the fire of the hotel increased. She slid along the wall until she came upon a group of men and women huddled in the same shadow. She started to speak, but several Mexicans rode suddenly into the alley. The group dashed around the corner, and Mary dodged the other way. Someone was shooting not ten feet from her. Trying to clear her eyes, she ran her sleeve roughly across them and saw a man wearing a sombrero. His back was to her, and he was shooting into the street. She ran again.

She paused, trying to get her breath. In a nearby window she saw a cardboard sign advertising BlueJay Corn Removers illuminated by the glow of the fire. Horses raced through all the streets, but the buildings around her were dark and silent, the doors locked, as if they had never been occupied, or never would be again.

Shooting was strongest in front of the hotel and east along the railroad tracks where the stockyards were. A bullet hit the adobe wall above Mary's head. She ducked and ran bent over. There seemed no safe place except around each next corner. She ran by a frame house and heard the crack of bullets hitting the wood. She kept going until she reached the corner, her breath rasping in and out like the sound of a cotton sheet tearing. She rounded the corner and collided with Julio Salazar, almost knocking him down. Her forehead bumped on his rifle stock.

"*Hijo de su!*" he said in surprise. He let go his rifle with his right arm and caught Mary around the shoulders, jerking her up roughly. She tried to get away from him, but she couldn't shake his grasp. She dropped her bag and pushed against him with both hands.

"*Cuidado*. Watch it," Salazar said, pulling her back against the wall. A bullet struck close by. "Son of a bitch," he said in Spanish.

A man rode up leading another horse. He was bareheaded and excited, and he was calling a name.

"*Aquí*, Antonio," Salazar said, holding Mary.

"What are you doing?" the rider asked in quick Spanish. "Shoot the *gringa* bitch, and let's get out of here. They are killing us all over town."

Salazar threw his rifle up to the rider and pushed Mary back far enough to swing his fist at her. He caught her on the cheekbone, and her legs buckled. He pulled her back to her feet. Her ears were ringing. She couldn't get her breath.

"We may need this one to get out of town," Salazar said. "Bring me the horse!"

The rider spurred forward. Four Mexicans came around the same corner, shooting behind them. The rider pointed Salazar's rifle at them, then said, "Listen. Get out. Get back across the border."

One of the four was hit and fell. Another, an older man, turned and saw Mary. "Why are you taking the girl?" he asked. It was Casoose.

Salazar pushed Mary up against his horse without answering, then lifted her easily into the saddle. A bullet cut her collar, and she almost passed out. Salazar caught the reins and swung up behind her. He put his arm around her waist, separated the reins between the fingers of one hand, and pulled the horse's head around.

"*Vámonos!*" he shouted. "Let's go!"

The bandits turned their horses north and cut through alleys until they were near the post office. They had to cross a street raked by gunfire, and, for a moment, they drew up and hesitated.

"Go first," Salazar shouted over his shoulder.

The other rider spurred his horse and raced across the street. In the confusion of shooting, it was impossible to tell whether or not he had drawn fire. He disappeared in the darkness. Salazar looked around, but the Mexicans on foot had scattered, trying to find a clear avenue back to their horses on the south side of town.

"*Vámonos!*" he said to the mustang and spurred him across the road. Mary gripped the pommel both to keep from falling and to keep from being pushed up on it and over the horse's head. She felt the concussion of a bullet in front of her face, but they reached the darkness beyond the post office without being hit.

"Are you there?" the other rider called tersely.

"*Sí*," Salazar answered, and they rode to the north before turning to the east. He meant to skirt the town in the darkness and thus get back across the border without being seen or pursued.

The cold wind revived Mary, although the pain in her cheekbone had spread until she felt each hoofbeat jolt in her temples. They were riding through brush east of town, both men looking for the railroad tracks. Mary brought her left leg up, hoping to throw her weight to the right, off the horse, but Salazar felt the heel of her shoe rise against his knee. He jerked the breath out of her.

"Let me go," Mary said in English. "I'm no use to you. I'll slow you down."

The other rider, riding not ten feet away, heard her voice and shouted, "Shoot her, Salazar."

"No."

"What are you going to do with me?" Mary cried, this time in Spanish.

Salazar brought his arm up to her breasts and pressed her there until she cried out in pain.

"I'll think of something," he said.

The brush opened, and they were at the tracks. Both horses slowed and leaped the rails. Mary almost fell, but the grip on her never relaxed. The sound of gunfire faded behind them. Ahead lay the border.

The preacher rode close in the shadows of houses when he could, but at the end of the street, he had to ride in the open. At the first intersection, three men spun around and one shouted, "*Quién vive?*"

The preacher reined in the horse to the left of the men, dropped the reins, and fired the Winchester at the closest man. Before the man had time to fall, the preacher swung his right leg over the saddle and dropped to the ground. The two Mexicans shot point blank at the horse, killing it. Backing away from the animal, the preacher fired rapidly at the men. He hit one of them twice. The other leveled his rifle to shoot, but was out of bullets. He threw down his Mauser and dodged away into the brush beside the road. The preacher sent two bullets after him, but could not be sure he hit the man.

There was a sudden burst of rifle fire up the sandy street, and the preacher heard horses. He cocked the rifle and ran toward the shadow of the nearer houses. He threw himself against the wall of one, the rifle raised beside his head, and waited.

Several horses raced by in the dark, only the shoulders and sombreros of the riders lit with the pale orange reflection of the burning hotel. The preacher let them go by, then turned his face north again, moving slowly up the street, his rifle in his left hand, his shoulder bleeding again and throbbing with each heartbeat.

He passed the house of a teller in the bank. The door opened, and a dark form appeared for an instant. The figure stepped back and closed the door again. The preacher went on. His arm was wet with blood, but did not feel cold.

At the end of the next street, he heard riders cross the road by the post office, and he stopped for a moment, breathing heavily, but the riders turned to the east away from him. Occasionally he heard bullets strike close to him. They seemed to be tearing through the town from every angle. Many were high, sometimes banging into tin roofs.

The preacher cut across the open street, keeping low, and again found the shadow of houses. Three more and he was in front of Marcos' house, half adobe and half frame. The windows facing the street were both broken, and the house was dark. The preacher listened against the wall for any sound. Almost all of the fighting was now concentrated around the depot and the barracks of Camp Furlong, but random shots could be heard from outlying houses. The sky was beginning to lighten in the east.

The preacher heard no movement or sound from inside the house as he stood under one of the broken windows. The rifle in his hand became suddenly so heavy, he thought he would drop it. He leaned against the wall and clenched his jaws, trying to keep his head clear. He felt a little nauseous and spit several times. He thought of the rough profile of his father, and the feeling passed. He was aware of cold sweat on his face.

"Marcos! Rosie!" he shouted hoarsely, like a forced whisper.

A pistol shot answered him. He bent down away from the window and grabbed his rifle with both hands. He thought he heard boots on the stone floor of the house, but he couldn't be sure.

He waited, breathing heavily. He couldn't remember whether or not he had ejected the last shell he fired. He looked back toward town. The noise was incredible.

"Marcos!" he called again, and this time he was sure he heard someone moving inside. Then he heard Rosie's frightened voice, "Go away. Go away!"

There was a deep growl, another pistol shot, a scream, and the front door was jerked open. The Mexican came out firing, but the preacher had not waited under the window. He had backed to the corner, and when the Mexican had come out shooting, the preacher kept his finger tensed and fired repeatedly, not raising the rifle to his shoulder. More certain of placement than the bandit, the preacher was more effective. The man jumped back, landed sitting up, then fell sideways and twisted, hit five times by the blunt .38-.40 slugs.

The preacher flung himself toward the open door, ejecting the empty shell. He had no idea how many rounds were still in the rifle, but he didn't care. He was afraid both Rosie and Marcos were dead.

"Rosie?" he called a third time, not mindful of his exposed position.

She answered, "Mr. Leggitt," and his relief was so great the preacher stumbled headlong through the doorway and fell.

The preacher felt his shoulders lifted off the floor, and he heard Rosie's voice, but it wasn't her hands he felt cradle him.

"Mr. Leggitt," Marcos said. "Are you hit?"

The glow of the fire came in the broken windows like moonlight, and the preacher could just make out Rosie's form kneeling in front of him.

"Yes," the preacher said. "I'm hit. Not too bad, but I think I've lost too much blood. Are you all right?"

"Yes," Rosie answered. "Marcos caught a bullet that bounced off the iron stove. I thought he was dead. When I screamed, the bandit came in looking for me."

A bullet hit the edge of a window frame and slapped against the far wall.

"Get down, woman," Marcos said.

Rosie lay on her side near the preacher. "You came at the right time, Mr. Leggitt," she whispered.

"With God's help," the preacher smiled in the dark. Then he said, "Marcos, retie the bandana on my arm. It feels like it has slipped down into the cut. Then reload my rifle. The bullets are in my pocket. You will have to use it. I don't feel very well."

"I can use it," Marcos said.

"Good," the preacher said and gasped as he felt the pressure of the knot Marcos made.

"Are we safe here?" Rosie asked.

"I don't think we are safe anywhere," the preacher said and let the back of his head touch the floor. Marcos leaned across him and picked up the rifle.

ELEVEN

SATTERWHITE caught up with Hampton and Tyler in less than a mile, and they rode closely abreast except when brush separated them. Then they would veer left or right, always letting Hampton take the lead.

Hampton rode high in his saddle, practically standing in his stirrups, but not. He watched for brush or outcroppings of rock directly in front of him, taking that necessity from Lady, and letting her concentrate on running. A delicate but firm twitch of the left or right rein told her what she needed to do. Hampton knew she could take the run, but he wasn't sure about the other two horses. He was separated now, alone, but confident. Tyler was behind him. He had never known anyone who could better place people in a battle than Tyler, who had an almost supernatural ability to know exactly where everyone was.

They tore across the desert. Tyler seldom looked at the horizon to see how far or close the town was, concentrating instead on the movement of Hampton's horse through the brush. Satterwhite likewise had little time to look up, finding that when he did, the glare of the rising flames blinded him for the shadows of the brush. He was so excited that he had no real conception of what he was doing or of what he was going to do when they reached Columbus.

In another two miles, by going due east, they came upon the Deming-Guzman wagon road. Hampton drew up and waited for Tyler and Satterwhite. They cleared the brush and reined in beside him.

"What is it?" Satterwhite said. "Why are we stopping?"

Hampton felt Lady's sides trembling between his legs. "Dismount," he said, like a command.

Tyler swung down.

"What for?" Satterwhite said.

"You're goin' to need that horse," Hampton shouted, almost as winded as Lady from the hard ride. "Dismount. We walk for a while."

Hampton started down the road, the gravel crunching under his boots. Tyler stepped up even with him. They were both looking at the fire three miles away to the left of the straight road.

"How about a fresh chew?" Tyler asked.

"You bet. I bleached that last one."

They could hear the gunfire now like an echo in their own pounding ears. Hampton tore off a chew and gave the plug back to Tyler. Satterwhite walked up even with them.

"What are we going to do when we get there?" Satterwhite asked. His voice was loud with nervousness.

Hampton didn't answer, then he said, "You just try to stay alive."

Tyler bit off a chew and folded the wax paper back over what was left. He tucked it in his shirt pocket and buttoned the flap.

"The thirteenth cavalry is there," Hampton said, working his chew. "With any luck, they might be takin' the fight away from the townspeople."

"If the army was on top of it, there wouldn't be no fire," Tyler spit.

"Uh-huh," Hampton said.

The road dipped down slightly, then rose again. At the top of the rise, Hampton stopped and said, "Mount up!" All three stepped back to the stirrups of their horses. One by one they swung into the saddle. Satterwhite saw Hampton slip the leather thong off the hammer of his Colt and did likewise on his own pistol. Hampton unbuckled the strap on his Winchester and pulled it out. Like the preacher's, it was a Model '92. Hampton cocked the lever and put a round in the chamber.

"Let me ride ahead," he said. "Give me about fifty feet. Satterwhite, you come in next, but off to the left. I get into some trouble, you flank me. Don't ride behind me. You understand that?"

"Yes, sir."

"You think you can't do this, say so now. I don't want to get into town and have to take care of you."

"I can do it."

"Uh-huh. If I go down, you drop back behind Bud. You hear that? If I go down, you watch Bud's back."

"All right."

"And don't worry about him. Don't even wonder where he is or where he'll be. He'll know where you are. Got that?"

"Yes, sir."

"Bud?"

"Yeah, Hamp?"

Hampton spit. "Let's do her," he said.

The fire on the main street of town was at its peak now, encompassing the hotel, the store, and several neighboring buildings. The fighting had begun to spread out as the bandits fled the killing light of the fire, but most of the civilians in Columbus either lay on the floor of their dark homes in terror or had escaped them to shiver in the brush outside of town.

When Hampton reached the first house, a small group of horses appeared suddenly to his left. He raised the Winchester, but the horses were without riders. He spurred on, watching carefully for any movement, keeping his eyes on the ground in front of and around him to avoid the blinding glare of the fire.

There was a shot from the drainage ditch that paralleled the road. Hampton let the reins slide and slack through his hands. He brought the rifle up to shoot but had no clear target and hesitated. There was another shot, as high as the first.

"Sing out!" Hampton called, waited a heartbeat, and fired at the point where he had seen the flash.

There was another shot. Hampton felt a tug at the wing of his coat. He fired again and spurred forward. Lady was steady but excited beneath him. There was no return fire from the ditch.

Ahead was a mass of movement across the road toward the west. Hampton pulled up, then jumped from the mare's back.

"Satterwhite!" he called over his shoulder. Satterwhite rode forward. "Hold the reins. I'm going ahead on foot. Hit the brush to the left if there's too much shooting. Keep Lady behind you. Don't let her tangle you up."

Hampton crouched and ran forward. Men and horses were crossing the road in groups and singly. He dropped to his knees and could see them against the pale light of the predawn sky.

"*Quién vive?*" he called.

"*Viva Villa!*" came a return shout.

Hampton opened fire, shooting quickly into anything that moved, then rolling to the left and shooting again. The road erupted in gunfire. Hampton heard Satterwhite dash for the brush as he rolled behind a drift of sand against the stump of a dead mesquite. Bullets hit the road and sang away toward Deming.

Hampton rolled to the left again and fired, but the movement was still rapidly to the west. The bandits were not making a stand. Hampton fired again. A bandit on horseback broke away and charged up the road toward him, screaming and shooting wildly with a pistol. Hampton ejected the shell and pulled the trigger, but the hammer fell on an empty chamber. He dropped the rifle and went for his pistol, getting to his knees to do so. The bandit was abreast of him on the road and saw him. Before he could shoot, a rifle cracked behind Hampton, and the bandit flipped backwards off his horse.

Tyler rode up and spit. "Dammit, Hamp," he said. "I'd shy away from stuff like that if I was you. I don't see as good in the dark as I used to."

"But good enough," Hampton said.

There were scattered shots, way off their mark, from the brush to the west of the road, but the road ahead was empty again. Tyler pulled on the reins and faded back into the night. Hampton picked up his rifle. He whistled sharply twice, hoping Satterwhite would have sense enough to know he was being called.

Satterwhite was beside him almost immediately, pulling Lady along behind him. Hampton went to the bag tied behind his saddle and pulled out a box of shells. He began reloading the rifle.

"You did good, Satterwhite," Hampton said.

"I thought you bought the farm when those greasers opened fire on you."

"Almost did," Hampton said, sliding the last cartridge home. "Old Apache trick: shoot and move. You all right?"

"One of those bullets took my hat."

"Good thing there was nothin' in it. Same plan. Let's move."

Hampton caught the reins from Satterwhite and climbed back on Lady. The smell of smoke hung in the air with the sound of rifle fire, but morning was coming. That would make things both better and worse for them as they rode into town.

Hampton moved forward with more caution now, since there was ample cover on either side of the road, but the firing was drawing steadily away from him to the south and the west. He could distinguish the sound of the army Springfields from the flatter crack of the Mexican Mausers and Winchesters. The Mexicans were evidently retreating, beating it back to the border as fast as they could.

Hampton came to the spot where the bandits had crossed the road and slowed Lady, his rifle ready. In the increasing light of the early dawn, he saw two bodies beside the road and a third in the edge of the drainage ditch. He looked at each body carefully for signs of movement. On the road behind him, Satterwhite drew up and looked around for Tyler, but didn't see him. Satterwhite drew his pistol.

The body at the edge of the road bothered Hampton. He swung down, and holding the reins in one hand and the rifle in the other, he walked over to it. The bandit was lying on his back, his arms extended above his head. Hampton crouched beside him and saw that he was just a boy. His dirty face was smooth and innocent. "Goddammit," Hampton said softly.

He stood and went to the other two. As he approached the second, the bandit rolled over and fired a pistol up at his head. Hampton let go the reins and jerked to the side, firing once as he moved. It only took one shot.

Satterwhite spurred forward and caught Lady. Tyler appeared suddenly from the drainage ditch.

"Brush is clear," Tyler said. "They're hightailin' it back to Mexico."

"See the kid?" Hampton asked.

"I saw him."

Hampton took the reins from Satterwhite and climbed back on Lady. He was starting to feel tired and hungry now. His mouth was dry. He untied the water bag behind him and took a long drink, holding his chew against his cheek. The water was cold.

"All right. Let's go," he said.

They separated again and rode into town. It was light enough now to distinguish colors in the landscape and to see the blackness of the smoke that drifted over the western part of the town.

The firing was south toward the border. Colonel Slocum, the commanding officer of the troops at Camp Furlong, stood atop the only high ground in Columbus, a rocky hill just west of the depot. Before him crouched or lay a dozen troopers, firing at the retreating Mexicans who were clear targets in the growing light. In the camp, horses were being rounded up and saddled for pursuit under the command of Major Tompkins who had been stranded in his house during most of the fight. Everywhere civilian men and troopers moved through the sandy streets checking the dead or wounded bandits and looking for those cut off from retreat and hiding.

Hampton rode through the smoke and stopped when two troopers excitedly raised their rifles at him.

"Don't do that," he said, and spit.

The soldiers lowered their rifles and went on across the road into town. Hampton sat his horse until Satterwhite and Tyler rode up with him. All around them was confusion and carnage. Horses and mules lay dead and scattered about, some with bandits dead beside them. Equipment, rifles, hats, and pieces of clothes littered the road and the ditches.

"It's not a pretty picture," Tyler said quietly.

Satterwhite's eyes were wide and staring. He still held his pistol in his hand, and he was shaking.

"War never is," Hampton said.

He eased Lady forward gently, and they rode to the corner by the depot. The sun was coming up beautifully, as it always did in the desert. Almost immediately it began to warm the riders. They turned at the depot, looking at bodies as they rode. There were many more

Mexicans than troopers. Some of the troopers wore no shirts or shirts that were not tucked in. The loose tails caught the soft breeze and lifted.

About thirty mounted troopers appeared suddenly from the camp and came up the road toward them. The three moved over and let the soldiers pass.

There was a crowd in the street in front of the burning hotel, but most were just watching it burn. It was too far gone to save.

Hampton stopped. He was suddenly tired, and he felt empty inside. He knew the feeling and knew he would just have to wait until it went away. He looked at Satterwhite and was surprised to see tears on his scared face.

"You can imagine it all you want," Hampton said slowly, "but killin' and burnin' is always hard, always."

"It's terrible," Satterwhite said. He rubbed his coat sleeve across his face.

Hampton did not look at him again. "Come on," he said. "Let's go see the preacher."

They crossed the main road again and turned north on the street where the preacher lived. The shooting continued to the south of the town, and people were stepping out of their houses the way they do after a storm, shaken and looking at the damage. The destruction of the storm was everywhere, but the storm had gone as quickly as it had come.

At the preacher's house, Tyler veered off and got down to check the Mexican the preacher had shot. He was dead. Hampton and Satterwhite dismounted at the house. Hampton was still carrying his rifle, but Satterwhite had put up his pistol.

"Stay outside," Hampton said. "I'll check the house."

He went in and came back out again.

"The preacher must have had some trouble, but he ain't here. I think I know where he is."

"You going to get him?" Satterwhite asked.

Tyler walked across the street and joined them.

"Yep," Hampton said.

"Mind if I wait here?" Satterwhite said.

"Suit yourself."

Hampton got back in the saddle, and he and Tyler turned up the street again. At the intersection, they rode around the dead horse and the three bandits the preacher had killed.

"The preacher?" Tyler asked.

"Could be. He's got it in him. He followed his daddy during the Indian wars."

When they drew up at Marcos' house, Tyler said, "There's another one."

Hampton looked at the body of the Mexican on the ground in front of the house. The sand beside him was stained with his blood. The door of the house was shut, but the glass in both windows on either side of the door had been broken by bullets.

The door opened, and Marcos stepped out. His face was dirty with dried blood and he still held the preacher's rifle. "Is it over, *Diego?*" he asked.

"For now," Hampton said, getting down. He tied the left rein to a porch post and let the other drop. "They may come back again tonight. You got a preacher in there?"

"Mr. Leggitt is here. He's been shot."

Hampton felt a cold lump in his stomach, but he said, "Looks like you caught one too."

Marcos nodded and put his fingers gingerly to his head. They went inside. The preacher was lying on the bed in the back room, drinking a cup of coffee slowly, as if each swallow were painful. Rosie stood up from a chair beside the bed.

"Hello, Preacher," Hampton said. "I need to cut that arm off or do you still want it?" Relief made his voice seem loud in the small room.

"I still want it," the preacher said.

"Uh-huh. Rosie, you wouldn't have any more of that coffee, would you?"

Rosie looked at him, and he saw the tenseness in her dark eyes lessen. "For you," she said, "I think so."

"Thank you, Rosie," Hampton said in a softer voice.

He and Tyler moved aside as Rosie left the room. Tyler took off his hat as she passed him. He looked at the preacher, then looked through one of the windows on the south side of the room. Occasional shots could still be heard.

Hampton took Rosie's chair and sat down heavily.

"What's going on out there, Hamp?" the preacher asked hoarsely.

"The army has them running back for the border," Hampton said. "The center of town is on fire. It's a big mess."

"Villistas?" the preacher asked.

Hampton nodded.

"Why?" the preacher said. "What could they gain?"

"I don't know," Hampton shook his head. "Maybe they just wanted to stir things up. Wilson will have to do something now."

The men were silent a minute, then the preacher said, "How bad is it? There was an awful lot of shooting."

"The Mexicans took a beating from what I saw," Hampton said. "I don't know how many of our boys they got."

The preacher closed his eyes and swung his arm to the left with the cup. Hampton took it from him and put it on the small table beside the bed. When the preacher opened his eyes, he said, "Can you take me back to my place?"

"Can you ride?"

"I think so."

"Well, rest a minute. I want some of that coffee." Hampton and Tyler went into the kitchen that already smelled like tortillas and coffee. Marcos sat at the table with the rifle across it. There was a pan of water in front of him, and Rosie was washing his face.

"Folks are goin' to think Rosie tried to scalp you, Marcos," Hampton said, pulling out a chair and sitting down. He took his hat off and laid it on the table.

"She has tried before," Marcos said without smiling.

"Maybe again one of these days, soon," Rosie said.

Tyler sat down, and Rosie gave the rag to Marcos while she got them coffee.

"I needed that," Tyler said.

"What happened?" Hampton asked, and listened while Marcos

and Rosie told him. He nodded. "Did you know anything about this, Marcos?" he asked.

"I heard some rumors about a border crossing," Marcos said, touching at the cut on the side of his head. "There is always rumors."

"What would Marcos know?" Rosie asked sharply.

"Rosie, there's goin' to be some hard feelin's about this. Folks are goin' to be scared, and they're goin' to act crazy."

"Because we are Mexican, they will think we are a part of it? They should have been here last night if they think we are a part of it," Rosie said.

Hampton nodded. "Anyone says anything, you let me know, that's all."

Rosie's face lost its hard lines, and the men looked at her. "Drink your coffee," she said, "or I will have all of your scalps."

"She means that," Marcos said.

Rosie put her hand on Marcos' shoulder. "And you first of all," she said with a smile. "Sleeping on the floor when Pancho Villa himself was forcing me. *Hijo!* I was afraid."

As they finished their coffee, the preacher appeared in the door. His face was pale, and his blue eyes were large.

"We're ready," Hampton said, standing. "Remember what I said, Marcos."

"I will, *Diego*. Thank you."

Hampton and Tyler lifted the preacher up on Lady. He gripped the pommel and winced with pain.

"This is his rifle," Marcos said.

"You need it?" Hampton asked.

"I have my shotgun."

"But no bullets," Rosie said.

"Get some," Hampton said. He took the rifle and put it in his own scabbard then untied Lady.

Hampton walked slowly down the street leading his horse. Tyler walked beside him. People were moving in and around houses, filling the streets, standing in little groups sharing stories.

"You feel like ridin' south, don't you?" Tyler said, listening carefully for the faint gunfire.

"A little bit," Hampton said. "Feels funny not to be in it."

"I know," Tyler said.

When they got to the preacher's house, they put him in his bed, and Hampton helped him take his coat and shirt off. Tyler and Satterwhite built a fire in the stove to heat water and cook some breakfast. The coffeepot still sat on the stove, the coffee cold now, but made. Sudden sounds from outside kept pulling Satterwhite nervously to the shattered window.

Hampton cleaned the preacher's arm with hot water, aware of the knot of covers the preacher gripped in his hand.

"That hurt?" Hampton said.

"You ever been shot, Hamp?"

"A few times."

"Yes. It hurts."

"It's a clean wound, Preacher. Had a little bit of cloth stuck in it, but I got that out. Looks like you been cut with a knife, but you'll have a hell of a bruise there. You'll have to watch out for infection."

"My father's medical bag and instruments are in the wardrobe," the preacher said. "There's iodine and alcohol in the satchel."

"Get ready for some punishment, then," Hampton said.

Hampton scalded the wound with alcohol, then iodine, and wrapped it firmly in clean bandages made from an old cotton sheet. Tyler had the coffee hot, but all the preacher wanted was cold water.

"Got some eggs fryin'," Tyler said from the doorway.

"Sounds good," Hampton looked up. "I'll be right there."

Hampton looked at the preacher. He had never been good at watching someone close to him suffer, but he was glad the preacher was alive.

"How is it?" he asked quietly.

"Throbs, but it feels better."

"You got some headache powders?"

"I think so."

"We'll find them. You'll need to sleep. You lost a good bit of blood."

Hampton watched the preacher drink the last of the water and took the glass. After a minute, he said, "I reckon you'll have a lot of preachin' to do in the next few days, but your father would be proud of you if he could have seen you in action."

The preacher looked at him and smiled weakly. "I felt like he was standing beside me the whole time. I heard his words telling me what to do."

The preacher closed his eyes again. Tears squeezed out of the corners and rolled through his sideburns. Hampton looked down at the satchel on the floor by his chair. He could hear Tyler and Satterwhite talking in the kitchen. Horses trotted by in the street.

"Well," he said. "I'll go look for those powders."

TWELVE

BY nine o'clock, the preacher had fallen asleep. Hampton left him and joined Satterwhite and Tyler in the kitchen. He sat down heavily at the table. Tyler pushed the last cup of coffee toward him.

"Satterwhite," Hampton said, "I want you to take the horses around the back and water 'em. Loosen the cinches, but don't unsaddle."

"Yes, sir." Satterwhite stood up and checked his pistol.

"And don't shoot 'em," Hampton said.

"I wasn't going to."

Satterwhite stomped out of the room. Hampton started to call out after him, but didn't. He got up, looked in on the preacher, then came back to the table carrying his rifle. He laid it across the table and reached a cup towel off the cabinet.

"Preacher goin' to be okay?" Tyler asked quietly.

"He'll keep the arm."

"He's a different sort for a preacher," Tyler mused. The hair on the down side of his part was sticking out perpendicularly from his head where his hat had been.

Hampton ejected the bullets onto the tabletop and pushed down on the lever of his rifle to hold the breech open. He held the rifle to the light and looked in it for sand. He blew into it several times, then worked the lever back and forth without dry-firing it.

"He was trained the other way," Hampton said. "Raised out by himself. Got big early. After his mama died, his daddy followed the army, fixin' troopers about as often as horses and mules. I reckon the preacher could have made a pretty fair horse doctor himself, but his mama was religious. He went that way on account of her, seems to me. He's good at it. He understands that stuff pretty well."

Hampton rubbed the entire rifle with the towel and added, "He could stand toe to toe with the Reverends Hampton and Tyler."

"He did last night," Tyler said.

Hampton heard Satterwhite saying something to the horses through the broken window, and he was restless. Too much had happened for him to be sitting idle over a cup of coffee. When he thought about the ranch, he felt a knot of worry in his stomach. He hadn't heard anything from that direction in the night, but who could say where the bandits had scattered before daybreak. He also had a great curiosity about what was happening in town and with the army. He began to pick up the bullets that lay scattered over the table, and he slid them into the magazine.

Tyler recognized the determination in Hampton's movements and finished his coffee. He stood up and went to the shattered window. He could just see the rump of his horse to the left.

"Satterwhite," he called softly.

Satterwhite's head appeared. He was holding his pistol. "What is it?"

"You loosened the cinches on them horses?"

"Not yet."

"Then don't. We're goin' into town."

Tyler turned away from the window and picked up his hat off the cabinet where sunlight played on shards of glass. Hampton stood up with his rifle in his hand.

"Figures," he said. "There are some things you can depend on Satterwhite for. Let's go."

Satterwhite remained behind in case the preacher needed attention, and Hampton and Tyler rode back toward town. Troopers on horseback were dragging the dead raiders to the edge of town where their bodies would be soaked with kerosene and set on fire. The dead stock would be next.

When they reached the depot, they found that the Deming militia had arrived. Horses and men were everywhere. Soldiers moved back and forth through the town on cleanup and security details. The black smoke from the fires still rose in the morning sky. The only gunshots to be heard now were those killing wounded animals. A buckboard passed them loaded with rifles, hats, ammunition belts, pistols and knives collected from the dead raiders.

Hampton paused and sat his horse for a minute, watching the activity.

"What?" Tyler asked.

"I'm startin' to get irritated," Hampton said. "There is no excuse for this. That murderin' son of a bitch. I hope the army drives him straight to hell."

Tyler knew who he was talking about, and looking around, he felt the same way. He wanted to be riding to the south. He wanted to shoot down every Mexican he saw. He squinted toward the horizon. No. He knew the difference between an outlaw and a common man.

"Let's go over to the customs house," Hampton said. "Looks like a powwow goin' on."

When they had dismounted and walked up into the shade of the customs house porch, several men turned to greet Hampton. The rest were listening to Colonel Slocum, who, with a secretary, sat at a table on the porch, asking and answering questions. Slocum was five years older than Hampton and had a farmer's face with sharp, intelligent eyes. A short, unlit cigar protruded from under his moustache, and his campaign hat was worn at a slight angle to the left.

"Gentlemen," he was saying, holding a paper before him, "by my count, I have seventeen dead, eight of whom were troopers, nine of whom were civilians."

"God have mercy," Hampton said. "I wonder who?"

"Of the Mexican bandits," Slocum continued, "I do not have a final count, but my men have collected well over a hundred corpses here in town, and there are dead men throughout the brush between here and the border." Slocum put the paper down on the table where his secretary picked it up and placed it inside a leather-bound folder. He took the cigar out of his mouth and spit a piece of it out to the side.

"It is assumed," Slocum said, "that Pancho Villa led this attack. My men have found wallets belonging to Villa on one of the dead bandits. Washington has been notified, and we are awaiting their instructions. In the meantime, Major Tompkins has crossed the border in pursuit of the bandits. I have no idea at this time whether or not we can expect help from the government troops in Palomas. My guess would be not."

"Colonel, what about reinforcements in case they come back again tonight?" one of the townsmen asked.

"I have no official information on reinforcements at this time, Mr. Bailey, although the militia in the surrounding towns have come to our aid. I have a man at the telegraph in the depot and another with Mrs. Parks in the telephone office. I will keep all of you informed as the day progresses."

"Just keep yourself informed," another townsman said in a voice choking with anger and emotion. "If your men hadn't been scattered all over creation playing polo and getting drunk, this never could have happened."

The man broke down. Someone close to him helped him through the crowd. Colonel Slocum raised his chin and watched the man's back. The secretary looked at the folder before him.

"What about that, Colonel?" another man said.

"My men are alert and ready. There was no way to know Villa would attack here last night. I had a patrol on the border the whole time. My men will be ready should there be another border crossing."

"What about those in the hospital?" the same man said. "I heard they locked the doors and hid themselves throughout the attack."

"I haven't heard that," Slocum said.

A lieutenant pushed through the crowd, walking with a noticeable limp, a smoking pipe clamped in one corner of his mouth. He stepped up to the porch, saluted, then sat down on the top step.

"It's true, sir," the lieutenant said in a quiet, firm voice. "There were some men in the hospital who barricaded the doors. They were ill and unarmed."

"I will want the names of those men, Lucas," Slocum said.
"Yes, sir."

The crowd of men talked among themselves. Hampton watched

the faces of the men, seeing the fear and the anger on them, then he looked back across the wide road at the smoke of the fires, drifting lazily now in the slight breeze. Men were cleaning up, searching among the buildings for clues to what had happened in the dark.

Hampton noticed a rider coming at a trot down the Deming road. Tyler followed his stare. It was Mr. Frank. Hampton stepped through the men and waved at him. Mr. Frank swung over and dismounted.

"Hamp. What on earth? What's happening?" he asked as his feet touched the ground.

"Villistas attacked the town, burned some buildings, and killed about twenty people."

"Where are they now?"

"Across the border. Anything go on at the ranch?"

"No, Hamp. It was quiet around the house. Everyone is all right there. I had to come in and see what had happened."

"It's not a pleasant sight," Hampton said, relieved. "We saw the fire and came in to help. I'm afraid the cattle have gone to hell and back by now."

"Forget them. What is this?" Mr. Frank said, tilting his hat up at the crowd of men.

"Powwow," Hampton said, and they stepped up to listen again.

"They apparently split their forces as they came into town, one column attacking the camp while another isolates targets in the town," Slocum was saying.

"What was their purpose?" a townsman asked.

"Other than to murder and to pillage, I cannot guess."

A trooper appeared from across the road and pushed through the crowd. At the steps, he saluted the lieutenant, then stepped up to the colonel. He saluted the colonel and handed him a red book. They talked quietly for a few minutes, the trooper once pointing back toward the smoke in town. The colonel nodded and set the book aside. The trooper saluted again. Lucas took his pipe out of his mouth and spoke to him as he went by. The trooper nodded. Lucas went back to smoking. He had spent the last hour picking grass burrs out of his feet.

"The marshal is accepting volunteers for a posse to pursue and capture any bandits found on American soil. He will be at the Gaines ranch, where I believe he has relatives, most of the day."

Hampton and Tyler exchanged looks.

"I'd hate to be an honest Mexican after this," Mr. Frank said.

A newspaper man spoke up above the crowd. "Colonel Slocum, have you had any response from President Wilson?"

Slocum did not answer but instead picked up the book given him by the trooper. He read the title on the cover, then opened the book. On the first page in a careful, looping hand, was a name written in ink.

"Excuse me," Slocum said, "one moment. A trooper has discovered a woman's valise on the ground behind what is left of the Commercial Hotel. The contents were scattered somewhat. Among them was this book. There is a name inside that perhaps some of you know. It is Mary Alison Wells. If you know this person, you might help us determine whether or not she was in the hotel or lived here in town, and where she is at present."

"Hold on!" Mr. Frank called out in a strangled voice. He gave his reins to Tyler, as did Hampton, and both men pushed up to the porch. "Let me see that book," Mr. Frank said.

"Who are you, sir?" Slocum asked.

"Frank MacPherson. I have a daughter by the name of Mary."

He and Hampton went to the steps. Lucas stood up, looking solemnly at the two men. Mr. Frank took the book from the colonel. The small crowd was quiet. Almost all of them knew Frank MacPherson and remembered his daughter. Opening the cover, Mr. Frank stared at the signature.

"Is it Mary's?" Hampton asked quietly, the same knot returning that had been forming and lessening since he first saw the glow of the fire.

"Yeah, it could be. I think it is. But she wouldn't have been in town."

"You said she was comin' home, Frank."

"Sure, but we didn't hear anything. She didn't say when. There was no way of knowin'."

120

"Excuse me, sir," Lucas said, behind them. "I met your daughter last night. We came in on the same train."

"What's she look like?" Mr. Frank asked, disbelieving.

Lucas looked down, then he looked up at Hampton. "Young, about so tall, dark hair, a face like the Lotta Miles girl in the Kelly-Springfield advertisements."

"What did she say?" Hampton asked.

"She said it was too late to go out to the ranch, she would just stay in town."

"Where?"

"She started toward. . . ." Lucas hesitated. The crowd was staring at him.

"Where?" Mr. Frank repeated.

"The Commercial. I'm sorry, sir."

The crowd murmured. Mr. Frank stared at Lucas until Hampton said, "Thank you, Lieutenant. Come on, Frank."

Lucas nodded. The men watched them return to their horses, where Tyler stood, grim and silent.

"It don't mean she was in the hotel, Frank," Hampton said. "The trooper said her valise was found behind the hotel."

Mr. Frank was opening and closing the book, looking at the cover, then the signature. It was such a strange-looking book that he could not associate it with his daughter.

"We got to find out," he said finally.

They mounted up and rode across to the street behind the hotel, looking for the trooper who had brought the book forward. They found him, still sorting through assorted possessions looking for identification. He showed them the valise, but there was nothing in it Mr. Frank recognized.

As Mr. Frank turned through the possessions of a young woman, Hampton felt more and more empty. He remembered in vivid flashes the dark-haired girl who had followed him around the ranch, learning as much as a young girl could about what went on. He remembered the first time he saw her without pigtails. He remembered the times he had helped her into a saddle, or the times she had curried Lady for him while he sat chewing tobacco and braiding a lariat for her. These things Mr. Frank turned over in his hands had nothing to do with the girl he had always known as Little Mary.

"I don't know, Hamp," Mr. Frank said finally.

"Do you want this stuff, sir?" the trooper asked.

Mr. Frank looked at him. It was clear he didn't know what to say.

"Yes, Trooper," Tyler said. "I'll carry it, Mr. Frank."

"Let's look around," Hampton said.

They rode their horses from house to house, asking the residents if they had seen Mary, if they had a wounded young woman in their house, but at each door they were met with a silent shake of the head or, if they knew Mr. Frank, with shock and condolences. Eventually, there was no place left to look, no one left to ask.

A little after noon, the troops under the command of Major Tompkins returned from Mexico, short of water and ammunition. The government troops at Palomas had bristled upon their return, but had neither helped nor hindered them. It was just as well. None of them was in any mood to be trifled with.

Hampton and Tyler sat with Mr. Frank in the shade of the depot platform where Mary's trunks awaited claiming. The men were going through possibilities both silently and out loud. Since Mary was not in the town, she could be somewhere between it and the ranch on foot. She could have died in the hotel fire. She could have been taken a hostage. No other possibilities made sense, but the first was unlikely, and the other two were horrible.

"I think we should operate on the first theory," Hampton said. "She may be in the desert waiting to see what happens next, or maybe hurt. I say we split up and look."

"I don't know what I'm going to tell Constance." Mr. Frank shook his head.

"You don't have to tell her anything yet. Let's go."

Tyler put the valise on top of Mary's two trunks, but Mr. Frank held on to the book, carrying it with him in the saddle. They returned to the preacher's house to find him awake but Satterwhite asleep.

Hampton told the preacher about the book, then he asked quietly, "How do you feel?"

"Like a bad case of influenza. My arm hurts."

"It'll pass."

"Hamp," the preacher said, "those men I killed. . . ."

"Don't think about it, Preacher," Hampton said firmly, remembering the boy beside the drainage ditch on the way into town. "They brought the fight to you."

"I feel like I should pray for them."

"You got any prayer left in you, use it for that girl's sake," Hampton said.

"Think there's a chance of finding her?" the preacher asked hoarsely.

Hampton took his hat off and looked at it, then put it back on. The preacher watched him with his sad eyes and waited, but Hampton couldn't speak. He went back into the front room and kicked Satterwhite on his boot.

"Wake up, goddammit," he said. "We got ridin' to do."

THIRTEEN

"**F**RANK," Hampton said, "you and Satterwhite ride to the north, like you're goin' back to the ranch. Fan out on either side of the road."

They were sitting their horses in front of the preacher's house. A boy ran by in the street dragging an empty bandoleer on the ground behind him and howled like an Indian.

"That's a big area," Mr. Frank said.

"Yeah, it is," Hampton said, watching the boy run up the street. "But if she's there, you'll find her." He faced Mr. Frank and said, "You'll also be headin' back toward the ranch in case there's more trouble."

"Goddammit, Hamp, I just . . . I just don't know what to think. I can't get my breath."

"We'll find her, Frank," Hampton said. "Me and Bud are going to look south of town. One way or the other, we'll catch up with you. Be on your guard. There's no tellin' what's lyin' out in that brush."

Hampton gave Satterwhite a meaningful look, and Satterwhite nodded. Hampton gathered the reins and turned Lady to the south. Tyler followed closely as they rode down the street. The smell of the fire in town combined with the smell of the burning bodies outside of town in an odor Hampton would never forget. He was anxious to get out of Columbus.

"This girl means a lot to you, don't she?" Tyler asked as they rode along. He watched their shadows on the sandy ground.

Hampton felt Mary's memory push forward like guilt, a nag-

124

ging sense of not having done something, or having done it wrong. "I used to know her," he said.

"Pa used to preach a hell of a good sermon on the lost lamb. Wonder what it is about a man that makes him that way?"

"A man hates to lose things," Hampton said.

"Funny situation, considerin' he's born to it."

"I'll tell you somethin' about Little Mary. She was always partly lost."

They crossed the El Paso & Southwestern tracks and rode past the depot, south out of town. In Camp Furlong, to their left, mounted troopers were pulling the carcasses of horses out of the adobe stables.

"Hamp," Tyler said after another hundred yards. "Before we even start to do this thing. . . ."

"I don't want to hear it, Bud."

Hampton drew up. He looked down the valley toward Mexico. Haze drifted on the mountains south of the border. With his back to town, the desert seemed quiet and peaceful and ordinary.

"I got to believe she's out there. I can't explain it, and I don't think I have to."

"All right."

"I'll look east," he said. "Keep your eyes open."

"I been doin' a lot of that lately," Tyler said. He looked at Hampton and gently turned his mustang into the brush to the right of the road.

Hampton moved at an angle to the road. He was full of purpose, but a sense of dread and defeat lay inside him too. It was hard for him to deal with the fact that fate had put Mary in Columbus, after being gone for five years, on the very night of the raid. It was also hard not to ask why, although he had long ago realized that why was a child's question. The only real questions that mattered now were what and how and where, but those questions had no answers either.

He continued in a southeasterly direction, crisscrossing through the low scrub, investigating shadows, riding around cactus, and through flats of dried grass. There were plenty of horse tracks in the sand, and he came upon two horses, both dead, one with a saddle, one without. A mile and a half from the border, he saw the first body.

Hampton approached the man carefully, but he was dead, his face covered with flies, beginning to swell. He wore a dark jacket and dark pants; his hat was under his head, held there by a string around his throat. Across his chest was a bandoleer, mostly empty. He had the long hair and features of a Yaqui Indian. Hampton looked at him with no feeling and circled out around him, thinking to find others.

A little farther on, he saw a leather case in the sand and stepped down to look at it. It was a pair of army binoculars. He tied the strap on behind his saddle and remounted. Tyler was nowhere to be seen back toward the road. Troopers were afield, doing the same thing Hampton was, but faster, less thoroughly.

A mile from the border, he saw movement under a mesquite and drew his pistol. He got down and tied Lady to the limb of a thorn bush. He worked his way around to the other side of the mesquite. A man had pulled himself up in the shade and was lying on his back, his shirt covered with blood. The man was coughing and drawing one leg up on the sand and pushing it back out again.

It was Casoose.

Hampton lowered his pistol and walked up to him. Casoose held his eyes shut, coughing, but when he opened them, he gave a startled jerk of his body. He recognized Hampton and lay still.

Hampton put his pistol in his holster and squatted beside him. "Casoose," he said, "looks like you got yourself pretty messed up."

"It hurts bad, *Diego*," Casoose said, speaking painful English. "Very bad."

Hampton lifted the man's shirt to see where the wound was, then let it go and wiped his fingers on his pants. He stood up and went to his horse for the water bag.

"You probably don't need this, and it'll probably kill you, but I suspect you want it."

"Yes. Thank you." Casoose drank, then said, "I am a dead man, *Diego*."

"I don't see how you lasted this long," Hampton said, taking a drink himself. "What the hell you doin' out here all shot up?"

"I was in the fight, of course."

"On whose side?"

126

"The Division of the North."

"Casoose, goddammit, you ain't no Mexican. You got citizenship same as me."

"It's not the same," Casoose said. He closed his eyes for a long time, then he said, "My grandfather was Mexican, and my father, on this same land. It was all ours once."

"You want it back, is that it?"

"No. We don't want it back, but we want something."

"Not what you got, I'll bet."

"You talk pretty hard to a dead man, Diego," Casoose said.

"I've seen some hard things this mornin'. I don't feel like bein' sweet. Those were my people you were killin' back there last night. Hell, they were your people."

"Yes, my people were killed too. They always are."

Hampton set his jaw and looked at Casoose with his face impassive. A bird twittered away through the brush, and the flies buzzed.

"You been listenin' to too many speeches, Casoose. The ones who make the speeches never lie gutshot in the desert waitin' to die."

"*Diego*, I have something to tell you, then you must do me a favor."

"What kind of favor?"

"You must shoot me, Diego."

"Somebody already did that. What do you have to tell me?"

Casoose lay still with his eyes closed again, and Hampton thought he was dead until he saw the fresh trail of blood wet the shirt. He brushed flies away from Casoose's face. The movement made Casoose open his eyes.

"Where did you go?" Casoose asked.

"It was you who went," Hampton said. "What did you have to tell me?"

"Listen. Last night, during the fighting, I saw someone I think I know. It was a woman, but not much of a woman, still much of a girl."

Hampton set the water bag on the sand and leaned forward. "Who?"

"It was the daughter of Mr. Frank."

127

"Where, Casoose?"

Casoose closed his eyes. "I don't remember," he said.

"In town?"

"Yes. It was in town, close to the fire. God, what a fire. It killed us, that fire. The *máquina* saw us."

"Was she dead?" Hampton asked, his throat tight.

"No. The man who makes dolls had her. He was putting her on his horse."

"What for?" Hampton asked, unable to restrain his need to know everything.

"I asked him why, but he didn't answer."

"What do you think, Casoose?"

"I think he wanted to use her to get out of town alive, but the *máquina* has no eyes for a *gringa*."

"Who was this man?"

Casoose faded in and out while he talked, and it took him a long time to say what he had to say. Talking was painful to him, but too much pain is numbness sometimes and after a moment Casoose would go on. Each sentence cost him a flow of blood.

"Who was the man, Casoose? I don't understand about the dolls."

"He makes dolls," Casoose said. "He is blessed. He makes the Virgin. She is his destiny."

"Who is he?"

"Salazar. Julio Salazar, the maker of dolls. He is the chief of his own bandits."

"What happened to the girl?"

"I cannot tell you. They rode away, and we were separated by the bullets."

"Will he kill her?"

"I don't know."

"Where does he live?"

"In the desert, in the mountains. Wherever it is necessary to live."

"Damn," Hampton said, but now he knew that she had not died in the hotel. There was a chance she was still alive.

"*Diego*, you must shoot me. I cannot take this pain, and it is a sin for me to kill myself. You must give me the mercy shot. Give it to me, *Diego*. Give it to me, quickly."

A rider came through the brush. Hampton got to his feet too quickly, and his head spun for a moment. It was Tyler.

"You was hunkered down too long," Tyler said. "I had to come investigate. Who's this?"

"Casoose. We met him on the trail."

"A raider?"

"Yeah."

"What's he sayin'?" Casoose was chanting softly, "*Démelo, démelo, démelo.*"

"He wants me to finish him. He's been gutshot."

"Are you goin' to do it?"

"I can't, Bud. I could have twenty years ago, but I can't now. I know him too well."

"Would you shoot me if I needed it?"

"Yeah, but only because I know you better. I know him too well, but not well enough."

Tyler spit and put his hand on his pistol butt. "I'll do it," he said. "I don't know him at all, but I know how he feels. There were times when I wanted somebody to shoot me. The doctors wouldn't do it. Neither would the nurses."

"You don't have to, Bud. He won't last much longer anyway."

Tyler looked at Casoose for a minute, listening to him mumble, "*Démelo, démelo.*" He spit and looked around the desert. The closest troopers were two miles away.

"He needs it, Hamp. I know how he feels."

Hampton picked up the water bag and turned away. Almost at the instant of his turning, he heard and felt the pistol shot. He went on to his horse without hesitating. He didn't look back.

Tyler walked up to him and spit. "Hell of a thing," he said.

"Thanks, Bud."

"Have any luck?"

Hampton finished tying on the bag and looked up at Tyler. "In a way. Casoose saw Mary last night. Said a bandit chief put her on his horse and rode out of town with her as some sort of shield. Doesn't know what happened after that. They were separated."

"Did he give you a name?"

"Salazar."

"So you think she might be alive?"

"It's enough to hang your hat on. It's a place to start."

Hampton watched some troopers moving west of them. They had not heard the shot. He looked down. Tyler pushed his hat back on his head and spit.

"What do you reckon they'll do with her?" Tyler asked quietly.

"I don't know," Hampton said. "Before last night, I think somethin' like this would have been just a matter of talkin' to the right man or handin' over a little money. I can't say what they'll do now."

"It's hard when it's somebody you know."

Hampton pulled the rein from the mesquite limb. He let it slide upward in his hand, feeling the frayed edges of the leather between his thumb and index finger. He worked the leather in his hand and looked toward Mexico. A gust of cool wind blew up around him, then pushed away, stirring the hollow stalks of dry grass.

"I'm goin' after her," he said abruptly. "If she's alive, I'm going to bring her back. If she's not, well, I don't care very much what happens. After all this, my life at the ranch won't be the same."

Tyler nodded. "You goin' right this minute?"

"As soon as I can."

"Be better to go back to the ranch, get a few things, another packhorse."

"I'm not tellin' you to go with me on this one, Bud." He looked toward the border. "That's a hard, war-torn country over there. Once there, you're on your own. There's no guarantees."

"Reckon not," Tyler said.

"You want to go on to Texas, why, maybe I'll join you later if I can."

"You think you're ready to go to Texas?"

"I don't want any more of this," Hampton said.

The men were silent a minute, neither of them looking toward the spot where Casoose lay. Lady tossed her head and switched her tail.

"Think there's a chance of findin' her?"

"There's a chance."

"I reckon I'm with you then. You'll be needin' somebody to watch your back."

Hampton looked at Tyler. "A while ago, I was wonderin' why Mary came to be in Columbus last night of all nights, but, you know, I never wondered why you happened to come along just now."

"Probably means somethin', don't it?"

Hampton shook his head, then clapped his friend on the shoulder. "Let's go back to the ranch," he said. "We got some hard ridin' to do."

On the way through town, they stopped in at the preacher's. Rosie was sitting in the front room, looking at one of the preacher's books.

"How is he?" Hampton asked.

Rosie smiled at him. "He sleeps, but the pain wakes him up, so he naps."

"Any bleeding?"

"Very little."

Hampton told her about Mary, then he said, "When the preacher wakes up, tell him I said to do what he has to do."

"I will."

"You goin' to be all right?"

"Sure," Rosie said. "I'm a little worried about Marcos."

"Have him stick close to the preacher for a few days. People in town are scared right now. That gets in the way of their thinkin'."

Rosie nodded and glanced at Tyler. Tyler ducked his head and smiled at her, and the room changed. Hampton looked in on the preacher. He was sleeping on his side with a blanket over his shoulder. Hampton watched him breathe for a minute, took a slow breath himself, and walked outside.

"She's right to worry," Tyler said when they had climbed back in the saddle.

"Whoever touches them will have to deal with the preacher."

"That's somethin' to think about."

The ride back to the ranch was too long for both men, already having spent most of the previous night and day in the saddle. Traffic was heavy on the Deming road. Some of the horsemen wanted to talk to Hampton and Tyler, but the automobiles, rattling by and throwing up dust that lingered in the air like smoke, spooked the horses.

Billy was sitting on the top board of the corral waiting for them when they rode up to the barn. He jumped down and ran to take the reins.

"Any luck, Mr. Hampton?" he asked eagerly.

"She may be alive, Billy. That's all we know."

"Mr. Satterwhite told me all about it. He said it was really something."

"Uh-huh," Hampton said. "You take care of these horses now. Plenty of feed and water. Take the saddles off and turn 'em on their sides to dry the sweat. Brush Lady down. Mr. Tyler will take another horse."

"Yes, sir."

"And be careful with my stuff."

"Yes, sir."

Hampton and Tyler went right on up to the big house. Mr. Frank met them at the door.

"Let's go inside, Frank," Hampton said.

Mrs. MacPherson, Betty, and Tom Dunbar were in the front room along with two other men who lived nearby. Dunbar and the two men sat uncomfortably on a horsehair sofa. Betty stood beside Mrs. MacPherson's chair. Satterwhite walked into the room from the kitchen and leaned against the door jamb.

"Hamp?" Mrs. MacPherson said weakly.

Hampton took his hat off. He looked at Mr. Frank. "I came across a man who had seen Mary during the fight. A Mexican put her on his horse and rode back toward the border. Since she hasn't been found, my guess is she is still alive and somewhere around Palomas."

Mr. Frank shook his head solemnly, trying to reject or deny the information. Mrs. MacPherson began to cry again and shake her head questioningly, as if she were confused by what she had heard. Betty knelt beside her and put her arm around her shoulders, but she watched Hampton's face. Satterwhite straightened away from the door.

132

"The army should be told at once," Tom Dunbar said. "Let the army know."

"What good would that do?" Hampton said angrily, turning on Dunbar.

Dunbar shook his head and was quiet. The other two men looked at the floor.

"What should we do, Hamp?" Mr. Frank asked.

Betty was watching Hampton's face.

"Me and Bud are goin' after her. We need some things, but as quick as we can get them, we're leaving."

"I'll go with you," Mr. Frank said.

"Think that's wise?" Hampton looked him in the face. Then he answered for him, "No. You need to be here. If Mary can be gotten, me and Bud'll do it."

"I'm going with you," Satterwhite said.

Hampton turned on him. "You don't know what you're talkin' about, Satterwhite," he said. "It's rough down there, and we can't be takin' care of. . . ."

"Try to stop me."

Hampton looked at him for a minute, angry. Then he said, "All right, Satterwhite. But you understand this ain't no Oklahoma City hayride. And you do what I say."

One of the men on the couch stood up. "Let us know how we can help," he said.

"Thanks," Hampton said. "We'll need some good horses, oats, water, and all the ammunition the ranch can spare. We need it now."

"Come on, J. P.," the man said, turning to the other.

Dunbar got up too. "I'll help Billy," he said, and the three men went out.

"The packhorse was at the gate when I got back," Mr. Frank said. "We'll get the packs off him and get you ready. I can't thank you enough, Hamp, or you Mr. Tyler for. . . ."

"Save it till we get back," Hampton said.

"Sure. I'll . . . I'll get the ammunition."

Mr. Frank went toward the kitchen. Tyler said, "I'll go over to the house and pack up."

"I'm comin' with you," Hampton said, but Mrs. MacPherson called him back. Tyler hesitated at the door, watching over his shoulder, then he went out.

"Yes, ma'am?"

"Do you think she's all right, Hamp? Please tell me. I'll believe you."

Hampton still had his hat in his hands. He did not like looking down at Mrs. MacPherson, so he crouched in front of her.

"Constance," he said, using her first name. Her red eyes looked into his. He was aware of Betty and of Satterwhite who still lingered in the dining room. "Constance, Mary is fine. I know she is. She can speak Spanish, and she was born and raised in this desert. We just have to bring her back. We will bring her back."

"Thank you, Hamp. God bless you."

Hampton stood up. "I'll see you soon," he said.

Betty followed him to the door. She was as distraught as Mrs. MacPherson, but she showed it differently. She was calm, but her eyes were wet.

"Hamp," she said.

Hampton looked at her, then said, "Pack me a full load, Betty. We'll need it. Bud says he would like some onions if we got any."

Betty looked at him, and her lips trembled at the edge of a smile. "Will you come back, Hamp?" she said.

Hampton looked down and took a deep breath, letting it out slowly. "I wouldn't lie to you, Betty. I don't know. I don't know what to expect."

"If anyone could do it, you can," Betty said softly.

Hampton turned and looked at her with gentle, tired eyes. "Goodbye, Betty," he said.

She drew close to him, put her fingers around his thick right arm, and, standing on her tiptoes, she kissed him on his whiskered cheek. Before he had time to respond, she was gone back into the room, and he was alone on the front porch with activity all around him. He felt half as young and twice as old.

FOURTEEN

A S Salazar neared the border, other horsemen swung in beside him, and the low brush seemed full of men on foot. Their dark faces turned toward Mary, then were gone in the dim light. It was all Mary could do to hold on to the saddlehorn. She felt weak and detached, as if she were drunk or barely conscious.

They turned to the west, away from Palomas, and crossed the road. For another three miles, they paralleled the border, then turned toward it.

Mary was aware of increased shooting, but she did not know what it meant. Riders breasted them and fell back. The sky was growing pale. Stars remained only in the low western horizon. She tried again to throw herself off the horse, but Salazar was still at the peak of his adrenalin and was strong and determined. She felt the bandoleers against her back and smelled the man who held her. It was a rich, smoky, old-wood-and-sweat smell that made her clench her eyes shut when the change in breeze made it too strong. There were times when his chin was on her shoulder, and she could smell his breath.

They pulled up. A thick-chested man with double bandoleers and the round features of a playful grandfather trotted up to them.

"How does it go?" the man asked.

"Well, General," Salazar answered, spurring ahead enough that he did not have to look over Mary's shoulder at the other man. "We killed the *gringos* everywhere, but the machine guns were too much."

"Good," the general said. "The *gringos* will not sleep tonight, not in Columbus or in Washington."

"Nor anywhere," Salazar said.

"What do you have there?" the general asked, then turned his head abruptly and shouted orders at a group of men on horseback. The horsemen reversed and raced away toward the west.

"A prisoner of the Division of the North," Salazar said proudly, but with a leering tone.

"Be careful," the general said. "We will have to move fast. If you have ransom on your mind, it will be difficult to collect."

During their exchange, both horses were moving and tossing their heads so that the two men were sometimes not even facing each other. Mary watched the other man's face.

"Tell him to let me go," she said in English.

"Madam," the general said in Spanish, "that matter is not in my hands. I do not give orders to any of my chiefs except in battle."

"Please," Mary said.

The general shrugged.

Salazar said, "Is she begging for her life again? It is like a song in my ears."

"*Hijo!*" the general said, "look at what a fire! *Andales, muchachos! Viva Mexico!*"

"My men are going to the mountains now, General," Salazar said. "We will see you again."

"Good," the general said. "Thank you. It is a great day for Mexico. Good luck."

The general spurred forward to meet two riders. Mary saw that she was now surrounded by men on horseback, and she was sure she heard the shrill, quick voices of Mexican women too. Salazar called for another horse several times, then gave his reins to the closest man. He got down and pulled Mary with him. Her legs were shaky.

"I can ride forever," Salazar said, "but not with you in front of me. I am going to put you on a horse. You understand me, don't you? How does a *gringa* learn the Spanish language? Do you like *Mexicanos?*"

Mary squeezed her eyes shut, then opened them. She shook his grasp loose and pushed the hair out of her face.

"Please let me go," she said in Spanish.

"Uh-oh," Salazar said. "*Mexicanos* don't like to hear that."

An empty horse was brought forward to Salazar. "Whose was this one?" Salazar asked, firmly gripping Mary's arm and pulling her beside him.

"Tomás," the man said. "The ugly one."

"He was a brave fighter," Salazar said.

"Yes, but ugly."

"Good," Salazar said. "Listen, *gringa*, you will ride the horse of the ugly one, but you will not try to get down or get away or we will kill you. *Comprende?*"

"Please," Mary said. The pins had come out of her hair, and it was long and tangled down her back.

Salazar shook her. "Enough of that. If the time is right, I will let you go. If I get what I want, I will let you go. If you try to get away from me, I will kill you. My men want to kill you now. Do you understand?"

"Yes."

"Good. Get on the horse."

Salazar pushed her ungently into the saddle. Two women wearing bandoleers and men's hats pulled up on either side of her. She was given the reins, and she held them tightly in her hands. Salazar remounted and looked around him, then back toward Columbus.

"What a fight!" he said happily. "But now we must ride."

The others let him spur to the lead, then they followed him. The women at her side urged Mary forward, the one on the left pointing a rifle at her, and she went, freer now, her head clearing with the morning light.

In a short time, they reached the fence that marked the border and crossed through the cut wires. Mary could not tell how many riders were in the group, but the number seemed to grow as they rode. Every man and woman she saw was armed, either carrying a rifle or a pistol. A leather bag tied with a loop to the saddlehorn in front of her bounced back against her leg.

They rode south, meaning to avoid the town of Palomas and the small troop of government forces there. To Mary's left, the sun rose across the desert, changing the texture and feel of the sweet air that washed over her face and lifted the wings of her hair at her temples. Her legs were chapped and sore from the ride to the border, and her skirt bunched up in front of her, but she began to relax and move with the horse rather than against it, controlling the chafing of the leather on her stockinged legs. She was surprised how easily it all came back to her — being in a saddle, the feel of the reins, the wedding of horse and rider as the horse jolted across the soft desert sand.

But while her immediate physical ordeal had lessened, the hopeless fear in her thoughts and emotions had not. She was a prisoner of Mexican bandits in a country so wide and empty that each man could become his own government, doing as he wanted with no one to say otherwise or even to know. Although Salazar did not seem angry or fanatical, she had no doubt of his cruelty. She had read accounts of Americans tortured and executed on Mexican soil. The revolution was their conscience and their brain, and the revolution was violent and bloody.

As the sun rose away from the horizon, and the drop of the land hid all but the thinning cloud of smoke from Columbus, the band slowed down to a walk. The men and women sheathed their weapons, some by slipping a homemade sling over their shoulders. There was easy and excited talking among them, those closest to each other going back over their part of the battle.

"Listen," one said ahead of Mary. "I think we should have taken the train."

"That train almost killed you, Eliseo."

"No, it did not. I was too quick for it, but I could make a lot of use of a train like that."

"In the desert? How will you drive a train in the desert?"

"There are tracks."

"Not where we are going."

"Then an automobile," Eliseo said eagerly. "We could drive around like the big men do."

The other man shook his head. "A horse is better," he said.

"I almost had me an automobile," Eliseo said. "The *gringo* was trying to get inside. I shot him."

"Where is the automobile then?"

"I had to leave it. There was too much shooting, then I could not get back to it."

They rode in silence a while, then the second man said, "A train for Eliseo!" and laughed out loud.

Salazar turned down a sandy draw and led the band into its deepest part. There they stopped and dismounted.

"Get down, bitch," the Mexican woman to Mary's left said, reaching for her reins.

Mary got down. The woman pulled her horse ahead where the other horses were. Mary stood alone, looking around her as riders passed, some reaching down and catching the loose ends of her hair and flipping them up. One rider rode directly at her so that she had to jump to the side. He laughed as he rode by.

Mary pulled her coat together and moved to the side of the draw where the sandy banks had eroded and left benches of rock and silt. She sat down and tried to catch her breath.

A man walked up to her, holding his rifle casually at his side. He had a small, tight Indian face with eyes so black they seemed the eyes of a dead man. Mary looked at him without turning her face to him. The man stepped closer and grabbed her left arm. Mary tried to wrench it free, but the man was strong. He held up her arm and looked at the plain, gold band on her finger. He slid his hand down to hers, pinched the ring, and jerked it off her finger. The sunlight flashed on it for a moment, then he put it in his pocket.

The man stepped past Mary, so that she was between him and the others, and squatted beside her, guarding her. The other men were gathered around Salazar, evidently talking over their situation. The women pulled goatskin water bags off several horses and circulated among the men. Others unwrapped dry tortillas and jerky.

One man lay on the sand, shot twice and bleeding badly. Two men crouched over him, looking at him. One raised his head and shook it at the other. The other nodded, then shrugged.

Mary looked at the ground in front of her, trying to avoid contact with anyone's eyes, trying to think clearly. She had crossed a border not just into Mexico, but also into a strange and emotionally empty world. She felt totally alone, totally dependent on people who cared nothing for her, perhaps even hated her — people who knew nothing about her at all.

Her eyes burned, but she did not raise her hand to them. A

muscle in her right leg was trembling. She massaged it, wanting it to stop. Tears ran quickly down the side of her face, but unless anyone was close to her, they could not tell that she was crying.

Against her will, she thought of her mother and father and the ranch. They were so far away now. No one would know where she was. She barely knew herself. She had spoken to the one soldier when she got off the train and to the hotel manager. What were the chances that they were still alive? And if they were, why would they remember her? She was nothing anyway, no one. A girl raised on an isolated ranch who read far too many books, who failed in her marriage, who at twenty-four was running home like the child she had tried so hard not to be.

The movement around her slowed down. Her guard did not look at her. She was nothing, no one. She was like smoke from the end of a match, neither match nor flame, but smoke, a ghost. She licked a tear from the corner of her mouth and looked down. Her loose, dark hair hid her face.

The man lying on the sand died.

FIFTEEN

WHEN Hampton walked in the door, Tyler was sitting in the front room with a duffel bag between his feet. Clothes were spread over the arm of the next chair. He was looking at the chair without moving, as if a snake lay coiled there. Tyler turned and looked up at Hampton as he closed the door.

"You know," Tyler said. "I was just thinkin' — I don't even own a chair. I'm fifty-six years old and don't even so much as own a chair."

Tyler shook his head and lifted the duffel bag again. "I was tryin' to figure what I'll need," he said.

"You been on enough of these rides to know you don't need half of what you take and do need plenty of what you don't take."

Tyler threw an old pair of jeans on the arm of the chair next to him and dropped the mouth of the duffel bag. For a moment he sat still with his hands empty and his chin on his collarbone.

"I'm too tired to think," he said.

Hampton nodded. Now that he was back in his own house, the pace had slowed down, and he could feel the loss of sleep, the hours in the saddle, the killing. He took off his glasses and rubbed his hand over his face. "It will take a while to get everything ready," he said. "I'm going to heat some water and wash up, maybe try to rest a minute."

"All right," Tyler said, turning toward the bunk in the corner where he had slept his first night there. "Sounds good."

Hampton started a fire in the stove and put on the big kettle full of water. He took a deep wash pan down from the nail in the wall

141

where it hung and put it on the table. While he waited, he looked around the kitchen for things he might need.

There wasn't much. Everything he owned was useful in ranching but not in making war. There was nothing very personal among his possessions either, except those small things he had carried with him from his youth: the shaving mug his father had used, a Ranger badge cut from a silver peso, three photographs, his father's Bible, a jackknife that had belonged to Homer, his little brother. He wouldn't be leaving much behind him if he never came back. Tyler had probably been thinking the same thing.

The kettle eventually began to steam. He mixed the hot water with cold in the wash pan and bathed with it. He called Tyler when he was finished, then went to his room and lay down on his bed. He was asleep immediately and slept until he felt Tyler shaking his shoulder.

"Everything is ready," Tyler said.

"Good." Hampton reached for his glasses and slid them on. The room had a late-afternoon feel. "Let's go."

Everyone was in the yard when Hampton and Tyler walked up, both carrying a small bag. Their horses were saddled. Tyler and Satterwhite had fresh horses, but Hampton had insisted on taking Lady. He knew she was tired, but they would be going easy the first night and day trying to pick up the trail, and he trusted her. He didn't want to be on a strange horse if they ran into a gunfight.

"Hamp," Mr. Frank said, "we've got every water bag on the place full and ready to go. Billy and Tom put the pack frames on the horses to make it easier for them to run if you have to move fast. It's all ready," he finished.

"You've got about a thousand rounds of .38s and about that in .45s," one of the other men said.

"That much?" Hampton asked.

"We took up a collection," the man said.

"I'll tie that bag on for you, Mr. Hampton," Billy said.

"Wish you was goin' with us, Billy?"

"Yes, sir," Billy said. "Satterwhite brought me a rifle he found in the desert."

"He did, huh?"

"Yes, sir."

Satterwhite turned from Hampton's glance. Betty stepped close and said, "I'd let him go if it would help bring you back."

"He's a good man, Betty," Hampton said.

Billy looked over his shoulder and smiled.

One by one, those staying behind took leave of those riding out. The goodbyes were hopeful but solemn. For all any of them knew, they would never see each other again.

Finally, Hampton mounted. Satterwhite and Tyler were leading the packhorses. Hampton looked at Satterwhite. He was wearing a wide-brim felt hat with a low crown and a woven leather hatband. It was white and new.

"Where'd you get that hat?" he asked.

"I've been saving it," Satterwhite said self-consciously.

"For what?" Hampton said. He looked at Mr. Frank and nodded, then he lifted the reins and said, "Let's go."

The sun was tilting down as they rode away from the ranch. It was Hampton's plan to ride in a southwesterly direction and cross the border below the Gibson ranch. He did not know what patrols the army had out but figured they would be staying close to town for the night.

"We won't even have the support of our own army," he said as they rode. "They catch us tryin' to cross the border, they'll stop us sure as the world."

"Reminds me of another time," Tyler said, referring to the time Captain McNelly had ferried his Rangers across the Rio Grande without the permission or support of the army.

"It's the same plan," Hampton said. "I just hope we don't get pinned down again like we did that time."

"What're you talking about?" Satterwhite asked.

"Texas," Hampton said. "You wouldn't understand."

After they crossed the border, they would continue south until they found a low place to make camp. They each needed rest, and they needed time to watch and listen in order to pick up Salazar's trail. It wouldn't be easy. They would be in his country among his people, people who most likely looked at him as if he were a hero.

When they crossed the railroad tracks, Hampton saw the dust of troopers circling the town, and they moved farther west. The wind had changed back to the south and was in their faces as they rode, a wind that would be cold when the sun had gone completely.

At the border fence, Satterwhite dismounted and cut the wires, loose and rusting on spindly posts. Hampton and Tyler crossed over.

"Should I tie it back?" Satterwhite asked.

"Want to come back through it?"

"Here? Will we be coming back this. . . ."

"Leave it," Hampton cut him off.

Darkness fell on their shoulders, and they pushed south in silence. The moon was already past zenith and threw some light in the shadows of brush and shallow draws. The horizons were the same, as was the landscape, but crossing the border made a difference in the feel of the land. It was not home anymore.

At the edge of a long flat, Hampton dismounted. "Time for a smoke," he said. He had made sure to pack all the tobacco he had in the house.

The others got down. Satterwhite stepped forward in the darkness. "I've got plenty," he said.

"Uh-huh," Hampton said. "So do I."

Satterwhite lowered the pouch in his hand and started to turn away. Tyler noticed the move.

"I could use some of that, Satterwhite," he said.

Hampton looked at Tyler. "Yeah, me too," he shrugged. "I don't remember where I packed mine."

They stood by their horses passing around the tobacco and papers in the darkness, rolling cigarettes.

"You know they make these already rolled," Hampton said.

"I'd rather roll my own."

"Cheaper," Tyler said.

"Strike that match against the saddle. We don't know who's watchin' out here."

"Think somebody is?" Satterwhite asked and felt a chill.

"May not be anybody. May be a whole bunch of somebody."

They lit their cigarettes and smoked for a while in silence. Then Satterwhite said, "How come you always call me Satterwhite instead of Rueben. Rueben is my name."

144

Hampton smoked. He said, "Rueben. That an old family name?"

Tyler said, "Rueben."

"Give me a smoke, Rueben," Hampton said.

"Come along, Rueben," Tyler said.

"Bring up those horses, Rueben."

"How about a drink, Rueben?"

"What's that over there, Rueben?"

"How do you do, Rueben?"

"All right, all right," Satterwhite said. "Forget it."

"Anything you say, Rueben."

They walked their horses for a while. The sound of the hoofbeats was muffled in the sand. The frames on the packhorses creaked as did the leather of the saddles, but it was a soft, natural sound in the darkness of the desert.

"What do you think is the best way to do this?" Tyler asked.

"How do you mean?"

"Ride at night and lay up during the day or vice-versa?"

Hampton walked a minute, then said, "We travel at night, we can probably go a good ways without being spotted 'less we stumble up on somebody."

"I vote for that," Satterwhite said.

"You ain't old enough to vote," Hampton said. "And I'm not finished. Look around you. Go ahead. See them shadows? How many men do you think could be lyin' in them shadows waiting to cut your throat?"

Satterwhite looked around him. The landscape became scary and threatening. Every thorny bush or cactus clump seemed to be disguising the shape of a black sombrero.

"Easy, Hamp. You'll have him seein' banditos in his sleep."

"He better. This ain't no camp meeting we're ridin' into."

"Maybe we better ride during the day," Satterwhite said, shaking off a shiver.

"All right," Hampton went on. "You move in daylight and you raise dust that can be seen from the desert around you. Or anyone on high ground can pick you out. And they know who you are, because this is their back yard. All they have to do is wait till you bed down

145

for the night and slip up on you. Before the sun rises, they'll be ridin' five new horses."

"That's the way I figured it," Tyler said.

"Then what do we do?" Satterwhite wanted to know.

"How far do you think we've come since the border?" Hampton asked.

Tyler stopped walking and looked around, placing landmarks on the dark horizon. "I don't know," he said. "Four or five miles."

"Uh-huh. Let's look for a low place to camp. I've gone about as far as I want to go today."

"What do we do?" Satterwhite said again.

"Whatever we have to," Hampton said. Then softer, "Whatever it takes."

They found a sandy cut with a wide, level bottom, and made camp. Before he went to sleep, Hampton allowed himself to think about Mary, something he had been avoiding since the afternoon. He could not picture her as she was now. He could only remember the girl she had been, long, soft, dark hair and gray eyes with a faraway look in them.

He rolled over on his side and felt the tiredness in his back and shoulders. The cold pressed around his collar. He pulled an edge of the blanket over his ears. They probably should have taken turns keeping watch, but they each needed the sleep, and it would be at least a day before anyone knew they were in Mexico. It wouldn't take long, and then what? *Whatever*, he said to himself again.

Before he went to sleep, he remembered one summer night years ago when he had found Mary walking along the corral fence alone in the dark. She was trying to make up her mind about marrying the man from Tennessee. She had asked him about it.

"Can't say," he said. "Never tried it."

"Why not?" she looked at him in the dark, her hair blowing in the wind.

"Oh, I don't know. Never seemed right, I reckon. Gals was a lot more scarce when I was young, and there was always somethin' that needed doin'."

"Gals was," she laughed, imitating him. "You know you always speak ungrammatically to me when you are being serious. Why is that?"

Hampton shrugged. He hadn't noticed. "I'm not so sure men and women were made to be married," he said. "I think sometimes they were meant to live on opposite sides of town and meet in the brush every now and then."

"Is that what you did?"

"You can set more traps than anybody I ever knew."

She had followed him to the windmill and stood silent while he set the brakes on the fan. An owl flew out of the barn and screeched overhead, and Mary had stepped close to him. He remembered leaning closer to her, as if to hear something she had to say, but she hadn't said anything. She had just been frightened, and he had known it.

"Would you miss me if I went to Tennessee?" she asked him.

"It's not my part to do the missing," he told her.

"You wouldn't, then?"

"That's not what I said."

"Tell me what to do, Hamp."

"Nope. You got to walk that valley by yourself."

They had stood in the shadow of the water tank in the warm, dark night and talked. Then she had said good night and gone back to the house, her hair catching the wind, leaving the smell of some kind of perfume in the air behind her.

Hampton closed his eyes and waited for sleep. She was somewhere under the same stars, he thought, surrounded by bandits. He opened his eyes with a start. A shooting star burned out above the northern horizon. Without his glasses on, it looked pale and sad.

SIXTEEN

AS the morning wore on, Mary was offered no food, but was given a drink of water by her guard when she asked for it. Six more riders joined them. One of them, a short man with a heavy black beard, had been shot through the arm. A woman put a poultice on the wound and wrapped it for him while he told Salazar of the Thirteenth Cavalry's pursuit into Mexico after the raiders.

"They were weak," the man said.

"All Americans are weak," Salazar shrugged. "They and the Chinese. That is why we must kill them."

"They may come after us again," the man said.

"Let them. They will find only what they have left us with — the empty desert."

"Villa is a great general," the man said. "He has shown the Americans who has the power in Mexico."

Shortly after, they mounted up. Mary was given a different horse, one with a cut on its right flank, and again rode between two heavily armed women. The band traveled southeast in the open desert toward the Casas Grandes River, which was little more than a stream at that time of the year, but it flowed east, the direction Salazar planned to travel, and allowed for ample water.

When they reached the river, Salazar followed it until he found a wide, grassy, level place below a cut bank. He gave the order to make camp, and they dismounted.

The short man who had guarded Mary that morning took her to where the women were preparing the meal and pushed her down on the ground. She lay still until the man walked away, then she sat up.

Dust from the horses blew across her face and powdered her cheeks and hair. She was hungry and tired. Her legs were chapped and sore. She was sure she had a black eye.

For a while she sat perfectly still, watching the movement in the camp, the picketing of the horses, the unloading of packs and saddlebags, the women rolling out tortillas. The men were tired but excited. They talked in laughing voices about the battle. The women were more reticent, but occasionally laughed out loud.

"Hey *gringa*," one of the women said.

Mary looked at her and pulled the wings of her coat together. The woman was younger than the others, with a strong nose and wide mouth. Her hair was in a single braid down her back.

"What do you think of our family?"

The other women looked at her while they worked. Some of them were curious, but others looked at her with cold eyes.

"You are lucky to be with your family," Mary said evenly.

"She speaks Spanish very well for a *gringa*."

"Bitch. Whore," one of the other women said. "*Gringa*."

Mary looked at the speaker. She could not tell how old the woman was, but she must have been beautiful once. She had the broad face and high cheekbones of an Indian, but was light-skinned. Although her face now was dirty and one cheek scarred, the premature wrinkles could not hide the proud lines. The woman cut her a look of hate.

Mary turned back to the younger one. "What is your name?" Mary asked her.

"Natalia," she said. She was rolling tortillas on a heavy cloth spread on the sand. "And you?"

"Mary."

"What a name for a whore," the older one said.

"What is your name?" Mary asked her, her voice even and cool. She wanted to be able to talk to them. It made her forget the dull ache of fear that felt like hunger in her stomach.

"I have no name for a whore like you."

"She is Carmen," Natalia said and raised her eyebrows behind the other woman's back. "She is the wife of the dollmaker."

"I am not a whore," Mary said.

"You are American. It is the same thing," Carmen said.

Mary watched the woman work for a minute without speaking, then she looked at Natalia. "Can I help you?"

"No," Carmen said. "Shut your mouth, or I will call Julio to shut it for you."

Natalia shrugged and went back to rolling out tortillas.

The sun went down. Fires were built around the camp, fueled with salt cedar and octillo stems. Everyone ate while Mary watched. When they were through, Natalia dropped two half-eaten scraps of tortilla and some jerky in Mary's lap. Mary looked up at her, but Natalia went quickly by. Mary ate fast, sure that anyone else would slap the food out of her hands if they noticed she was eating.

The food did not push aside the empty ache of fear. The possibility of her death was very real to her, but death itself did not mean much. She had already left behind everything she had to leave. It was the brutality that would precede death that she feared. Her breasts were still sore where Salazar had gripped her.

When she finished eating, she leaned back on her arms, trying to ease the stiffness in her back. She pushed her legs out in front of her. The night was cold, and her hands were cold on the rocks beneath them, but the soreness in her back was greater.

A man appeared suddenly in front of her. He pulled out a sheathed knife, bent quickly, and ran the knife under the hem of her skirt. Mary gripped a rock in her right hand and sat up. The knife was sharp. The hem parted. Mary tried to pull her legs up, but the man caught her thigh in one hand and kept sliding the knife forward. The lines of his face were highlighted by the nearest fire. He was grinning, watching the path of the knife as it split the skirt.

"Please don't," Mary said.

When the man continued, she raised the rock in her hand and swung it against his temple. He lurched backward, lost his balance, and sat down hard on the ground. Mary rolled to the left and stood up, still holding the rock.

The man growled at her and pushed up onto his feet, but Salazar stepped forward before the man could reach Mary.

"What is it?" he said abruptly, with authority.

"The *gringa* tried to kill me."

Salazar saw the knife in his hand, the rock in Mary's. The breeze opened her split skirt. He smiled. "So you want to kill her?"

"Yes. Right now."

"No. Not now," Salazar said again with authority. "Not now. Go on."

The man spit at Mary and turned away. Most of the camp had not noticed what had happened. The fires burned, and the talking continued unbroken.

Salazar looked at Mary. There was nothing in his face, not even interest. Mary returned his stare, her knuckles white around the rock in her hand.

"Do you want to die now?" Salazar asked.

"I would rather die than be assaulted," Mary said.

Salazar nodded and looked at her skirt again. "You will be assaulted before you die," he said. "Do you want it to be now?"

"No."

"Then do not provoke my men."

Salazar looked at her, then glanced at the other women close by.

"Please let me go," Mary said.

"No," Salazar said. "I want you to come sit by the fire with me."

Carmen looked up quickly. Smoke stung Mary's eyes. She was tempted to throw the rock at Salazar, but she didn't. She opened her fingers and let it drop to the ground.

"What do you want the *gringa* for?" Carmen asked, an edge on her voice.

"We must find out who will pay for her," Salazar returned.

Salazar stared at Carmen for several seconds, his face hard and set, then he looked at Mary and indicated with a nod that she was to follow him. They crossed the camp to Salazar's fire, where Salazar sat down on his saddle and pointed to the ground for Mary to sit. The men circling the fire got quiet. Mary could feel their eyes on her face like the heat of the fire. She sat with her left side to the fire, facing Salazar.

"Now, *compadres*," Salazar said. "What do you see here?"

"A woman," said Eliseo, who had no wife.

"No," Salazar said. "You are wrong."

"She has the breasts of a woman."

Mary looked down, then got angry and looked across the fire at the man.

"It is true," Salazar said.

"You should know," Mary said sharply, taking a chance, her voice loud.

"Shut up," Salazar growled. "You are not here to speak unless you are asked a question." Salazar looked toward the women, then said, "No. This is not a woman. This is ten thousand dollars."

"Ah," Eliseo said. "Of course. Pesos do not have breasts."

"She is not to be harmed unless she tries to escape. It is my order." The men around the fire continued to stare silently at Mary. Salazar had a small collection of twigs and grass at his feet. In the silence, he picked up two twigs and made a cross of them, tying them together with tough, dried grass.

"General Villa is riding south. We will join him soon, but first we need bullets and guns. This woman can buy them for us. That is why she must not be harmed."

Mary shifted her weight and listened. The fire was warm in the cold night.

"I will need someone to ride back across the border with a message to the people of this *gringa*."

"I will go," said a man across the fire.

"Good," Salazar said. He bent forward and picked up a handful of dry grass. He gathered the grass around the twigs.

"What is your name?" Salazar looked at Mary.

"Mary."

Salazar's hand stilled at his work. He looked at her closely, and the men around the fire spoke softly to each other.

"What are you called?" Salazar asked again.

"Mary."

"It is bad luck, *jefe*," one of the men around the fire said solemnly.

Salazar looked at Mary, then looked at the man. He shrugged. "No," he said. "It is a good omen."

Mary looked from one to the other without understanding. The fire crackled for several minutes while Salazar stared at the stuff in his hands.

"It is a good omen." His fingers went back to work. "Good," he said. He turned to Mary. "What is the name of your husband?"

"He will not pay for me."

"Listen," Salazar said, his fingers still. "Your life depends on your answers. Answer me directly."

"My husband will not pay for me."

"Why not?"

"He . . . he lives in Tennessee."

"Tennessee? I do not know this Tennessee. Where is that?"

"Another state of the United States."

"Who then?"

"No one."

Salazar shook loose a long stem of dry grass and wound it around the twigs and the grass in his hand. The other men around the fire were silent, watching.

"I do not believe you," he said. "You can tell me the truth now, or I will let Antonio make you tell me the truth."

Salazar nodded across the fire. Mary turned and saw the man who had cut her skirt staring at her. He was smoking a cigarette and staring impassively at her face. She dropped her eyes again. A shift in the breeze blew smoke around her figure.

"My father," she said.

"What is his name?"

"Frank MacPherson."

"Where does he live?"

"He has a ranch north of Columbus."

At the sound of the town's name, the men shifted and laughed. Salazar sorted through the small pile of grass at his feet for short pieces.

"Good," he said. "We will send him a message that you will write. You will tell him to bring ten thousand dollars for your return."

Mary did not think her father could raise the money, but at least he would know what had happened to her. "All right," she said.

Mary was brought a piece of paper from a carton of smoking tobacco and a pencil. She wrote the message by the light of the fire, saying only that she had been taken prisoner at Columbus and was being held for ten thousand dollars ransom. When she was through, she gave the paper to Salazar and watched his face. As she thought, he could not read it.

"Good," he said, after a minute. Those around the fire nodded and smiled. "Here it is, Manuel. Go when you are ready, but soon, eh?"

"*Sí, jefe*," the man said. He stood up and took the paper. He looked at it, then put it inside his shirt.

"For you," Salazar said, holding out his hand to Mary. In it was a crude doll, its face and skirt made of brown grass. "It is Mary," Salazar said.

Mary took the doll and held it in her cold fingers for a moment, looking at it, then she turned abruptly and threw it away from her into the dark.

For two days they camped by the river, while riders left and came back again. In the afternoons, when the sun warmed the air, the men went down to the river and bathed while the women washed their clothes. The women bathed too, some openly, the married ones shyly alone or with their husbands. In idle moments, the bandits sat in groups looking through the loot they had taken in the Columbus raid. For each item, there was a separate story.

Mary was left alone. Antonio and several others glowered at her, but they did not approach her. Nor did they change their minds about her being bad luck. Her eye swelled where Salazar had hit her, but it quickly went down again. The Mexican women made fun of her for the way she looked, often with cruel allusions. No one stood apart and guarded her. She had nowhere to go.

She washed in the edge of the river and braided her hair the way Natalia had hers. At night she slept on a saddle blanket that smelled heavily of mule hair and shivered in her clothes and the two extra blankets the women gave her. If she was too cold to sleep, she lay thinking of her life, of the tree-covered mountains of the Cumberland or of times spent with her family. She remembered in detail her room at the ranch and talks she had had with Hampton. When she thought of him, she wondered if he remembered her or missed her. It made her sad that she would never know.

All the time they were there, not far from the border, Mary hoped that someone would rescue her. In her mind, it was not anyone in particular, just armed men coming to take her back, but she knew it was in vain. All she could do was wait, live each moment as if it were her last.

On the third day, the man called Manuel rode back into camp with his news. Mary was sitting alone in the hot sun when the rider came in. She recognized him and walked over, a tight feeling in her chest.

"What news?" Salazar asked.

"Plenty, but not good for us."

"The American will not pay?"

"I never spoke to him," Manuel said. "The border is crawling with soldiers. There was no way to get across without being stopped, and no one to speak for me if the soldiers caught me."

"Coward," Salazar spit on the ground.

"What would be the use?" Manuel said quickly. "To lose a soldier for nothing? Not even a mouse could cross the border now."

"Tell me about the soldiers, then, mouse."

"There are many hundreds. The talk is that they are preparing to cross the border after those in the raid of Columbus. They will track down Villa."

"They will try," Salazar said.

"Yes, *jefe*."

Salazar looked up and caught Mary's eyes. "You have heard then, eh *gringa*? There will be no ransom now."

"Then let me go."

"No." Salazar turned to the men who had gathered around him. "It is time for us to ride again. There will be no money for the *gringa* now, so we must take our bullets from the Carrancistas as we always have."

"What of the *gringa*?" Antonio asked. "She is bad luck."

"There are other Americanos in Mexico who will pay for her. That is their way. *Vámonos*. Pack up."

The bandits packed their horses with the studied pace of long

155

practice. Mary was put under the charge of Natalia, and the band pushed east, following the banks of the river.

During a rest stop, Mary asked Natalia where they were going. Carmen answered, "Shut up. What difference does that make to you?"

They crossed the road to Colonia Dublan, the site of a once thriving Mormon colony, and turned south. At sundown, Mary looked across the desert behind them. It was empty and still. Not even the low clouds to the north were moving.

SEVENTEEN

JUST before daybreak, they were all three out of their bedrolls and stamping their feet to get warm. The temperature had dropped below freezing in the night, and it was too cold to sleep as the sky lightened in the east.

"Damn," Tyler said, shivering. "I'm glad this is the desert. Otherwise it might be cold."

"Go along the draw and break off some dead limbs for a fire, Satterwhite," Hampton said. "Be sure not to get any green ones. We want as little smoke as possible."

"The water in my canteen is frozen solid," Satterwhite said.

"I know that. Get some wood."

Satterwhite walked away holding himself with his arms across his chest. Hampton and Tyler were both wearing their work gloves, but the cold air was still numbing their fingers.

"Be all right, once the sun comes up," Tyler said.

"Yeah. Maybe. The wind's out of the northwest again. It's liable to be cold all day."

After the fire was built, Satterwhite put his canteen beside it, and the men stood close to the small fire waiting for some of its warmth to thaw them out as well. Hampton and Tyler turned their backs to the fire on opposite sides of it and watched the desert. Satterwhite, intent on the progress of the fire, did not notice.

When the coffee was made, the three crouched next to the coals and held the warm, metal cups in their gloved hands. The sun was up, but there was a haze of clouds on the horizon.

"What do we do now?" Satterwhite asked.

Tyler knew the question was not aimed at him. He sipped his coffee and waited for the answer.

"I don't know," Hampton said.

"Well, we got to do something. I'm freezing my backside off out here."

"Cold all over, are you?"

"Yes," Satterwhite said.

Tyler gave a short laugh. Satterwhite looked up, but Tyler's face was straight again.

"How about we cook some breakfast?" Hampton said. "Smoke won't show with those low clouds."

"I suppose you want me to get the stuff?" Satterwhite said.

"Uh-huh," Hampton said, and he smiled, but later as Tyler and Satterwhite tied the packs on the horses, he stood apart, grim and thoughtful. What was there to do but ride and keep their eyes open? He did not know this man Salazar, had no idea where in the Chihuahuan desert to start looking for him, which direction to take. If the Carrancistas caught them, they would at the least be detained and their horses taken from them. If any of the bandits loyal to Pancho Villa caught them, they would be killed.

Mary became almost an abstraction when he thought about their chances of finding her. If the bands split apart and went their separate ways, the desert would be laced with tracks. If Salazar were killed, it was possible she could be in the hands of a single captor. Hampton felt spun around, dizzy, as if he were in an East Texas fog. He could not, no matter how much he thought about it, see the right way to go.

"Ready, Hamp," Tyler said softly, standing behind him.

"All right."

Hampton cut himself a chew of tobacco and slipped it in his cheek. He squatted and pulled a limb off a dead thorn bush.

"Y'all look," he said. He drew in the sand with the limb. "Here's the border. This is the road from Columbus through Palomas and on down to Colonia Dublan and Casas Grandes."

"How far are them towns?" Tyler asked.

"Hundred and fifty miles, maybe more. They ain't far from one another."

Tyler nodded.

"We're here, west of the road," Hampton went on. "If we keep headin' south and east, we'll hit the Rio Casas Grandes that snakes around like this and ends in a lake — I don't remember what the name of it is. East of the lake is salt flats, sand, and low hills when you get close to Juarez. In other words, nothin'. Except the Mexican railroad crosses below the lake on its way from Juarez."

"Hook up with the El Paso and Southwestern at the border?" Tyler asked.

"Yep."

"Is that important?" Satterwhite asked.

"Nope. Just wanted to know."

"South of Colonia Dublan is the Santa Maria Valley, pretty place. To the west are the Sierras, serious mountains with snow this time of year."

Hampton spit, and they all looked silently at the map in the sand. Hampton switched the stick in his hand back and forth. "Now, you tell me," he said finally, "what we do."

"Maybe we should go down here to these towns and look there," Satterwhite said.

"I thought of that. Carranza probably has forces at Casas Grandes. It would be my guess Villa's bunch wouldn't be ready for another big fight this soon."

"What about the other town you said?"

"Not much there. Mormons settled it. They wouldn't have anything Villa would want. Besides, it's right at Casas Grandes. Any shooting there would be heard by the Federales."

They were quiet again. Hampton spit. "Bud?"

Tyler shook his head. "I don't know. Too many spies in a town, and an American woman would draw attention. Did the old Mexican tell you anything about this man's territory?"

Hampton remembered what Casoose had said about Salazar. "He said he lived in the desert or in the mountains, wherever he had to."

"I'd say the desert then," Tyler said. "He would be travelin' light and would need to stay close to water. That would be this river here. What did you call it?"

"Rio Casas Grandes."

"Sounds good to me," Tyler said.

Hampton dropped the stick in the sand and kicked at the map with his boot. The wind caught at the edge of the red bandana around his neck. He stood with his hip to the side, one hand on the cocked hip, the other on the butt of his Colt.

"All right," he said. "Let's do her. Ride easy to keep the dust down. Watch the horizon."

They mounted up and rode out of the shallow cut where they had made camp. The sun was still hidden behind a gauze of clouds. The wind was chill and steady, picking up little puffs of dust as they moved through the scarred and broken desert.

By afternoon they hit the Casas Grandes River and let their horses drink. They were farther south than they had planned to be, but it would be easy to follow the river north and east looking for signs of the bandits.

"How much daylight we got left, Bud?" Hampton asked.

"About two hours."

Hampton was standing beside Lady as she drank from the cold river. His coat was open now with the sun, and his hat was pushed back on his head. As far as he could see, there was nothing but desert.

"Let's make camp here," he said.

"I think we should push on," Satterwhite said.

"Be my guest, Satterwhite."

"I mean all of us," Satterwhite said.

"My horse needs some rest. So do I. Time we scout this area for sign, it'll be dark."

Satterwhite looked around him. "I didn't think about that," he said.

Hampton looked down. After a minute he took a deep breath and blew it out. He shook his head.

"I'll go left," Tyler said. "Satterwhite, you ride south."

"What am I supposed to be looking for?"

Tyler stepped back up in the saddle. "Anything that ain't bald, naked desert."

Tyler jerked the reins and eased along the shoreline. His outline was erect and determined. In the saddle he looked twenty years younger.

160

Satterwhite got back on his horse grumbling and rode off quickly. The packhorses lifted their heads and watched him.

"Come on, girl," Hampton said when he was alone. "This is as far as we go today."

Taking his time and keeping a part of his senses trained on the desert, Hampton stripped the horses and picketed them on the dry grass along the river bank. The ground was gravelly where he unloaded the packs. He was glad. Gravel was better than sand to sleep in if he dug a depression for his hip and shoulder. After the horses were taken care of, Hampton built a smoke and walked to the top of the bank where the river sometimes rose in July when flash floods hit the desert.

He could not see either man, nor any sign of dust from them or from anyone else in the desert. Low clouds were moving in again from the south. The new front had been a cold but weak one. By noon the next day, the wind would be cutting out of the east. Hampton had never liked the east wind. It seemed colder than any other wind in the winter. He had once thought the wind would be out of the east on the day he died.

He lit his cigarette, looked around once more, and turned back down toward the river to look for firewood.

Hampton had a good stack of wood, mostly branches, when Satterwhite came back. At the sound of the horse, Hampton had dropped a handful of wood and waited, one hand on the butt of his pistol.

"See anything?" he said, as Satterwhite got down.

"No, sir. Not even any hoofprints along the water."

"Uh-huh," Hampton said. "I'm not goin' to have to go look myself, am I?"

Satterwhite gave him a hurt glance. "I told you I wasn't ever going to try something like that again," he said.

"Uh-huh. Well, take care of your horse and let's get ready for supper before it gets dark."

Tyler rode in with a different report. "There's been some movement of stock up river. The trails are well worn and distinct. Any ranches around here?"

"Could be," Hampton said. "Why?"

"I don't know. I had the feelin' I'd see an old ranch house any minute."

"What made you think that?"

"I don't ask myself anymore where my feelin's come from. What's holdin' up that coffee?"

"Dark," Hampton said.

They ate a cold supper of jerky, bread, and canned peaches. Betty had put in several packages of sweet chocolate, and Hampton split one of them with Tyler and Satterwhite. None of them was very hungry. Later they might be, but the tiredness and the cold took away their appetites. They ate mainly to keep up their strength and did not relish what they ate. Coffee they did relish, and the pot remained on the edge of the small fire after they had eaten.

They sat close to the fire with their blankets over their shoulders and their backs to their saddles. Hampton put his cup on the ground in front of him and rolled a smoke. His glasses reflected the flames of the fire. Satterwhite noticed it once or twice and thought to himself that the devil would look the same way.

The wind had laid, and overhead the sky was bright with stars. The moon was lower on the southwestern horizon than it had been at the same time the night before. The men did not look at the stars, though. Their eyes were on the small fire.

"Everything seems pretty far away out here," Tyler said softly.

"Is," Hampton said.

"Up in Denver, I thought I'd never see nights like this again."

"You should be out here in the summer when the rains come. Whole different place."

"I'll bet. Wouldn't be as nice as Texas though."

"Different," Hampton said again.

"Are you going to Texas?" Satterwhite asked.

"Maybe," Tyler said. "Tryin' to get Hamp to go with me."

"You goin'?"

"You'd like that, wouldn't you, Satterwhite?"

"I just asked."

They were silent a minute, then Hampton said, "We'll see how this mess comes out first."

"Do you think Mary is all right?" Satterwhite asked after a while.

"I prefer not to think about it."

"Do you reckon those bandits. . . ."

"I prefer not to think about it," Hampton said again with an edge on his voice.

They sat silent, thinking about it anyway.

"Did you know her very well?" Satterwhite asked. "I only saw her about twice when we were little. She was older than me."

"Everybody's older than you," Hampton said.

"It's not my fault," Satterwhite said.

"I knew her well enough," Hampton said, smoking and remembering. "She was just a girl, but she could out-feel any woman I ever knew. Maybe all young girls can."

"I think they learn to hide it when they get grown," Tyler said.

"Could be. Little Mary could get turned around by the simplest things — flowers, rainbows, sunsets, baby animals, what to do next."

"I always thought she was pretty," Satterwhite said.

Hampton smoked.

"Didn't you think she was pretty?"

Hampton smoked. He took a last puff and threw the cigarette in the fire.

"Is," he said. "Is. And don't you forget it."

EIGHTEEN

I N the morning, Tyler was reluctant to leave his blankets. The sun
rose, tinting the desert with its reddish light, and an east wind
blew up the river from the hazy West Potrillo Mountains. Hampton
and Satterwhite built a fire and made breakfast, but Tyler only sat up,
pulling the blankets around his shoulders as he did so. His face was
flushed and drawn, and his hair was peaked from sleeping on it
wrong. He shivered.

"What is it, Bud?" Hampton asked, walking over and crouching down beside him.

Tyler shook his head. "Don't know. Guess I'm just beat."

"Fever?"

"I think so. Can't stop shakin'."

Hampton worked the muscles of his jaw. If Tyler were to get
pneumonia now, they would have to turn back. It made Hampton
feel weak to think about it.

"How about the chest?"

"Can't say. It's sore like everything else, but breathin' don't
hurt."

"I'll get you some coffee. You keep them blankets around you."

"They feel thin as lace."

"I'll give you mine, too."

Hampton went back to the fire for a cup. Satterwhite was stirring the canned bacon in an iron skillet. He looked at Hampton out
of the corner of his eyes.

"What's the matter with him?" he asked.

Hampton poured a cup of coffee. "Don't know. Tired, maybe. Exposure. Don't know."

Satterwhite watched Hampton take the cup to Tyler. He too had a hurt feeling in him when he thought about Tyler being seriously sick. He stirred the bacon again but didn't feel hungry anymore.

"Drink this. It looks dark enough to stand you up," Hampton said.

"Thank you."

Hampton stepped over to his bedroll and jerked the blankets off the ground cloth. He shook them out, then wrapped them around Tyler's shoulders.

"Sorry about this. Give me a minute," Tyler said. "I think I can ride."

"You ain't ridin' anywhere today, Bud. When I need you, I'm goin' to need all of you."

"I'd be all right if I could get warm."

"Uh-huh. You just sit tight. We could all use some rest today, I'm thinkin'."

"No, you ain't. You're thinkin' about that girl."

"A man does what he can. No sense wearin' yourself out worryin' about what you can't help."

Tyler nodded. "Coffee's good."

"There's plenty. Feel like eatin'?"

"Don't smell good to me," Tyler said, nodding at the fire where Satterwhite was cooking.

"All right. I've got some headache powders. We'll see if that brings the fever down."

"Thank you, Hamp. I'm sorry about this."

Hampton shook his head, negating the apology. He stood and went back to the packs, looking for the medical kit Betty had packed. As he looked for it, he thought about Betty and the way she had of stopping her work and watching him while he talked to her. It was a shame she was married to Tom Dunbar, but she had been close to thirty and her family was anxious that she not be a spinster, so they pushed her into it. Now that she was married, she always would be until one of them died. That was the kind of woman she was.

He found the kit in a cotton flour sack with a drawstring sewn in. He went through it until he found the box of powders. Taking three of the papers out, he put the rest away again, and carried the powders to Tyler.

"Take these with your coffee. They may help."

"I feel dizzy as a swung cat."

Tyler opened the papers with shaking fingers and took the powder with his coffee. When the cup was empty, he lay back with the blankets around him, and Hampton could see them trembling.

Hampton and Satterwhite ate the bacon and biscuits without talking. Then Satterwhite said, "He looks bad."

Hampton nodded. "Pushed him too hard. Should have known better. Neither of us is young men anymore. Takes longer to get over strain."

"I feel pretty tired myself. I can imagine how you two feel."

Hampton looked at Satterwhite from across the fire.

"I just meant. . . ."

"Uh-huh. Well you can just save that old man crap for somebody else."

"You said it yourself."

"I'm entitled to," Hampton said, "but you ain't. You ain't earned the right yet."

Satterwhite huffed and blew and looked at the sunlight on the river for a while. Hampton let his gaze drift over to Tyler. The blankets were still. Tyler had gone back to sleep.

"Now what?" Satterwhite said finally.

"We rest."

"That doesn't do Mary much good."

"Listen," Hampton said, getting to his feet and stepping close to Satterwhite, "you let Bud hear you say somethin' like that, and I'll knock your goddammed head off. You understand me?"

"Yes, sir."

"All he's got is what he can do. You start tellin' him he can't do nothin', then he ain't nothin'. You understand that?"

"Yes, sir."

Hampton stepped back. Satterwhite was staring at him. Hampton took a deep breath to calm himself.

"You better understand it, or you'll have to deal with me. Book, chapter, and verse. Let's get these dishes cleaned up before the fire goes out."

While Satterwhite did the dishes, Hampton repacked what was extra in case they had to move quickly. He untied the horses and led them down to the river to drink. Lady was looking thin, but he knew she was strong. He moved them up river and staked them apart where there was enough dry grass for them to browse on.

Satterwhite packed the skillet and the utensils, but he left the cups out. The sun was beginning to take the chill out of the air. The east wind was dying.

"Spread the coals to kill the fire. Sprinkle 'em with water a little at a time. Douse 'em all at once, and we'll have too much smoke."

"Yes, sir."

"You can drop the sir. I'm over it now. Wouldn't hurt you to think once in a while, Satterwhite."

Hampton made a cigarette while Satterwhite spread the coals and put out the fire. Tyler had not moved, but the steady rise and fall of his blankets told Hampton he was sleeping easy. Hampton took a kitchen match from his shirt pocket and lit his cigarette.

"That's good enough," Hampton said. "Those left will keep the coffee warm if Bud wakes up and wants another cup."

"What about the smoke?"

"Too thin to be seen far on a day like this. Anyone close enough to see it can hear us talkin'. The wind is out of the east. There's no reason for anyone to be west of us to smell it."

"That's the way we came. I'll guarantee you there's no one out there."

Hampton started to question Satterwhite's guarantee, then decided to let it pass.

Satterwhite stood up. He poured the rest of the water on the gravel and watched it roll away. He dusted his hands on his pants. He folded his arms and looked around, carefully avoiding Tyler's bedroll.

"Should we saddle up and look around?" Satterwhite asked finally.

"Can't sit still, can you?" Hampton threw his cigarette in what was left of the fire. "Me either. Let the horses be. We can walk."

Brush was thick in places next to the river. In other places, the bank was bare sand or rock. It was hard to get high enough to see beyond the tops of the brush where it grew thick, and Hampton got a closed-in feeling, but at the same time he was glad for the cover.

"Let's get up away from the river," he said. "Might be easier to see."

They stepped up the bank and walked east into the wind. Dead, dry limbs brushed at their pants' legs as they moved. Hampton was more interested in the skyline than in the immediate area, but there was nothing moving.

"Look here," he said once, pointing. "Bud's tracks."

"How can you tell?"

"Only one goin' our way. The sand hasn't filled them in yet the way it would old tracks."

"Should we have left him alone?"

"He'll know where we are if he needs us."

"How does he know stuff like that?"

"He keeps his eyes open, I guess," Hampton said.

In another hundred yards, Hampton picked out an opening through the brush and cactus. It was a trail, well worn by cattle and burros, and it twisted around back toward the river. They followed it until they stood on the bank of the river again.

"This must be what Bud saw that made him think a ranch was close by. A trail this distinct means animals kept in the same place a long time."

"You think someone lives around here?"

"Could be. Let's go on back."

They retraced their steps to camp. Everything was as they had left it, except Tyler was sitting up in his blankets, throwing them off.

"Got the sweats," he said as they walked up.

"Leave one of those blankets on, or you'll get the chills."

"It's freeze or fry out here."

Tyler's hair was wet with sweat, as was his lined face. His eyes were red, and his arms trembled on the blanket.

"Get my groundcloth, Satterwhite. We'll rig him some shade. How do you feel, Bud?"

"Like my horse has been walkin' around on me all night. Even my clothes are sore."

"Chest?"

"No, Hamp. You can put that out of your mind. I know what that feels like, and I haven't got it."

"Glad to hear you say it, Bud."

"Me too."

They made a lean-to with Hampton's groundcloth, and Tyler sat up for a while.

The day wore on. Hampton remained watchful. Tyler drank water and dozed. The sweats left him toward the middle of the afternoon, and he awoke abruptly.

"How do you feel now?" Hampton asked.

"Hungry. What we got to eat?"

"We'll make something."

They built up the fire, and Hampton heated up a can of chicken soup. Tyler ate it eagerly, drank more water, and wanted a smoke.

"I'll roll it," Satterwhite said.

"I'm startin' to like you, Satterwhite," Tyler smiled.

"Don't spoil him. We have a long way to go yet."

Satterwhite started to say something, then didn't. He spilled the tobacco on the paper and smoothed it out with his finger. He rolled the paper and licked the edge.

"Here you are," he said.

"Thank you." Tyler took the cigarette, lit it, and inhaled deeply. "I think I'll live," he said.

Satterwhite smiled and pushed his hat back on his head. He and Hampton were sitting on the gravel in the sun next to Tyler.

"I guess I just got too tired," Tyler said. "Feel all right now, just weak."

"We all needed the rest," Hampton said.

"I mean," Tyler said. "We been pushin' it pretty heavy the last few days."

They were quiet for a while, each thinking how much more they would have to push it.

"We've been lucky so far," Hampton said.

Satterwhite pulled out his pistol and turned it over in his hand.

"So much for luck," Hampton said.

"What you got there, Satterwhite?" Tyler asked.

"Army Colt, .38," Satterwhite said. "It was my father's."

"Your father's? He in the army?"

"No. He owned a drygoods store in Oklahoma City. He gave it to me when I moved out here."

Hampton took out his plug of tobacco. He bit off a chew and put the plug back in his pocket.

"Think maybe you were goin' to run into Indians?" Tyler asked.

"Shoot," Satterwhite laughed, "there's more Indians in Oklahoma than there are out here."

"Let me see that piece," Tyler said. He took the pistol from Satterwhite and looked at it. He held it like he was going to shoot it, then lowered it. He pulled the hammer back to half-cock and rolled the cylinder. "I prefer the .45 model myself," he said. "Got more heft." He handed the gun back to Satterwhite.

"You know how to use that?" Hampton asked.

"Sure," Satterwhite said. "I intend to do my share."

"Uh-huh. I hope you don't get the chance."

Hampton checked the horses and walked slowly around the camp until he felt the lazy tiredness rise in his muscles. He found some shade under a ragged salt cedar on the bank above the camp and lay down. At first, he couldn't make his eyes close without thinking of Mary, then he was asleep without knowing it and dreaming of a town he had never been in. The wide streets were lined with brick buildings several stories high, and the sidewalks were full of people all walking in the same direction. Before he could find out where they were going, Satterwhite shook him awake.

Hampton blinked up at him through his glasses, but Satterwhite wasn't looking at him. He was facing the river, and his attitude was tense. Hampton sat up and looked. Across the river was a man sitting his horse, a half-starved mustang pony.

"I don't know where he came from," Satterwhite whispered. "I just looked up and there he was."

Hampton threw a glance at Tyler. He was on his side, his eyes closed.

"All right," Hampton stood up. "Stay behind me. Don't grab for that pistol unless I grab for mine."

Hampton walked forward past the fire circle and stopped, facing the man. He was a *campesino* from his dress, but there was a Winchester hanging from his saddle by a homemade sling.

"*Buenas días*," Hampton called. "Come and join us."

"Don't let him come into camp, Hampton," Satterwhite hissed behind him.

"Shut up," Hampton said, without taking his eyes off the man.

The pony nickered softly and tossed his head, but the man sat perfectly still, watching Hampton.

"We are friends," Hampton said in Spanish. "Hunters. We will not harm you."

The man looked up and down the banks of the river. Hampton followed his looks, but nothing was there. After another pause, the man kicked at the pony and turned him down the bank toward the river. Hampton watched him cross and ride up to them. The man kept his eyes on Hampton's.

"*Quién es?*" the man asked. "Who are you?" He had a hard, dry face hidden in a black beard.

"Hunters," Hampton said again.

"Hunters for what?" the man asked.

Hampton looked at the man without answering. He knew the man's sense of hospitality made the answer optional.

The man looked around the camp, then said, "Will he shoot me?" He tossed his head up, indicating Satterwhite.

"If he does, I will shoot him," Hampton said.

The man smiled and swung down from the pony. On the ground, Hampton could see how short he was.

The man looked past Hampton at where Tyler lay. "Is he drunk?" he asked.

"No. He is sick."

"What is it?"

"A fever," Hampton said.

The man nodded. He looked around again, then asked, "Have you seen my children?"

"We have not seen anyone," Hampton said.

The man nodded. "I do not believe you are hunters," he said. "I think you are here because of the fight at Columbus."

Satterwhite heard the town's name. "What is he saying?" he asked.

"Shut up," Hampton said, without turning around. In Spanish he said, "That is true."

The man nodded. "It was bad, the fighting?"

"Yes."

"Were your people killed?"

"Yes."

The man nodded. "The fighting is very bad. You are here to take revenge?"

Hampton had already decided to tell the man the truth. He had seen something in his eyes when he crossed the river that made Hampton think he was no part of any Villistas.

"No."

"No?"

"An American girl was taken prisoner. We are here to get her back."

The man nodded. "This girl, she is your daughter?"

"No. She is the daughter of the man I work for."

"You would come here to look for another man's daughter?"

"Yes."

The man nodded. He looked at the packs. "You have coffee?"

"Some."

"Some to spare?"

"A little."

"I could use some coffee," the man said.

"Satterwhite," Hampton said over his shoulder, "find something to put coffee in and give this man half a pound of what we've got."

"What?"

"Do it."

Satterwhite went to the packs.

"Thank you," the man said. "I have been a long time without coffee."

"This is your ranch?"

"Yes, it is my ranch."

"It is very dry," Hampton said.

"Yes. The grass is hard to find."

Satterwhite measured out about half a pound of coffee in a small bag and gave it to the man.

The man nodded. "Thank you," he said.

Satterwhite stepped back behind Hampton. The shadows where they stood were growing long and deep. The sun was low on the horizon. Hampton, groggy and tense at first, was now awake and relaxed.

"I could use some tobacco too, if you have any," the man said.

Hampton turned his back on the man and went to his war bag. He pulled out two pouches of tobacco. When he bent over to get them, he glanced sideways at Tyler. Tyler winked at him.

"Here you are," Hampton said, stepping up to the man.

"I am in your debt," the man said.

"It is nothing," Hampton said.

The man shook his head, still holding the pony's reins in one hand and the coffee and tobacco in another. In such a position, Hampton had all of the advantage unless there were others in the brush across the river.

"No," the man said. "It is not nothing when it would have been just as easy to shoot me."

Hampton shrugged.

The man nodded. "This girl you are looking for, do you know who has her?"

"If I do and say his name, perhaps you are his brother."

The man smiled and nodded. "I do not trust you, either," he said. "But I will say this: no one of the Columbus raid was my brother."

"If that is true, then we can trust each other," Hampton said.

The man nodded. "I have been a rancher here on the Casas Grandes for many years. It is all I know. I do not know about the fighting. That is far away for me. Then one day, an army rides up to my door. You must join us for the fighting, they say. I say no, but they take me anyway. I am a prisoner until it is time to fight. Then they give me a rifle with five bullets. I escape and come back. I do not know where my wife and children are. My house is very quiet at night. But now I have coffee and tobacco."

"I am sorry for you," Hampton said in Spanish where the words say that he felt sorrow for the man rather than that he pitied him.

The man nodded. He looked away, then spoke softly to his pony. He glanced up at Hampton. "The revolution is not for me," he said. "I never wanted the quiet nights."

Hampton looked down. "Listen," he said, "I am looking for the man who makes dolls. His name is Salazar."

The man nodded, but did not say anything. He stepped back to his saddle and tied the coffee to it. He put the tobacco inside his shirt, then mounted the pony.

"Thank you again," the man said. "I am looking for my children. They too have been taken for the revolution. Still, I look for them. I look east along the river, always east until the river goes south. If I find the children, they will be all right. At least I hope so. They are all right now, but who can say tomorrow."

"I think you are not talking about your children."

"You can think that," the man said.

"Thank you very much," Hampton said.

The man nodded. "The night is too quiet without the children," he said. He turned the pony and rode slowly back across the river. Hampton watched him until he was out of sight.

"What was that all about?" Satterwhite said. "I thought you were going to give that greaser the whole camp."

"Don't call him a greaser," Hampton said.

Tyler threw back the blanket and sat up. He was holding his rifle. Hampton went over to him and crouched down.

"You sleep with that thing?" he asked.

Tyler's eyes were clear, and his color was right, nut-brown from the sun. "She sleeps good, long as she don't snore."

"Uh-huh. You catch what that hombre said?"

"I didn't," Satterwhite said.

"Some," said Tyler. "But my Mex ain't as good as yours."

"He said the revolution took his children. He has no love for the Villistas."

"Did he ever hear of Salazar?"

"I think so. He said he would look east, then south where the river turns. He seemed to think she was all right."

"How would he know?" Satterwhite asked.

"You ever hear of an *avisador*?"

"No."

"Uh-huh. It's a man who sends messages across the desert with a hand-held mirror. These people been doin' it for centuries. Nobody knows the codes they use, but they can relay messages across a hundred miles in just a few hours."

"What's to stop him from telling everybody about us?" Satterwhite cast a quick glance across the river.

"Are you listenin' to me or not?" Hampton looked up. "This man has lost everything because of men like Salazar. He isn't going to give them anything else."

"So you think she's all right?"

"If I read him right, that's what he said. And we have our directions, like we figured. Yep, she's all right. For now."

They were silent for a minute, each thinking about the man who had lost his children. Then Hampton and Satterwhite turned at the same instant and looked at Tyler.

"I'm ready," Tyler said.

NINETEEN

BY Sunday following the Thursday morning raid, the smoke that had hung over Columbus turned to dust. The buildings in the center of town no longer smoldered, nor did the dark piles of human bodies and animal carcasses outside of town, but the road from Deming was thick with troop movement, the arrival of curious sightseers, the departure of Columbus residents, some forever, and the competitive swarming of newspaper reporters. The little town had become known all over the world.

Trainload after trainload of troops poured through the station. Rows of tents grew in the camp south of the depot. A landing strip was cleared east of the tents, waiting for aeroplanes from San Antonio. While Washington tried to make up its mind about the course of action to take, the border armed itself.

The preacher delivered a sermon to only a handful of listeners that morning. His message was about the trials of earthly living and the promise of a better existence in heaven, taken from the funeral sermons he had given at three separate ceremonies the day before. When it was over, Herbert, the schoolteacher, approached him and invited him to dinner at one of the cafes in town. The preacher was hesitant to accept, but he had eaten enough meals alone and didn't look forward to another.

The cafe was noisy and crowded with strangers. As the preacher ate, he overheard conversations from nearby tables. Most of the talk was of war, but some of it had more to do with genocide than combat. The preacher looked at the speakers as he sipped his coffee. They were older men, easily identified as businessmen by their clothes and manner. The preacher reflected that it was easy for them to talk. They hadn't been in the raid or at the funerals of those killed, and they wouldn't be the ones who crossed the border to do battle if it came to that.

Herbert was uncharacteristically silent during the meal, perhaps because of the noise, but when they were outside again in the dust and sunlight, their hats pushed firmly down on their heads and their coats buttoned, the schoolteacher said, "It doesn't even look like the same town, does it, Mr. Leggitt?"

"Some of it does."

"Yes, some of it does," Herbert agreed. "But I don't know any of these people."

The preacher looked at the crowds in the street, mostly men, mostly troopers. His eyes lit on an automobile. He watched it come down the street toward them and listened to the noise of its engine. He remembered how his father had liked the automobile when it first came out and how he had talked about getting one someday. His father had died of a heart attack walking from the barn to the house on a bright fall afternoon. The automobile went by, the men in the front seat looking neither left nor right as they passed.

"Thanks for sharing dinner with me," the preacher said.

"Sure," Herbert said. "Are you going back to your house?"

"I think so. If anyone wants me, he can find me there."

"I'll walk with you. The truth is, I want your opinion about something."

"All right."

They turned down the street and walked toward the charred rubble of the Commercial Hotel. Nearly every building they passed had windows broken by bullets or bullet holes in the wood or adobe walls.

"I'm thinking about quitting my job at the school," Herbert said abruptly.

"What?"

"I may just quit. I don't think any of the children will be coming for a while anyway. They have too much to do helping their families."

"I guess so," the preacher said as he walked.

177

"My brother needs help with his hauling. He has a chance to make a lot of money freighting for the army, not to mention the businesses in town. They're selling out of their stock already with all these people coming in."

The preacher looked at the remains of the hotel as he passed it, thinking of the girl Hampton had gone to find. He felt nervous and anxious when he thought of Hampton in Mexico, and he half wished he had gone with him. His arm was still sore, but it was healing.

"What do you think?" Herbert asked. "I trust your opinion."

The preacher dropped his eyes.

They rounded the corner before they came to the railraod tracks but had to wait to cross the dusty street.

"Are you sure you want to?" the preacher asked while they waited for some men on horseback to pass. The men were wearing pistols.

"What do you mean?" Herbert looked at him. His narrow face was reddened by the cool breeze.

"You wouldn't miss the children?"

The preacher started across the street before Herbert could answer. They turned northwest and crossed the bridge over the deep drainage ditch beside the Deming road that divided the town.

"No," Herbert said. "And I'm sure they won't miss me."

"Oh, I don't know. They might."

"I'm pretty sure they wouldn't."

"Well, I think you are better off working with your brother then."

"That's what I thought. We could really make some money. I never planned to live in Columbus forever."

Two boys ran by. One of them stuck his tongue out at the schoolteacher. He didn't see it, but the preacher did.

"I never thought I would either," the preacher said.

"Are you planning to leave, Mr. Leggitt?"

"I've been thinking about it."

"But you can't."

"Why not?"

"What would we do for a preacher?"

The preacher looked at him, then looked ahead, up the street.

He could see his house. No smoke was coming from his stovepipe, but there was no reason why any should.

"What are we going to do for a schoolteacher?"

"They'll find somebody. There's always somebody."

"You can find another preacher just as easily."

"It's not the same," Herbert shook his head.

"Why not?"

"God doesn't make schoolteachers, but He chooses preachers, don't you think?"

"Maybe so, Herbert. Maybe so."

Herbert left the preacher at his door and went on toward his brother's house.

Inside, the preacher built a small fire to take the chill out of the house. He sat before the stove and closed his eyes. The faces of people he had buried or visited with or watched during the last three days crowded across his mind's eye.

Where before there had been a resting fullness on Sunday afternoons, there was only emptiness and the throbbing pain in his arm. He could hear the noises in the town as the east wind brought them against the walls of his house, but the aggressive bustle of the town and camp only reinforced his feeling of loneliness.

The town was strange to him now. It had been the object of an act of war, and that fact seemed to change the texture, even the colors of paint on the buildings. The town had been violated, a sense of home and security had been destroyed forever. The tall hotel sign fronting the tracks at the edge of town took on an ironic significance, as did a line of washing, bullet holes through the sheets. Like a child looking at his world through a bit of colored glass, the preacher saw each bright outline or shaded depth of Columbus in a completely different light. It was a tinting that would never fade.

The preacher slipped lower in his chair and stared at the wood heater. He wanted to ride out to the MacPherson ranch in the same way a smoker would habitually reach for his tobacco, wanting it without thinking about it. But Hampton would not be there, would perhaps never be there again. When the preacher thought in those final terms, he felt even more restless. Mexico was no place for Hampton to be.

The preacher lifted his eyes to the rifle he had leaned against the door to his bedroom, and he thought of his father and the life they had had together. Hampton was a lot like his father. The preacher was sure they would have been friends if they had known each other.

The rattle of barrels in the back of a wagon passing in the street broke into his thoughts, and he got to his feet and went to the window. He raised his eyes to the hazy sky above the town as if he saw something there, but there was nothing. He dropped his eyes to the street again and looked out his window. He felt a prisoner behind it.

Even if Hampton was gone, the ranch would hold his memory, and perhaps the MacPhersons had heard something. A visit to the ranch would do him good, he thought. He had to get away from the town.

Despite the springs under the seat, the ride out to the ranch jolted the preacher's arm, as did the pulling of the reins. It was a constant, throbbing ache, but the preacher did not find it unbearable. Although his arm was black with the bruise of the bullet's impact, the wound was clean, and he had had no fever. The more he used it, the faster it would heal.

There was no one in the yard when he got there. He drove the buggy up to the big house, got down gingerly, and tied the bay to a cottonwood. Hampton's little house looked empty even from the outside. He walked up to the big house and knocked on the door. Mrs. MacPherson answered his knock and showed him in to the parlor, where he sat down on the sofa.

"It's good to see you up and around," she said. "We had heard that you were wounded in the attack."

"I was very lucky, Mrs. MacPherson. Next to what you must be feeling, I am ashamed of my discomfort."

Mrs. MacPherson put a hand to her throat. Her brows knit in a confused way. "I just don't understand it." She shook her head. "I don't know what's happening any more."

The preacher looked at her. "It is hard on all of us, but the men who make war seldom stop to consider how difficult it is on the women. I pray that your daughter is all right."

"Thank you," Mrs. MacPherson said. Then she asked, "You never knew her, did you?"

"No, ma'am. I guess she was married and gone before I got to Columbus."

Mrs. MacPherson turned her confused look on a small table beside her chair. "I have some photographs in the album. Would you like to see them?"

"Of course I would."

The preacher leaned forward as Mrs. MacPherson carried the album across the room to him and sat down beside him. She opened the heavy, leather-and-brass-bound book and turned the pages slowly, looking.

"Here she is when she was nine. That was her first horse, a pet really."

The preacher saw a brown photograph of a young girl with long hair sitting astride a tall horse. The girl's eyes were large and smiling. She had dimples at the corners of her mouth.

"Yes," the preacher said.

"Here she is just before her wedding."

Mrs. MacPherson started to turn another page, but the preacher stayed her hand. "Excuse me," he said, looking closer at the photograph. Mary was standing in the sunlight just in front of the porch outside. Her hair was long but pulled back. She had a half-smile on her lips. Her eyes were almost alive on the paper.

"She's very beautiful," the preacher said, and he tried to believe she might still be alive. "Did she marry a local man?"

"No. Mr. Wells was from Tennessee. We telegraphed about Mary."

The preacher was suddenly aware that tears were on Mrs. MacPherson's face.

"What is it?"

"I don't know what to think. Mr. Wells wired back and said that Mary was, well, Mr. Leggitt, she was divorcing him." She whispered the word.

"What?"

Mrs. MacPherson nodded. "I just don't know what to think," she sniffed. "Oh, excuse me. Here I go again."

"Mrs. MacPherson. . . ."

"No. I'll be all right. Please excuse me."

She hurried out of the room toward the kitchen. The preacher looked after her, then gathered the album into his lap. He looked again at the picture of Mary before her wedding, then at others throughout the album. Each time he saw her face, he saw it as Hampton must have seen it, the kind of face that made a man want to gain her approval or want to protect her.

Finally, he put the album aside and stood up. Mrs. MacPherson had not returned, and there was little he could say to her anyway. He crossed the room and went outside. The bay looked at him, expecting to go somewhere, but the preacher went past the buggy and walked slowly over to Hampton's house.

Inside, he closed the door and looked around. The sun had warmed the house, but there was an unused chill in the air of it. The house, with Hampton gone, was just a place to be for the preacher. So used to finding comfort there and now finding none, he walked into the front room and sat down heavily in one of the captain's chairs.

Tyler's extra clothes were still on the bunk he had claimed. They seemed to have been there forever. Hampton's spitoon was on the floor next to the heater in a layer of fine ash dust.

The preacher took a deep breath. He could see the face in the photographs before his eyes. *Mary*, he thought. She was divorcing her husband and coming back home. Now she was somewhere in Mexico, perhaps already dead.

A door opened, and the preacher looked up quickly, expecting to see Hampton lean his Winchester in the corner. It was Betty.

"Hello, Preacher," she said, coming awkwardly into the room, as if she had been summoned to appear before a court. "Constance said you were here and that I was to apologize for her just running out on you like that. She has done nothing but cry the last three days, seems like."

The preacher got to his feet. "I wish there was something I could say to her. I'm afraid not everyone has my trust in the Lord."

"Don't get up," she said. "I don't mean to bother you." She

182

looked around the room for a moment, her hands along the edges of her apron.

"Come here, Betty," the preacher said.

She stepped up to him, and he put his arms around her. He hugged her hard, then held her lightly.

"I'm so worried about Mary and our Hamp," she said.

"So am I, Betty. Has anyone heard anything since they left?"

Betty shook her head. "No, and the worst thing is, we may never hear."

"We must not underestimate Hamp or his friend," said the preacher, hoping to give reassurance he did not feel.

"I don't, Preacher. I don't underestimate the Mexicans either."

Betty pulled away and sat down in Hampton's chair. She was neither self-conscious nor apologetic about her feelings for Hampton. She and the preacher had been friends too long to be coy with each other. Betty touched at her eyes with her apron, then was still.

"He was here with news about Mary, then gone. I didn't have time to think about what he was going to do. Tom suggested letting the army deal with it, and Hamp just about bit his head off. Of course, Hamp wouldn't be likely to act on anything Tom said."

"I gather Mr. Frank's daughter was kind of special to Hamp."

"There were times when I could have been jealous of her, if I was the jealous type." Betty shook her head. "I guess that sounds funny to you."

"No," the preacher said.

"She was special to all of us. She was just that sort. She made me think of somebody that famous painters would paint. She had that kind of look about her."

"Mrs. MacPherson was just showing me some photographs of her."

"Then you know what I mean. But then, you always do. You're like Hamp in that respect."

"Thank you," the preacher said.

They looked at each other for a minute, then the preacher's eyes drifted to the wall behind the wood stove. They were quiet, their faces became long and thoughtful. A quick step on the porch made them raise their eyes. The door opened again.

183

"Mama?" Billy asked, coming into the room. "Hello, Mr. Leggitt."

"Billy," the preacher nodded.

"Have you heard anything about Mr. Hampton?"

"No, Billy," the preacher shook his head. "I thought one of you might have heard something."

"Wish I was down there," Billy said, remembering his hat and taking it off. He looked at his mother. "I wanted to ask if I could go into town, Mama."

"What for?"

"Just look around. I only been there once since the battle."

While they talked, the preacher looked at the cold wood stove. His restlessness grew into a resolution. Why not go into Mexico? He did not see how he could keep on in Columbus when his heart was not in it anymore. His whole life had been a record of passively losing one person he loved after another. Hampton might need him, if he could find him. If not, what did he have now that he would not have then? After a silence he looked up at the other two.

They were both looking at him, then Betty's expression changed. She said, "You're going after him, aren't you?"

The preacher looked at her, but did not answer.

"Let me go with you," Billy said quickly.

"Hush, Billy."

"Aw, Mama. It's Mr. Hampton."

Betty seemed to waver, then said, "No." But it was a soft no, the kind that a mother needs to say sometimes, knowing it won't be heard and spoken like a wish without any hope of being obeyed.

The preacher stood up. He felt weak for a moment in the face of his decision, but then he felt stronger than he had since his father died. He stood taller.

"When do we start, Preacher?" Billy asked. "I got my own rifle and everything."

A smile ghosted Betty's trembling lips, and she dropped her eyes.

TWENTY

IT was their third day in Mexico, and the low, red sun was in Hampton's eyes as he laid the saddle across Lady's back. Although the temperature was already rising, the morning air was cold, and Hampton's hands were stiff inside his work gloves. Lady turned her head and looked at him when he bent to reach for the cinch straps.

Behind him, Tyler and Satterwhite were tying the packs on the horses. Hampton had loaded the bags the way he wanted them while the other two had finished their breakfast and saddled their horses. He was restless and impatient to-be riding again. They were in the bowl of the desert with very little cover, and they had stayed in one place too long.

Tyler seemed to be his usual self. He ate well and joked around the fire, but Hampton saw him steady himself when he stood up. He hoped the light-headedness would pass with the warmth of the day, was pretty sure that it would. He felt rested himself. Even the split watch with Satterwhite the night before had not taken the edge off the previous day's rest.

When Hampton finished, he led the horse over to the others. Satterwhite tied the reins of one packhorse to the frame of the other, then gathered the reins of the second packhorse and his own horse and pulled them forward to where Hampton stood. Tyler ran his fingers through his graying hair several times before putting on his hat, then stepped up to the other two. The desert was bright, and the wind was calm, but Tyler had an impression of a cold, gray East Texas afternoon with miles to go before turning in to the home gate.

"We know where we're goin' now," Hampton said, "so we don't

have to waste any time. But we're not goin' at a full gallop. Bud, you ride point. I'll bring up the rear. Stay spread out, Satterwhite, and don't let those horses get away from you. They know what they're supposed to do, so don't surprise 'em. If Bud runs into trouble, you drop back to me. If we all run into trouble, we'll either ride or make a stand. I'll tell you which. Got that?"

"I got it, but. . . ."

"But what?"

"How come nobody's around? I keep expecting to see whole armies of greasers. All we've seen is one old man."

Hampton raised his eyes to the western horizon. "We been lucky," he said. "Either that, or the Villistas aren't stickin' around Chihuahua to see what happens next. After Columbus, I imagine they're interested in findin' a place to hole up for a while."

"Our bunch must have split from the main army. The way they're goin', I'd say they still had ransom on their minds," Tyler said. Hampton nodded, then said, "Uh-huh. Way I figure it, too. But don't start relaxin' and takin' naps in the saddle, Satterwhite. If there's nobody in this whole desert but us and that one bunch, there's still that one bunch."

"I know," Satterwhite said.

"Good. Don't forget it. Let's go."

Tyler mounted and rode up the bank away from the river, shifting easily in the saddle as his mustang cleared the sandy top. Satterwhite moved off after him about a hundred yards behind. Hampton paused before mounting and looked across the shallow, green river at the point where the Mexican had disappeared through the brush, thinking back to every detail of the encounter to make sure he had not missed anything that could mean a trap. Then he mounted and swung up through the brush to flank the other two riders.

They moved slowly through the day, searching for signs of Salazar's band, but, still too far west of where Salazar made his first camp, they found no evidence of the passage of horses or men. At noon, Tyler stopped and waited for Hampton and Satterwhite to catch up.

"See anything?" Satterwhite asked.

"Plenty of real estate I wouldn't give a plug nickel for," Tyler said.

"Let's go down to the river and eat," Hampton said.

They found a sloping bank covered with dried grass and thinly shaded in one spot by the lacy limbs of a salt cedar. They led the horses down to the river's edge. While the horses drank, Satterwhite untied the sack Hampton had packed with jerky and crackers and carried it over to the salt cedar. He dropped the bag on the ground and stood resting in the shade with his hands on his hips. Hampton and Tyler brought the horses up from the river and tied them to low bushes nearby. Before Hampton joined the other two in the shade, he pulled the Winchester out of the saddle scabbard and carried it with him.

He leaned the rifle into a fork of the cedar and looked at Tyler who was crouched with his elbows on his knees and his hands loosely twined. "How do you feel?" Hampton asked him.

Satterwhite was sitting with the sack in front of him. He paused in slicing jerky to hear the answer.

"Good. Whatever it was came and went. I guess the good Lord was just remindin' me how mortal I am."

"Uh-huh," Hampton said. "Could have been the devil seein' how much meat you had on you."

"That's a comfortin' thought," Tyler said. He looked up at Satterwhite, then pushed his hat back on his head. "Don't mind if I do," he said.

They sat in the thin shade and ate without much appetite. The horses nibbled at the dry grass with the same lack of enthusiasm.

Satterwhite fidgeted for a few minutes, then asked, "If we do come up on the bandits, and they have Mary, how are we going to go about getting her away from them?"

"That has to be your longest question yet," Hampton said, chewing. He spit out a hard edge of the jerky.

"I believe it was," Tyler said.

"Well, have you thought about it?" Satterwhite said with an accusing edge in his voice.

"Yeah, we have. Hamp and me both think that was your longest question yet."

"That last one was a medium-sized question," Hampton said.

Satterwhite sat trying to think of something to say, but couldn't, so he stood up and went up through the trees away from the river, mad.

"There he goes, walkin' away," Hampton said.

Tyler and Hampton passed a sleeve of crackers back and forth for several minutes, then Tyler said, "You goin' to try to *habla* with 'em, or surround 'em and go in shootin'?"

Hampton swallowed and took a drink from Satterwhite's canteen. "I don't know, Bud. We go in shootin', and they'll kill her. We walk into camp with nothin' to trade, and they'll kill us all."

"We'll have to use their plan and sneak up on 'em in the dark."

"There's somethin' wrong about fightin' in the dark, seems to me," Hampton said. "But that's the way they always do it — horse thieves, outlaws, bandits. Suits their way of life, I guess."

They heard Satterwhite coming back through the grass. He stopped, then he came a little quicker.

"Better come look," he said.

Tyler and Hampton were on their feet at once. Hampton reached the rifle into his hand as he moved. They stepped through the dry grass to the higher ground.

"What is it?"

"Look there," Satterwhite said and raised his arm to point.

To the northeast was a trail of dust in the desert, moving steadily parallel to them.

"Get those binoculars off Lady, Satterwhite. Quick."

Satterwhite got the binoculars Hampton had found and brought them back. Hampton gave his rifle to Tyler, took them, tried to focus, said, "Damned glasses," and passed the binoculars to Tyler, taking back his rifle. Tyler focused them and watched.

"One rider," he said. "Moving pretty fast. If the river keeps goin' the way it's goin' now, that rider will hit it."

"Tell anything about him?"

"Can't even see him. I can just tell it's one."

188

"A messenger or spy," Hampton said. "Been to the border and comin' back with his report."

Tyler lowered the glasses. "He's gone. Lay of the land hides him."

"How far do you reckon?"

Tyler turned the binoculars over in his hand and thought. "Three or four miles."

"Camped?"

"That'd be my guess."

Hampton nodded. He turned and looked at Satterwhite, who was leaning forward, squinting at the desert, his pistol in his hand.

"Hey," Hampton said. "You want to put that pistol up? I'll tell you when you'll need it. You shoot it off now by accident and we might as well head back for the border."

Satterwhite holstered the pistol and looked at the ground. Hampton could see how tense he was. He glanced at Tyler. Bud returned the glance and shrugged.

"You done good, Satterwhite," Hampton said, softening his tone. "Let's finish eating and powwow."

In the shade again, Tyler jerked tight the drawstring on the cotton sack, then leaned back. One after the other, they took out their tobacco pouches and rolled cigarettes.

"I'm starting to like these things," Hampton said.

"My father never would let me smoke back in Oklahoma, but I got the habit out here."

"You're too young to smoke."

"I'm twenty-one."

"I said smoke, not vote."

"You said vote the other day."

"Maybe I meant live."

"Doctor up in Denver told me a steady diet of cigarettes would ease the chest pain."

"That right?" Hampton said, turning away from Satterwhite.

"Yeah. Another doctor told me the next cigarette I ever smoked would be my last."

"Was he right?" Hampton asked.

"I don't know. He didn't say which next. It might be this one."

Satterwhite blew out smoke in the way all young men do, as if the blowing were the whole point of smoking. "You can get mad at me all you want," he said. "I'm getting used to it, but I got to say something."

"Go ahead," Hampton said.

"It's a free country," Tyler said.

"Not this one."

"Oh, yeah. You take your own chances around here, Satterwhite."

"That's it right there," Satterwhite said. "There's I-don't-know-how-many greaser bandits camped just over yonder, maybe holding my cousin, Mary, maybe killing her this minute, and you two sit around cracking jokes like it was Sunday afternoon."

"It is Sunday afternoon," Tyler said.

Satterwhite shook his head and smoked. "I'm scared. I admit it. I'm scared, and I'm worried. I just don't see how you can joke at a time like this."

"What do you want us to do, Satterwhite? Piss in our pants? Run around like a chicken with its head cut off? What good would that do?"

Satterwhite shook his head again.

"You tell me I'm not worried about Little Mary," Hampton went on, "and I'll shoot you right now. I know that girl. I have that girl right here," Hampton said and touched his chest. "But I won't do her any good if I'm runnin' around in circles sayin' 'Oh my, oh my, what are we going to do? What are we going to do?'

"Listen," Hampton said. "When Bud and me was your age, we'd already been fighting Mexicans south of the Nueces River in Texas. And they were runnin' fights too, with no cover and not enough bullets to fill your shirt pocket."

"Sharps .50 caliber single shot," Tyler said. "I'd give a pretty for one of them guns right now."

Hampton nodded. "And we learned that if you want to stay alive, you have to face what is, and you got to use your head. If my gun jams in the middle of a fight, I have to face that. I can't stand there saying, 'Why did this have to happen?' I have to face what is and use my head to get myself where I want to be. You have to stay calm, Satterwhite, so you can think, and so you can act when the time comes. Book, chapter, and verse."

"The time is now," Satterwhite said.

"No it isn't," Hampton said. "We don't know where that camp is or how many are in it. We go stompin' along the river lookin', and they'll spot us. We been runnin' that risk all day, but that was because we had to and we didn't know where they were. We don't have to now. All we have to do is wait for dark. Then we'll ease forward on foot until we see firelight."

Satterwhite dropped his eyes. He finished his cigarette and mashed it out under his boot. Hampton looked at him a minute, then stepped on his own cigarette.

"I'm going up for another look," Hampton said. He picked up his rifle and walked toward the higher ground away from the river.

Satterwhite followed him with his eyes until he was gone. He shook his head. "So I'm wrong again," he said. "I get the feeling he would just as soon see me dead."

Tyler was smoking his cigarette slower, like he did most things. "You're wrong yet again," Tyler said quietly. "Hamp is actually quite fond of you."

Satterwhite looked at Tyler for signs of sarcasm on his face. Tyler's brown eyes were serious.

"I don't even care whether he likes me or not. I just get tired of always being wrong."

"I think you do care. You should. In case you haven't noticed, that's no ordinary man we got ridin' with us."

"I can't do anything right around him," Satterwhite said, avoiding Tyler's eyes.

"He's a little hard on you, maybe, but I'll bet he ain't never told you anything that wasn't right."

"According to him."

"Let me tell you somethin' about Hamp. He used to have a little brother named Homer. About the best lookin' kid I ever saw. Had the face of an angel, and by the age of three, he could charm the spokes off a wagon wheel.

"Hamp's pa was a preacher like mine, and they both had to hit the circuit back in those days, holdin' prayer meetin's wherever they could, so he was gone a lot. He left Hamp in charge of Homer. Hamp was kind of a big kid, never got away with anything, never had many friends, so he spoiled that little Homer pure rotten. Let him do anything, and never said no. Even took the blame for stuff Homer did wrong.

"When they was older, they'd go out huntin' together. Homer was completely wild by then, wouldn't listen to anybody, not even Hamp. They was camped out on the Trinity River in East Texas, one time, and that river was floodin' the game out of the bottoms. An island was in the river there with game trapped on it. Homer decided he would swim across to that island and shoot all he wanted. Hamp tried to talk him out of it, but Homer wouldn't listen. He tied his rifle on his back and jumped in. Before too long, he got in trouble. Hamp jumped in to try to save him, but Homer went down before Hamp could reach him. They never did find the body."

Tyler put his cigarette out. "Hamp blamed himself for lettin' Homer get away with too much, and he never was the kind to make the same mistake twice if he could help it. I figure that's why he's so hard on you."

Satterwhite reached down and pulled a dead grass stem out of the ground. He stretched it between his hands and looked at it. "Just my luck," he said.

Tyler stood up. "You listen to him, and you might come out of this alive. And one other thing: if Hamp didn't think you were worth the trouble, he wouldn't give you the time of day. I'm goin' to check on him."

"Thanks, Bud," Satterwhite said.

They spent a long afternoon under the salt cedar, waiting. The country was too open for them to cross on horseback without being seen, and Hampton was against looking for the camp on foot in daylight. But finally the waiting was too much, and they walked their horses along the river, using the natural cut for cover. After a mile, they lost the sloping bank and had to stop. They ate another cold meal and smoked.

When it got dark, they mounted up and rode slowly abreast of each other along the river, but away from it. They rode for about an hour, then Hampton drew up.

"Let's tie the horses here and go ahead on foot," he said.

They tied the horses, pulled their rifles out of the saddle scabbards, and filled their pockets with bullets.

"Put the rifle rounds in your top pockets," Hampton told Satterwhite. "Carry the pistol rounds in your pants."

They moved from shadow to shadow along the banks of the river, spread out to the limit of whispering. It was slow going and nearly midnight before they broke into the clearing where Salazar's band had camped. They were tired and cold and disappointed.

"This is it," Tyler said. "They been gone several hours. The coals are cold."

Hampton stared ahead in the darkness.

"Reckon they left a rear guard?" he said.

"Doubt it. My guess is they was waitin' for word about a ransom and didn't get it, so they moved on. After a raid like Columbus, they'll be needin' more ammunition, maybe more soldiers."

"Uh-huh. How many in the band, do you think?"

"Can't see the layout well enough in the dark. Have to wait till mornin'."

"Was Mary here?" Satterwhite asked.

"Can't say till mornin'," Hampton said. "If they killed her before pushin' on, we'll know then."

Tyler and Satterwhite both looked at Hampton. He swung the rifle up and down in his hand, took a deep breath and faced them.

"Well," he said, "no sense backtrackin' to make camp. I'll get the horses. We can camp here."

For a minute, none of them moved, then Hampton said, "Damn!" and kicked at the cold ground with his boot.

"I'll get the horses," Satterwhite said.

Hampton turned and looked at him.

"I'll get them," Satterwhite said again, even though he felt the chill of walking back through the desert alone in the dark.

"Thanks, Satterwhite," Hampton said quietly. "I'm feeling a little blowed."

Satterwhite moved off in the dark. When he was gone, Tyler stepped up to Hampton.

"I'm sorry, Hamp," he said. "If I hadn't gotten the shakes, maybe we'd have found her."

"Or gotten ourselves killed," Hampton said.

"We'll find her."

"I don't know," Hampton said. He shook his head. "I get a bad feelin' from this."

They walked around the camp in the dark, then moved up against the bank and sat down to wait for Satterwhite. Hampton never raised his eyes from the ground in front of him.

TWENTY-ONE

MARY woke up. Without stirring, she looked at the shapes of the women close to her, wrapped in blankets. Beyond them, dead stalks of century plants pointed their crooked fingers at the pale, gray sky which was starless and sunless and cold. Mary shivered. Her hip was sore, and her shoulder felt numb from lying on the hard ground. Strands of hair, heavy with dust and dirt, tickled down across her cheek and brushed her eyelash when she blinked.

She was glad another night had ended. She tolerated the days, but the nights were filled with endless shivering minutes and imaginings and memories more closely related to fever dreams than conscious thought. She shifted under her dirty blankets to take the weight off her hip and shoulder, and she heard the crunch of gravel and the jingle of conchos that meant one of the men was awake and moving around.

Mary concentrated on the movements of the man. He walked to the edge of camp and stopped. He coughed, cleared his throat, and spit. Another man said something, and the first man spit again. The second threw back his blankets, cursing. Mary pulled the blanket up close to her cheek. Now they would all be awake.

Mary squeezed her eyes shut, but found she could not keep them closed. There was talking all around the camp now, and the sounds of movement increased. The sky began to take on the faint, fleeting rosiness of sunrise, and Mary could smell smoke from new fires, built on the coals from the night before by putting tufts of dry grass on them and blowing until flames appeared.

From across the camp came a call so urgent that even Mary

rolled over to look. Antonio was kneeling beside the blankets of one of the men who had been wounded in the Columbus raid. He was looking over his shoulder at Salazar, who, hatless, wearing a blanket instead of a coat, walked quickly through the others toward him. Antonio threw back the cover and let Salazar see that the man was dead.

Mary sat up, keeping her arms under the blankets, looking from one to the other of those around her, each frozen. From the shallow draw where the horses had been tied came another alarm. Salazar turned away from the dead man and went to the edge of the draw. Antonio followed him.

"What is it?" Salazar called.

"One of the horses is dead."

"So what?" Salazar called back angrily. "Four of those horses should have been dead two years ago."

"It is the horse of Marcelino," came the reply.

Antonio jerked his head around and looked at the blankets where the dead man lay rigid, his pockets already emptied. Antonio's head turned slowly until his eyes rested on Mary. He raised his arm and pointed at her.

"It is the bad luck," he said.

Everyone looked at Mary. She tried to hold their eyes, then looked down. Salazar walked up to her. He pulled the blanket off his shoulders and threw it on the ground. The others stood in a half-circle behind him.

"Stand up," he said to Mary.

Mary got to her feet, holding the blankets against her breasts. Salazar reached forward and snatched the blankets away from her. Smoke passed between them, then blew away.

Mary forced herself to stand up straight and look only at Salazar. "What are you going to do with me?" she asked.

"It is a good thing you do not ask Antonio that. He says you are bad luck. He thinks you should die."

Mary raised her chin two degrees but did not say anything.

"Maybe he is right," Salazar ran his eyes up and down her figure.

"She has been bad luck for us from the first," Antonio said.

"From the first what?" Eliseo asked.

"Shut up," Antonio looked at him.

Mary continued to look at Salazar. She felt weak from the sleepless, cold night and the strain of being a prisoner. Her breath came quickly, and she smiled.

"You are your own bad luck," she said.

Salazar's face turned ugly and his eyes widened. "You make me want to cut your throat," he said.

"Do it, then."

Salazar pulled his knife and stepped close to her. Mary stopped breathing but did not take her eyes off of his. Tears formed in the corners of her eyes and blurred her vision. "Do it," she said.

Salazar raised his knife so that she could see the dirty blade. She remembered El Paso and how quickly it had been over.

"Do it," she said again.

Salazar turned the blade in the air, his wakened face rough and angry.

"Wait!" Natalia called.

Salazar turned and looked at her. "Why, woman?"

"Her name is Mary. You cannot kill her. It would be the worst bad luck for us all. It was the mother of Jesus who sent you the stone and the vision," Natalia said. "It would be bad luck to kill her now, after you know her name and have made the doll."

"Mary was also the name of the whore," Carmen said, pushing up from behind the men. "It is not bad luck to kill a whore."

"This one is not a whore," Natalia said.

Carmen slapped the younger girl. Natalia's cheek burned in the cold air.

"Stop it," Salazar said. He looked back at Mary who had turned her head to stare at Natalia. He could feel the truth of what Natalia had said. If he killed the *gringa* thinking of her as a whore, it would be a lie, and he would know it was a lie when he did it. Mary, the Mother of God, would know it was a lie, too. That is what would bring the bad luck.

Mary faced Salazar again. She could feel her breath cut her lungs.

"Kill her," Carmen said.

"No," Salazar said. "Natalia is right. It would be a sin to kill this one. It would make very bad luck, like killing a child cripple. You remember when Rodrigo killed the cripple on the train from Juarez. He had cactus thorns stabbed through his eyes when his horse pitched him for no reason."

"Rodrigo was a drunkard," Carmen said.

"It was the bad luck," Antonio said.

Carmen gave him a narrow look. Salazar dropped his knife hand to his side. Sunlight touched his face and shoulders, but his eyes remained dark.

"Tie her up," he said to no one. "Tie her hands."

He turned away from her, pushed a nearby man out of his way, and crossed the camp to one of the smoking fires. Carmen was beside him immediately. He shook his fist at her and told her to leave him alone. She finished what she had to say, then turned her stare on Mary.

Mary looked away, trembling. Natalia stepped to one of the food packs and snatched up a piece of rope that lay on the ground. She went behind Mary and caught her left wrist, then her right one, to tie them together. Mary did not resist, but stood still trying to get her breath. She blinked to clear her eyes.

Antonio and the others turned away to the fires. The dead man was dragged down into the draw where the sand was deep enough to bury him.

"Thank you," Mary said softly.

"Do not thank me. I did not stop him for your sake. I have seen bad luck before. We do not need it where we are going."

"Where will you go?" Mary asked, looking sideways and down.

"What does that matter to you?" Natalia asked, looping the rope and tying it.

"I only asked. I am trying to understand what is happening."

Mary felt the knot pulled tight.

Natalia stepped around and faced her. Her eyes were cold, but sad too. She shrugged.

"Salazar wants to attack a village where Carrancistas have guns. It is El Indio. We have been there before."

"Will he kill them?" Mary asked.

"Of course. It is the revolution."

"When will it end?"

Natalia looked over her shoulder and stared down a man who was watching her from where he squatted by a fire, smoke blowing over his face. She looked back at Mary.

"Maybe it never will. It is exciting for us. Before, we had nothing. Now we have the revolution."

"What will they do to me?"

"I do not know."

One of the other women called to Natalia and pointed at the cooking pot near the fire. Mary turned away and faced the north. She had no hope of help. The only thing left to think was that it would end as soon as possible.

Mary sat down on the ground after a while. Her fingers felt numb. She was given nothing to eat or drink. After the others finished eating, they squatted in a close group around Salazar to wait for his decision. The women moved away and began packing the food and blankets.

Although Mary tried not to look at the men, her eyes were drawn back to them again and again. She could not hear what they were saying, but Salazar talked for a long time. One of the men shifted, and Mary saw that Salazar was making a doll. It was working its effect on the men. Finally he stood up. The men got to their feet, each talking to his neighbor and smiling.

Two men crossed the camp and jerked Mary to her feet. She felt her breath quicken with the cold fear that settled in her chest. There were so many things that could happen, she thought, so many men who could save her. All they had to do was ride in now, before the men could take her across the camp. She didn't care if she was shot in the battle. She just didn't want things to happen the way Salazar had planned them. She didn't want to be hurt. She could die. It would be easy to die, but she didn't want to be hurt.

The men dragged her past the edge of camp toward the draw where the horses were tied. Each gripping an arm, they slid down the gravel bank with her. She saw past the horses where a man was digging a grave. He paused to look at her. The dead horse lay on the sand in front of her in the deep shadow of the draw. The rest of the bandits came down the slope behind them.

Mary was taken to a dead mesquite tree that slanted out from the bottom of the draw. One of the men held her while the other untied her wrists. He pulled the rope free, and Mary felt the sting of blood returning to her hands.

Through the hair that fell across her face, Mary saw the other bandits crowd in front of her. Her left wrist was tied again, and that arm was pulled close to a limb of the tree behind her. Another piece of rope was put on her right wrist, and that arm was tied to another limb so that she was stretched between two limbs of the tree.

They meant to crucify her.

She began to cry without control. It was a deep, tearing sound that was more animal than human, horrible to hear. The figures blurred in front of her. Carmen stepped up to her and struck her repeatedly in the face with her fists. Some of the other women spit on her and tore her shirt open. The sateen waist was torn as well, and Mary felt her nakedness. The blows had stopped her crying, which had sprung from her helplessness. She could deal with the pain easier than with the anticipation of the pain. She felt the sting of dirt thrown on her. Fresh horse dung was thrown at her face.

Her ears were ringing so loud the sound drowned out the cheers and laughter of the band. She tried to get her breath, then realized one of the men was urinating on her skirt. She screamed at him, but was slapped into silence. Rocks hit her, one on her temple that knocked her unconscious.

When she came to, she dimly saw Salazar standing in front of her. She could not see any of the others, but she could hear them.

"So," Salazar said. He gripped her chin and shook her head. "There will be no bad luck now. We have not killed you. We have left you as a monument."

When Salazar let go of her chin, Mary felt his rough hand pull at the waist of her skirt. She tried to look at him. Her breathing was shallow and rapid. He held the skirt away from her skin and pushed a thorny doll into it. Mary gasped.

"Now, bitch," he said, "you understand the revolution."

200

She felt his hand across her face and tasted blood in her mouth. Then she was left alone.

In her mind, Mary went to another year in her life. People were talking to her. She was sitting on a couch with her legs drawn up beside her the way she used to sit covered with a quilt when she was a girl and the winter winds swept across the desert. She could not understand what the people were saying. Leonard appeared before her holding a broken plate in his hands. Another man was coming across the room toward her, and the people moved aside for him. She looked up to see his face, but she couldn't.

The sound of horses pierced the dream, and a mantle of pain fell about her shoulders again. The beat of hooves vibrated through her, and she smelled dust. When the horses were gone, she strained against the ropes that cut her wrists and tried to get her feet under her. Then, panting, she surrendered to the pain.

A white-wing dove landed in a bush near her and began to sing in a hollow, sad voice. When the sun came into the draw, it flew away.

TWENTY-TWO

HAMPTON was up before the dawn had turned the deep, blue-black sky to gray. He put on his coat and work gloves and his hat, and he gathered some of the wood the bandits had piled close by but had not used. Breaking off stems the diameter of a pencil lead, he made a small pile in one of the black fire circles and set it aflame with a kitchen match. The glow hurt his eyes for a few seconds, then he was used to it. He added larger limbs until the fire was big enough to warm his face as he squatted beside it.

It had been close to freezing in the night, but the water in Satterwhite's canteen was only cold, not frozen. Hampton poured it in the coffee pot and set the smoke-blackened pot at the edge of the fire. He was not worried about anyone seeing the fire. The bandits had pulled out and were at least a half-day's ride ahead of them.

Hampton rolled a cigarette, although he did not favor the way they tasted before he had eaten. When it was rolled, he lifted a small, forked twig and put the end of it in the flames. He lit his cigarette and tossed the twig on the fire.

He began to feel warmer. His thoughts turned to Mary again, like to the lines from a song that stick in the mind and play themselves over and over whether a person wants them to or not. He remembered her best in the spring when the desert bloomed briefly before turning dry again until July. There was something about the budding green and the bright orange and red blossoms of the cactus that suited her, added to her. He remembered her crossing the barnyard on some errand, perhaps with a bucket in her hand, coming back from town on the wagon seat beside her mother and father, stepping up on his porch with a bright, checkered cloth covering something Betty had baked and sent him, always a hesitant look on her face, a question on her mind. She had a way of getting around in front of him to watch his eyes when she talked to him, her words carefully spoken, sounding just right. She wondered about so much, could sit down with a copy of some current magazine and wonder about what she read, or the pictures she saw. And in the evenings, when the twilight was warm and alive with the voices of insects and nighthawks, he remembered sitting on his porch, listening as the sound of her playing the piano came through the open windows of the big house.

The life he had led before the raid on Columbus seemed as far away as the memories of Mary as a girl. Something had changed for him, and earlier transient feelings of becoming a stranger in his own house had turned into reality. Squatting by the fire in the Mexican dawn was a step backward into a previous life, and it made his present existence meaningless. He had thought of living out his days at Mr. Frank's ranch, perhaps moving into Columbus to retire if he began to get in the way of things at the ranch, but now that seemed unlikely.

He knew he could die in the desert and had been ready to do so the moment he learned Mary had been taken, but if he got back across the border, it could only be by killing men. That was a border which, he knew from the past, could never be recrossed.

He heard Tyler stir behind him and swiveled on his heels to watch him get out of his blankets. Tyler pulled on his coat and joined Hampton at the fire. He sniffed.

"Cold," he said.

"Yep."

Tyler sniffed again and touched the lid of the coffee pot. It was still cold. He shook his head in disappointment.

"Won't be long," Hampton dropped his cigarette in the fire. "How do you feel?"

"Fit. You?"

Hampton shrugged his shoulders.

Tyler yawned. "Used to, I'd know what you was thinkin'. Now I see the sign, but can't follow it."

After a silence, Hampton said, "That's because I don't think anymore. I spend my time rememberin'."

The fire crackled softly, occasionally sending smoke across their faces. Hampton squinted and held his breath until it shifted to another direction.

"Listen," he said, "if I was to get shot and die today, what difference would it make to anybody? Who would even know who I was, 'cept maybe you and the preacher?"

Tyler looked at the fire and watched the smoke curl away from the flames.

"I spent my whole life just leavin' behind things I did. I never had kids, never planted a tree nor built a house. If I wrote a will, it would only be one sentence long. I don't know, Bud. People nowadays have things. They don't measure a man by what he does. They look at what he has. A man has a big spread and rides around on rubber tires, people say what a great man he is. No one could say the same about me."

"I could," Satterwhite said quietly from behind him.

"Hell," Hampton said with a wry smile, "I'm worse off than I thought."

By the time it was light enough to see the ground, they had finished breakfast. Hampton walked from fire circle to fire circle, stooping now and then to look at something that might have been dropped. Tyler was doing the same thing at the fringes of camp, looking at horse tracks and droppings, trying to estimate how large the band was that they were following. Always out of the corner of their eye, they looked for some sign of Mary, whether something she owned, or her body.

"Hamp?" Tyler called.

Hampton crossed the campsite. Tyler held out a rough figure made of twigs and grasses. Hampton took the doll and turned it over in his hands.

"All right," he said. "This was them. There's nothing here to say Mary was with 'em, but there's nothing here to say she wasn't. Can we track 'em?"

"A band this large? With my eyes closed."

"Let's do her," Hampton said. He turned away, then turned back. "How large?" he asked.

"Twenty or thirty."

"That all? Let's do her."

They followed the tracks away from the camp, letting their horses walk. The tracks were easy to see, but walking the horses would raise less dust. Hampton and Tyler rode abreast. Satterwhite trailed behind, leading both packhorses. At the road to Colonia Dublan, they drew up, considering the tracks on the road as well as those that crossed it. Tyler moved out in a loop on the other side of the road, then came back.

"They cut across and turned to the south," he said.

"They'll hit the river again and cross it most likely," Hampton said. When he looked at the desert, he had the feeling someone was calling his name.

"Did they cross here this morning?" Satterwhite asked, his face tense and shaded by the wide brim of his hat.

"Yesterday," Tyler said. Then, "It'll be noon in another hour. You want to stop, or push on?"

"Push on," Hampton said, searching the desert to the south, "but carefully. We don't want to come up on them without plannin' to."

Before they moved off again, Hampton handed the field glasses to Tyler and had him scan the horizon.

"Nothin'," Tyler said.

"Keep 'em. You can see better with 'em than I can," Hampton said.

They came to the river and let the horses drink while they filled the water bags. On the other side of the river, the ground changed to rock and gravel, and the trail became less distinct. Were it not for the fact that the bandits had ridden single file around thick cactus clumps, Tyler might have lost the trail altogether. As it was, he was able to see the upturned rocks and the occasional droppings fairly well.

Every mile, Hampton drew up while Tyler searched the horizon with the glasses. Hampton looked at the desert sky and sniffed the air. He had an increasing feeling of danger and was taking no chances.

Tyler pointed out the buzzards before they found the camp. Ten of them were circling in the air above a draw. Hampton pulled up.

"What do you think?"

"Horse, probably."

"Their camp?" Satterwhite asked, riding up.

"Probably," Tyler said again.

Hampton straightened his back. He tried not to think of Mary.

"They're gone, though. They wouldn't stay where something was dead, and the buzzards wouldn't circle that low if men were movin' around."

"All right," Hampton said, pulling his rifle from the scabbard. "Let's go in, but keep your eyes open."

The buzzards circled higher the closer they rode. Hampton and Tyler both held their rifles ready, their eyes spotting even the slightest movement of leaf or bird in the brush.

When they rode into the clearing, Hampton was in the lead; Tyler was off to the right behind him, Satterwhite to the left. Hampton's eyes scanned the fire circles, one of which still showed a thin ribbon of smoke, then went to the lip of the draw. A buzzard flew up out of it and flapped away to the south. Hampton pulled the hammer back on the Winchester and kicked Lady forward. His heart was beating fast, and his mouth was dry.

He saw the dead horse, then saw Mary tied to the mesquite and forgot everything. With a harsh, throaty yell, he urged Lady down the gravel slope. He jerked the reins to the left and let the hammer down on the Winchester by holding it with his thumb and squeezing the trigger. He pulled back on the reins and was out of the saddle before Lady bucked to a stop. He threw the Winchester in the sand as his boots touched the ground.

"Mary," he said, reaching for his knife.

Her chin was touching her chest and her face was hidden by her dark hair. One knee was bent, the other leg supporting her, keeping the ropes from cutting into her wrists.

She raised her head and blinked at him, not sure if he was real or not, disinterested almost, too empty to care about finding out. Then she was sure Hampton really was there, and her eyes filled with tears of pain and shame and rage, and relief. She had once wondered how she would go to him when she saw him again, if she could approach him as the woman she was or the girl she had been. Now she looked at him, her lips forming a word she never spoke, and her eyes blind with unshed tears.

Hampton put an arm around her and cut loose her left wrist. It fell limply at her side, and she slumped against him. Behind him, he heard Tyler and Satterwhite slide down the gravel slope on foot. He shifted the knife to his left hand and cut the other rope with one clean, downward slice. Mary dropped into his arms. He could feel her stomach quivering as she cried into his shirt.

"Little Mary," he said in a deep, husky voice, and that was how she went to him.

He bent and picked her up. When he turned, he saw that Tyler had caught Lady and was leading her forward. Satterwhite stood staring, his mouth open, his pistol in his hand.

"Is that Mary?" he asked. Hampton looked at him and pushed by him, heading out of the draw. "Is she all right?"

Hampton stepped up through the loose gravel as if it had been steps in a staircase. Mary's left arm dangled in front of them, the cut end of rope brushing the top of Hampton's boot as he moved.

Tyler walked up to Satterwhite. "Come on, Satterwhite," he said. "Hamp's goin' to need some help."

"What's going on?" Satterwhite asked. "How come they just left her? Where are they?"

"They're gone," Tyler said and spit. "Come on."

When they came out of the draw, Hampton was kneeling by the smoking fire circle, holding Mary in his arms. He looked down at the beautiful face he remembered and saw it clearly through the bruises and swelling and dirt.

"Here," Tyler said to Satterwhite, "take the horses and tie them up. We'll need the medical kit and some blankets."

Tyler knelt in front of Hampton and looked at Mary. When he saw her face, he glanced up at Hampton, and the two exchanged hard looks. "Is she conscious?" he asked.

"I think she can hear us," Hampton said. "Get those goddamned ropes off her wrists."

Tyler pulled at the knot on her left wrist. It was wet with blood.

He untied it and threw it on the smoking coals. He did the same with the other. Mary moaned, but did not open her eyes when they moved her arms.

Hampton looked at Satterwhite. "Bring those blankets over here. Make a bed there where the rocks have been cleared, then build up this fire and get some water cookin'."

Satterwhite spread three blankets folded in half on the ground. Hampton moved and laid Mary out on them. He straightened her legs and pulled her blouse and coat together across her sunburned chest.

"Get her other hand, Bud. We got to get the circulation goin'."

While Satterwhite built up the fire with dried century plant stalks and anything else that would burn, Hampton and Tyler worked the long, slender fingers between their rough hands. Mary's face was in the sun, and Hampton moved so that his shadow fell across her. She moaned and sobbed quietly. Tears ran out of the corners of her eyes.

Hampton concentrated on what he was doing. His face had taken on a hard, flinty set from the moment he had first seen Mary. As he worked the small hand in his, he noted the cuts on her wrist. They were not deep, but the skin had been worn off, especially on the soft underside.

Satterwhite filled the Dutch oven with water and set it on the fire. He took his first look at Mary. "Goddamn those bastards," he said quietly.

"Get the medical kit and some rags and towels," Hampton said over his shoulder. "We'll talk about bastards later."

Mary abruptly pulled her hand out of Tyler's fingers. She folded her arm across her chest like a wing.

Tyler looked up. "Should I be insulted or glad?"

"Glad," Hampton said. "Be sure Satterwhite gets me some soap."

"You want us to rig a lean-to?"

"Let me clean her up first."

Satterwhite and Tyler got the things Hampton asked for and set them beside him.

"Will she be all right?" Satterwhite asked.

"We'll see. Better scout the area, Bud. We may have to stay the night here."

"Don't worry about it. Come on, Satterwhite."

"And bring me Satterwhite's canteen and another blanket," Hampton added.

He took the blanket from Satterwhite and spread it over Mary, then went to work on her. He took off her coat, lifting her gently to do so. He did the same thing with her torn blouse and sateen waist. He put them in a pile on the sand beside him and covered her again with the blanket. He removed her shoes, hose, skirt and drawers the same way, gently, then covered her again with the blanket. When he saw the doll and the abrasions it had made on her lower stomach, he swore and threw it on the fire. The doll didn't burn at first, then it did.

Mary stirred. She put an arm across the blanket to hold it to her.

Hampton looked at her. "Mary," he said, "can you hear me?"

She nodded slightly and brushed hair away from her face with the back of her hand but did not open her eyes.

Hampton unscrewed the cap of the canteen and slid an arm under her back. "Take a drink, Mary."

She drank a little, then turned her head away. He let her down again. "Do you know who I am, Mary?"

Mary nodded again.

"Say it, Mary. Say my name."

Mary moaned, then said, "Hamp," in a cracked, hoarse whisper.

Hampton looked down at the face turned up to his. She had smeared blood on her forehead with her wrist.

"Mary, I'm goin' to bathe you now. Would you rather do it yourself?"

Mary was still, then shook her head. Her dirty forehead knit with pain.

Hampton pulled the Dutch oven off the fire and dipped the towel in the warm water. He rubbed soap on it and began to bathe her. As he did so, he did not think of her as a woman. She was still the child to him. He scrubbed her cuts and abrasions, then dried that part and covered it with the blanket again. At times she struggled and closed herself up with pain, but Hampton spoke to her soothingly and went on. The knees of his pants got wet.

Her chest was badly sunburned, her breasts tender and swollen. He cleaned her carefully, then had her roll over on her side so he could wash her back.

Her face and hair were last. He soaked the towel, wrung it out, and laid it across her cheekbones. She moaned. He lifted the towel, turned it over, and laid it across her eyes. The water stung in the cuts. She tried to snatch the towel away, but Hampton did not let her.

"Don't fight me, Little Mary," he said.

As her face came clean, Hampton could see again how beautiful she was. He put the Dutch oven behind her head and lifted her with one hand so that he could wet her hair. Her neck was stiff, and she winced when he lifted her. He wet her hair and soaped it but had trouble rinsing it. At least it would smell better. He wrapped her hair in a towel and let her down. When the sun hit her face, she squeezed her eyes shut.

"Are you cold?" he asked.

"No," she said in a cracked voice. Then she said, "A little."

"I'm going to doctor you now," Hampton said. "It'll burn."

Mary did not respond. Hampton took a brown bottle of boric acid and some cotton swabs out of the medical kit. Starting with her wrists, he cleaned the abrasions and cuts with the boric acid. She tried to jerk away when Hampton touched her with the cotton. He was patient and careful, oblivious to everything around him but Mary. Finally, he put a rough hand on her forehead to hold her steady, and he swabbed the cuts on her face.

Mary cried out and twisted her face away.

Satterwhite and Tyler looked up from where they stood by the packs, smoking, and watched Hampton. Hampton waited, then started to work again. Satterwhite and Tyler exchanged glances and went back to smoking.

"I'm going to have to use iodine now, Mary," Hampton said softly.

"Why not just shoot me?" Mary cried. She still had not opened her eyes.

"I'll think on it," Hampton said.

When he was through with the iodine, he tossed the swab into the fire and let Mary cry for a few minutes. He wrapped her wrists with bandages and laid them across her.

"You are going to be all right, Mary," Hampton said, quietly. "There's just one more thing. I need to know if you are hurt on the inside. Any ribs or bones or other hurts. Mary?"

The tears that squeezed out of her eyes were not accompanied by sobs. She sniffed and took a deep breath, sliding her hands down her sides and across the smooth, flat plain of her stomach. She shook her head, then said, "My heart is dead."

Hampton took off his glasses and rubbed his hand over his face. He put his glasses back on and put the medical kit back together.

"I don't have anything here for that," he said.

He looked at her, her eyes still closed, her face discolored by bruises and iodine. He put a rough hand on hers. The skin was warm but dry.

Mary slipped her thumb out from under his hand and pressed it across his knuckles. Someone had come for her, and it was Hamp. She didn't know who else was with him, whether her father was there or not, but it didn't matter. Hamp had come for her, and she was alive.

"Little Mary," she heard him say, and something like a smile played briefly on her lips. "You rest now."

Hampton slipped his hand out from hers and stood up. His legs were stiff. He walked over to Tyler and Satterwhite. "Anybody think to roll me one of those?" he said.

"Matter of fact," Satterwhite said and handed Hampton a rolled cigarette.

Hampton took it and lit it.

"I really want to thank you for what you have done for my cousin," Satterwhite began.

"Goddammit, Satterwhite," Hampton interrupted him, "why do you always have to follow a good thing with a stupid one?"

"What?"

"Don't ever try to thank me for helpin' Mary again. I'm not doin' it for you. Go rig her some shade so she can rest."

Satterwhite picked up another blanket and walked away.

"How is she?" Tyler asked quietly.

Hampton drew deep, then blew out smoke. It made him a little dizzy, but he wanted that. "She'll be all right," he said. "Physically. She's been brutalized, though. That'll take longer to get over than the bruises."

Tyler nodded.

"How does this place look for tonight?"

"We're in a bowl, so we can't be seen from the desert. Someone high up could spot us, but it's a long way to those hills. The bandits went out of here south still. There's a shallow grave beyond that dead horse."

"We may have to rig somethin' for tomorrow then, or I can carry her. I don't feature campin' by no dead horse."

"If we head for the hills to the east, we could probably find a canyon to hide in," Tyler suggested.

"That's not a bad idea. Mary's not fit to ride for the border now, and the higher ground would make it easy to keep track of movement. We're practically at the Potrillos now."

Tyler nodded. Then he said, "It sure feels good to have that girl."

Hampton had stood with his back to her while he talked, but then he turned and looked at her. Satterwhite was walking back toward them.

"I feel like killin' somebody," Satterwhite said.

"You ever done it?" Hampton asked.

"No, but. . . ."

"Then don't talk about it. Our obligation now is to get the hell out of here as soon as Mary can ride."

They looked at her small figure on the ground by the fire. She was on her side, facing away from them, her knees drawn up, and the line of her hip distinct under the blanket.

"You got some extra clothes, Satterwhite?"

"Yeah. Why?"

"Mary'll need 'em. You're closest to her size. What about a union suit?"

"Sure, but. . . ."

"She'll need that too. I'm burnin' the rest of her stuff while she sleeps. Get them clothes. Let's get something to eat."

Mary slept until the sun started down and the air began to cool. While Satterwhite and Tyler laid out the food and utensils for their first cooked meal in two days, Hampton dressed Mary. She helped him, but she was like a person hypnotized. She obeyed his orders but did not open her eyes. When she was dressed, Hampton rolled the blanket Satterwhite had used for shade and put it under her head for a pillow.

"Feel better?" he asked quietly.

She didn't answer. He looked at her carefully. Chances were that she was suffering from exhaustion, dehydration and trauma, as much as the superficial bruises. It was hard to judge her color in the waning light of day, but her skin felt dry, and her breathing seemed shallow.

"Get me some water, Bud. Put it in a cup with a pinch of sugar and a little salt. Not too much."

In a moment, Tyler handed him the cup. The water was still warm from the sun of the day. Hampton lifted Mary's shoulders.

"Mary, I want you to drink this. Drink this."

When he put the cup to her lips, she opened her mouth and drank. She shook her head after three swallows.

"Drink it all, Mary," Hampton said. "You got to drink it all."

Mary drank, coughed several times, and wanted to lie back down. Hampton eased her back and pulled the blanket up to her throat.

"Too bad we didn't bring any whiskey," Hampton said. "She could use a shot, if anybody could."

"Your pa did his preachin' too good," Tyler said.

"Uh-huh," Hampton looked at him. "I see your war bag full of whiskey, too."

"Think she'll eat anything?" Satterwhite asked.

"I'll make her," Hampton said.

"You treat her like she's a baby," Satterwhite said.

Tyler nodded. "That's the worst part of bein' laid up."

They were all tired, but the excitement of finding Mary and the tension of her care gave them an appetite. Satterwhite built a stew in the cleaned Dutch oven as darkness took the desert sky. Hampton heated another can of chicken soup, put more salt in it, and held Mary up while Tyler fed it to her. She responded well physically, but she didn't talk or open her eyes.

Over coffee, Hampton said, "Well, she's asleep now and breathin' easy. Guess we can count our blessin's."

"Imagine just finding her like that," Satterwhite said. "I'd have thought they would have killed her."

"You think they spared her because we came along and found her? They didn't know about us. They thought they was killin' her, the hard way."

"Yeah. I guess so. Those bastards," Satterwhite said, still trying to understand it.

They were quiet a while, sipping their coffee. The small fire crackled and sent wavering shadows across the ground. A night bird cried over the desert and was silent.

"What do you think the bandits did?" Satterwhite asked.

"Anybody's guess," Hampton said. "The closest targets for another raid would be El Indio to the south or the Mexican Northwestern Railroad. They were headin' the right way for either one."

"How come you know so much about what they might do?" Satterwhite looked at him.

"I cut my teeth on bandit tactics, Satterwhite. But those are only guesses. They might be sittin' around right now thinking about comin' back for Mary."

"I wish they'd try."

"No, you don't. They'd have us easy, like fish in a barrel."

"Speakin' of which," Tyler said, "I think I'll take the glasses and have a look around."

"Good idea. Wouldn't hurt to go ahead and let the fire die, either."

They finished their coffee and stood up. Tyler got the field glasses and walked away into the dark, his boots soundless, even on the gravel.

"Rinse that stuff out with river water, then try to get some sleep,

Satterwhite. I'm goin' to keep watch over Mary for a while. May need you later."

"Let me know."

"I will."

Hampton walked quietly over to Mary and crouched down beside her. His muscles were tired from the draining tension. The night was cold and still. He took off one of his work gloves, tucking it behind his suspender strap, and put his hand softly on her forehead. It was cool, and the skin was soft. He brushed his hand up over her hair, dry now and full. Her breathing was even and deep.

A little while later, Tyler walked back to the dwindling fire. He bent over it, warming his hands. Hampton got up and joined him, taking Mary's torn and stained clothes with him. He dropped her blouse and stockings on the fire. They smoked, then caught, making the camp lighter.

"She all right?" Tyler asked. He reached for the coffeepot and shook it. There was about enough for one more cup, not counting the grounds.

"Sleepin' easy."

"You done more doctorin' than shootin' on this trip."

"I'm no doctor. How does the desert look?"

Tyler poured his cup. Hampton watched the texture of the material change as it burned. He put her waist and drawers on the fire.

"Looks like desert," Tyler said, watching the undergarments catch the flame. "There was a ghost of a light to the south. Thought I saw it but couldn't find it in the glasses. Didn't see it again."

"Movin'?"

"Couldn't tell. Don't think so."

They were quiet a while. Tyler drank the coffee carefully. Hampton put Mary's skirt on the fire. It made a lot of smoke before it caught.

"Sorry about Mary," Tyler said. "If there was ever good reason for killin' a man, that would be it."

Hampton nodded, but didn't speak. He was watching the skirt burn.

Tyler threw the grounds on the sand and stood up. "I'll be right over there," he said.

"I know," Hampton said.

Hampton picked up a short stick and stirred the ashes of Mary's clothes with it. The breeze blew them red and added yellow, wavering flame to them. He looked past the fire and watched Tyler shake out his blankets. Everything about the camp and the people and the night took on a sudden brilliant clarity, the clarity that danger or battle had always given him. For a moment, he wished he were alone in the desert with just his horse and his guns. But he wasn't, and the moment passed. When the ashes were unrecognizable as clothes, he threw the stick on the fire and stood up.

He carried his saddle over and set it down easily a few feet from Mary's head. He looked at her again, then sat down and leaned back against the saddle. The lining of his coat felt cold against his back at first, then warmed. He stretched his legs out and crossed his arms over his stomach.

An hour went by. Hampton was lost in thought, almost asleep, when Mary gave a sudden jerk and cried out. Hampton rolled over on his knees and put a hand on her shoulder.

"You're all right," he said quietly, rubbing her shoulder gently. "Hush now."

Mary opened her eyes for the first time since he had found her. He saw the pale light of the stars reflecting in them.

"Hello, Mary," he said and smiled.

She started to cry.

"Now don't start that," Hampton said. "This is the desert. You need them tears."

"I'm cold," she said.

Hampton pulled his saddle closer and lifted Mary's shoulders into his lap. He tucked the blankets around her chin. She was shivering but felt warm against him.

Mary nestled her head against his chest and sniffed. "You came, Hamp. How did you know?"

"We found a book with your name in it. Some kind of book about monkeys and a man named Tarzan. A trooper in the camp said he had seen you get off the train."

"It was so awful, Hamp."

"Don't talk about it now, Mary. Keep it a secret a little bit longer. I know it was bad."

"Do Mother and Father know?"

"Yeah. I told them I would bring you back."

"Who else is here?"

"Friend of mine and your cousin, Rueben."

"Rueben's here?"

Hampton smiled. "I know it's kind of hard to believe."

"I can't stop being scared, Hamp."

"You were never scared."

"I'm scared now."

"Even with me here?"

Mary turned her face against his coat and cried. She sniffed. Hampton held her and rubbed her shoulder lightly, smoothing the blanket across it, gripping her to let her know he had her, then smoothing the blanket again.

"Talk to me, Hamp," she said in a muffled, crying voice. "Tell me things."

"Well, first of all," he said slowly, "it's like steppin' back in time to see you."

"I was gone a long time," Mary said, raising her face against his chest and looking out across the dark desert. "Tell me about the ranch."

He started telling her things about the ranch that she would know about and what had changed. He told her about Bud Tyler, and the preacher, and things they did and the way they talked. He told her about the widow woman in town who had set fire to her house because she kept seeing lights in it at night and figured it was haunted. He told her about a dog that Mr. Frank had that wouldn't bark at anything except buzzards. He told her about a snow they had had two years before and how Billy Dunbar built a snowman in front of the barn with it.

Her shivering stopped, and her breathing was easy, no longer punctuated by sobs. Hampton was quiet for several minutes, thinking she was asleep. The temperature was still dropping, but Hampton, holding Mary against him, ignored the cold.

"I went to the town in Tennessee where you told me you were born," Mary said abruptly, remembering her homesickness for him the first year she lived in Tennessee.

"Did you?"

"Yes. I didn't know where your house had been. It was a beautiful little town."

"Seems like it was, but that was a long time ago, and I was pretty young when we left it."

"I don't think until right now," Mary said slowly and sniffed, "I ever realized how much I missed you."

"Me?"

"Yes. Remember our talks?"

"I remember doin' a lot of listenin'."

"Sometimes, on Sunday evenings, you would come into the house, and we would have coffee and cookies that Betty had baked. I would play the piano. Remember?"

"Yeah."

She rubbed her hair gently against his coat. "I would talk you into sitting by me on the piano bench, and we would sing hymns."

"I could never sing," Hampton said.

"But you did," Mary said. "My favorite was 'Sweet By and By.' Sing that for me, Hamp."

"You're embarrassin' me."

"You don't have to."

Hampton hesitated, then began singing the hymn in his deep, rough voice. He sang it slowly, quietly, all three verses. When he was through, he gripped Mary's shoulder. "You need your sleep, Little Mary," he said, but he started on the first verse again. Mary picked out a low peak on the eastern horizon and stared at it until her eyes watered. Hampton looked beyond her at the horses while he sang the hymn. The sprinkle of stars overhead reflected in his glasses.

"You hear that?" Satterwhite whispered to Tyler. "Sounds like two voices singing."

"Must be an echo from the draw," Tyler said.

As he sang the words, Hampton remembered hard benches and his father's voice stirring hot East Texas air, a lantern hanging from a limb behind his head throwing yellow light on his open but seldom-looked-at Bible. He remembered sitting in the back of the church in Columbus, alone at one end of a pew, listening to Mary and the other children sing when she was fourteen.

Mary's chin dropped, and she went back into a troubled sleep.

From their bedrolls, Tyler and Satterwhite listened to the refrain of 'Sweet By and By' until the voice singing it faded away in the cold empty night.

TWENTY-THREE

T HE very first light of the new day was in the cloudless sky. Mary's left eye was swollen shut, but with her right, she saw some distant gray mountains to the southwest. She had a confused sense of place at first, then remembered where she was.

She lifted her head and looked at Hampton, the worn tan of his coat, partly covered by two blankets someone had put over him in the night, the darker corduroy of his collar, the wings turned up against the cold, and his face in sleep, the graying beard, the gold-rimmed glasses slipping a little on his nose, and his hat firmly on his head. She could hear someone breaking sticks behind her, but she did not turn her eyes from Hampton. An image of Salazar came into her mind abruptly, and she felt sick to her stomach. She wanted Hampton to open his eyes and look at her.

"Hamp," she called softly.

She felt a hand on her shoulder and turned her head to see the brown eyes and worn features of Bud Tyler. She saw a shadow cross his face when he looked back at her, reacting to the bruises and the swelling.

"Don't wake him up," Tyler whispered. "Not just yet. He had a long night."

Mary blinked at Tyler without changing her expression.

"How do you feel this mornin'?"

"You're Mr. Tyler."

"Bud, ma'am. I'm one of those men who never feel comfortable with the mister."

Satterwhite stepped up behind Tyler and looked over his shoulder at Mary. "I'm Rueben," he said. "Do you remember me?"

"Yes." Mary said, blinking up at him. "You've become a man."

"Not yet," Hampton said, throwing off his blankets.

Satterwhite gave Hampton a hurt look and stomped back to the fire where he and Tyler had started breakfast.

Mary turned her head and looked at Hampton.

"Whose blankets did I end up with?" Hampton asked.

"Me and Satterwhite both donated one after you went to sleep," Tyler said.

"Uh-huh."

Hampton took off his glasses and a glove and rubbed his face with his bare hand. He put his glasses back on and leaned toward Mary. Without speaking to her, he felt of her forehead. There was no fever. Then he reached under the blankets and caught her forearms. He looked at her wrists, checking for bleeding.

"Hamp here is studyin' on becomin' a doctor," Tyler said. "Up until now all he's had to practice on is lizards."

Mary did not smile but looked back at Hampton. Her sense of security changed to one of vague guilt, as if she had done something Hampton did not approve of but would say nothing about.

"Did you comb your hair this mornin', Bud?"

Tyler ducked his head. "Satterwhite's idea," he said.

"Uh-huh."

Hampton stood up with Mary watching him and stepped around to the fire. Tyler looked away, then nodded and followed Hampton. Satterwhite did not look up at them.

"What do you think?" Tyler asked, watching Hampton fill a cup of coffee.

"I think we need one more goddam cup lyin' around fillin' up with sand."

Satterwhite glanced up at the tone in Hampton's voice. From her blankets, Mary looked at Hampton's back.

"There's somethin' I'd like to show you," Tyler said. "I'd like you to look at the rear leg of that young packhorse."

"If it's lame, shoot the son of a bitch," Hampton growled.

"I want you to look at it," Tyler said again and walked toward the horses.

Hampton looked up at the horses, then fell in behind Tyler as he stepped quickly away from the fire. When they were on the other side of the horses, Tyler stopped and looked at Hampton.

"You have a mighty rough edge this mornin'," Tyler said.

"What's wrong with the horse?"

"There's nothin' wrong with the horse. I just wanted you away from them two children so I could find out what's bitin' you."

Hampton drank from his coffee cup and looked away across the desert. A low bank of clouds rode the western horizon like an army. He sneezed and shook his head.

"I woke up from a nightmare. There was killin' in it and dyin'. I saw bandits without faces hangin' a man, a young cowboy. I felt like it might have been Satterwhite. Guess I woke up wantin' to fight back."

Tyler looked at the horse beside him and put his hand on its rump. The horse moved away a step.

"I'm just an old soldier," Hampton went on. "I don't know nothin' about doctorin' and makin' people feel better. War is the only thing I ever been good at." He shook his head and looked at his friend.

"I know better than that," Tyler said. "You ain't done nothin' *but* the last few days. Fact is, you been carryin' all of us up to now. I don't blame you for buckin' a little bit."

Hampton looked down. "Hate the way it feels. Man ought to be able to do it, or, or just get away from it. I'm sorry, Bud. It won't happen again."

"Don't worry about me, Hamp. I know the difference. It's them other two need a little reassurance."

"I ain't got any of that. We're a long way from home with a hurt girl. The men who beat her up have a happy memory, but all she's got is hurt, and all I got is a hate inside me so thick I can barely swallow. Damn. I can't shake last night."

Tyler was silent.

Hampton looked up at him. "Let's get breakfast over and see about gettin' out of this desert. I'm all right."

When they walked back up to the fire, Mary was out of her blankets.

"She said she had to see a man about a horse," Satterwhite said. "You teach her that?"

Hampton started to answer, then said, "That's a good sign. Breakfast smells good, Satterwhite. You ever think about goin' into cookin' full time?"

"Not hardly," Satterwhite said tentatively, watching Hampton's face.

The bacon was on a metal plate, and Satterwhite was cooking biscuits. When they were ready, he would make gravy. Hampton and Tyler squatted by the fire, waiting. When the biscuits were ready, and Mary had still not come back, Hampton put down his cup and went to look for her.

He found her standing in the desert a hundred yards the other side of the camp. She was looking toward the hazy blue outline of the Potrillos, a blanket wrapped around her, and her loose hair rolling across her shoulders in the slight breeze.

"Mary?" he said.

Mary raised her chin but did not turn her head.

"I'm sorry if I'm trouble," she said in a cracked voice. "I didn't ask for any of this, and if I did, I wish to high heaven I had not. Everybody would have been better off if you hadn't found me. By this time, surely, I would have been beyond caring. In fact I am now. So you don't have to do anything else for me. You've done too much already. Just forget about me and go on your way."

Hampton took a deep breath and put his hands in his coat pockets. He looked toward the rising sun, then said, "I earned that. How are you doin' this mornin'?"

"Why should you care?"

"Well, I do. I want to know."

He could see, as he stepped closer to her, that she was breathing fast, swallowing her breaths. She turned her head and looked at him through her hair.

"I can't live with this, Hamp," she said. "I don't know how."

Hampton was beside her now. He felt like saying her name, so he did. Then he said, "There's a lot of people would be sorry to hear you say that."

"I don't care about them."

"I'm one of them."

"I told you my heart was dead."

She shook back her hair, and Hampton looked away from her bruised face. Pieces of a small skeleton were under the edge of a creosote bush nearby. He looked at them, then looked up at the sky. A single bird flew high overhead, an eagle perhaps.

"Are you cryin'?"

"Yes."

"Don't that hurt?"

"Yes, it hurts," Mary said in an ugly voice. Then, softer, she said, "You're talking ungrammatically."

"I could shut up."

"No, don't. Don't ever."

Hampton stepped closer to her and passed her his red bandana. She held it in her hands without using it, then she gave it back to him.

"Wipe your face," he said.

"You do it."

Hampton looked at her. He refolded the bandana until it was smooth, then touched her face with it. Her gray eyes watched his.

"Yesterday, it was like I had never been away," Mary said. "Today I feel like I never saw you before in my life."

"Bad as that?" Hampton said.

Mary studied his face. She saw what she was looking for. "No," she said. "Not any more. Oh, Hamp, make me care again."

He looked at her, then looked down at his bandana. He put the bandana in her hands. "You keep it," he said. Then he asked, "How do those clothes fit?"

Mary dropped her eyes to the bandana in her hands. She turned it over and over, refolding it. "Can I borrow a pair of your suspenders?"

"Sure. Can you ride a little today?"

"Are you taking me home?"

"Depends on you."

"I don't think so. I feel sick."

"Let's go back. Get you some breakfast, and then we'll look for a better place to hide while you mend." Hampton stepped back as if he were in front of a door and had moved aside to let her walk through it. As they picked their way around clumps of cactus, Hampton looked sideways at Mary's profile. There were reddish tints in her hair.

"I'm sorry about the way I made you feel when I got up. Sometimes I wake up mean."

Mary nodded but did not say anything.

They ate breakfast. Talk was strained, both Satterwhite and Tyler glancing at Mary out of the corners of their eyes while she ate. They had been a threesome so continuously that it was difficult to adapt their rhythm to a fourth. The sun warmed the camp, but the breeze was still cold.

"Eat as much as you want, Mary," Hampton said. "Satterwhite can always cook more."

"Thank you," she said.

The men looked at each other.

They were loaded and ready to go when Tyler came back into camp with the field glasses in his hand.

"I can't understand why nothin's movin'," he said.

"There's not much tellin' what's happenin' in the rest of the world," Hampton said. "I would just as soon nothin' moved but us until we were out of Mexico."

Hampton stepped up to Mary. She had put on a pair of his wide suspenders and was wearing the red bandana in her dark hair.

"How do you want to do this?" he asked.

"Can you carry me?" she looked at him.

"Wouldn't be the first time."

Hampton mounted. Tyler helped Mary up beside him. She gasped when she was on the saddle.

"The stiffness will pass," Hampton said. "We'll go slow."

They followed the edge of the draw toward the mountains to the east. As they rode, Hampton glanced to the north, thinking how near the border was, but each step Lady took seemed to bring a response of pain from Mary. He couldn't make up his mind to put her through that long a ride even though his better judgment told him that they needed to get back across the border. On the other hand, if they were careful, there was no reason anyone should notice them or pay attention to them.

After two hours, they stopped, and Tyler helped Mary down. She could not stand up at first, and Tyler held her until Hampton was down.

"Easy now," Hampton said and helped her sit.

Her face was sunburned and swollen. The sun was hurting the bruises. Hampton took off his hat and put it lightly on the top of her head.

"I'm goin' ahead to scout the foothills," Tyler said. "You ever been in these hills?"

"Been by 'em is all."

"I'll find a good place."

"Be careful."

After Tyler rode away, Hampton called Satterwhite. "Listen," he told him, "you keep your eyes peeled for dust. I don't like sittin' out here in plain sight."

Satterwhite stood watch while Hampton crouched beside Mary, covering her with his shadow.

"How are you makin' it?" he asked.

"I hurt."

"I know. We'll make camp soon."

Hampton looked at her. In profile, the right side of her face looked well, but he knew the soreness she was feeling in her arms, back, and head.

"You think we should ride for the border, don't you?" she asked.

"We'll be all right in the hills for a while."

Mary put her hand on the warm rocks beside her and leaned on her arm. The sore muscles would not support her, and she sat up again. When she thought about the ranch, she felt sick to her stomach, but she was not sure why. She wanted to avoid going home as long as she could. There was something in the back of her mind that was keeping her from wanting ever to see Columbus again.

The sun was high in the southern sky when Satterwhite saw Tyler riding through the cactus and yucca toward them.

"Here he comes," Satterwhite said.

Hampton stood up and waited.

"Found it," Tyler said. "There's a narrow canyon to the south. I didn't follow it all the way back, but it has steep sides. May have water too. The floor is hard rock the farther back you go."

"Sounds good," Hampton said. "Mary?"

"All right."

When Mary was in the saddle again, she leaned back against Hampton, the soft brim of her hat bending up against his chest. She could smell smoke and tobacco in his shirt and the other smell that cotton takes on when it is worn in the sun. She watched Tyler move easily across the ground ahead of them, then turned and watched Satterwhite moving abreast of them twenty yards away, looking back over his shoulder at the packhorses the way a child looks back at the wagon he is pulling.

A haze drifted over the sun. Mary faded into her thoughts. She felt scared, but she wasn't sure what she was scared of. Each time she thought of Salazar, she pushed his image immediately from her mind, but there was another face she could not shake. It was Leonard's face. She did not think of him with regret or emotion, but with fear, and that was what she could not understand. His memory filled her with anxiety and dread. She leaned back against Hampton, but the feeling would not go away.

TWENTY-FOUR

THEY made camp half a mile into the canyon, which had high, crumbling rock walls sometimes further broken by dry pour-offs that ended abruptly a hundred feet above the canyon's floor. Erosion caves, some deep, were in the walls of the canyon, most reachable only from the top. The canyon had a quiet, graveyard feel to it that both Hampton and Tyler were aware of immediately, but it would be a good place to hide and rest, especially if there were water farther back.

They unloaded the horses while Mary watched from the sandy shade of an overhang. Then they joined her there, Tyler and Satterwhite stretching out on their backs or sides. Hampton sat with his back to the canyon wall, his legs out straight on the sand and gravel.

"You know, Mary, you're a funny picture sittin' there with an old man's campaign hat on, a lady's coat, and Satterwhite's striped pants."

Mary looked at him. "It must be the hat," she said.

"I think it's the shoes," Tyler said. "You didn't mention them slippers."

"What's wrong with my pants?" Satterwhite asked.

"Nothin', when Mary wears 'em," Hampton said.

"What about my shoes?" Mary asked Tyler, speaking to him for the first time since she asked his name that morning.

Tyler blushed and ducked his head. "Maybe they should be boots," he said weakly.

228

"Mary used to have a pair of boots with a big star on them," Hampton said. "Didn't you, Mary?"

Mary looked at Hampton. The desert silence of the canyon was almost palpable.

"They were your Texas boots. It was Texas Mary when you wore those boots."

Mary held Hampton's eyes.

"I had some of those too," Satterwhite said. "Pa ordered them from Dallas."

Tyler looked at Satterwhite and smiled.

"Texas Rueben," Hampton said. "Yeah. I can picture that."

"How are your mother and father?" Mary asked him.

"Fine, I guess," Satterwhite said. "I don't get time to write much."

"He means he don't know how," Hampton said.

"What made you want to be a New Mexico rancher?" Mary asked him.

"I don't know," Satterwhite said. "I didn't want to work in the store all my life. I like being out in the open, riding around, seeing things. Besides, me and Pa weren't getting along too well. I got tired of him always telling me what to do."

Satterwhite looked over at Hampton. Hampton looked back at him, then sniffed.

Mary took off Hampton's hat, looked at it, and set it on the sand beside her. She took off her coat and put it on the sand and lay back with her head on it. The suspenders widened around her breasts and bunched the tops of Satterwhite's pants at her waist. Hampton looked at her, then looked away. Tyler and Satterwhite did the same.

No one said anything. In ten minutes, they were asleep.

Hampton and Tyler woke up at the same time. They had stopped taking turns keeping watch while the others slept since there was no sign of pursuit or other movement in the desert, but neither slept well unless someone else was awake.

The shadows in the canyon had deepened. Above them the wind blew. The canyon was strangely empty of birds. Hampton stood up with a stifled groan as his muscles stretched. He stepped quietly around Mary and Satterwhite, and Tyler joined him at the horses. They rolled a cigarette without talking.

Hampton lit his and said, "I'd like this a lot better if it was New Mexico."

"She looks a sight," Tyler said, glancing at Mary's sleeping figure. "You never said she was such a pretty gal."

"Never thought about it, I guess. Every time I look at her, I see a little girl."

"That ain't no little girl," Tyler said. He lit his cigarette and shook out the match.

"This is a good place, Bud," Hampton said. "We need to see how far back this runs. If we're lucky, it's a box canyon with a pour-off at the end. It would mean the chance of water."

"I'll take Satterwhite's canteen and my rifle and go find out," Tyler said.

"Feel like it?"

"Sure. I might find me a pot of gold back there."

"Or a bear."

"Thought of that."

Satterwhite sat up. The sun was in his face. "Take Buster with you. Make him carry one of the empty water bags just in case."

"He's not a bad kid," Tyler said, watching him wake up.

"Uh-huh. Just born too late to know what it means to be a man."

"He might get the chance to find out."

"Yeah," Hampton said, "that's what I'm afraid of."

Tyler and Satterwhite walked off up the canyon in the ribbon of sunlight that lay on the rocky bed. Hampton took one of the water bags and set it in the shade. He sat down and watched Mary until she woke up.

She sat up abruptly, looked around, then put her face gingerly in her hands.

"Hurt?" Hampton said.

"Yes."

"Got some headache powders." Hampton got to his feet and dug through one of the packs until he found the medical kit. He gave Mary two papers and the fresh water bag, then sat down on the sand again.

"I feel terrible," Mary said.

"Hungry?"

"No."

Mary stretched her back, feeling the soreness in her neck and along her spine. She looked at Hampton who sat against the canyon wall, sifting his fingers through the gravel beside him. He looked older sitting down.

"Mind if I join you?" Mary asked.

"Go ahead."

She moved over beside him and took a deep breath. The breeze blew the loose ends of her hair.

"Where are the others?" she asked.

"Scoutin' the canyon. Deep as this thing is and the way it twists, there could be a whole army around the next bend and we'd never know it."

"You would know it," Mary said.

"Probably."

Mary rubbed her neck, her fingers disappearing in her hair.

"I've been curious about something, Little Mary," Hampton said. "What made you decide to come home this time of year? It's too late for Christmas and too early for Easter."

Mary folded her hands in her lap and looked at the stained bandages on her wrists.

"I was homesick," she said quietly.

"Uh-huh."

She looked at him. "I was," she said.

"I believe you."

Mary pushed away from the rough rock wall behind her and stretched her back painfully. She looked at Hampton and slid over against him.

"That's much better," she said.

"One of the benefits of old age," Hampton said. "It makes a man comfortable. I guess that's so he can hold his grandkids in his lap."

Mary was quiet. Hampton could see her hair without seeing her face. He looked over at the horses. Lady had one of her hind legs cocked, resting.

"Hamp," Mary said, "do you remember the time you killed that rattlesnake in the barn?"

"Yeah."

"It should have been killed, shouldn't it?"

"Bad idea to let one live. They have a way of showin' up on you again."

Mary was quiet. One of the packhorses put his head over the mane of the other one. The other one shook it off.

"I was coming home to stay," Mary said. "I was leaving Leonard."

Saying his name made Mary feel tight in her chest. She shifted her back against Hampton. He looked at her hair.

"That so?"

"Yes. Does that disappoint you?"

"It doesn't surprise me. You been gone five years and don't have any kids."

"He didn't want children."

"Some men don't," Hampton said. "Do I need to go to Tennessee and shoot him?"

"No. It was my decision."

"Probably needs shootin' anyway, a man that would let you get away. I never liked his looks."

"Why didn't you say something?"

Hampton looked at her hair. "Wasn't any of my business."

"You didn't care, you mean," Mary said sharply, like she was saying a line from a play.

Hampton looked across the canyon. "There's some things you just have to find out for yourself," he said.

"You could have stopped me."

"Wasn't my place."

Mary turned her face to his. Her bruised eye squinted at him. "I wish you had," she said. "Maybe I wouldn't feel like I do now." Tears formed in her eyes, and she turned her face into his shoulder.

Hampton put an arm around her and rubbed her shoulder. "Maybe I should have," he said.

"I can't go back," Mary cried. "I don't belong anywhere anymore. Please don't make me go back."

232

Hampton rubbed her shoulder and put his chin on her hair above the red bandana.

"I'm sorry," Mary cried.

"Now, now," Hampton said, "you don't have anything to be sorry about."

"I feel ugly and dirty and wrong," Mary cried.

Hate grew in Hampton's chest, but he held her lightly. "I won't listen to that kind of talk," he said.

"It's true," Mary cried.

"No it isn't."

"They were so cruel."

Something was changing inside of Hampton, born out of the agony of the girl and his hatred for the men who had brutalized her. He never had much in his life, but he had been taught honor by his father and kindness by his mother, and they were the things he lived by. He could not conceive of a man who could hurt someone like the girl he held.

When Satterwhite and Tyler returned, Mary was still, perhaps asleep again. Satterwhite held up the water bag. Hampton could see that it was full.

"Good news," Tyler said quietly. "This is a box canyon, and there are a couple of good *tinajas* back there, deep ones, with good water."

"Bath time," Satterwhite said. "Is Mary all right?"

"Would you be?" Hampton said.

Tyler looked at Mary, her face against Hampton's shoulder. Satterwhite lowered the bag to the ground and looked at her too.

"Well, what are we going to do about it?" Satterwhite asked.

"Get her out of here as soon as possible," Hampton said quietly and evenly.

"And just let that son of a bitch run wild to do it again?"

"What do you want to do? You want to ride after him and get killed? You think that would make her feel better?"

Satterwhite looked at Hampton, then turned away toward the packs.

"Where are you goin'?" Hampton hissed after him.

"To get wood for a fire, if that's all right with you."

Mary stirred and sat up. "What is it?" she asked.

"Your cousin is walkin' away again," Hampton said.

Tyler, who had remained silent and watching, looked away and walked to one of the packs.

Mary pushed her hair out of her face and looked at Hampton.

"Everything's all right," Hampton said. "I'm goin' to have a look at the desert before it gets dark."

He got to his feet and stooped to pick his hat off the sand. Putting it on, he passed Tyler and said, "Bring them glasses, Bud."

Hampton and Tyler walked to the mouth of the canyon, then climbed up the slope to get on top. Before they were even with the rim of the canyon, Tyler paused, then nodded at Hampton toward the desert.

"Great God Almighty," Hampton said.

Miles away on the floor of the desert was a column of dust that stretched from the north along the road to Colonia Dublan across the Casas Grandes and due west. The light of the sun was hazy through the dust.

Tyler had the glasses raised.

"What do you see?" Hampton asked.

"Dust closer up," Tyler said, lowering the glasses. "Looks to me like the army."

"That's more than any soldiers from Camp Furlong. Reckon Wilson declared war on Mexico?"

"What do you think?"

"Doesn't sound like him, but the Mexicans don't have any army this far north that could raise that kind of dust."

Tyler raised the glasses again. "Looks like they've already passed us," he said. "We could have hooked up with that line and gotten out of here," he said.

"Yeah," Hampton said, "but with that much movement of our troops, you can bet the bandits are long gone."

"What about Carrancistas?"

"I don't know. God help us, I don't know."

Tyler lowered the glasses, and they watched the dust drift away to the northeast. Hampton had a mild sense of relief.

"Wish we was ridin' with 'em under different circumstances," Tyler said.

"We had our chance at that," Hampton said. "Let's go back."

That night, the mood in their camp was different. They ate well. The possibility of their getting back safely was greater. The fire was big enough to warm them. The only one who did not seem affected was Mary. She remained quiet and thoughtful.

"Did them greasers feed you at all, Mary?" Satterwhite asked.

"Scraps," Mary said, "dreadful scraps with spit still on the edges of the tortillas where they had taken a bite out of them."

Satterwhite shuddered. "It must have been pretty bad," he said.

Mary looked at Hampton in the firelight. "It was," she said.

The men rolled smokes. Mary sat on Hampton's saddle, holding a cup in her hand and sipping the strong coffee.

"Let me have one of those," she said abruptly.

"Not good for you," Hampton said.

"Let her have one," Satterwhite said. He gave his to Mary, then lit it for her with a stick from the fire. He built a new one, and they all smoked for a few minutes. Hampton watched Mary. Her face looked strange in the firelight. She coughed briefly.

"Another good supper," Tyler said. "You're goin' to make a fine wife some day."

"That does it," Satterwhite said. "I'm not cooking anymore."

"Take it easy," Hampton said.

Satterwhite cut him a look across the fire.

"Why do you let Hamp tell you what to do all the time when you said you got sick of Uncle Oliver telling you what to do?" Mary asked.

"That beats Satterwhite's longest question," Tyler said.

"Believe so." Hampton smoked, half listening for an answer.

There was a long pause, then Satterwhite said, "It's different. And just because he tells me, doesn't mean I'm going to do it."

"You better," Hampton said.

They smoked a while, Mary glancing at Hampton from time to time.

"Besides," Hampton said, "you get married, you'll have to get used to being told what to do."

"How do you know?" Satterwhite asked.

"A lucky guess."

Hampton got up and went to the edge of the firelight where the packs were. The medical kit was on top of the nearest pack. He lifted it by the string that tied it shut and walked back to Mary.

"Time to change those bandages," Hampton said. With his free hand, he picked the cigarette out of Mary's fingers and threw it in the fire. Mary looked at him as he sat down in front of her, sideways to the fire and the others, but she didn't say anything. She put her coffee cup on the sand and held her wrists out to him. When he took them, she turned her head to Tyler.

"Were you ever married, Bud?" Mary asked him.

Tyler ducked his head. "No, ma'am."

"Were you ever in love?"

Hampton looked across the fire at Tyler. Satterwhite gave a short laugh, and Hampton cut his eyes to him. He turned back to Mary, picking carefully at the knot on her left wrist.

"Matter of fact, I was once."

"Tell me about it," Mary said.

Hampton untied the knot and unwound the bandage.

"It was a long time ago," Tyler said quietly and slowly. "We was in Arkansas for a few years on our way to Texas. What was the name of that town, Hamp?"

"Don't remember."

"Me either. We had to go to a school there part of one spring. It was one of them little old one-room schoolhouses with a potbellied stove up near the front. The teacher was an old widow woman with more sticks than a cedar tree. She used to get kind of impatient when somebody didn't learn fast enough."

"I had a teacher just like that," Satterwhite said.

Hampton threw the bandage in the fire. He bent Mary's hand down to look at the cuts. They were dry around the edges, but still alive where the bandage had blocked the air.

"Did you?" Tyler asked.

"Yeah. Her name was Mrs. Woolley, and she had. . . ."

"Let Bud tell his story," Mary said gently, not looking at Hampton.

Hampton unwound the other wrist. It looked better than the first.

"Sure," Tyler went on, "I don't remember this lady's name, but she had a rule that I remember very well. The schoolhouse had three doors, one at the front for the teacher to use, one at the back for the girls to use, and one at the side for the boys."

"What?" Satterwhite asked.

"Well, she had a worry that if the boys and girls used the same door, there would be some mischief on the way in from recess. When she rang that bell we had to line up at our door and come into the room. The boys sat on one side, and the girls sat on the other.

"There was one little gal sittin' on the end of a row of desks across from mine that caught my eye after a while. She wore the same dress every day, and I never saw her wearin' any shoes. She wasn't very tall for her age, but I never was neither. She had a face that seemed to me as pretty as Helen of Troy."

"Who's that?" Satterwhite asked.

"She don't live around here," Hampton said. Mary looked at him. He had taken out the cotton swabs and was dabbing at her wrists with iodine.

"This little gal had black hair and brown eyes and the sweetest way of lookin' out of the corner of her eye at me."

"What was her name?" Mary asked. She flinched when the iodine burned and clenched her fists. Hampton held her clenched hand as he cleaned her wrist.

"Hallie," Tyler said. "I don't remember what her last name was. You remember, Hamp?"

"Nope."

"What about her?" Mary asked.

"Well, we got to kind of lookin' at each other while the teacher was puttin' the irons to some other kid."

"Probably Hampton," Satterwhite said.

"Shut up, Satterwhite."

"Did you get together during recess?" Mary asked.

"Nope. Them little gals always had plenty of whisperin' to do,

237

and the boys was always gettin' into contests to see who was fastest or who could jump the highest. There was one kid said he could jump over another boy with the other boy standin' straight up. We argued it a while, then he tried it. He kicked that boy right in the teeth."

"What about Hallie?"

"Aw, nothin'. I never knew where she lived and only saw her at school. I sure looked forward to that. We'd just look at each other. Sometimes she would smile."

"You never talked to her?"

"Bud's been shy all his life," Hampton said. "Born that way."

"He's talking to me."

"Can't figure that," Hampton said. He reached into the bag and pulled out the roll of gauze. He would make the bandages lighter this time to let the air get through.

"You never talked to her?" Mary asked again.

"Nope. But we got to linin' up at the doors so that I'd turn the corner at the same time she got there. Then we'd walk beside each other between the desks until we got to ours."

"That's all?" Satterwhite asked.

"Well. There was one other thing. One time I came around that corner and she was lookin' right at me, then she kind of put out her hand when I got beside her. I took it and held it for maybe three or four steps until some of the kids behind us got to gigglin', then I let it go. It's a funny thing, but I can still feel her little hand in mine."

Tyler threw his cigarette in the fire and watched it burn. Mary looked down at her hand in Hampton's and was quiet, thinking about the little barefoot girl.

"She would have been a lot like you when she grew up," Tyler said quietly.

"Thank you, Bud."

The fire crackled with muffled snaps. Hampton cut a length of gauze and tied it on Mary's left wrist. Tyler poured himself another cup of coffee. The cold night air pressed down on them, the breeze finding its way with chilling accuracy around the bends in the canyon.

"I was in love once," Satterwhite said. "There was this girl in a saloon in Oklahoma City. . . ."

"We don't want to hear about no saloon girl," Hampton said, cutting another length of gauze with his knife.

"Hamp," Mary said.

"I'd go there sometimes and we'd dance." Satterwhite stopped, and after a pause, Mary asked, "Then what?"

"That's all. We'd dance. She was real pretty, too."

Mary looked down and smiled. Hampton tied the bandage on her wrist. Mary caught his hand and he glanced up at her. Their eyes held for a moment, then Hampton said, "Oh, no. No, sir. Don't even ask."

"Mary wants to know," Satterwhite said.

Hampton looked at Mary. The light of the fire was in her good eye. He squeezed her hand and slipped his out of her grasp. "She'll just have to wonder," he said.

"No I won't," Mary said after a pause. She lifted her hands, pushed them over Hampton's shoulders, and slid off the saddle into his arms.

Satterwhite and Tyler looked at them for a minute, then looked away.

"We found her," Satterwhite said quietly.

Tyler nodded. "Yep," he said.

Part III

MARY'S
WAR

TWENTY-FIVE

HAMPTON was awake when he heard Mary stir from her blankets and get up in the darkness. He rolled over on his side and watched her walk toward the mouth of the canyon, pulling one of her blankets over her shoulders. He reached for his glasses inside his nearer boot and put them on. The rims were cold against his nose. Mary's slender shadow disappeared past the horses.

Hampton pushed off the ground and rested on his elbow for a minute, waiting for her to come back. There were no sounds in the canyon at all, neither bird nor insect, and when Mary did not come right back, he threw off the blankets and sat up. The night was calm, but cold. He pulled on his boots, shivering. He could tell they were higher here than in the desert by the feel of the air. He put on his coat and hat, sat still, thinking, then pulled his rifle from the saddle scabbard on the ground by his bedroll.

Tyler's voice came quietly in the dark. "Hamp?"

"It's all right, Bud. Mary's gone for a walk." Hampton stood up and looked toward the mouth of the canyon.

"You know what I think?" Tyler asked quietly, rubbing the blanket edge against his gray whiskers. "I think she's well enough to travel, but she don't want to."

"I think you're right. I'll be back."

Hampton crunched away across the sand and gravel. Tyler rolled over on his back and watched him fade into the night. He yawned.

Hampton walked slowly, expecting to see Mary the next step, but he didn't find her until the mouth of the canyon. She was standing alone in the dark, looking out across the desert. Hampton paused, satisfied just to keep an eye on her. Then something in the lonely way she stood prompted him to walk up to her.

She turned when she heard his step, then looked away again. Hampton stopped a little behind her to the left, the rifle held easily in his hand. He scanned the desert, but it was like an empty floor in a dark room.

"I get the feelin' you're drawin' me out," he said. "You got a purpose for it?"

"I couldn't sleep, that's all."

"Cold?"

"A little."

"It'll be colder before the sun comes up."

Hampton shifted his feet in the loose rock and dead grass at the mouth of the canyon. He swung the barrel of the rifle up and down, feeling the weight and balance of it in his left hand.

"Are you cold?" Mary asked.

"Nope."

"In the winter, you always wore a flannel shirt that was brown plaid. Whatever happened to that shirt?" Mary asked, not looking at him.

"I don't know."

"It was my favorite. It looked so warm when you wore it."

"You used to have a blue dress with a waterfall of white lace down the front. That was my favorite."

"I never knew that," Mary said, shifting with the cold, shrugging the blanket around her neck. "I used to wonder what dress you would like when Mother and I went to Deming to the store."

"Is that right?"

"Yes. I would pick something out, but you would never say anything. Sometimes I could tell which ones you liked though."

Mary was quiet for a while, shifting her feet on the cold rocks. Then she said, "It's strange to talk about it."

"Maybe we shouldn't."

Hampton looked across the desert. He yawned with the cold, and his eyes watered. He shook his head.

"Maybe we should," Mary said. "It's so dark and empty out here, I feel like I'm in a dream."

Hampton suddenly remembered the dream that he had had about a girl with her hands tied and her lip bleeding. It had been Mary in the dream. The thought made him shiver.

"You can say anything you want to in a dream, can't you?" Mary said.

"I reckon."

"It's so easy to talk to you. I would try to talk to Leonard, but he never understood me. He never just listened to me and knew what I was saying. I would tell him some simple thing, and he would either look at me like I was crazy, or he would think I was accusing him of something. It was like we were talking two different languages."

"I suppose bein' married had something to do with that. Talk between a man and a woman gets different when . . . when marriage is involved."

Mary tucked a lock of loose hair behind her ear and looked across the desert at the low stars above the horizon.

"He just sat there when I told him I was leaving," Mary said.

Hampton slid his free hand inside his coat pocket and clenched his fist. His fingers were stiff.

"What did he say?"

"He didn't say anything. He just sat there."

"Hard to imagine," Hampton said.

"I felt like someone had stepped on my grave," Mary said. "Or taken me from my home and placed me here."

"Yeah."

"I saw a woman murdered in El Paso," Mary said.

Hampton took his hand out of his pocket and rubbed the cold metal of the rifle. At the edge of hearing came the rapid cluster of coyote calls. The density of the night air took the sounds away again.

"Close up?"

"It was in the lobby of a hotel. There was a woman and a little boy. She was a prostitute according to the policeman I talked to — a nice man, you would have liked him — and she was trying to run away from her husband. Hamp, I could see what was going to happen. There were others in the lobby, but nobody lifted a finger to stop the man. I tried to, but I couldn't."

"Shoot her?"

"Cut her throat."

Hampton looked out across the desert and put his right hand back in his pocket.

"I'm not a little girl anymore, Hamp. I've seen things. I know the world isn't always a nice place. God, that seems stupid to say. But I can't get over the fact that no one did anything, that Leonard just let me walk away."

Hampton sniffed and looked at her.

"Am I wrong, Hamp? Have I just read too many romances?"

"You ain't wrong, Mary. I think a woman needs to know her man will fight for her. I hear folks talkin' about honesty between a man and a woman, all this suffragette stuff, stuff about men and women bein' equal. But I'm not sure they are. Or maybe they are equal, just not the same. Seems to me sometimes, a woman would rather hear a strong lie than a weak truth, rather miss a hero for a week, than spend the day with an ordinary man."

"Where did you get all the answers?"

"They ain't answers, Mary. They're just opinions."

"You're speaking ungrammatically again."

Hampton laughed and looked down. "You always get me with that, don't you? You goin' to be a schoolteacher one day?"

"No. I'm not going to be anything."

"Sure you will."

"No, Hamp. Not after what has happened."

"This Leonard was just one fella in a million. You got a long way to go before you're nothin'."

"I'm already there."

Hampton was quiet a while. He could feel his anger rising, but he wasn't angry at Mary. He took a deep breath and blew it out.

"Any chance that I had ended the night those. . . . I wish they had just killed me."

"That's a hard thing for me to hear from you," Hampton said.

"When I think about it, I just want to be dead."

"That's about the last time I want to hear that."

"You could never understand how I feel."

Hampton felt his anger rising, but she was right. He couldn't argue with her. "You're puttin' yourself in a place where I can't follow you," he said.

He took his hand out again and put it on her shoulder. She shook it off. Hampton clenched his jaw and looked out across the dark desert. Mary stood apart from him, then turned and leaned against him, her head on his shoulder, her blanket warm against his coat sleeve.

"I'm sorry. I don't know what makes me act like that. I want to be in that place where you can't follow, but you make it hard. I keep looking over my shoulder and seeing you there."

Hampton pulled his hand out of his pocket and put his arm around her shoulders. He stared at the western sky where Orion stood guard.

"You just keep on seein' me standing there because that's where I'll always be," he said.

Mary put her arms around his waist and held on to him. "You think I'm worth something, don't you?" she asked.

"Sure."

"What are we going to do now?"

"The best thing for us to do is point our horses to the north and get the hell out of here."

She pushed away from him, his hand sliding off her shoulders with one edge of the blanket, and she shook her head. "We can't," she said.

"We're in a country split apart by revolution. We don't belong here, and we won't be safe until we're out of here."

"No," Mary shook her head. Her voice cracked.

"Mary," Hampton said quietly.

"No, Hamp. We can't just leave. It isn't finished yet."

"It was finished when I found you."

"No it wasn't. Don't you see? It isn't complete if we just ride away."

"Revenge is what you're after."

"It's finishing what that man began."

"Mary, you don't know what you're sayin'. How could two old

men, a big-mouthed kid, and a girl have any chance against a gang of Mexican bandits on their own ground?"

"Oh, Hamp," Mary said, beginning to cry. "I feel like I've been cut loose from the universe, and it hurts, Hamp. It hurts with every breath I take. It has to end. It has to be finished. I can't explain it, Hamp, but if you don't help me, I know I will die. I can't bear to live in this world if no one will fight for me."

"That's hysterical talk. You can't get by me with that."

"I'm entitled to it," Mary said, whipping the blanket at him, her voice rising. "Every minute for the last week, I've been thinking I was about to die, or worse. Someone just can't do that to someone else, Hamp, and be let alone to do it again."

"Mary."

She spun away from him. "It chokes me to think about it."

"I can't take you into something I know will kill you, Mary."

She turned back to him. "Hamp, listen to me. I'm dead already if you don't do something. That man is like the rattlesnake you killed. He has to be stopped, or he just comes back again."

Hampton felt a coldness slip inside his chest. "That bunch is probably out of the country by now," he said.

Mary stood looking at him in the darkness for a few minutes, sobbing, then she shook her head and tried again to make Hampton understand.

"God, I can't stop being emotional," she cried. "I haven't been able to cry for two months, and now I can't seem to stop."

"Mary."

"Listen to me, Hamp. All that time I was in Tennessee, when things would go wrong, I would think of you and my life on the ranch. We always knew what to do, didn't we? When something went wrong, we always did what we had to do to fix it, didn't we? We did something, Hamp, because not to do something was worse than what was wrong. I never ever heard you or Father say, 'Oh well, these things happen. We just have to accept it.' You never did. You always did something, even when it hurt to do it or you didn't want to do it. What is the matter with this world?" Mary cried. "I don't know what is going on. People don't do things anymore. Hamp?"

Hampton stepped up to her and pulled her to him. She cried against his coat.

"Oh Hamp. It hurts so much," she sobbed. "Tonight, sitting around the fire with you and Bud and Rueben — it was so sweet to me, but I am so scared. As long as he lives, it will never be over. Oh, Hamp. Help me."

Hampton slid his hand up Mary's back until it was in the hair that fell across her shoulders. He felt her trembling against him, and he knew, without putting it into words, how sometimes the wrong thing could be the right thing.

"All right," he said. "I ain't got nothin' in this world to lose, except maybe the people I love most."

Mary clung to him. "Hamp," she said quietly. "All my life you have been the one person who always looked after me, who always knew exactly what I was feeling. You didn't feed me or clothe me, but you always gave me what I needed. I need this now. Don't make me feel wrong, and don't hate me for it."

"All right, Mary," Hampton said again. "I'll ask the other two and see what they say. I'll go with you, but I won't tell them what to do."

"You won't have to," Tyler said.

Hampton released Mary and turned. He could see Tyler and Satterwhite standing about twenty feet away in the dark.

"You was gone a long time," Tyler said, ducking his head.

"I'm with you," Satterwhite said.

Hampton looked at them. Mary wiped her face on the blanket and stepped up beside Hampton again.

"You know what this means, don't you, Bud?"

Tyler scratched his bare head and shrugged. "Yeah. Well, I ain't got anything all that pressin' that needs doin'. If Mary wants us to go to war, I reckon I'm willin'."

Hampton looked down, swinging the rifle in his hand. Mary slipped away from him and went to Tyler. She put out her hand to him, and, ducking his head, he took it. She did the same with Satterwhite, then she returned to Hampton and stood in front of him, pulling the blanket around her shoulders.

"It scares me," she said, "and it's evil, but, thank you."

Hampton closed the distance between them. She put her arm around him and kissed his bearded cheek. He looked at her in the dark, trying to see her eyes, then turned her gently back toward camp. As the four of them walked silently through the darkness, Hampton had a very clear memory of his little brother's face. *Damn,* he thought, *it's Homer all over again.*

TWENTY-SIX

MARY joined Satterwhite at the fire, Hampton's red bandana folded across the top of her head and knotted under her hair as if the bandana had been a hair ribbon.

"Just show me where everything is," she told Satterwhite, "and get out of my way."

Hampton and Tyler sat across the fire on their saddles, coffee cups in their hands.

"You bet," Satterwhite said. Then he asked, "Are you sure you want to?"

"I'm sure."

"Empty out that food pack on a blanket, Satterwhite," Hampton said. "We need to take stock."

"Taking stock is something I know a lot about," Satterwhite said.

"Uh-huh," Hampton said. "That doesn't surprise me."

While Satterwhite spread the food out on a blanket, Mary picked out a can of bacon, the flour bag, and a can of condensed milk. She hesitated, then picked up a sixteen ounce can of yellow hominy.

"Let's celebrate," she said.

"I hate that stuff," Satterwhite said.

Mary looked across the fire at Hampton. He nodded at her.

"She's wound up this mornin'," Tyler said, watching Mary with a slight smile on his face.

"Looks better, too," Hampton said.

The bruises on Mary's cheekbone had begun to lose their darkness, and the swelling had gone down. Her sunburn was peeling.

"Hard to figure a woman," Tyler said, aware that he was being trite. "She's all wound up and happy while we sit over here like a couple of deacons on Sunday night."

"Uh-huh," Hampton said quietly, watching Mary work at opening the cans, aware of the quantity of provisions Satterwhite was laying out on the blanket. "I'd buy that, if I didn't already know you're about as wound up as you ever get."

"I admit I'm excited."

"You just show it different. Satterwhite's excited too, but he's the only one of the four of us who doesn't have any idea what we're about to get into."

"He done good the other night when we rode into Columbus."

Hampton nodded and sipped his coffee. "He got his feet wet anyway. That don't mean he knows how to swim." Hampton looked at the fire and thought of Homer again.

"What are you two whispering about?" Mary asked.

"Probably me," Satterwhite said.

Tyler shrugged, but Hampton kept looking at the fire. Neither of them answered.

While they ate, they were quiet, except for "Pass me" and "Hand me" talk. The sun was warm. The day was going to be mild, perhaps even hot. Hampton finished his third cup of coffee and stood up to shake the grounds out in the fire.

"I think you just lost a job, Satterwhite," Hampton said.

"Suits me."

Mary was crouching by the fire with her back to Hampton. She had taken off her coat and rolled up her sleeves. Hampton saw the flex of his suspenders across her narrow back. Her hair swept down to just above the X.

"That was good, Mary," he said.

"What's the plan?" Satterwhite asked.

"You in a hurry to die?"

"I just wondered what the plan was."

Mary looked over her shoulder at Hampton, but he was looking away. She felt she could almost read his thoughts.

"We need to get cleaned up," Hampton said, "for one thing. These packs will have to be moved to one horse. Put 'em on the bay.

252

Mary'll ride the other one, and she'll need some kind of blanket rig for a saddle. But that's tomorrow. These horses need to browse and drink and rest today. Once we start movin', we'll probably keep movin' til we're dead or out of here."

Hampton looked down at Mary, who had turned now and was facing him. Her expression was serious, and her face had the curves again that Hampton remembered. The collar of Satterwhite's shirt was open, and he could see the gray neck of the union suit.

"And Mary needs a hat," he said.

"Can't I wear yours?"

"Did yesterday. But a man's hat ain't somethin' he wants to get in the habit of loanin' out."

"It ain't?" Mary said.

"No, it ain't," Hampton said.

He took his hat off and swatted at her with it as he walked by toward the horses. He untied Lady and moved to the next horse. Tyler untied the other three, and they led them back into the canyon to the first and most accesible *tinaja*. While the horses drank and nudged each other, Hampton and Tyler rolled a smoke.

"You got some big doubts about this, don't you?" Tyler said.

Hampton lit his cigarette and blew out smoke. "You don't?"

Tyler lit his cigarette and shrugged.

"I don't feel good about it," Hampton said, watching the muscles in Lady's flank roll as she walked around one of the packhorses. "Not with Mary along. I'd be there already if it was just us."

"You startin' to get superstitious on me?"

"Always been, Bud. A man keeps his eyes open, he gets to where he can track somethin' that hasn't put a foot down yet."

Tyler nodded and smoked. "Got a strange feelin' myself," he said. "But not about this. I feel like somethin's steppin' on my tail."

"Somebody followin' us?"

"Feels like it. May just be nerves."

Hampton blew smoke out and looked at the horses. "You see anything?"

"No," Tyler said.

"True?"

"True."

One of the packhorses started to turn back, satisfied with water and looking for forage. Hampton stepped forward and caught the lead rope. They gathered the reins of the rest of the horses and walked back.

"There's somethin' else," Hampton said.

"What's that?"

"I keep thinkin' about Homer. It's the same action, Bud. I'm the one who could stop this, and I'm not doin' it."

"I don't think you could," Tyler said. "I don't think you could have stopped Homer, and I don't think you want to bad enough to stop this."

Mary was finishing the dishes when they walked back into camp, but they didn't stop. They took the horses to the mouth of the canyon and staked them out in the brush that had gained a hold where the silt flowed out of the canyon in heavy rains.

"I don't want an open running fight," Hampton said. "If there was some way we could contain them, I'd like it a lot better. They could probably shoot better in an open fight than we could. Mary can use a rifle, but she's used to a rest. I don't know about the Oklahoma Kid."

"You want to ambush 'em?"

"Not in the desert where they can scatter."

"Maybe we could send 'em an invitation to come here."

"It would have to be a hell of an invitation after all the dust we saw yesterday."

They checked the horses, then looked across the desert. Heat waves shimmered off the rocks.

"Then we'll have to give 'em what they gave Columbus," Tyler said. "Go in at night before they can get to horse."

"Seems cowardly," Hampton said. They turned back up the canyon. "But like Mary said, they started this. If they never thought somebody'd come lookin' for her, that's their mistake."

"That's the one thing we got workin' for us," Tyler said.

"We'll need it," Hampton said.

The day got warmer and drifted into hot. The men took turns going to the big *tinaja* in the rocks that was ten feet deep with dark rainwater from some other month. They took along the collapsible water bucket they used when they watered the horses to rinse off with after they had soaped down. Water was too precious to the animals of the desert to bathe in the *tinaja* itself. They each washed their clothes too, doing it first so the clothes would be almost dry when they were through with their bath.

Mary was last, and nobody said anything when she picked up the soap to go. When she was out of sight, Satterwhite said, "Mary seems to be doing a lot better."

Hampton nodded, but did not say anything for a while. Then he said, "She's been through more than any girl should ever have to go through. She's crossed more than one border since last Thursday, and she's countin' on us to bring her back. It won't be easy."

"It's what they deserve," Satterwhite said, thinking about the bandits.

"Uh-huh," Hampton said. "For once, I agree with you."

"It sure turned into a warm day," Tyler said.

"Yeah," said Hampton.

"Yes, it did," Satterwhite said, and then they were silent and restless until Mary's slender form came around the bend and joined them in the shade of the canyon walls.

"It's time to talk, Mary," Hampton said, cutting a piece of tobacco and slipping it in his mouth.

Mary knew what Hampton meant. She sat down on her blankets, her hair wet but drying and her face more revealed and bare.

"All right, Hamp."

Satterwhite moved closer to Tyler, who sat beside Hampton.

"Tell us about it."

"Everything?"

"As much as you feel like. We guessed what happened in Columbus."

Mary nodded. She ran her fingers through her hair down to the tangles in the damp ends. The bandages on her wrists were gone.

"I got off the train late at Columbus, so I stayed at the hotel. When the Mexicans broke in, I hid in a bathroom until they set the hotel on fire. I couldn't imagine what was happening or why. The smoke began to stifle me, so I ran down the stairs."

"Did you have your bag with you? It was found behind the hotel someplace."

"I think so. I think I had the idea that I would try to get out of town on foot and walk to the ranch."

"Little Mary," Hampton said.

"Bullets were everywhere. I remember that. They were hitting the walls everywhere I went. One cut my collar."

Hampton stopped chewing and watched her face, then he went back to chewing.

"I turned a corner in an alley and bumped into the leader of the bandits, Salazar. He hit me when I tried to fight him, and he put me on his horse." Mary's hand worked through her hair over and over again while she remembered.

Hampton said, "Easy."

Mary looked at him, squinting her eyes a little at the memory. "We rode toward the border and waited for the rest of his men. They put me on a horse. At daybreak we rode south for several hours, then stopped while Salazar waited again. We rode east until we came to a shallow river and camped there for several days. Salazar made me write a note to Father. He gave it to a man to deliver, but the man couldn't make it across the border."

Hampton watched Mary's fingers working the same strands of hair over and over. He spit to the side and thought about getting up but sat still.

"We moved camp, east then south. The bandits were already planning another raid. That morning a man and his horse died. They blamed it on me. They wanted to kill me, but they thought I was bad luck, so they. . . ."

"That's enough, Mary," Hampton said.

Tyler was looking at the ground in front of his boots. Satterwhite was biting on a fingernail and looking at Mary.

"They tied me up and kept hitting me and throwing things at me," Mary said. Tears rolled down her cheeks. She stopped her hand and looked at Hampton. To her, his face was like a warm fire on a cold night. She dropped her eyes and took a deep breath. She shuddered and was still.

"Did the bandits say where they might go?"

Mary didn't look up. "One of the women said they were going to raid the Carrancistas at El Indio."

"Where were they going when they left you?"

"I don't know."

"How many were in the band?"

"Twenty-four, mostly, but riders came and went, sometimes men I had never seen before."

"How many women?"

"Eight."

"Were the women soldiers?"

"They all carried rifles."

"Would they fight?"

"Yes."

Hampton spit to the side. "All right," he said. He thought a minute. "El Indio is two days' ride from where I found you. They would probably move easy and scout the village before raiding it. It was Monday when I found you. Today is. . . ."

"Wednesday," Tyler said.

". . . . Wednesday. That means they would probably reach that area late today, moving slow, and scout El Indio tomorrow. My guess is they would head south then. With the movement we saw, most of the bandits will be looking for mountains as soon as they can find them. They would cross the Mexican Northwestern Railroad tracks and head for the Rio Santa Maria."

"How far is that?" Satterwhite asked.

"Don't know, but it's all salt flats down that way."

"What if they stayed around El Indio enjoyin' themselves?" Tyler asked.

"They might," Hampton said. "Depends on how hard they have to fight when they get there."

"One of the women told me they had taken it before," Mary said.

"Then it might be easy, unless they have strengthened the force there. On the other hand, the Carrancistas might have moved out altogether."

Hampton and Tyler were thoughtful, working it out in their minds.

"So what's the plan?" Satterwhite asked.

Hampton shook his head and spit. "Nobody will give a damn about four riders with everything else that's happenin'. We could probably ride to El Indio unnoticed and see what the situation is. Bud?"

"Don't know what else to do until we find them."

Hampton looked at Mary. "Mary?"

She raised her eyes, clear now, and met his. "When?" she asked.

"First thing in the mornin', if I can't talk you out of it."

"You can't."

"That's it then. Satterwhite, go get the horses."

Satterwhite got up. Tyler followed him. "I'll help," he said.

When they were gone, Mary went to Satterwhite's pack and dug through it for a comb. When she found it, she returned to her blanket and combed out her hair. Hampton looked at the ground in front of him, chosing his targets each time he spit. Mary watched him, drawing the comb roughly through her hair.

Hampton looked up and met her eyes. After a minute, he said, "You're lookin' better. Goin' to war must suit you."

Mary combed and looked at him. "I feel almost normal again," she said evenly. "My hair felt like a mule's tail."

"Uh-huh. Mine too."

Mary looked at the canyon wall behind Hampton, then returned to Hampton. She looked down, then looked at him again.

"I know what this means to you," she said.

"Same here."

"Thank you, Hamp."

Hampton nodded and spit. "Thank me when we get home."

"Home," Mary said with wonder. "I don't know if any place will ever seem like home to me again."

"It will."

Mary combed her hair.

"Mary, there's somethin' I ought to tell you," Hampton started. "It may not make sense to say it now, but I thought of it, so I might as well."

Mary looked at him. "What is it?"

"I might not be stayin' at the ranch if we ever get back. Bud wants me to go to Texas with him, buy some bottom land and raise cotton."

Mary smiled, then she stopped combing her hair. She held the comb in her hand on her lap and looked at it.

"I was tryin' to decide when all this happened, but I think it would probably be best," Hampton went on. "I've gone about as far as I can go in this life, and I've been kind of standin' on the border of somethin' else for a good while now. I reckon it's time I crossed over and went on to the next thing."

Mary looked at the comb in her hand.

"It's hard to think of the ranch without you there," she said.

"Might be better," Hampton said quietly. "We spent a lot of time together when you were a little girl. I always figured I must have done somethin' good along the way somewhere, and you were my reward. There's a lot of things about this old world I'd have never known but for you."

"Hamp. . . ."

"But now," he said, cutting her off, "you ain't a little girl anymore. I'm afraid if I kept hanging around, you'd get to the point where you wished I wouldn't. I don't believe I could bear that."

Hampton looked at a flat, round pebble and spit on it. Mary put the comb on the blanket and stood up. She crossed the sand to Hampton and stopped in front of him. He looked to the side, wishing he were with the other two.

"You are like the hero in the book I was reading," Mary said quietly. "You came after me. You found me. You doctored me. And now you are fighting for me. If you will be happier in Texas, then I understand about your going. But until then, I want you to do one more thing for me."

Hampton looked up at her. "What's that?"

"I want you to let me be your Little Mary still."

Hampton nodded but didn't say anything. He stood up, and Mary fell against him, her arms around him. He felt the slim weight and press of her body, and his whiskers cut into her soft, damp hair. The clean scent of soap on her sun-warmed skin made him close his eyes.

Early the next day, they loaded one packhorse and put two extra blankets over the other one for Mary. They left the second pack and most of the canned goods in the canyon under a thick shield of dry brush.

"Will you be all right until we can get you a saddle?" Hampton asked Mary.

"Yes."

"If not, Satterwhite can give you his."

"Why mine?"

"Youngest man always has to give the girl his saddle."

"Oh sure," Satterwhite said.

"If we run into trouble, you and Satterwhite drop back. He knows the routine. I want you to wear my .45 so you will always have something. Know how to use it?"

"I've used it before."

"Good. Our chances are better if we can catch them at El Indio or just south of there, so we need to ride pretty steady. You get tired or start to hurt, you let me know. Bud?"

"Yeah, Hamp."

"You ride point. Ready?"

"I been ready."

"All right." Hampton helped Mary across the packhorse and passed her the reins. He patted her thigh and looked at her. "Here," he said, and gave her his hat.

"Hamp."

"You wear it. You need it worse than I do."

Hampton stepped over to Lady and swung up into the saddle. "All right," he said again. "Let's do her."

TWENTY-SEVEN

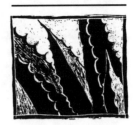

TYLER drew up, took his hat off, and wiped his forehead while he waited for Hampton to come abreast. When Hampton rode up, Tyler was fitting his hat firmly back on his head.

"How much farther?" Tyler asked.

Hampton sat his horse and squinted at the horizon. The desert stretched away flat in all directions, broken by unseen gullies and ravines. As far as the eye could see, there was no sign of a village or of any human life at all. Satterwhite and Mary rode up.

"What is it?" Satterwhite asked.

Hampton glanced at Mary. Her face had a patient, tired look that was close to being grim, but her eyes were clear, and the clothes she wore, rather than making her seem boyish, made her seem that much more feminine.

"We may be too far south," Hampton said. "El Indio is a little place with low hills all around it, easy to miss."

"I thought you knew where it was," Satterwhite said.

"Only been there once. It must be to the northeast. We haven't crossed the railroad tracks yet, so we haven't gone all that far."

Tyler untied the field glasses and scanned the horizon to the northeast. They had moved south the whole day before, camping in a low spot in the desert, and had continued south when the sun came up. It was mid-morning now, hot in the sun, cold in the shade.

"Land rises," Tyler said, pointing, "there to the northeast. Looks more broken."

"That's it," Hampton said. "Ground around El Indio looks like a brick factory blew up there. Feel like goin' on, Mary?"

Mary pointed to Satterwhite's canteen, waited for him to give it to her, drank, wiped her lips gingerly, then said, "Yes."

They moved northeast until past noon, and when the land became more hilly and broken, they crossed several well-used trails and a primitive roadbed. The land was broken hills and twisting arroyos. They made an effort to keep low rather than ride the hilltops, so their route was circuitous and slow.

The sky became overcast, and a chill wind blew in their faces. In another half hour, Hampton smelled smoke, and they stopped.

Tyler carried the field glasses to the top of a hill, with Hampton behind him. They approached the rim carefully and peered over. Below them were the first adobe buildings on the edge of El Indio. Smoke was coming from the chimney of one of the buildings. The roof of another had caved in with fire and was smoking. Two women were standing in front of the first adobe, shawls around their heads, talking.

Tyler raised the glasses and went from adobe to adobe. Outside the burned one, he saw the first body. It was on its side against the wall of the house. In the street were scattered pieces of equipment and clothes, broken clay jugs, and torn blankets.

Tyler lowered the glasses. "Looks like they been here," he said. He took his tobacco out of his shirt pocket and bit off a plug.

"Uh-huh," Hampton said. He looked to his right. "Let's move to that other hill. Get a better picture of the whole village."

"Reckon they left any soldiers?" Tyler asked, stepping carefully down the broken rock of the hill.

"They would have been standin' around lookin' mean if they had."

At the bottom of the hill, Mary was sitting on a rock as big as an automobile tire, her elbows on her knees. Satterwhite was standing in front of her, looking up the hill, his rifle in his hand.

"What did you see?" he asked.

"They've been here," Hampton said. "We're on the west end of the village. Can't tell if any of the bandits are still here or not."

Mary turned and looked at Hampton over her shoulder, her dark hair flowing out from underneath his hat brim. Her eyes rested on his face, her expression tense, but she did not speak.

"Wait for us here," Hampton said, and he and Tyler followed the draw to the next hill and climbed it.

"Think they might still be here, Mary?" Satterwhite asked.

"I don't know," she said and looked down again. She felt a little scared and sick to her stomach, but she tried to think like a soldier, not like the woman she had been raised to be.

In the main street of the village were more bodies. The roofs of three more adobe houses had been set on fire, and people were moving about in the gray light of the chill afternoon, mostly women, small girls, and older men. There was no sign of soldiers either alive or dead.

"Looks like they rode in and shot the place up just for the hell of it," Hampton mused. "Some of the villagers must have been armed. Those bodies in the street are most likely bandits. The villagers would have gathered their own dead in by now."

"None of the corrals got any stock in 'em," Tyler said. "Either the bandits took the animals or the remainin' men formed some kind of misguided posse."

"We're the misguided posse," Hampton said, his eyes moving from thing to thing in the small desert village.

"Now what?" Tyler spit.

"May as well go on in and have a look at it. I don't think there were any Carrancistas stationed here for whatever reason. These people got no quarrel with us. They're mostly Indians."

Hampton and Tyler returned to the horses. The sun was lost behind low gray clouds. Hampton untied his coat from behind his saddle and put it on. He turned the collar up.

"We're goin' in," he said. "These people won't hurt us. If we're careful, we may find out somethin' that could help us. Be on your guard, though. They been hit hard."

One by one, they mounted, then waited on Hampton to lead the way. Satterwhite carried his rifle across his saddle. Mary slipped the leather thong off the hammer on Hampton's pistol that hung heavy on her hip. Hampton skirted the hill, and they rode into the village.

The villagers could tell at a glance that these new riders were neither bandits nor soldiers, but the women turned their backs on them. The children stared without expression or ran for doorways.

As Hampton rode, he nodded at the faces turned up to his, but he did not speak. At the smoldering adobe, he stopped and got down. He turned over the body against the wall and looked at him. The man's possesions had already been stripped from his body, and he had nothing in his pockets, wore no coat, and his boots were gone. Hampton looked at Mary.

"This one of Salazar's?"

Mary rode forward and looked at the body. It was Eliseo, the bandit who wanted to drive a train across the desert. Mary turned away. "Yes," she said.

"Hamp?" Tyler's voice warned him.

Two men approached from the main part of the village. Both were carrying Mausers, but they were carrying them one-handed, not shouldered.

Hampton stood up and stepped away from the body. He turned toward the two men and waited. Before they were close enough to hear him, he said, "Mary?"

"No."

"Hello, gentlemen," Hampton said in Spanish. "What has happened here?"

The first man to speak was older than the other, his hair and moustache white.

"Villistas came riding in before the sun was up, shooting and killing us and burning down our houses."

"Where are the soldiers of Carranza?" Hampton asked, when they were close.

"They have gone," the old man said.

The younger one held his Mauser with two hands now and was watching Tyler.

"Who are you?" the older man wanted to know.

"We are Americans. We have business south of here. I am James Hampton. I have been here before with the American cattleman, MacPherson. We shipped cattle out of here five or six years ago."

"I remember," the older man said.

"Is there anything we can do to help you?" Hampton asked. "We have some medicine in the pack. Are there wounded?"

"Some," the old man nodded, looking away from Hampton to those on horseback.

"Show them to me," Hampton said, and, holding the reins in his hand, he led Lady forward.

As they walked away, the younger man followed. Satterwhite looked at Tyler and started to dismount, but Tyler shook his head, and turned his horse slowly after the three on foot. More people came out of their houses as they rode up the single street. Tyler looked from doorway to doorway when they passed each building.

"What happened?" Hampton asked the old man as they walked.

"The bandits came in the night," the old man said. "They came from the south like you did so that no one heard them until they were already among us shooting and screaming. There are some of us who have rifles. We fought back, but they set fire to the houses that showed gunfire. We had to leave the village and hide in the hills until they were gone."

"What did they want?"

"The same as always — anything that is not theirs."

They stopped outside of one of the larger adobes in the village.

"The ones who were shot are in here," the old man said. "There is nothing we can do for them. We will be grateful for any help you can give them."

Hampton looked over his shoulder. "Bud, you and Satterwhite wait with the horses. Mary, bring me the medical kit."

Tyler let Satterwhite dismount, then swung down himself. Mary slid off the blankets and went to the packhorse. Satterwhite eased over to Hampton.

"What did he say?" Satterwhite asked.

"They were hit, just as we figured, in the dark. Never were any soldiers here. I offered to help his wounded."

"Be careful," Tyler nodded.

Mary walked up with the cotton sack holding their medical supplies. She watched Hampton's face.

"After you," Hampton told the man.

They went inside the adobe. The air was warm and smoky, and the room was dark. Four men and one woman were on pallets on the floor. An older woman crouched by the firepit and watched them.

"These four are ours," the old man said. "The girl is from the bandits. We were going to shoot her, but no one wanted the bad luck."

"Uh-huh," Hampton said. He turned and took the bag from Mary. "You take a look at the woman while I look at these other four."

"All right," Mary said, and when she spoke the old man looked quickly at her and nodded.

Hampton knelt down by the first man and pulled the blanket back from his chest. His blouse was dark with blood. Hampton touched his throat.

"This one is gone," Hampton said. The old man crossed himself, as did the woman at the fire pit.

The other three had taken bullets at close range. One had been shot in the head. Hampton knew there was nothing to be done for him. The other two had been hit in the extremities, one in the forearm, the other in the calf. In both cases, the bone had been shattered, leaving ugly wounds.

Hampton took his coat off, and, with the assistance of the woman, started to work on the leg wound.

Mary crossed the room feeling as if she were watching someone else cross the room. The woman lay on her back on a rough pallet, with a blanket of heavy weave over her. Mary knelt beside her in the gloom and saw at once that it was Natalia. The girl's eyes were closed, but she was breathing evenly. Mary pulled the blanket back. Natalia's blouse was ripped on the left side, and was wet with blood. Mary tore a handkerchief-sized square from the blouse and carried it to the pot of hot water the village woman had set beside Hampton.

Hampton glanced at her. She dipped the bloody cloth in the water and squeezed it out, feeling the hot water go into the cuts on her chapped hands. She nodded and went back to the girl.

The bullet had pierced the girl's side at an angle, so that the exit hole was barely two inches from the first hole. Other than the danger of bleeding and infection, the wound was not a serious one. As Mary cleaned it, Natalia opened her eyes. She sucked in her breath and slid away from Mary's fingers.

"It's all right, Natalia," Mary said in Spanish. "I am not going to hurt you."

Natalia crossed herself. "Are you dead?" she asked.

Mary raised her chin two degrees. "You see I am not."

Natalia stared at Mary, who continued to clean the wound. Slowly she relaxed. She looked around the room.

"They were arguing over who should shoot me," she said.

"No one will shoot you now," Mary said.

"Not you?"

"You helped me when no one else would. I will not shoot you."

"I have never been shot before," Natalia said, and her voice sounded scared. "I do not like the revolution very much anymore."

Mary remembered Salazar's words, "Now, bitch, you understand the revolution." She bit her bottom lip gently and looked at Natalia. "The revolution was never a place for you," Mary said. "Did you ride with Salazar because you had a husband or lover who rode with him?"

"No." Natalia flinched as Mary cleaned the wounds. "I had no other place to go. My mother was killed by Carrancistas, the same ones who took my father to fight for them. I was a little girl then. My brothers and I joined a Villa band who promised us food and gold. Last year, I rode with Salazar. My brothers are dead now. Only I remain."

"Will you fight again?" Mary asked her.

"I do not want to die," Natalia said, her expression more that of a child than a woman.

Tyler and Satterwhite were surrounded by old men, women, and children of the village when Hampton and Mary finally came out of the adobe. Hampton carried his coat over his arm. The medical kit hung down from his hand by the drawstring.

"Thank the Lord," Tyler said. "I'd about used up every Mex word I knew a hundred times."

"Well say *adiós*, then," Hampton said, "because we're not stayin' for supper."

Hampton swung the bag at Satterwhite and told him to tie it on.

He slipped into his coat and shook it up around his neck. Mary did likewise.

"How does it look?" Tyler asked.

"Two dead, two crippled for life, and one *Adelita* who may live to have kids in some village like this some day."

"What about Salazar?"

Hampton nodded. "We rode all around him. Benito here says he's camped between two hills about five miles to the southwest. Says there's a seep spring there."

"The truth?"

Hampton looked up and down the street and at the people who watched them silently. "I think so, considerin'. Let's go."

Satterwhite helped Mary on her horse, then mounted his own and sat looking at Hampton. Tyler crossed to his and stepped up into the saddle.

"Thank you very much," the old man Benito said.

"Don't hurt the *muchacha*," Hampton told him. "It would be very bad luck to do so now."

"She will not be molested," Benito said. "You are going to ride after the man who makes dolls?"

"We will see," Hampton said, and climbed on his horse.

"Sure," Benito said. "It is fortunate you found the girl. I heard you were coming, but I heard only one man and a boy. Good luck to you."

Hampton looked at him. *Avisadores* were fast, if not accurate. "And to you," Hampton said.

They rode slowly through the villagers, who moved aside to let them pass, their faces empty even of curiosity.

TWENTY-EIGHT

TYLER picked up the trail of the bandits a mile out of the village. The northeast wind had swung around to the northwest and was getting colder. They followed the trail another mile, then stopped against a low hill in the lee of the wind to eat and talk.

Mary had become somber and quiet during the afternoon. Hampton watched her face as she crouched to tie the reins of her horse on a creosote bush. She caught his eye when she stood up, and she walked over to sit beside him. Tyler and Satterwhite unwrapped jerky and opened two sleeves of smashed crackers.

Hampton took out his knife and wiped the blade on his pants. He glanced sideways at Mary. "Doin' all right?" he asked.

Mary took off his hat and held it with both hands in front of her, crown down like a beggar. Her hair, since she had washed it, was full and shiny with strands that would not be contained either by the bandana or by Hampton's hat.

"I feel like I'm hanging from the side of a cliff, and I can't let go or get back on top."

"Other than that?"

"This is such a sad country, Hamp. It's so hard and lonely. It breaks people down into only a handful of soul, then leaves them like that. It makes me sad."

Tyler cut the jerky and passed it around with the crackers.

"We can still beat it out of here. We don't have to go on," Hampton said.

"Yes we do," Satterwhite said, his mouth full of crackers.

"I have to," Mary said.

"Well, hell," Hampton said, "I guess we'll be doin' a lot of people a big favor if we can stop this rattlesnake."

"You trust old Benito?" Tyler asked.

"Yeah. After what we did. Those hurt were on their conscience. We doctored them, so if they suffer or die now, it is our fault, not Benito's."

"I don't want that," Mary said.

"Don't worry about it," Hampton told her. "I was in charge, so the obligation is really all mine."

"Sometimes I don't have any idea what you're talking about," Satterwhite said and shook his head.

"I've noticed that," Hampton said. "Benito said something else, too. He said the American army was in Mexico. If we wanted to leave right now, we could ride easy to the border."

"Why do you keep saying that?" Satterwhite asked.

"Maybe we should," Mary said in a low voice.

"And after we got home?" Hampton asked.

"I'm just one person," Mary said.

"Not anymore," Satterwhite said. "I don't think I could ever bear to look at myself again if we just turned around and rode home."

"I can't bear to look at you now," Hampton said.

They ate without enjoying it. Tyler kept glancing over his shoulder and finally went to his horse to get the field glasses. He walked up into the wind to search the desert. Hampton got up, folded his knife, and followed him.

"What is it?"

"Somethin' keeps steppin' on my tail," Tyler said. He lowered the glasses and shook his head. "I can't figure it. It doesn't feel bad, but it must be bad or it wouldn't bother me."

Hampton looked out across the empty desert.

"You know how when you're huntin' at the edge of dark and you see a deer, but you can't tell if it's a buck or a doe?"

"It's always a doe," Hampton said.

"That's right. Because when it's a buck, you always know it. Well, that's how I feel right now. I can't tell if it's a buck or a doe, but I can't trust my experience either. Too much at stake."

"I'm glad Satterwhite ain't listenin' in on this talk," Hampton said. "All you can do is what you're doin'. Keep alert. Keep watchin' our back trail."

"Yeah," Tyler said. "Just wish I knew what it was."

"Me too."

They rejoined Satterwhite and Mary. Tyler took a fix on landmarks so they could travel after the sun went down. Hampton and Satterwhite pulled out all the guns and untied the ammunition from the packs. Mary laid the boxes out on top of a flat rock.

"How do you want to do this?" she asked.

"Break the boxes of the .38s and divide the cartridges," Hampton told her.

"Three ways?"

"No. Four. I want you to have as many as the rest of us in case one of us goes down. Divide the .45s the same way."

"Let me use a rifle," Mary looked at him.

"No, Little Mary. Rifles are for the charge. You won't be in the charge. You'll be behind the biggest rock I can find, and you'll have my .45. All you need to worry about is whatever comes your way."

"I want to be in on the charge," Mary said.

"Don't push me on this, Mary," Hampton said. "We have to go in, we'll go in fast on horse or on foot, shootin' from the hip in the dark. You think you can do that?"

"I don't want to be left behind."

"You won't be. You'll be right there, but, by God, you'll be where you'll have a chance and where you'll do some good."

Mary looked at him. "Don't be mad at me," she said.

Hampton looked at her, his eyes still stern, his face set. "I'll be whatever I have to be to keep you alive," he told her.

It was cold and dark when they pulled out of the draw into the desert again. Hampton turned his collar up to keep his ears warm. They left the packhorse tied where anyone could see it if none of them were alive to come back for it. Satterwhite tied the medical kit on his saddle.

Hampton and Tyler rode together with Mary and Satterwhite close behind them.

"Are you excited?" Tyler asked.

Hampton nodded in the dark.

"Me, too," Tyler said. "Damn, I'm excited. I wish the Captain was with us."

"Yeah," said Hampton.

"You know," Tyler said, "the only times in my life I ever felt good about myself was when I was helpin' someone or when I was goin' to war."

"Well, you ought to feel real good now, because you're doin' both."

Hampton dropped back until he was beside Mary. "You warm enough?" he asked.

"It's a cold night," Mary said. "Want your hat back?"

"Nope."

Satterwhite looked around Mary, trying to hear what Hampton was saying. Neither of them paid him any attention.

"Mary," Hampton said, "I want you to promise me something. If we all go down, I want you to promise me you'll get out, try to get back home."

"I can't promise that, Hamp," Mary said.

"Uh-huh. I knew you were goin' to say that. Guess I just had to ask it anyway."

Hampton spurred ahead. Mary watched his outline against the cold night sky. Every line of his silhouette meant strength and comfort to her.

"What did he want?" Satterwhite asked.

"He was just checking on us," Mary said.

"Sometimes he gets on my nerves," Satterwhite said.

"What does that mean?"

"He's so bossy, so sure of himself."

"He's like a father to everyone who knows him," Mary said.

They rode a while in silence, Mary watching Hampton's outline against the stars that occasionally broke through the thinning clouds.

"He acts like he wishes I was dead," Satterwhite said.

"If you really believed that, you wouldn't be riding behind him now, Rueben. He's not like any man I have ever known. He belongs to an older breed. There's few like him left. I can't imagine the world without him in it."

272

Then, as soon as she had said it, she realized how true it was. She kicked the horse and rode to Hampton's side.

"We don't have to do it, Hamp," she cried. "We don't have to."

"We're already doin' it, Mary," Hampton said.

Mary turned and included Satterwhite in her appeal. "Just all of us be careful. Please."

"Hamp," Tyler said and pointed.

Ahead of them as they topped a rocky hill was the glow of fires in the desert, perhaps a half a mile away.

"There they are," Hampton said. "Benito was right."

They pulled down into a draw and tied the horses. Hampton helped Mary down. While he still held her, he looked at her face in the dark and said, "Mary?"

"Please don't let anything happen to you," she said.

"I didn't come down here to die," Hampton said. "You watch your own hide."

He let go of her abruptly and went to his horse, pulling out his rifle, and unslinging the pouch with the cartridges in it. He began slipping them loosely into the pockets of his coat. Tyler and Satterwhite were doing the same. Mary had already filled her pockets with her share of the bullets.

"All right," Hampton said, dropping the empty pouch on the ground. "From here on, let's move in single file. Satterwhite, you follow me, then you, Mary. Bud will be behind you. No one shoot until I shoot or unless you have to save your life. Them fires are burnin' too bright for the banditos to be asleep. We'll want to look first, then wait till they bed down. Bud?"

"Sounds good," Tyler said. He had taken a fresh chew of tobacco and was ready.

"You scared, Satterwhite?" Hampton asked.

"Hell, yes."

"Good. The Captain used to say if a man was pale before a fight, he'd do a good job. Let's go."

They walked carefully over the broken ground of the draw. Volcanic boulders blocked their path every third step so that they had to wind around them, at the same time avoiding the sharp points of the Spanish dagger that competed with the boulders for space.

The right bank of the draw curved around like a cat's tail and ended in a rocky slope. The nearer bank did the same, while the delta passed between the two hills and opened into a flat. The Mexicans were camped in the gravel of the flat on the south side of the hills, and their fires lit the draw ahead of Hampton when he got there. He held up his hand and waited for Tyler to move forward.

"What about sentries?" Hampton whispered.

"Checked already. They ain't any."

Mary and Satterwhite huddled close to hear. The wind was wrong for noise to come to them from the camp, but the fires were still too bright.

"What the hell can they be burnin'?" Hampton said.

They sat down close to one another to wait. Hampton kept his eyes on the opening between the two hills where the draw spilled out into the desert. His heart was beating fast, and his mouth was dry. Mary knelt at his feet, looking up at him, her hand on the butt of the .45.

Gradually, the light wavered and weakened until it was only a ghost of a glow ahead among the boulders. Hampton signaled Tyler again.

"I'm takin' Satterwhite with me," he said. "We're crossin' to that next hill. You and Mary stay with this one. Once the shootin' starts, don't let 'em scatter into the desert."

"Let me go with you," Mary said.

"No. I can think better if you're with Bud. He can keep up with you better in the dark than I can, too. Do what he says and do it like you mean it."

"You'll be fine," Tyler said. Then he held out his hand to Hampton. "Good luck, old partner," he said.

Hampton took his hand. "Same to you, you old bear hunter."

Tyler shook Satterwhite's hand. "You let anything happen to Hamp, and I'll shoot you myself," he said. He smiled in the dark. "Good luck."

"Thank you, Bud. I'll do my best."

Mary hugged Satterwhite and looked at him. Then she looked at Hampton. He stood up and looked down into the shadow his hat brim cast across her face.

274

"I'm not going to hug you until this is over," Mary said.

"Fair enough," Hampton said. He reached down beside her and pulled the leather thong off the hammer of his pistol on her hip. "Come on, Satterwhite," he said, and turned away.

Mary watched them move cautiously forward. "Should I have told him goodbye, Bud?" she said, quietly.

"Let's move up the hill," Tyler said, touching her arm. "Place your feet before you put your weight on them."

Hampton and Satterwhite moved forward until they could see the first fire, little more than coals now, and the first dark forms wrapped in blankets. They edged around the rocks until they could see the whole camp. There were five fires, but Hampton couldn't tell how many people were asleep on the ground.

He turned and looked behind him, trying to see whether or not Tyler had reached the top of his hill, but he and Satterwhite had gone too far around the slope.

"All right," he said, whispering close to Satterwhite's face. "Over yonder is where we want to be, but we got to cross this open ground to get there. The best way to do it is just to do it. Go hunched over. Go quietly, and don't look at the camp. A sleepin' man can feel the eyes of an enemy on him. Got that?"

"I'll be right behind you. No, wait. All right. I'll be right behind you."

"Let's do her."

Hampton bent over and crossed the open ground slowly and carefully without looking to the left at the camp. Satterwhite came behind him. Once in the shadow of the next hill, Satterwhite took a deep breath and let it out slowly.

There was no sound from the camp.

"You done good, Satterwhite. Let's climb this hill and see what we can see."

At the top of the hill, they separated, each finding a rock to crouch behind that would also allow them a good field of fire. Satterwhite released the grip on his rifle and felt in his pockets for the extra cartridges.

Hampton took off his gloves and put them on top of the rock in front of him. Below him, he saw the five distinct fires, burning dimly down to breeze-fanned coals. Each fire had several sleepers around it, and the restive, dark shapes of the horses were tied at the edge of the flat to a picket rope stretched between two willows. His heart was beating fast from the climb, but now he felt only tenseness like that he felt as a boy when he stood frozen over a lizard he was trying to catch. He thought of the Mexicans moving up in the dark on Columbus, then on El Indio, and he remembered the way Mary had looked when he found her.

He glanced to the left in the darkness and made out Satterwhite's shape huddled down behind a rock. He pulled back the hammer on the Winchester. "Ready?" he whispered.

"No," Satterwhite answered, then waved his hand.

Hampton stood up and stepped about ten feet from the boulder. He would begin shooting there, then move back to the safety of the boulder. He raised his rifle to the night sky, and screamed in a rough, ragged voice that brought chills to Satterwhite. He touched the trigger on the rifle, brought it down, and fired into the camp.

Instantly the bandits rolled out of the blankets. As Hampton had hoped, it was impossible to tell the women from the men. He could not discern the rifle sights in the dark and pointed the rifle like an arm at his targets. He fired at a bandit below him who was bending over trying to pick up his gun. The man dropped, and Hampton levered another round and fired at the next moving figure. He was aware of shots coming from the next hill and from Satterwhite to his left. The first shots began to flash up from the camp, as the bandits crouched, their rifles in their hands.

Hampton moved back to his left and regained the boulder, levering shells and firing as he moved. The firing was almost continuous until Hampton emptied the magazine. He ducked down to reload and heard for the first time the crack of his .45. It fired, then fired again in a steady pace, and Hampton knew Mary was picking her targets.

Satterwhite stopped firing, and Hampton rammed cartridges into the spring lever. "Satterwhite?" he called above the firing from below. Bullets were whistling off the rocks around him.

"I'm all right," Satterwhite answered.

Hampton counted nine rounds before he turned and fired

down the camp. Before he had shot all nine rounds, every bandit in the camp was down and still. He levered the hot Winchester and stood up.

There was no way of knowing whether or not some of the bandits had run into the darkness of the brush, but Hampton knew he had not seen any. He had shot at those closest to the edge of camp first. Smoke drifted away from them. The horses pitched and pulled at the picket rope. He looked at them twice, but failed to see what had drawn his attention there. He reached in his pocket and reloaded the rifle.

"Satterwhite? You all right?"

"Is it over?"

"I don't know."

Hampton whistled shrilly in the dark. An echoing whistle came from the next hill. "Thank God," he said. Then he said, "Come on, Satterwhite. Let's go check the damage."

They slipped easily down the south side of the hill, working off the adrenalin of the gunfight.

"Why did you scream like that?" Satterwhite asked.

"Wanted to warn them. Didn't have to, but I wanted to."

"I never heard anything that terrible in my life. It nearly made me piss in my pants."

"Man I knew once taught me that yell. He fought for the South in the Civil War."

At the bottom of the hill, Hampton led the way around the bend of the draw into the camp. Packs and blankets were scattered everywhere, as were the bodies of the bandits.

"Be careful," he warned Satterwhite. "You never know which of these bandits will be lyin' on a pistol ready to shoot you when you walk up."

They entered the camp, Satterwhite moving to the left, while Hampton worked to the right. Almost immediately, a bandit rose across the camp, but before he could shoot the unsuspecting Satterwhite, a shot rang out from the top of the hill, and the bandit fell back, dead. "Keep your damned eyes open," Hampton hissed.

He was near the second fire circle. A man rolled, then was still. Hampton held his rifle on him and crouched beside him. The man was still. There was no pulse. The skin on the back of Hampton's neck prickled. He stood up and moved on, working around to the picket line where he met Satterwhite.

"Looks like we cleaned them out," Satterwhite said, his voice shaky.

"How do you feel?"

"Not too good. At least I'm glad all the women were on your side of the camp."

Hampton turned and looked across the camp, and in the same instant, he knew what he had missed before. He looked at the horses. There were less than ten of them. Benito had mentioned a seep spring below the draw, but this wasn't it, and there were no women. The rest of the band was in the desert behind them.

"God damn," Hampton said. "Get out of here. Get out of here! Run, Satterwhite!"

Hampton pushed Satterwhite ahead of him, and they ran across the camp, sidestepping the corpses. Before they cleared the camp, the first shots rang out behind them. The firing was loud and continuous. It sounded like a hundred guns at once.

Hampton turned and fired from the hip, moving backwards and levering the shells at the bursts of rifle flame.

"Get in the rocks!" Hampton shouted. His relief at getting through the first part of the fight dissolved. They faced an unknown now, something he had not planned for, but his mind was calm, as he had trained it to be, and he resisted the memory of Homer that tried to push through his concentration. This would not end that way, if he could help it.

From the top of his hill, Tyler shouted, "Get out of there, Hamp!" and levered shells into the brush as fast as he could move his wrist back and forth.

Hampton started to turn, then felt a blow to his right shoulder as strong as if someone had hit him there full swing with a claw hammer. The impact threw him off balance. He lost his grip on his rifle and went down.

"Hamp!" Mary screamed. She jumped to her feet and ran forward on the hilltop, emptying the .45 in her hand as she went. Tyler grabbed her around the waist and pulled her down as bullets cut the air above them. Mary felt the world drop away from her.

"Don't do that again," Tyler said roughly, as he rose and continued firing.

For a minute, Hampton felt the cold gravel and sand against his cheek. He rolled over on his back and looked up for the stars, but there were not any. The night was black, and the explosions of rifle fire did not diminish. He took a deep breath and lay still. His eyes closed.

Satterwhite made the protection of the rocks and fell behind a boulder, breathing hard and aware that he could hear Mary's voice above the shooting. He looked out into the camp from behind the boulder and saw that Hampton had gone down.

"Hampton," he shouted, adding his voice to that of Mary's.

The shooting was furious, but misdirected, so that the real danger came from a stray bullet rather than an aimed one. Satterwhite went down behind the boulder again. "What do I do now?" he said aloud. He jammed his hand in his coat pocket and brought out a handful of cartridges. He slid them in the rifle until it would hold no more, then, barely thinking what he would do, he stood up and ran back for Hampton.

He was ten feet from Hampton's form before he was noticed. He dropped to his belly to the right of Hampton and fired as quickly as he could. He heard two screams, then heard Tyler firing with lightning action from the top of the hill, all the time yelling, trying to draw fire away from Satterwhite.

Satterwhite got to his feet again and ran to Hampton. He dropped the rifle, put his hands under the arms of the big man and dragged him backwards as fast as he could move. Bullets hit close to him, one of them ripping the top of his boot, but he did not hesitate, nor look up. At the base of the hill was a boulder as big as a horse trough. Satterwhite stumbled in behind it, pulling Hampton after him, and fell. His breath was tearing in and out of his lungs so fast and so deeply, he thought he would pass out or die before he could breathe normally again.

Tyler fired in a sweeping line at the edge of the camp where the shadows could hide someone, and out beyond in the desert, where the land was brushy and uneven, and where other bandits could be moving up. When he exhausted the magazine of the rifle, he gave it to Mary to reload while he shot his pistol into the darkness at his left flank, hoping through accident to keep the bandits in front of him.

Mary worked without thinking or feeling anything, forcing herself to remain useful and deadly. When she saw Satterwhite pull Hampton out of the open, her resolve hardened again. Tyler had never known but one better comrade in arms than the one Mary became.

Satterwhite scrambled to his knees and crawled to Hampton. He touched his chest and felt it rise and fall beneath his hand. "Oh sweet Lord," he said. He pulled a bandana out of his coat pocket and pressed it against Hampton's shoulder where even his coat was wet with blood.

Bullets hit the rocks around him. A man on horseback broke through the camp at a run, firing as he came, hoping to drive Satterwhite out of the rocks. Satterwhite grabbed for his pistol, but his holster was empty, his gun gone. Hampton had given his pistol to Mary. Satterwhite fell back against the rock, waiting to be found.

The horse was close enough for Satterwhite to hear him snorting when Tyler shot the bandit, hitting him twice before he fell. The horse galloped by into the draw, but the bandit rolled against the rocks and was still.

Satterwhite took a quick look and saw the man's rifle close by. He dashed for it, drew fire, and dived behind the rock again. To his dismay, the rifle was a Mauser. Whatever was in the magazine was all the firepower Satterwhite had. He would have to pick his shots with care.

Tyler and Mary were forced to withdraw from the crest of the hill. Tyler had done too much shooting to be elusive, and the bandits, scattered in the brush beyond the camp, concentrated their fire at him.

"Come on, Mary," he said, reloading as they moved down the north side of the hill in the dark. "This hill isn't safe for us anymore."

"We have to find Hamp," Mary said.

"Him and Satterwhite are all right for now. Satterwhite found a good place to defend. We got to do the same."

"Did you see him get hit?" Mary asked. "How bad do you think it was? Do you think he is dead?"

"He's not dead, but that's all I can say. Watch that cactus there."

At the bottom of the hill, Tyler turned at the sound of horses, then pushed Mary low and fired rapidly as two riders came up the draw firing pistols at any shape larger than a rabbit. One went down, then the other.

"Damn," Tyler said. "Good thing these bandits fight at night, or they'd never have a chance."

When Satterwhite left his cover to get the bandit's rifle, he gave his hiding place away, and round after round chipped rocks, cut cactus, or whined away around him. He slid closer to Hampton and pressed the bandana again, hoping to slow the bleeding, although he could not believe it would make any difference. Something had gone wrong, and now they were pinned down. As soon as the sun came up, they would be dead men. Perhaps he could save the Mauser for the two of them. He knew he did not want to be captured alive. His wet fingers felt cold, but when he looked in the darkness at Hampton, he felt a hard calm replace his fear. *All right*, he thought. *Let it be what it will be. I'll do whatever it takes.*

Tyler found a good place along the bottom of the draw that could be defended from every direction except facing the bed of the draw. It was formed by the cleft of two boulders on edge. He helped Mary in between the rocks and sat down beside her, reloading his Winchester.

"Well, Mary," he said. "Looks like we let you down, after all. Hamp saw them horses was short the same time I did, but who would have figured they would split their camp?"

"It's my fault," Mary said.

"I have a feelin' Hamp knew you would say somethin' like that. That's why he sent you with me — couldn't bear to hear you say it."

"I insisted."

Tyler rolled out, waited for a rifle flash that would tell him the bandits had reached the top of the hill he and Mary had just left, then fired twice at the first one he saw. He dropped back behind the rocks.

"Yeah, you did insist," he said, listening as he spoke. "And here we are. But live or die, I feel good about myself, and that's thanks to you, Mary. It isn't every day that a man gets a chance to go into battle for a girl like you. That may sound silly, but there's lots of men in this old world that'd change places with me at the drop of a hat."

The shooting continued, above and around them. Salazar had roused his men from the spring where they had gone with the women and was now leading them through the camp. Shouting and waving his arms, he ordered an attack up the side of the hill where Tyler had been. He had no idea who his attackers were or how many, but he knew he had somehow gained the advantage. If it was the men from El Indio, he would make them very sorry.

The bandits raced up the south side of the hill, firing randomly, trying to draw return fire that never came. From his hiding place, Satterwhite heard the shouts and the firing, but, for the moment, it was moving away from him. He put his hand on Hampton's shoulder again.

Tyler waited, hoping to draw the bandits into skylining themselves on his side of the hill, but another rider through the draw saw them, and Tyler was forced to shoot, hitting the horse with the second round. The rider tried to crawl away. Tyler exposed himself long enough to stop him. Bullets hailed down on them from above.

"This may be it, Mary," Tyler said, squinting against the noise. "If worse comes to worse, do you want me to shoot you?"

"Could you?"

"If worse comes to worse."

"Yes," Mary said. There were tears on her face, but she wasn't crying. "I wish I had told Hamp goodbye."

Tyler nodded and spit.

The gunfire moved down the hill on top of them. Tyler rolled out and fired, then dropped back and waited for another opening.

Abruptly, with a totally new sound, a machine gun opened up from the top of the opposite side of the draw. It brought a momentary pause to the firing above them.

"Damn," Tyler said. "That's it, Mary."

But as the machine gun continued to rake the hill, it remained high. There were screams above Tyler and Mary as some of the bandits were hit.

"Wait," Mary said. "That gun is on our side."

"Sure," Tyler said. "That's what's been steppin' on my tail."

He rolled out and fired up the hill whenever a man skylined himself against the graying early morning sky. Mary tried to see across the draw, but the machine gun was well placed, and she could not see its fire.

Tyler moved up the hill in pursuit of the now retreating bandits. Mary stepped out, too, hoping to use the distraction to find Hampton and Satterwhite. To the left was the mouth of the draw, but no firing was coming through it. Mary crawled around the boulders, carrying Hampton's pistol, loaded and ready. Tyler was aware of what she was doing but was pinned down by a man thirty yards above him.

Then, as abruptly as the machine gun had started, it stopped, and was replaced by more accurate rifle fire. Three bandits, including the one who had Tyler pinned, broke their cover and retreated back toward the camp.

"Hello the hill!" a voice rang down.

"Is that you, Preacher?" Tyler shouted back.

There was a cheer from the top of the next hill, and the firing began again.

From his hiding place, Satterwhite heard the change in the battle and dared enough of a look to see what was happening. In the dim light, he could see the southern edge of the camp, where two men spun on horseback as if performing in a rodeo, and he saw another man and a woman on foot, running toward the two riders. There was shouting amid the gunfire. He could not see the opening of the draw and had no idea who had joined the fight or what the machine gun meant.

Mary reached the bottom of the draw and, keeping low, she ran for the opening across which Hampton had led Satterwhite. In one place, the gravel of the bed of the draw ran smoothly against a sheer boulder twenty feet high. Mary ran along the boulder, then stepped out into the open.

Across the camp, she saw Salazar on horseback and recognized him immediately. There was firing from the top of the hill to her left, and bandits were running for the picketed horses. No one noticed her as she stood in the gray light of the coming dawn. Her heart beating like the sound of the pitching horses, Mary raised Hampton's .45 and fired at Salazar. The bullet disappeared in the air. Mary pulled the hammer back and fired again. She missed her target, but this time Salazar noticed her, and, leveling his rifle, he spurred toward her.

Mary shook Hampton's hat off her head and fired again, hitting Salazar's horse in the face without meaning to. The horse went down. Across the camp, two women climbed into saddles and tore away through the brush. Salazar jumped from the stirrups as the horse fell, and he rolled clear, then scrambled for his rifle. Mary fired again, aiming carefully in the confusing light. The bullet threw gravel just beyond Salazar's back.

On the hill above her, Tyler saw Salazar reach the rifle, and Tyler aimed a careful shot. The hammer fell on an empty chamber. He brought the Winchester down and slapped his pockets frantically. They were flat on his hips, empty. "Mary!" he shouted.

Satterwhite heard Mary's name and lurched across Hampton's body for the Mauser. He grabbed it up and slid the bolt back, then rammed it forward. He stood up and jumped out from behind the boulder.

Mary pulled the hammer back, lowered the front sight, and fired. The bullet cut the shoulders of Salazar's coat. He sat up quickly with the rifle in his hands and levered a round in the chamber.

"Mary!" Tyler shouted again, moving down through the rocks.

Salazar pointed the rifle at the girl, his mouth twisted in a snarl. He could not imagine how she had come to be there, but she had proven bad luck after all. As his finger closed on the trigger, he saw a man appear suddenly beside her. He was a *gringo* cowboy with long brown hair, and his arms were tied behind his back, the same cowboy he and his men had hanged before the raid at Columbus. The rifle twitched to the side, and Salazar, his eyes wide and disbelieving, shot at the ghost.

Without flinching, Mary pulled the hammer back, and the

cylinder brought the last round into place. Salazar got to his feet and fired again at the image of the dead man. Mary sighted down the short barrel of the .45. Above her, Tyler's boot turned on a rock, and he went down on one knee, his rifle stock hitting the ground like a supporting cane. To her right, Satterwhite raised the Mauser, and he and Mary fired at the same moment.

Salazar jerked. His legs buckled, and he went down. As his vision turned liquid and blurred, he saw the ghost of Clay Smith grow dim and distant. In death, Salazar's face still carried the look of disbelief.

There were no other bandits in the camp, but someone was still shooting. Tyler got to his feet and moved down the hill. Satterwhite took a deep breath and looked back toward the boulder where Hampton lay.

Alone in the dawn, Mary was aware for the first time that she was cold. She shivered and her eyes watered, but she broke the action on the .45 and reloaded it, her fingers doing what her eyes could not see to do.

TWENTY-NINE

T HE morning broke across the desert in tints of orange and pink and rose. Birds twittered from bush to bush. An eagle cried once above the hills and veered south. Mary slid the last .45 in the cylinder and looked at the body of Salazar on the ground sixty feet away.

Tyler and Satterwhite reached her at the same time.

"Are you all right, Mary?" Satterwhite asked.

She reached down beside her and picked up Hampton's hat. "Hamp," she said.

"Yeah," Satterwhite swallowed. "Come on."

Satterwhite led the other two up into the rocks where Hampton lay on his back, his face pale and set.

"How is he, Rueben?" Mary asked, stepping up beside Satterwhite.

"I don't know. He took a good hit, but it didn't go through. He's only bleeding here."

"Let me have a look," Tyler said, squatting against the rock.

He opened Hampton's coat, then pulled back the shoulder of his shirt. There was a clean hole two inches below his collarbone, and the surrounding flesh was purplish with bruise. Tyler wiped his hand on his pants and put it over Hampton's heart. The beat was strong and steady.

Mary caught Tyler's eyes. He winked and nodded.

"What do you think, Bud?" Satterwhite asked.

"I think I seen some stuff in my lifetime, but I never saw anything as brave as you goin' back for Hamp."

286

Satterwhite smiled slowly, then glanced at Mary. His face went solemn again.

"Hamp!" a voice called from the draw. "Hamp! Mr. Tyler?"

Tyler whistled and stood up. In a moment, the preacher appeared below. He was wearing a rough, brown coat and a black hat and carrying his rifle. Behind him were Billy and a Mexican. At first Tyler did not recognize the Mexican, then he remembered the visitor to their camp who had lost his children.

"Where's Hamp?" the preacher asked, his voice hoarse.

"Here," Tyler said. "He's been hit."

The preacher hurried forward. Billy and the Mexican began going from body to body. Satterwhite stood up to let the preacher close to Hampton.

"How bad?" the preacher asked when he saw the blood.

"Bad enough. He's carryin' the bullet."

"I'll get my father's bag," the preacher said.

"Let Billy get it," Satterwhite said. "Billy. Get the preacher's medical bag."

"Why me?" Billy asked.

"Youngest man always gets the bag."

"Who says?"

"Me for one," Satterwhite told him and choked. "Now get it. Mr. Hampton's been hit."

"Yes, sir," Billy said and hurried away.

The preacher looked at Mary's face beneath Hampton's hat. He smiled in spite of the circumstances. "You must be Mary," he said.

"Can you help him?" she asked.

"I think so. Bud, help me carry him down to a level place. We'll need to build a fire."

"I'll get this side," Satterwhite said.

The preacher led the way out of the rocks, and Tyler and Satterwhite carried Hampton into the Mexican camp. Mary and the preacher grabbed up some blankets, shook them out, and spread them on the ground by a fire circle. Mary avoided the dead bandits with her eyes, afraid she would see a face she remembered.

"Put him down here," the preacher said. "Get a fire going.

Mary, help me get his coat off. We'll use it for cover. These blankets are filthy."

"I'll get the horses," Satterwhite said.

Tyler gathered enough sticks to build a fire on the coals of the night before. Billy returned with the worn, black valise that the preacher's father had used for thirty years. Satterwhite came along behind him leading the horses.

The preacher opened Hampton's shirt and doused the wound with boric acid. Hampton's body flinched, but he did not open his eyes.

"Do you know what you're doing?" Mary asked.

"Yes. In fact, I've seen more operations on the ground than in a hospital."

While the preacher cleaned the wound with antiseptic, Satterwhite and Tyler filled the preacher's Dutch oven with water and put it on the fire.

"This is the last time I want to do this," Tyler said.

"Is he going to be all right?" Satterwhite asked quietly.

"We'll see," Tyler answered. He followed the Mexican man with his eyes as he roamed around the camp.

Billy walked up. "Some fight, huh?" he said.

"Where the hell did you get a machine gun?" Tyler asked.

"It was his," Billy said, pointing at the Mexican. "He stole it from the Villistas in the battle of Celaya. He said he was going to use it if they tried to make him fight again. He only had four clips, though. He said that was all he could carry."

"Where did you get him?" Satterwhite asked.

"He's our guide. He helped us find you. Otherwise we would still be wandering around looking for you."

"Let's get these bodies over on the other side of the camp," Tyler said. "It's bad luck to leave 'em lyin'."

"Now," the preacher told Mary, "put some chloroform on this cloth and hold it lightly over Hamp's nose and mouth. If he stirs, let another drop fall on the cloth."

Mary looked at the serious eyes of the preacher and felt reassured, the way she would have if she had looked at Hampton's eyes. She did as she was told, and the preacher probed for the bullet. When he found it, he rinsed a pair of long, thin forceps in the boric acid and pulled the bullet out. He threw it sideways on the sand.

"It was spent," he said. "Didn't go in far enough to tear much. He should be awake, but it's just as well he isn't. I'm going to sew it up."

When the preacher was finished, he washed his hands. Mary still held the cloth to Hampton's face, watching the breeze move strands of his hair. The preacher put a gentle hand on hers and lifted it away.

"What now?" Mary said.

"We wait for him to wake up."

"What if he doesn't wake up?"

The preacher looked at Mary, the memory of the feel of her hand still fresh in his mind. Despite his own misgivings, he said, "Have you forgotten this is Hamp we're talking about? He'll wake up. I'm sure he was exhausted before he was hit. Most times, a hit like that wouldn't even slow a man up, much less put him down. He needs rest and time."

"Preacher," Tyler said, "that man means more to us than we can say."

The preacher was still looking at Mary. Her eyes were on Hampton's face. She bit her lip and looked away.

"Let's get some coffee on," the preacher said. "We could use some."

Mary sat by Hampton with her hand on his wrist while the sun found its way into the flat. Her shadow threw shade across his pale face. She remembered a time when she was twelve and had sat on her porch watching Hampton sitting on his own porch as the summer twilight turned to dark. They had been aware of each other, but neither had signaled the other to come over. After a while, they had each gone in, Mary with a lingering impression of having had a conversation.

Now, in the still-cold Mexican morning, Mary knew she had been right to leave Leonard, but, with Hampton lying unconscious before her, she did not think she was right in insisting they find Salazar. It had been Hampton who taught her the value of a code and the kind of sickness that breaking the code led to. She had learned the lesson well, but it had never before meant losing someone she cared about. Perhaps love was more important than justice or duty, and she had selfishly broken the code after all.

"So I didn't see just sitting around waiting," the preacher was saying. "Billy volunteered, and we crossed the border in the dust of Pershing's troops."

"Daddy never would have let me go if half the soldiers in the United States weren't already down here," Billy said, poking at the fire.

"Are we at war?" Tyler asked.

"You know Wilson better than that. The official term is 'punitive expedition.'"

"Me and Hamp saw the dust a few days back."

"We drifted around asking ranchers if they had seen you, but no one had until we came across Cipriano."

Cipriano looked up and nodded. He was smoking a cigarette and drinking a cup of coffee.

"He remembered you. He said he had been looking for his children and thought if he helped us find this 'other man's daughter,' as he called Mary, it would bring him luck. We never dreamed he would have a machine gun hidden in his house. He led us to El Indio, where we found out you were coming here."

"You sure came at the right time," Tyler said. "Them banditos was puttin' a squeeze on us."

Mary felt Hampton's wrist stir beneath her hand. She looked down quickly and saw him open his eyes. He blinked up at her, then winced and turned his hand so that it was holding hers.

"Little Mary," he whispered. "I saw Homer go down, but there was nothin' I could do. I couldn't have stopped him."

"No, Hamp," Mary said, crying. She bent down and kissed his forehead, ending nearly forty years of guilt. "I'm sorry I made you come down here, Hamp. I was wrong."

"It had to be done, Mary. Bud and me were figurin' on it all along. We just didn't know what to do with you. We pretended you talked us into it for your sake."

"Hamp, I thought they had killed you."

Hampton gripped Mary's hand. The others had heard Mary

speak and now gathered around them. Hampton's eyes went from one to the other, taking roll. "Is that the preacher and Billy? Am I back home?"

"Practically," Mary said. She told him what had happened.

Hampton felt around on the ground with his left hand, then started to push up, but the pain laid him back down again. When the sharpness had turned to throbbing, he opened his eyes. "Satterwhite," he said.

Satterwhite crouched down beside him.

"Listen," Hampton said, looking at him, "thanks for comin' after me. It took a man to do that. Book, chapter, and verse." He held up his left hand, and Satterwhite took it.

Mary looked across at Satterwhite and saw his cheeks flush red.

"One more thing," Hampton said. "I sure could use one of them smokes."

In the middle of the afternoon, they loaded the horses with extra guns and all the stolen goods that were in the camp, and prepared to return to El Indio. Hampton sat propped against a Mexican saddle, his arm in a sling. Mary came up to him with something behind her back. Hampton looked at the pants and shirt, the way the suspenders came off her shoulders, and her face beneath the brim of his hat. He was sure he would never see a prettier girl in his life.

"I've got a present for you," Mary said and smiled.

"Uh-huh," Hampton said. "What is it?"

Mary brought a narrow-brimmed gray Stetson out from behind her back and held it out. The crown had been squashed, but Mary had shaped it up again.

"Where'd you get that?"

"It was part of the stuff the bandits took from Columbus. It's for you."

"I already got a hat."

"Not anymore," Mary said. She knelt on the ground beside Hampton and put the hat on his head. It was a good fit. She looked at him and smiled.

"All right," he said.

Tyler helped Hampton up on Lady.

"I want to see which one was *El Hacedor de Munecas*," he said.

Tyler led Hampton over to the edge of the camp by the willows where they had laid out the bodies and covered them with blankets. He stopped by one and pulled the blanket back by the corner. Hampton looked down into the dead face for a minute, then said, "Now it's finished."

They started back for El Indio. Mary rode beside Hampton, Tyler just ahead, holding the reins.

It was dark when they rode into the village. Benito found them an empty adobe for Hampton, and they all moved into it. Hampton had a low fever, and the pain made him see double images.

With the constant attention of the preacher and Mary, Hampton beat the fever, but it was several days before he had the strength to ride. On the second day, Tyler and Satterwhite rode for the other pack they had left behind in the canyon. Cipriano left on the third day, taking Natalia with him.

Mary saw them packing their horses and went out to say good-bye. Cipriano had an extra sack of coffee and tobacco on his saddle. He turned to Mary.

"Mary," he said, calling her "*Maria*," "you have been very much luck to me, and I can understand why so many men have come to look for you. Tell your father he should come next time. So many men should not have to look for another man's daughter.

"This one I take with me. She is not my daughter, but they do not want her here. Now there will be no more quiet nights."

Cipriano took off his hat and kissed Mary on the cheek. Mary smiled at him, then looked at Natalia. For several seconds Natalia held a sulky, resentful look on her face, then she dropped her eyes.

"Thank you for your help to me," Mary said. "I and my family owe you a debt of gratitude."

Natalia looked up at Mary then and smiled. Her face looked younger and prettier, almost innocent again. They mounted their horses and rode slowly out of the village.

Tyler and Satterwhite returned and with Billy spent their time helping rebuild the roofs and burned interiors of some of the adobes fired by the bandits. Mostly, however, they all rested, idling in to sit with Hampton, then wandering out again.

On the fifth afternoon, Hampton and the preacher stood at the only window of the adobe watching Mary who sat in a doorway across the street talking with some children.

"She is an incredible young woman," the preacher said.

"Uh-huh. She is that."

"I don't need to ask what they did to her, do I?"

"Nope," Hampton said. "It doesn't matter. What matters now is that she is made to feel as important as she is."

"You have been awfully close to her, haven't you?"

"Yeah," Hampton said. "But I reckon I'll be headin' to Texas with Bud if we ever get out of this desert."

"I hate to hear that, Hamp."

"You stayin' in Columbus?"

"I don't know. I may see if the army could use me. I'm not returning to the church."

"Too bad. Church needs some preachers who are men, leaders in their own right."

"Well. . . ."

"Don't doubt it, Preacher. You saved more than one life when you came down here."

Hampton watched Mary tease the hair of one of the children who then leaped in her lap.

"Look at that," he said. "She's goin' to need some lookin' after."

"She's a beautiful girl," the preacher said.

Hampton turned back into the room and looked around at its dusty shabbiness. His shoulder hurt, and he felt old. "I'm ready to go back to New Mexico," he said in a rough tone. "Let's move out tomorrow."

On the twenty-third of March, fourteen days after the raid on Columbus, they swung wide of Palomas and crossed the border. They rode through the desert east of Columbus, watching the activity in the little town.

"Don't even look the same," Hampton said, the reins held easily in his left hand, his chin leaning into his collar to steady his wound.

"It's not the town we left," Mary said, riding beside him.

Hampton looked at her. "We're not the same people who left it either."

Mary nodded. Hampton watched her, then asked, "How do you feel, Little Mary?"

She let her eyes drift to his. After a minute, a slow smile came to her healed and beautiful face.

When they rode into the ranch yard, doors opened, and people poured out to greet them. Mary swung down, still wearing Hampton's hat.

Hampton watched Mr. Frank and Constance surround and embrace her, Constance crying, while Mr. Frank patted Mary's shoulder. Betty and Tom Dunbar met Billy. Satterwhite swung down, followed by the preacher and Tyler. Hampton sat his horse, watching everyone, wanting to remember them when they were happy.

Tyler stepped back to him.

"Need some help gettin' down?" he asked and spit.

Hampton looked at him, then said, "I wish I had a picture of this."

"It's a mighty pretty thing," Tyler said and nodded.

Hampton gripped the pommel with his left hand and swung down out of the saddle. He felt tired to his bones. Tom Dunbar began rounding up the horses to take them to the barn. Billy ran forward and took Lady's reins.

"I got this one," he said.

As the horses moved away, Hampton saw Mary and her parents looking at him. Mr. Frank stepped forward and shook his left hand.

"You all right, Hamp?" he asked.

"I'll mend. Yeah, I'm all right."

"Thank you, Hamp. I don't know what else to say. Thank you all."

Hampton nodded and watched them walk up to the big house, Mary's slim figure in Satterwhite's clothes hugged from both sides by her parents.

Betty stood a little to the side, a smile on her trembling lips. Hampton looked at her and smiled. She stepped to him and hugged him on the left side, wincing at the sight of the sling on his right shoulder. He held her a minute.

"Want some supper?" she said. "I'm cooking."

"In that case," Hampton said.

"Sounds good to me," Tyler said and ducked his head.

"Yes, thank you," the preacher said.

Satterwhite stood looking at the ground, then he glanced up at the big house.

"I'll get started right now," Betty said.

She walked toward Hampton's house, and, one by one, the men fell in behind her. Hampton was last. He took a few steps, then glanced at Satterwhite, who stood alone now in front of the big house.

"What is it, Satterwhite?" Hampton asked.

"Nothing. Only, I would kind of like to eat with you tonight."

"Uh-huh. Well, come on. You earned it."

Satterwhite grinned and followed Hampton to the house.

Before they had finished eating, Mary slipped in the door and stood behind Hampton's chair, her hands lightly on his shoulders. She was wearing a blue dress, and her hair was brushed.

"I told Mother and Father I needed to rest for a while and slipped out." Mary shrugged and bit her lip. "I thought you would be here eating. I guess I got used to being around you all." She bit her lip again and paused. Hampton felt the pressure increase on his shoulders. He was looking at his plate, and his chest felt tight. "I have to go back now," she said.

Her hands slid off Hampton's shoulders, and she was gone through the door before he could stand up.

"She was crying," Satterwhite said.

Hampton slowly sat back down. For a few minutes, everyone just looked at the food without eating.

Two nights later, Mary found Hampton leaning alone on the corral fence, holding a handful of oats out to Lady. It was just after dark, and the air, though chill, had a hint of the lingering warmth that would cloak the spring nights to come. The activity and celebration of their return was over, and the ranch was quiet again.

"She's a beautiful horse," Mary said. "Leave it to you to ride a mare."

"Old Lady's been good to me. She's taken me where I wanted to go and brought me back again."

"Are you going to take her with you?"

Lady nuzzled the last of the oats. Hampton patted her face and rested his left arm on the top rail of the corral fence.

"Yeah."

Mary leaned her back against the boards facing the other way. She was wearing a light gray skirt and a pink blouse, and she had on a suede leather jacket. Her hair was tied back with Hampton's red bandana. He could smell her, a thin scent of what it was that made her Mary.

"You get settled in all right?" he asked her.

"Yes."

"Is Constance givin' you a hard ride about the man from Tennessee?"

"She wants him to come out here so we can all talk."

"Uh-huh."

"I'm not going back to him," Mary said. "I want to find someone who doesn't have to ask me what's wrong when I'm sad, but knows. And I can't live in a place where the town is more important than the country."

Hampton watched the horses move about. "I'll vote for that," he said. Then he said, "About that other, you got that straight?"

"You mean Mexico?"

"Yeah."

Mary was quiet and serious for a minute. "Yes, except for the nightmares. It all seems far away now, like it happened to someone else."

Hampton sensed Mary's restlessness beside him, but he was silent, waiting for her to find the words he knew she was looking for.

"It was easier to talk in the desert," she said finally.

Hampton looked at the horses. Lady moved away to the water trough. He heard Tom Dunbar calling Billy. Billy answered. A door slammed.

"Always is," Hampton said. "Always easier to talk outside than inside. Never trust anyone who finds it easier to talk inside."

Mary was quiet. She took a deep breath, blew it out, and looked down. Then she said, "I'm not sure I can get along without you, Hamp." Tears were in her voice.

"You can. You have to. I'm not the man in your life, Mary. I would only get in the way of that man if I stayed around here."

"You've always been the man in my life, Hamp," Mary said.

Hampton shook his head. "No, goddammit," he said. "No, I haven't." Then he said, "Feels like I've missed so much in my life. Don't know what happened to me along the way. It seems like all the things I ever really wanted I could never have. And then there was you. Little Mary in the sunshine. We had some times, didn't we? Maybe if I hadn't known you so well as a little girl, or was younger myself — maybe then I could pretend. . . ."

Hampton stopped, unwilling to say the words. Instead, he said, "When I heard you had been taken by those goddamned bandits, something inside of me died. Never felt that way before, not even when I lost Homer. But I got you back, and here you are, and I'm all right now.

"I still have time left to build a life in Texas. Bud and me get along pretty good. And who knows, hell, there's liable to be some pretty East Texas widow woman over there who wouldn't mind takin' on an old guy like me. It's shady over there, Mary, and it rains year around. Good for corn. I love to watch corn growin'." Hampton was quiet, thinking about it, aware that Mary had more to say.

"Can I tell you something?" Mary said quietly.

"Now's the time for it."

"Sometimes, in Tennessee, when I was lonely or sad, I'd wonder what it would have been like if I had married you. I even wondered what our children would look like and what we would name them."

"You probably should have kept that to yourself," Hampton said. "But thank you."

"I used to think that the world was a fair place for people who were good," Mary said. "I don't think it's very fair anymore."

"You get into somethin' you can't see your way out of, think of me, think of what I'd do or say, and you'll be all right."

"And if that's not enough, can I come to Texas?"

"Yep, if you don't stay too long. I don't know how many more times I could say goodbye to you."

"I'll come in June," Mary said. "When your corn is ready.

I'll even pick us a dozen ears or so, and we'll have them for supper."

Hampton looked out across the corral and rubbed his chin on his forearm. She had stepped into another dream of his, and it made the difference he had been wanting. He pushed away and looked at her. She raised her face to his.

"I was wrong," Hampton said. "I haven't missed anything. All the things I will never have in my life I can let pass without regret because, for a little while, I have known you."

Mary looked at him. He raised his left hand and touched her face, gently cradling her cheek and touching the hair that partly hid it. She stepped up against him and hugged him around his middle, her face in his shirt.

They held each other in the desert darkness for a minute or more, then Mary took a troubled breath and whispered, "It's sad to love somebody, isn't it, Hamp?"

Hampton did not answer her. His eyes picked out a star above the barn, and he watched it grow brighter.

The door to the big house opened, and Constance appeared silhouetted there. She called Mary.

"Better go," Hampton said, releasing her.

Mary looked at him in the darkness for a moment. Constance called again, and Mary turned away. Hampton watched her until she was inside, then he walked through the darkness to his house. Tyler was sitting by the wood stove, drinking a cup of coffee.

"You know the best thing about bein' home?" Tyler asked when Hampton joined him. "Bein' able to lean back against somethin' when you sit down."

"That's old man talk."

"Damn right."

Hampton looked at the floor for a while, then he said, "I've said my goodbyes, Bud. I'm ready to go."

"Said goodbye to Mary?"

Hampton looked at the floor. "It came too late, Bud. We got different roads we got to walk down. We can't stand around forever wishin' it weren't so. Time for her to go on, and time for me to go on too."

298

Tyler sipped his coffee and looked at the wood heater. "There's few men ever get to stand in the light of a gal like that," he said. "We was lucky."

"I wish I had somethin' to give her, somethin' to leave behind."

"We ain't the kind that has things," Tyler said. "Remember? Besides, maybe we already gave her somethin' in bringin' her back."

Hampton ran a hand over his beard. "I guess so," he said. "Anyway, she's still got my hat."

On the first day of April, Hampton tied his last bag on the bed of his empty house. He and Tyler had booked passage on the train from Columbus to San Antonio, and they were leaving in two hours. Neither one of them felt like a long journey on horseback. Betty stood at the doorway watching him.

"I always knew you would leave this place one day," she said.

"Why don't you come with me?"

"Wouldn't you have a fit if I said yes."

"Somebody would."

Hampton picked up the bag and carried it to the door. Betty moved aside, and he carried it into the front room and set it by the front door.

When he turned around, Betty was in front of him. She put her arms around him, being careful of his shoulder. He patted her back lightly, but before he could say anything, she broke away from him and brushed by him on her way to the door. He turned in time to see her pull it open and step through it.

Hampton and Tyler said the rest of their goodbyes in front of the big house, except for Satterwhite and Mary, who were riding into Columbus with them. Then they saddled up and rode out of the yard for the last time.

"You didn't look back," Mary said, when they were on the road.

"Nope," Hampton said.

The preacher met them at the depot. The town was full of activity and movement.

"Look," Satterwhite said, "an aeroplane."

One of the spindly, smoking aeroplanes from San Antonio circled the camp south of town and landed.

Hampton and Tyler swung down, unloaded their saddles, then

stripped them off the horses. Hampton was taking Lady with him, and Mr. Frank had given Tyler his choice of all the horses in his remuda. An attendant took the horses down to the stock car. Another attendant helped them put their saddles and bags on an express wagon, to be taken down to the baggage car.

There was an awkward moment when each of them looked at the second car down from the locomotive, then Tyler took off his hat and put out his hand to the preacher.

"It was a pleasure meetin' you, Preacher. You done a good job in the desert."

"Same here, Bud. Thank you. Perhaps we'll meet again."

"That would be nice," Tyler said. "Satterwhite, you ever get tired of this desert, come to Texas, and me and Hamp'll let you ride for us, a dollar a day and found."

"Thanks, Bud. I'll see what happens here first. It was an honor to ride with you."

They shook hands in a strong grip, then Tyler turned to Mary. When he looked at her, he ducked his head, and Mary embraced him. "Take care of yourself, Bud," she said.

Tyler nodded, then sniffed. "Well," he said, "I reckon I'll pick up those tickets." He put his hat on and walked away.

"Hamp," the preacher said, "there's no way to tell you how much I am going to miss you, how much you've meant to me."

Hampton looked at the ground and kicked at the gravel. He looked up and shook the preacher's hand. "Same here, Nathan," he said. "Do what you have to do, and let me know."

"I will."

"Hamp," Satterwhite said, then he held out his hand. "I'll do my best."

"Uh-huh," Hampton said. "I believe you will."

They shook hands. Satterwhite nodded and looked down.

Hampton felt a rising in his chest and a tightening of his throat when he looked at Mary. Tears were on her face in the bright sunlight.

"You goin' to hug me goodbye this time?" he asked, stepping up to her and looking into her eyes.

"I don't know," Mary said with an effort at a smile. Then she reached her arms around his neck and pulled his face down beside hers.

She hugged him tightly, and he held her off the ground, trying to memorize the feel and smell of her. When he put her down, she leaned back and looked at him a long time, tears in her eyes.

"Goodbye, Hamp," she said.

"Goodbye, Mary."

THIRTY

IT was spring in Texas. The meadows were covered with new grass, Indian paintbrush, buttercups, and the first blooms of blue-bonnets. The smell of growing things was in the air, and the sky was alive with insects and birds.

Tyler swung down off his horse at the gate of the little cemetery on the hill above Burton in Washington County. The sun was low in the west, bright through the haze of spring pollen. From Lady, Hampton watched the wind sway the limbs of a solitary pine on the next hill. Tyler opened the gate, remounted, and they rode through the rows of monuments until they saw the one they wanted.

They got down and led their horses close enough to the monument to read it. The name on it made them still and thoughtful: *Leander H. McNelly*. They took their hats off in unison.

"Just thirty-three when he died," Tyler said.

"It may have been just as well," Hampton said. "Man like the Captain would be a little out of place in this world."

"I reckon so," Tyler said.

"Take my word for it. He'd have a different way to handle this border war, not to mention the war buildin' up in Europe."

"Think we'll get into that?"

"We won't, but there's a lot of youngsters who might."

They were silent a while, looking at the monument and at the name of the man who had been their captain forty years before, when they had been little more than tall boys.

"We had us some times, didn't we," Tyler said.

"After Homer, I didn't care whether I lived or died, and I think the folks felt the same way. That's why I joined up. I haven't figured out yet why you did."

"Did some thinkin' on that up in Denver," Tyler said. "There's some men that ain't a whole man by themselves. They have to be with somebody else to be whole. You were always that somebody else. I never was as good in my life as when I was with you."

"I suppose I could say the same."

"That's why I joined up. And that's why I ended up in Mexico with you."

"That raid on Columbus changed everything," Hampton said.

"You been thinkin' a lot about the folks in New Mexico, haven't you?" Tyler asked.

"Uh-huh," Hampton said. "Except when I'm asleep."

"Good people," Tyler nodded. "I miss 'em myself, and I only knew 'em a month."

"Satterwhite turned out all right, didn't he?"

"You kind of always thought he would, I'll bet."

"The preacher turned a corner he'd been standin' by for a long time," Hampton said.

"Good man."

"Satterwhite has something to teach Billy now, so he'll be all right too."

"That's the happy-go-luckiest kid I ever knew."

"Funny how one day everything is the same, then the next day it ain't, and there's no goin' back. It's like we all crossed a border into new territory."

A mockingbird set up a fuss in a still dormant mimosa tree at the edge of the cemetery. The sun sank a little lower over the hills of Washington County.

"You miss Mary most of all, don't you?" Tyler said.

"She told me something before we left that I can't shake," Hampton said.

"What did she say, Hamp?"

"She said it was sad to love somebody."

Tyler looked at the monument over the grave of Captain Mc-Nelly. He nodded his head.

"Reckon she was right," Tyler said.

"Feels like she was," Hampton said.

They put their hats back on, and, after a while, they saddled up and rode out of the cemetery. The sun was going down, and they turned their horses and rode away from it.